MW01122796

Nowhere to Go

3/31/2010

Blan

the second best
left handed golfer I know

RM Calabresa

Nowhere to Go

RON CALARESO

To order additional copies of this book, contact:
Xlibris Corporation
1-888-795-4274
www.Xlibris.com
Orders@Xlibris.com
54981

DEDICATION

Several years ago, there was a very popular movie, *The Perfect Storm*, based on a book written by Sebastian Junger. It is the true story of the *Andrea Gail* and her crew of Gloucester fishermen who lost their lives during a hurricane in October of 1991. This was not only a great movie; it was also a unique experience for me. There have been several occasions when I've been asked if I ever saw the movie *Titanic*. My response is always the same, "I really don't want to see a movie when I know the ending." Well, when I went to see *The Perfect Storm*, I was riveted by the story while knowing all the while how it would end.

I have visited Gloucester many times in my life, usually to enjoy a day of charter fishing and a great clambake at the Gloucester House, but I also returned twice while writing *Nowhere to Go*. On both of these occasions, I visited the monument of the Gloucester fisherman and the memorial to the men who have lost their lives at sea while working their chosen profession.

The thing that stuck me most during my first visit was that there are nine plaques displaying the names of those lost at sea and there were about six hundred names on each. Well over five thousand fishermen never returned home from the sea. I dedicate this book to those people and the families left behind to grieve their loss.

This marks the memorial to the Gloucester fishermen lost at sea.
The memorial overlooks Gloucester Harbor.

ABOUT THE COVER
AUTHOR'S Q & A

Q. **Where and what is *Public Alley 101*?**
A. It is an alley located in the North End of Boston and the site of an important event which takes place in this book.

Q. **When is *Public Alley 101* not *Public Alley 101*?**
A. On the cover of this book.

Q. **So where's the location of the alley on the cover?**
A. It is an alley in Grasse, France. The photograph was taken in the North African section of the Village.

Q. **Who is the photographer?**
A. The photographer is Jim Chamberlain. Jim was originally from Boston, Massachusetts, and is now a resident of Naples Florida; he has been a professional photographer for over 35 years. He travels the world and specializes in European landscape photography. Each of his images is hand-printed with acrylic pigment inks and nontraditional materials such as fine German watercolor paper, canvas and sheet metal. These unique characteristics make his landscapes come alive with a sense of color and design.

Authors comment: The moment I saw Jim's alley photograph, I knew it was right for the cover of *Nowhere to Go*.

FOREWORD

The Voyage

It was late in the winter of 1925 and three young Italians stood on a pier in Naples, Italy waiting to board a ship bound for America. Marco Silina, his wife Mary and his sister-in-law Rose had said their goodbyes to friends and family prior to leaving the only home they had ever known. The Silina roots in Gaeta went back several hundred years and would continue to do so for many hundred more in spite of their departure. Now they waited, surrounded by strangers from several regions of Italy, all headed for a new life in another country.

Although the Re d'Italia was not due to depart until late that afternoon, the passengers had started arriving at first light. They knew that the bureaucratic process of checking each passenger's paperwork would be long and arduous and arriving early would improve their chances of being among the first to get on board and staking out a good spot to settle in below deck.

The Silinas were able to get cleared early, pay the fare, which was the equivalent of forty American dollars each and get one of the better spots. They wanted to be close enough to the hatch to get the maximum fresh air and light without being so close that they would get wet if the weather turned bad. They were aware that the crossing would not be easy, but they knew that it would only be a week or so in duration and having one another would make it easier to endure.

The passengers were from several different regions of Italy and in many cases this made it difficult to communicate with one another since there are many different dialects in the Italian language. It did help that everyone seemed in good spirits since they were heading to America and what they thought would be a much better way of life.

There were two things about the passengers that concerned Marco. The large majority of them were men; Italian men, and he was traveling with two women, handsome women. He would keep them close and make sure neither of them ever moved around the ship alone. His other concern was that many of the men were Sicilians and many Sicilians were not to be trusted. They had no respect for other people's property, would steal from you in a second and had little concern for the life of another. He would keep an eye on them and never turn his back to them.

The Re d'Italia left port shortly before dark that evening. There were no passengers on deck to get a final glimpse of their homeland, or the setting sun. It had been made clear to all of them that they were to stay below deck unless the Captain allowed them to come on deck in the event of an emergency.

No one was expecting the voyage to be easy, but the first few days went as well as could be expected. Everyone, with the possible exception of the Sicilians seemed content; not so much for what they were experiencing, but rather because of the expectations of what was to come in their new home. To say that the accommodations were crowded would be an understatement, but there was enough room to allow the passengers to move around, get some exercise and strike up a conversation with some of their neighbors. There was nothing fancy about the food; pasta fagiole, lentil and minestrone soup, bread and water, but there was always enough to go around.

On day five things took a serious turn for the worse. Early that morning the sky was black and the wind was gaining in strength with each passing second. By noon it was raining and the wind was so powerful that the rain appeared to be coming from the north rather than the sky. The Re d'Italia was experiencing seas of fifteen to twenty feet and panic was quickly beginning to reign and show on every face.

"Marco, this is terrible, are we going to be alright?" asked his young wife.

"It is bad, but this is a far bigger boat than I have ever been on. It will be rough, but we will be fine."

He hoped he was convincing because he didn't believe a word he was saying.

They had not received lunch, but most of the passengers were losing what was in their stomachs from that morning. At that second Mary became part of that group. That didn't bother Marco, however what did was what he noticed happening behind her. The tumbling and rolling of the ship was causing the passengers baggage to become loose from their bindings and there was a real potential of them becoming dangerous flying objects.

He began looking around for anyone who was not sick and who might be able to help. Rose was his first recruit and he quickly added a half dozen men. He knew where the extra bindings had been stored after the boarding process and he and the others retrieved them and started securing whatever they could. Mary, along with some of the other distressed passengers saw what was happening and also started to lend a hand. Under normal circumstances what they did would have taken an hour, but with the prevailing conditions it took better than four hours of exhausting work to get things to a relatively safe state.

The storm continued through the night and half way through the next day before it measurably subsided.

"Hello, is everyone OK in here?"

The voice came from the hatch and everyone below deck looked up to see two men descending into what must have appeared to be a sewer, and smelled every bit as bad.

Marco recognized one as being the first mate. It was the second man who was talking. When they got to the bottom of the ladder, they got their first good look at havoc that the storm had wrought in the past twenty four hours.

"I'm Captain Ferretti, are there any injured among you?"

There were mumbled responses, which were inaudible and the Captain correctly assumed that to mean no.

He looked around and noticed the extra strapping securing the baggage.

"It looks as if you people have been busy."

Again there was no real response, but several people glanced in Marco's direction. This gesture was not lost on the Captain.

Once these passengers reached America they would become immigrants, but at this moment; in the eyes of Captain Ferretti they were fellow countrymen and would be treated as such.

"I want each of you to come on deck. I will have a crew come down here and get started on getting this mess cleaned up. I believe that the foul weather is behind us, but we have gotten a little off course, which will add a couple of days to our passage. In the meantime I will do whatever possible to make you comfortable."

The sun had broken through the clouds and the passengers, who had been below deck for over five days, had to shield their eyes from its glare. While doing this their bodies welcomed the warm rays it provided and their senses relished the first real fresh air they had had in nearly a week. Within the hour the galley crew came on deck with pots of hot soup, bread and water. Never had so little been so greatly appreciated.

True to his word the Captain put regulations aside and did what he could to make the trip more bearable. His greatest gesture was to allow the passengers on deck for several hours a day. Everyone took advantage of this unexpected gift, and seldom did anyone stay below deck for more than a few minutes.

It was because of this, that when on the eighth day of the trip, Marco became suspicious when he saw a man go below and not reappear for what seemed a long period of time.

"Mary, I want you and Rose to stay together, right here. I will return in a few minutes."

"Be careful, he's Sicilian."

"What?"

"The man that went below a while ago; that's where you are going, no?"

He marveled at her, his Mary was wise beyond her years.

Marco got to the hatch and looked in, but he could see little so he started moving down the ladder. They spotted one another before he got to the lower deck, so Marco jumped down the remaining rungs to the surface.

"What are you doing; that is not your property?"

The man moved his hand to his pant belt and came out with a knife.

"That is none of your business."

He moved towards Marco, who moved back in order to gain time and to determine the best way to deal with this.

The other man was not waiting. His knife hand was held below his waist with the blade angled upward. His first thrust was a bit wild and short of its target. Marco kept moving back, but now he had a plan. When the Sicilian's next attempt swept past his face; Marco's right hand shot up and grabbed his assailant's right wrist and his left hand sunk into the man's ribs. The man tried to turn away, only to expose his kidney's and paid for that by receiving three crippling blows to that area. The man was done. The knife dropped to the floor and he slumped down beside it. Marco reached down and retrieved the man's weapon and while there he delivered a message.

"We get off this boat tomorrow, if I see you before then I will kill you with your own knife."

He then stood upright, stepped back and delivered a crushing kick to the Sicilian's balls.

Marco knew he would not see that man anytime soon, but knew that he would have friends that might try to carry out his vendetta. That night he didn't sleep, but rather lay awake with the Sicilian's knife at his side.

Early afternoon the following day the Re d'Italia arrived at New York Harbor. The passengers were crowded along the ships railing in order to get a glimpse of the new home and the grand lady waiting to greet them. Marco turned to Mary and Rose and saw their eyes welled up with tears. He was a very happy man. Marco turned to the railing, removed the Sicilians knife from his coat pocket and dropped it into the harbor. He smiled to himself and thought, "I won't need that any longer. I just have to remember to stay away from those damned Sicilians."

PROLOGUE

The Dreams

The pain was excruciating. Why is this happening? It's been almost four years since the injury and almost that long since he had felt pain anywhere close to this. Johnny Silina felt the pain in his shoulder and remembered the pain of a dream coming to an end. At that point, the pain subsided as a new injection of morphine put him deeper into a drug-induced sleep. His last thought was of two bodies coming together at breakneck speed. Neither of the two were breaking stride or losing focus on the object that they pursued.

It was late April 1953, and PFC Johnny DeSimone lies in a MASH infirmary a scant few miles south of 38th parallel in Korea. The pain he felt in his right shoulder was not the result of a collision that happened four years earlier but rather from the shrapnel emanating from artillery fired by the Chinese Communist army just days earlier. The next several days seemed to fall into a strange pattern. The drugs would wear thin, and the dreams would return; and then mercifully, Johnny would receive yet another injection. Then at least for a while, he would not have to endure the horrors of what his dreams held for him. The dream of that collision returned on occasion, but the images that dominated his semiconscious state were those of heavy combat, exploding artillery, and mangled soldiers screaming in agony. He came to realize that one of those screaming solders was himself.

Johnny had arrived in Korea on April 6, 1953, and was assigned to Company F, Seventeenth Infantry as a replacement. Less than two weeks later, Company F was sent on a mission in an attempt to recapture Hill 255, or Pork Chop Hill as it had come to be known. They came under heavy attack from the Chinese forces from the minute they started moving up the hill. They soon found themselves about to be overrun, and only a counterattack by Company E saved

---

his company from certain annihilation. Soon thereafter, the evacuation of the wounded began; and while Johnny's injuries were both serious and painful, his were not horrendous, and he was one of the later evacuees.

All things good and bad come to an end, but it would be some time before that was the case with Johnny's dreams. That didn't occur until the decision was made to wean him off the morphine that was giving him relief from the pain resulting from his injuries. That did not happen until after he was evacuated from Korea to a hospital in Japan where he would undergo the first of three operations in an effort to reconstruct the damage to his shoulder. On the first day that he was able to think clearly, he asked himself in a tone only he could hear, "When is this all going to end?"

CHAPTER ONE

Roots

Johnny Silina didn't know when it would all end, but he did know where it had begun.

Gloucester is a city which is located in what is called the North Shore of Massachusetts. As the crow flies, it's no more than twenty five or thirty miles from Boston. It is the place where the Silina family would settle and live the rest of their lives. Marco Silina, his wife Mary, and his brother's wife Rose had come through Ellis Island in the spring of 1925. Two year earlier, Marco's older brother Santino had preceded their arrival to America, and he eagerly anticipated the arrival of Marco, Mary, and most assuredly his beloved Rose. All four were born in the same small village in Italy. Gaeta was on the coast between Rome and Naples. It was a fishing village, and no one could ever remember a Gaeta Silina who had ever been anything other than a fisherman.

The dream of the Silina brothers was not to come to the land of opportunity to gain access to the gold that lined the streets. Their dream was to come to America, earn a good living, and offer their children the opportunity to grow and prosper in this great country. When Santino departed Gaeta in 1923, he did not do so penniless as did so many others. The Silinas were not wealthy by any standard, but they were a family of hard workers, and they saved whatever money they earned beyond what it took to put food on the table and shirts on their backs.

The plan was simple. Marco would stay in Gaeta and provide for Mary and Rose, and before leaving for America, he was to sell their interest in their boat to their two partners. The partners were eager to do this since it would increase their income. The Silina brothers were happy to do so because the partners were married to their two sisters. Santino would go to the new country, find work as a fisherman, and find the place where they would settle. On arriving in Boston, he was to find the home of Dominic and Lena Patrano. The Patranos were cousins who had come to this country two years earlier. They had written Santino and told him that when he arrived, he would stay with them until the others followed. When he finally found them, Dom informed him that he could work, along with him, unloading fishing boats at Commercial Wharf. This would be fine for now, but the Silinas were fishermen in Italy, and they would be fishermen in America. It did not take Santino long to discover that the place that the Silinas would finally settle was the small fishing town of Gloucester.

After clearing Ellis Island, the three new immigrants boarded a train in New York and headed for Boston. A couple of days earlier, Marco had convinced an employee at Ellis to place a call for him to the home of the Patranos where Santino was living. The message was what Santino had been waiting weeks to hear. In two days, Marco, with the wives in tow, would be arriving in Boston's South Station.

It was late March when they arrived, but if you didn't know better, you would have thought it was Christmas. Santino came with gifts for all three, but the gifts became an afterthought as soon as the newcomers stepped off the train.

"Marco, Marco, how can I thank you?" the two brothers threw their arms around one another. It was not difficult to see the family resemblance. Both men possessed rugged good looks, sturdy builds; and Marco, at five nine, stood about an inch taller than this older brother. Their wives, however, would never be mistaken for sisters. While they were both handsome women, Rose was full bodied while Mary was tall, slender, and moved with the grace of an athlete.

"No, Santino, it is I who should be thanking you. I have been in Gaeta with family while you have been here alone." With that, Santino went past his brother and into the arms of Rose.

"I thought I might never see you again. What was I thinking when I left you for all this time?"

Marco put an arm around his wife who had tears steaming down her face.

"I could not have done that," said Mary, wiping the tears from her eyes. "We owe them both a great debt."

"You do what you must do" was Marco's reply.

Dominic had a friend who owned an automobile, and for the tidy sum of three dollars had consented to provide the Silinas transportation to Gloucester. The fee had been five dollars a month earlier when he had taken Santino there. He needed five dollars because his entire day would be lost while Santino looked for an apartment and jobs for him and his brother. Santino was successful on both counts. He found a two-bedroom apartment in the center of town and jobs for both of them as hands on the same boat.

When the Silinas arrived at their new home, the newest arrivals were in for a surprise. The apartment was spotless, with two large bedrooms, a bath, dining room, a bright airy living room and a good working kitchen. Unfortunately there was little else. Santino had purchased two beds, a kitchen table with four chairs, some dishes, utensils and a few pots and pans. Of course there was nothing in the house to be cooked. After the initial shock was over the three newcomers had a good laugh at Santino's expense.

It then began to dawn on the women that they had no idea where to start. Where do you go to find the bare essentials required for a household? A market for food? A place to purchase a dresser of drawers, or a sofa and chairs? Who do you see for ice for the ice box? Where is the Catholic Church? The questions kept coming with no answers. Then out of nowhere there was a knock at the front door. Rose went to see who it was and got her first glimpse of their landlady, Josie Scalise. Josie came armed with answers to all of their questions and a large pot of macaroni and meatballs. The five of them sat and enjoyed their first meal in the new Silina home in America. Marco let his elder brother have one of the four chairs and made due by sitting on a large piece of luggage.

They discovered that Josie had lost her husband, Cosmo, at sea ten years earlier, but he left behind not only Josie, but also seven children. Josie was not a lonely woman, but Santino made a mental note to purchase a fifth chair. He had a feeling that this would not be the last time they would break bread with their newest friend.

Things seemed to be too good to be true, and the news would only get better. Santino and Rose went out for a walk on the last Sunday in May. An hour later, Santino came bursting through the front door of the apartment. "I'm going to be a father!" he shouted. A minute later, Rose came through the same door and was in fact a strange sight. She, of course, started crying when she shared the news with her husband; and the crying intensified when she saw Santino's joyful reaction to the news. News he could not wait to share with Marco and Mary. Mary, of course, had heard the news the previous day. The combination of seeing Rose's tearstained face while she gasped for breath was a sight to behold. Santino had hugged and kissed Rose when she told him of her pregnancy but then turned and ran the three blocks home in order to share the news with his family. That story would be told countless times over the years. Anna was born just after the new year; and one year later on January 5, 1927, John was born to Marco and Mary Silina.

Chapter Two

A Dream Gone Bad

The Silinas were new to Gloucester while many of the other families had been working these waters for generations. In his two years in America, Santino had made an effort to learn the language and was beginning to get to the point where he could get by. Marco, of course, spoke not a word; and because of that, the brothers conversed in Italian only. It was clear that the locals were not about to anoint the newcomers into their circle, and there were long, cold looks as the Silinas walked the pier to and from the boat they were working.

This went on for several weeks until one unseasonably hot day in late May when Marco and Santino decided to have a cold beer at the Seamen's Club before returning home for the day. This was a first for them since they usually went directly home after returning from a trip that might have been as much as a week long. This, of course, was during the time of Prohibition. Prior to that, the Seamen's Club was the Seamen's Pub. The only thing that had changed, other than the name, was that hard liquor was no longer sold. Since the local police force was made up of brothers and cousins of the patrons, there was little or no chance of a raid. The cops were not on the cuff, but simply of the "see no evil" mentality.

When the Silina brothers entered the club, they found it filled with familiar faces; all turned their way and none smiling. The brothers didn't say anything to one another, but if they had, it would have been something like this; "Maybe this isn't such a good idea." They also knew there was no turning back. Doing so would mean that they would not only be leaving the pub but Gloucester as well. You didn't have to speak the language to understand this. They also knew something that the eight sitting at the bar didn't know. That back in Gaeta, the Salina family, the entire family, was known to be nice people, good fishermen, and tough. They also understood, as did the men at the bar, that you didn't have

18

to win, but you did have to fight. They did win that night. Not the fight, two against eight only works in the movies. What they did win was the respect of the people in the bar, including the other eight combatants. The story worked its way around the pier the next day and would be recounted for years to come. After that, they would stop at the club once a week or so. It wasn't so much that they wanted a beer, but more because this was to be their home, and they wanted to be part of the community. They were always greeted with a friendly turn and nod of the head. This was not a demonstrative group, but the Silinas were now accepted.

The Silinas' plan was simple. Work hard and save every penny possible; then with that money combined with that from the sale of their boat in Gaeta, they would first buy a boat and then a two-family home, which they would share. A good plan, but flawed. During the next four years, their families had grown so fast that the house had to come before the boat. By this time, there were five young Silinas, and God only knows where that would have gone if the Silina brothers hadn't decided to keep it in their pants. Johnny had a sister, Margaret, and Anna now had a sister, Annette, who had quickly followed Tony. Uncle Santino's second born was a boy and he and Johnny were inseparable from the time that Tony could get on his feet and chase after his cousin.

It was now late 1929, and suddenly, things took a turn for the worse. The country found itself in the grips of the Great Depression while Gloucester faced a new dynamic in the form of motor-powered vessels and the "otter trawl" which was a bottom-dragging net. These new innovations meant that the size of fishing crews was cut by half. Johnny stood in the kitchen and listened to his father and uncle talk, and while he was too young to understand, he could sense by the mood and tone of the conversation that something was wrong.

"We can get through this. It could be a lot worse." Marco would nod his head in agreement.

The Silina brothers were true Silinas, and aside from the three-thousand-dollar mortgage on their house, were debt-free with some money stashed away. *Stashed* being the operative word since the Silinas did not trust banks. "This is what I think we need to do," offered Marco. "One of us should stay here. We are good fishermen and hard workers. There will be work for one of us. The other needs to go to Boston and seek work, maybe on the wharf. We need to do whatever we can, not to lose our home." Santino liked the plan, but who is to stay, and who goes? Before he could ask, Marco cut in with the answer. "When we planned to come to America, you went ahead alone. Now I must do the same." It was decided, and all that remained was telling Mary of the plan.

This became very emotional. Mary knew that it was the right thing to do but had seen the melancholy that Rose had experienced during Santino's absence, and she begged Marco to not stay away for too long a period. He explained that he would not be making much money, and he would have to take a day's work anytime it was available. He did, however, relent and promised that his absences would not exceed a month at a time. On January 8, 1930, just a few days following Johnny's third birthday, Marco would catch a ride with a friend, Mike Gallo, who had also decided to seek employment in Boston.

He had ten one-dollar bills in his possession to tide him over until he was able to find work. He, of course, knew that he would be welcomed by the Patranos as would the few dollars he would offer whenever possible. As his family saw him climb into the truck, they had no way of knowing that this trip would trigger a chain of events that would change their lives forever.

Coincidentally, just three days before Marco arrived in Boston, Mayor Michael Curley was being inaugurated as Boston's leader for a third term. During a long and protracted speech, Curley outlined his plan to lead the city out of its current devastating state of affairs. He talked of jobs coming from preparations for Boston's tercentenary year and city projects such as road construction, building new libraries, and even a new golf course. The crowd cheered the popular mayor, maybe as much for what they hoped for rather than what they really believed.

When Marco reached the Patranos' front door, he was greeted by Dominic with a firm handshake and a smile.

"Again, the Silinas find themselves in your debt," Marco started. "A few years ago, you offered my brother a bed, and now you do the same for me, how can I repay you?"

"I'm ashamed to talk of repayment, but things are bad. I do not expect to profit from your stay, but I need your help to put bread on the table."

Marco nodded in agreement. "The first dollar I earn every day goes to your home. If I make only one dollar, that dollar goes to you and Lena." Dominic smiled again. He was relieved to have this talk behind him. "I know the Silinas. I know you are as good as your word."

"Now," said Marco, "let's talk of work, I was hoping to find work with you at the wharf."

"There is no work there. The boats with the motors come, and the jobs go away. The men from the boats have taken any work there was."

Now Marco was concerned for his friend. "Will you be able to keep your job?" he asked.

"For now, yes. I drink no more than two glasses of wine with dinner. I have worked the wharf six days a week, for ten years, and I show up every day able to work."

"You are OK then, I am glad to hear this."

Dominic shrugged his shoulders and spread his hands. "For now, yes, but it can get worse. The price of fish has been dropping, and the fishermen say that they would rather dump their catch than take any less for the fish. If this happens, there will be little need for me."

"I brought wine," said Marco. "Let's pour a glass." That night, Dominic had four glasses of wine but was still up at 4:00 AM the following morning. When he got to the kitchen, he found that Marco was there, finishing up a cup of coffee. He smiled to himself and thought, "Ah, those Silinas."

Marco soon learned that if there was work to be found, that it was best if you went to the municipal employment bureau where day work was sometimes available on a first-come-first-serve basis. Marco was always there early, but he discovered that *first come* usually meant the first person who knew someone. The worksheets were handed out very guardedly by the suits, as they had come to be called. There were certain people who seemed to get work on a regular basis. Never one to accept unfair treatment, he would shout out his protest to those given the responsibility of doling out the jobs. The fact that his protest were made in the broken English of an immigrant Italian didn't help his cause. It was more than a week before he got his first day's work, and only then because someone tired of his incessant complaining. Work or not, each night when he returned to his cousin's home, he put a one-dollar bill on the kitchen table.

Chapter Three

An Accounting

As promised, Marco returned home after a month's absence. He did so with mixed emotions. He was getting work on a more frequent basis, and he feared being away, even for a couple of days, might change that. Let's face it, he was not getting work because they liked him. On the contrary, it was his persistence that was getting him work. On the other hand, he missed his family terribly, and he had been looking forward to returning for the past several days. As a fisherman, he was often away for a week or more; but somehow, this absence seemed very different. With each week he was away, he came to better appreciate the sacrifice made by Santino when he came to this country in advance of the others.

It was Rose who spotted him first. She was returning home with an armful of groceries when she saw him getting out of a truck a block away. He saw her a few seconds later and started to wave, but before he could get his arm up, Rose had rushed into the house, shouting to Mary, "He's here! Marco is home!" Mary dropped the pan she was washing into the sink, and wiping her hands on her apron, ran out into the cold February weather to greet her husband. Marco saw her and ran toward her with any doubt as to whether or not he was doing the right thing gone from his mind.

Marco had planned his visit for this day because he knew his brother should be returning from a stay at sea. It was a Saturday, and if he didn't make it that day, then he should be in by Sunday. This was important not only because he wished to see Santino, but they needed some time to do an accounting of where they were at.

Marco had a great day. He spent the afternoon telling Mary of his stay in Boston, how the Patranos were faring, and how much he missed her and the children. He also spent hours with the five children. Margaret, who was not yet two, hung onto his arm and wouldn't let go of him. He then did something he had never done in all the years that he and Mary had been married. This old-world Italian went into the kitchen and cut vegetables while Mary prepared dinner. While he did this, Mary turned her face to him, smiled, and asked if he was OK.

As the afternoon passed, Marco started looking out the window, hoping to get a glance of his brother; and just after dusk, he spotted him coming up the street. He left the house and greeted his brother as he came up the walk.

Rose and Mary had prepared a feast, the likes of which Marco had not seen in over a month. First came a huge antipasto salad, followed by a bowl of pasta and gravy (Italians called it gravy rather than tomato sauce), and a main course of fresh mackerel and vegetables. Marco gave Mary a sideways glance when she explained to Santino that Marco himself had cut the vegetables.

Santino let out a belly laugh and said, "What happened to the brother I sent to Boston? Who is this imposter?" Marco did not laugh but took his older brother's joking good-naturedly.

After dinner was cleaned up and the children were in bed, the four Silinas sat in Santino and Rose's living room for a family meeting. In an Italian household, this was generally unheard of since this was man talk, but the brothers were in agreement with their wives that they should all be present. Santino started by discussing the accounts from the Gloucester standpoint. It was only he who was employed, but at least for now, his job was secure. There was some concern over what Dominic had told Marco of the anger the fishing owners had about falling prices for their catch, but for now things could not be much better. Gloucester was recording catch poundage at a record rate.

"We have had to go into our savings, but that is to be expected," stated Santino. "But we are paying our mortgage, and we are putting food on the table." Marco stirred around a bit uncomfortably since his accounting was not at all good.

"I am embarrassed to say that I have little to contribute," he started. "A month ago, I left here with ten dollars, and I return today with twenty. I have only ten dollars to show for a month away." He went on to explain that he was giving his cousin a dollar a day but added that their generosity far exceed that amount. "I'm sorry there is not more, but I have been working more of late, and next month should be much better." It was quiet for a moment, and as usual, it was Santino that broke the ice. "It may not seem much to you, but you forget that at least, we don't have to feed you." The four of them, remembering the huge quantity of food he had consumed at dinner, began to roar in laughter. Marco looked at his brother and thought, *I will never let you down, my brother. I will never let any of you down, no matter what.*

The next morning being Sunday, the nine Silinas headed off for Mass after which, Marco had a chance to see some of the men he had worked with before the layoffs. Some were unemployed and admitted that they should do as he had done, but they didn't have a brother to look after their families. They were hoping things would get better. Marco was tempted to tell them of his meager earnings, but decided not to because that was family business.

Marco's ride was returning to Boston at 7:00 PM, so the family had an early dinner, which matched the spread put out the night before. Marco reminded them that not having to feed him helped with the household expenses. The ride to Boston was a quiet one. Marco had a long time to think.

"What did you say?" asked Mike. Without realizing it, Marco had muttered half aloud. "I have to find a way."

CHAPTER FOUR

A Simple Prayer Answered

Until now it had been a cold, but clear winter; however, as the truck carrying Marco approached Boston, snow began to fall rather heavily. Both men knew what this meant. There would be work available tomorrow shoveling snow.

"We must be at the municipal building early," said Mike.

"No," said Marco, "we must be there very early. Let's go home and get some warm clothes and our shovels. We will then go to the damn municipal building and park the truck in front of their fucking door. If they want to get into the building, they will have to give us a work slip first." As warm as the two men were dressed, they didn't sleep much that night. They were sheltered from the snow and wind, but the temperature hovered around twenty degrees. It was only a few hours before other men started drifting in, some of who took refuge in the back of Mike's truck. When three suits arrived at 6:00 AM, it was a sight worth paying to watch. At first, they asked Mike to move the truck. His response was, "No capisce." They then looked for crawl space under the truck. The snow had been blown in drifts beneath the truck, and the suits wanted no part of this. At this point, the head suit approached the truck and asked what it was they wanted while knowing in advance what the answer would be. This time, it was Marco who answered. "We were the first to arrive. We want our work slips."

"Why didn't you say so?" he said, as he reached into the pocket of his overcoat and retrieved a pad of slips.

As if he read the mind of the suit, Marco leaned over to take the slips and asked, "Will we see you tomorrow?"

"Come without the truck, and slips will be waiting for you." As Mike drove off toward the work site, Marco could not help to think of the work slips coming

---

25

from the overcoat pocket of the suit. I wonder how many were handed out to others the night before?

February delivered close to a record snowfall, and each day there was work, there was a slip handed out to both Mike and Marco. There was no preferential treatment in play here because the two friends were always among the first to arrive, but their actions had delivered a message; Don't fuck with us. Of course, Marco was hedging his bet and would, on occasion, slip a dollar bill into the hand of the boss suit.

At the end of the month, Marco couldn't wait to get up the walk and to the front door of the Silina home. February had been a very good month, and he couldn't wait to share the news. Unfortunately, Santino was at sea and would have to get the news secondhand. There were some other things to discuss with the family, but since his brother was away, it would have to wait until his next visit. He passed through the front door and went directly to the kitchen where Mary and Rose were preparing a feast for that evening. Marco proudly placed sixty dollars on the kitchen table. Sixty dollars, meant that the family savings would go untouched for this month. The food that night was similar to that of the previous month but somehow tasted much better than it did then.

As is so often the case in New England, March came in like a lion but went out like a lamb. This came of no surprise to Marco and in fact was what he had wanted to discuss with the family during his last visit. He knew the heavy snow was a stroke of good fortune, and it would not last much longer, and there were only questions beyond that.

There was not as much bounce in his step during his visit the following month. He was very glad to be home to see the family, especially his brother who he had not seen in two months. He handed Santino forty-three dollars with the hope the family savings would go untouched for another month.

"I am going to play with the children for now, but we must talk tonight." With that, he gave Mary another kiss on her forehead and headed to the living room.

With dinner finished and the children put to bed, the family meeting was convened in the living room of Rose and Santino.

Marco was the first to speak. "These past two months have been good, but I am worried about what the future will bring. Almost all of my work had been with the snow, and now that is over. I don't know what will happen now. No one I talk to has heard of any work."

"How about the city's celebration?" asked Santino, referring to tercentenary year.

"That is the mayor talking. He has a lot of big ideas, but not the money to do it."

"Marco, whatever you bring, even five dollars, it's better than nothing because there is no money to be made in Gloucester."

"I need to do more, Santino, you carry too much of the load."

With that, Rose spoke up and said, "Marco, let us not forget who is making the sacrifice of being away from the family, you are doing more than your share." "And, yes," chimed in Mary, "let us not forget how fortunate we are. When we are at Mass tomorrow, look at the faces around us, the faces of our friends and neighbors. Most of them would swap places with us, given the chance."

The men shrugged and smiled. The good fortune the brothers shared was sitting in this room with them.

Chapter Five

A Turning Point for the Better?

The city of Boston was being rocked with a steady barrage of riots and demonstrations. The Mayor was being assailed from every direction. The major combatants were the labor unions and demonstrators, carrying banners, and extolling the virtues of Communism. There were battles within the union ranks as well, as union members were applying for jobs where other members had been locked out. Of course, where there were demonstrations, there existed the potential for violence, and the Boston Police were being accused of brutality. To Mayor Curley's credit, he was making every effort to appropriate money for projects that would create jobs.

Marco was having nothing to do with the politics related to joblessness; his concern was to find work wherever he could. At dinner one night in early April, Dominic told him of a new possibility. It seems that construction workers had been laid off and were being replaced by day labor. Several members of the Italian community had already found work there. The next morning, Marco was at the desk of the top suit at the municipal employment bureau.

"Why did you not tell me of this?" Marco reasoned that the five or six dollars a month he slipped the suit gave him the right to ask.

"It pays three, sometimes four dollars a day, I didn't think you would be interested?"

"Are you crazy? Yesterday, I made nothing, the day before that, nothing. I still pay for my boarding. How can you think I am not interested?"

"OK, OK, I'll give you a slip for tomorrow, and I'll make it up to you after that." Marco took the slip and forced a "thank you."

"I'll do what I can for you."

Marco quickly did the numbers; when he made three dollars, one would go to Dominic and Lena. On some of the days that he made four, he would slip one to the suit.

When he got to the work site the next morning, he was not surprised by what he saw. First of all, it appeared as if all of the replacement workers were Italian. There was also a heavy contingent of workers who had been replaced, none of whom looked Italian. In fact, there were some Germans, but predominantly they were Irish. There was plenty of shouting, threats, name calling, and ethnic slurs. Marco kept his head up, but his eyes looked straight ahead. He heard every word, and they stung, but he did not respond. Truth be told, if their positions were reversed, he would probably be doing as they were. It was quiet when they finished at the end of the day. The unemployed workers had long since tired of the jeering and determined that tomorrow was another day.

The suit was true to his word, and Marco had work almost every day, and when he went home at month's end, he had thirty-two dollars to contribute to the household. "I did not get a full month, so I expect next month will be better. The work does not pay well, but it is steadier than any other I have had. I think next month, I will bring home close to forty dollars."

Later, when the two brothers were alone, Marco shared with Santino what took place each day.

"Think of how it would be if you arrived at the pier tomorrow and there were men there taking work from you."

"You are right, Marco. I wish that I could tell you not to go back, but if I did, there would be fifty men waiting to take your place."

"I'm not sure that makes it right."

"You are right, Marco, you are right."

Marco was back at the work site on Monday morning, and to say that nothing had changed would not be accurate. With each passing day, the replaced workers became more frustrated and abusive. If it were not for a heavy police presence, things surely would have erupted long before now. Then one morning in about the middle of May, the shit hit the fan. Marco and the other workers were trudging through a gauntlet of abusive slurs when things got out of hand.

"Hey you, you fucking wop. I mean you with that stupid black hat. I met your wife last night, but she couldn't talk. She had my cock in her mouth"

This was followed by boisterous shouts of approval. Marco was the one with the black hat, and his anger rose to a dangerous level; but even at that, he was ready to let it pass. He did, however, turn his head to see the person responsible for the insults. When he did, the culprit let fly a large mouthful of saliva, which caught Marco flush in the face.

To say that Marco saw red would be an understatement. He started at the Irishman who stepped back and put up his dukes John L Sullivan style as if to say, "Watch me knock this guinea on his ass." He would have been much better off if he had turned and ran. The fight lasted only thirty seconds or so. It is hard to speculate how many punches were thrown in that time, and almost all of them found their mark. By the time the cops were able to get to the scene, the Irishman was a bloody mess and rolled into a ball in an effort to protect himself from further punishment. Even as he was being restrained, Marco managed to get in one last blow, which was a solid kick to the to the prone man's crotch. The cops dragged Marco away from the fray and toward a paddy wagon.

"How about him?" shouted one of the Italian workers, pointing to the Irishman who was still lying on the ground in the fetal position.

"He's had punishment enough," answered the cop. "We'll be taking him to Mass. General."

Marco was taken to the police precinct in City Square, Charlestown. Charlestown was a predominantly Irish community, and it was fortunate that word of the fight had not preceded his arrival.

Marco was booked for disorderly conduct and put in a cell by himself.

By this time, he had cooled down and began to wonder what would happen next. This was long before the right to a phone call, and even if he had one, who would he call? Santino had long since removed the phone at home in order to save a few dollars a month. His good friend Mike was in the same work party, and he would surely stop by the Patranos to tell them what happened, but they would have no way of knowing where they had taken him. He could only sit and wait. He did not have to wait long. Within a few hours, a policeman came to his cell door, opened it, and stated in a matter of fact manner, "You made bail."

Marco was stunned; he couldn't imagine how this could have happened. Who knew he was here? Who did he know that had the money to pay the bail? He was taken to the property room where he picked up belongings, which consisted of a wallet, one dollar, and a key to the Patranos' front door. He went past the desk sergeant and quickly out the front door; maybe this is a mistake, and they will call him back. When he got outside, he looked around, trying to get his bearings. There was no way he could have determined where he had been taken from the rear of the paddy wagon. He recognized the area as one where he had done some day work. Yes, go straight ahead to the bridge, and on the other side is the North End. As he started toward the bridge, he heard a voice call his name. "Silina."

Marco turned to the direction of the voice and saw a large man wearing a dark overcoat and a gray fedora. The man extended his hand, and after the slightest hesitation, so did Marco. "How is it that you know my name?"

"I always know the names of people I bail from jail."

"Why is it that you did this?"

"You ask a lot of questions for a man who has yet to thank me" was the response. "Please excuse my ignorance, thank you Mr.—?"

"Another question, my name is Joseph Pino. Why don't we talk as we walk? I believe we are going in the same direction."

Marco was impressed by the man. For a big man, he spoke in a low tone, but not so low that you had to strain to hear him; and his voice did not have a hint of an Italian accent.

"Now that we are away from the police station, let me answer some of your questions. I am a lawyer and I have but one client. You need not know his name at this time, but he is a very important man in Boston, and he has taken it upon himself to be a benefactor to the Italian community. When he heard of today's incident, he summoned me to see that you were treated fairly and met with no harm."

"When you next see this gentleman, please thank him for me. I don't believe it was by chance that I was delivered to the Charlestown station house."

"Neither do I, Marco. Let me ask you, what do you plan to do tomorrow? You certainly will not be allowed to return to any of the work sites. At the first sight of you, there will be a riot, or worse."

"You may be right," said Marco. "But I really have no choice. There is no other work to be had—"

"You may be wrong," interrupted Mr. Pino. "Your benefactor was quite impressed when he was told of your exploits today. He indicated that he may have something for you."

Marco may have been new to this country, but he wasn't completely naive. He knew there was much more to know beyond what he was being told, but he answered, "Tell me more of this work." Mr. Pino reached into his pocket and pulled out a business card and a pen. He quickly jotted down an address and handed the card to Marco.

"Be here at eight o'clock tomorrow morning. Ask to see Pete."

CHAPTER SIX

No Turning Back

There was not much sleep to be had that night. The fight, the arrest, and the quick release were enough to cause unrest, but the offer of work made sleep impossible. Marco really wasn't trying to sleep because he had a very important decision to make. Was it the right thing to do? What would he say to his family? Where would all this take him? Sometime before dawn, Marco would make two decisions. He would take the job, and he would tell only his brother what he was going to do.

The address that Mr. Pino gave him the night before turned out to be an innocent-looking storefront on Salem Street in the North End of Boston. Marco paused for a long minute as he looked at the store from the opposite side of the street. He knew, once he walked through that door, there was no turning back. This was not a man seeking employment; this was a man who has made a choice.

"Is Pete around?" he heard himself say.

"Who's askin'?"

"My name is Marco Silina, I was sent by Mr. Pino."

The guy made the connection right away. Pete had told him about the paesan who beat the crap out of this Mick yesterday. He looked at Marco with a new respect. "Yeah, Pete's here, follow me."

In the blink of an eye, Marco passed through a grocery store and into a room lined with desks and telephones. *Numbers,* thought Marco, *this is not going to be too bad.*

Pete looked up from his paper. He wasn't much for small talk and started right in. "You must be Silina. I'm Pete, what do you know about what I do?"

Mario looked around and smiled. "It looks like you're booking."

Pete looked around and said, "No, no, that ain't it. Didn't they tell you nothing? Let's get outta here and go someplace where we can talk."

They ended up at a club of sorts where you needed a key to get in and spent the next two hours drinking espresso and talking about the importing business. That was, of course, the importing of booze from Canada.

Numbers and women was good business for organized crime, but nothing in comparison to Prohibition. People had always wanted their booze, and once it was taken away, they seemed to want it more then ever. The Mafia bosses were only too happy to provide it to them, and John Q. Public was only too happy to pay the freight.

Pete told Marco that he would earn $35 every week, and on those weeks when traffic was especially heavy, there would be more. Marco realized that this was a huge amount of money and wondered how he could explain it to his family. He would have to think about that later.

Two nights later, Marco made his first trip north. It had been determined that he would be a driver. Pete was riding shotgun. He was doing so without a weapon.

There was a good reason for this. The "boss", known as the Don to those closer to him, had made the decision that these men would not be armed. While he expected them to do whatever possible to get the booze safely to one of his roving warehouses, he wanted it done without a shoot-out. Not that he ran a gun-free organization; nothing could be farther from the truth. His reasoning was simple. Every year, he would spread thousands of dollars throughout the Boston Police department. In return, the police would look the other way whenever possible. What they couldn't look away from was the killing of a federal officer. If the feds caught up with you, they more than likely would make an arrest, so little could be gained by killing one of them in the process.

Marco's first day could not have been simpler. They left Boston before sunrise, traveled to a location a few miles south of the Canadian border, made the exchange, and returned to Boston long after dark. He made another trip that week and two the next. When he went home that weekend, he had ninety dollars. He proudly put fifty on the table and was quick to explain that Santino had been right, and there was much more work to be had from the city's celebration than he had expected. Later that evening, while the women were cleaning up, he handed an envelope to his brother and told him what had occurred since his last visit. Santino was not pleased.

"What are you thinking? We may not be wealthy, but we don't have to resort to breaking the law."

"It's a stupid law."

"But the law nonetheless, and we don't get to choose which laws we obey and which we don't."

33

The men were talking in muffled tones, but the anger in their voices was evident. They heard their wive's voices become clearer as they approached the living room. "More on this later," said Santino.

"It doesn't matter," answered his brother. "It is done."

The two men hardly exchanged a word for the balance of the weekend.

In the months that followed, Santino's position softened. He rationalized that if he accepted the money, he then would have to accept the way it was earned.

During this time, Marco began to learn of the hierarchy of the organization. It started when he arrived for his third trip north to find that Pete was not there. When he inquired about this, he was told that Pete was a "made man," and that he had made the first couple of trips only to show the new man the ropes. Since all of the others seemed to know what was meant by a "Made Man," he was reluctant to inquire of the meaning. In the next couple of weeks, he listened closely to the others and was finally able to understand the language, so to speak. There was also talk of the benefactor, Dominic Belamonte, or the Don. Some of the other men, being from the North End, knew the Don from sight, but none of them had ever met the man. Unlike his experience with the Gloucester fisherman, Marco was quickly accepted as one of the guys. The tale of his battle with the Irishman didn't hurt in earning the respect of the others and neither did the fact that unlike the other drivers, he always gave a hand in loading and unloading the truck. What happened early that fall did nothing to harm his status in the group.

They were about an hour into a return trip to Boston. It was after nightfall, and there was every indication that it would be an uneventful drive. Marco happened to look into the rearview and spotted a car, which was quickly closing the gap between the two vehicles. He knew the truck couldn't outrun the trailing car, but he did increase his speed just to see what the occupants in the following car would do. When they also increased their speed, he felt for sure they were in trouble. Whatever little hope he held on to disappeared when the car started flashing lights and setting off its screaming siren. Marco's mind was racing; he knew he must try something, but what it was, he hadn't a clue. Suddenly, his mind cleared, and a plan started to form. He had used this route a couple of times, and if his memory was serving him right, they had a chance to escape. He reduced the speed of the truck and came to a stop. The other vehicle stopped about a hundred feet back, and four federal agents got out and, with guns poised, started walking toward the truck. Marco put the truck in gear and, when the feds got within twenty feet of the truck, put the pedal to the floor and left the agents eating dust and scrambling to get back to their car. Marco knew there was a crossroad about a half mile up the road, and the faster they got there, the better their chance to escape. He was also watching in his rearview mirror to check on the pursuit of the agents. He got to the crossroad and turned left while using the brakes as little as he dared. As the truck righted itself after skidding out of the turn, he quickly turned off the trucks lights.

"Tom, adjust the mirror on your side so you can watch for the car." Tom rolled down the window and responded, "I don't see anything."

"Good, pray that it stays that way." Marco needed to cover just a few hundred yards to the right-hand turn he remembered from his earlier trips.

"Do you see anything yet?"

"No, no."

"Hold on," warned Marco just before a second harrowing turn, this time to the right. He traveled just a few hundred feet before pulling onto the road's shoulder and came to a stop. He and Tom sat with their eyes glued to the rearview mirrors. Finally, they saw what they were hoping for when the car carrying the federal agents sped past the intersection, heading south toward Boston. Marco didn't hesitate a second. He immediately sped down a road with no idea where it would take him. It was another five minutes before he dared putting the truck lights back on. He drove another half hour before pulling to a stop.

"What are you doing?" asked Tom.

"I just thought of those guys in back. I hope they're in one piece."

When they pulled open the canvas that covered the back of the truck, they found the four helpers passing a fifth of scotch around and laughing their asses off. They got back to the warehouse about four hours late, but with the contraband intact. Well, almost intact.

When Marco arrived at the warehouse the next morning, he was met by Pete who slapped him on the back and said, "Come with me."

"Where are we going?"

"You'll find out, lets go."

Pete had a car waiting outside, and they drove to the same club where they had talked several months earlier. Again, they gained access with the use of a key. There were a half dozen men, drinking espresso and talking in Italian. Marco didn't fully understand the dialect but guessed it was Sicilian. He followed Pete across the room to a door leading to another room. He expected to see a room similar to the one at the storefront with a bank of telephones and men booking numbers. Instead, he walked into a plush office, rich with raised panel wood walls, leather chairs, and sofa and a desk large enough for three people. The man behind the desk looked up, and an almost imperceptible smile showed on the unmistakably Italian face. Several things had passed through his mind as he was driven here, but there was no way he could have been prepared for what was taking place. "Marco Silina, I want you to meet Don Belamonte." Marco was stunned; he was being introduced to the great man himself; the Don, his benefactor, the boss of all bosses. Marco was surprised by his age. The man seated behind the desk was much younger than he had expected, no more than ten years older than himself.

He somehow managed, "Don Belamonte, I am honored to meet you."

"Have a seat, please sit. Pete, could you leave us alone for a minute?" instructed the Don. Pete departed without a word. The man behind the desk was big, broad, and brought to mind a barrel of nails. This was not a man who made his living from behind a desk.

"Marco, I find myself in your debt. Your actions last night saved me a large sum of money, a truck, and a lot of legal fees." Marco could not think of a response, so he kept his mouth shut.

"Men in your charge spoke of your quick thinking and courage. Not to mention your ability to drive while using only two wheels."

The Don's attempt at humor surprised him and put him a bit at ease.

"This is the second time your actions have come to my attention," said the Don, in an apparent reference to the fight with the Irishman.

The Don paused for a second, but when it was obvious that he wasn't going to illicit a word from the other man, he continued. "I am always looking for good men who have the talents that you have shown. Would you be interested in perhaps another place in my organization?"

This was not what Marco wanted to hear. If his brother was angry with what he was now doing, what would he do if he were to accept the offer made by the Don?

Beyond that, it was something he himself wanted no part of. He could rationalize the driver's job in times like this, but to do more would be wrong. Has anyone ever said no to the Don?

"No," he blurted out. "No, I am quite satisfied with what I am doing, but I thank you for the kind offer."

He was sure he was holding his breath when the Don answered.

"I understand, but if you should ever change you mind, a job will be waiting."

With that, he reached to the corner of the desk where a white envelope sat.

"I always pay my debts. I want you to accept this." He handed the envelope to Marco, who took it, but suddenly didn't know what to do with it.

"Thank you, Don Belamonte; I too am in your debt."

The meeting finally ended, and Marco could not exit the room fast enough. He didn't bother to open the envelope but instead stuffed it in his pocket.

When he returned to the warehouse, he was greeted by the members of his crew.

"What happened, did he give you a new job?"

"No, he gave me a gun and told me to shoot the bastards who drank his whiskey."

There was a slight delay while the other men processed the information, and then laughter rang through the warehouse.

When he returned to the Patranos late that evening, he finally opened the envelope he was given that morning. In it, he found $150, which was the equivalent of a month's pay. *Oh my god, how will I explain this to Santino?*

CHAPTER SEVEN

Building Memories

It's July 4, 1931, and the Silina men are at the playground, overseeing the preparation of the evening's festivities. They had brought with them as much flammable material that they could carry. The residents were determined that the current state of affairs was not going to dampen the enthusiasm of America's celebration of independence. Even those who were not yet naturalized, like the Silinas, felt that this was their celebration because in their hearts, they felt as if they too were Americans. There had been talk for weeks of how this was going to be the best Fourth ever. While there would be fireworks, the centerpiece of any Fourth of July celebration was always the bonfire. The two elder Silinas sat on a bench and watched their two boys in their efforts to heave things onto the pile of flammables which, in about six hours, would be lighting the sky over Gloucester. The two men laughed as they watched the boys. Johnny was four and a half and Tony a year younger. Each boy would run to the location where people were dumping their contributions for the event. They would grab something, anything they could drag, and bring it to the growing tower of debris. They would then toss it as high as they could onto the pile. This, of course, was rather futile since the height of each toss never exceeded five feet or so. They would then turn and run for yet another piece of something. As soon as they did so, one of the older boys would retrieve their most recent effort and toss it to the top of the pile. Johnny and Tony seemed oblivious to what was happening.

"I want you to know that I am sorry for the way I acted when you took the job with the booze. I know you felt that you needed to bring more money into the house and, if not for that, you would not have gotten mixed up in this thing."

Nowhere to Go

"You know that I care only for the welfare of our family," responded Marco. "I have been doing this for more than a year now, and since that time, we have been able to not only pay our bills but also save some money."

"That is true, and when all this craziness is over, we should have no trouble buying the boat we dream of."

"Yes, but right now, I dream only of the feast our wives will bring here in a few hours."

Things indeed had improved in the past year, and it was more than just the money. Marco did not have to go to the employment bureau every day in the hope of finding work, but rather he would talk to Pete about which days he would be driving; and whenever he had a couple of days off, he would return to Gloucester. His schedule did not always coincide with Mike's, and when that happened, he was able to employ the services of Dominic Patranos neighbor for his transportation. This meant that he was home almost every week. This, of course, made Mary very happy, although she wondered at times what made this possible. While she wondered, she never asked. Instead she enjoyed having him around and took great joy in watching him make up for lost time with the children.

From time to time, Don Belamonte would inquire of Pete as to how this man Marco was doing. There was something about Marco that intrigued him. He knew that by most standards, Marco was making good money, but that was chicken feed compared to what others in his organization made each week. A few of his top earners like Pete were making close to what Mayor Curley took home, and even his street soldiers made double what Marco did. He knew that men talked of such things and that Marco knew how much better he could do, but never once did he call to asked about the offer he had been made.

The Don did, however, maintain a level of contact with Marco through Pete. He had heard that they shared a common interest in boxing and on occasion would send an envelope containing several tickets to him. The first time it happened, it became a special family event, and it was evident right from the start that it was to become a family tradition. Santino shared his brother's love for the sport, and although they thought that the boys might be a bit too young to grasp what it was all about, they decided to bring them along. Johnny always loved doing anything that included the elder Silinas, and Tony loved being with his cousin. Tonight would be the first boxing match for the boys, and they could hardly control their excitement. This was the first fight for their fathers since before the Depression, and they too were very excited. There were tickets for Mike and Dominic, so four men and two boys climbed into Mike's truck and headed out for the fights.

Heading for the fights generally meant going to St. Botolph Street and the Boston Arena. The really big headliners usually fought at the Boston Garden, but while these guys didn't qualify as such, they were pros and didn't leave any of their fight in the locker room. This was the Great Depression, and boxing was a way to make money for those who were tough enough and willing to risk an ass kicking to do it. Johnny wasn't yet five and had no idea what advantage the Silina gene pool would give him, but he loved what went on inside the square ring.

Both boys slept during the ride home, but Johnny was at his father's bedside bright and early the next morning with a dozen or more questions about boxing, what they had witnessed the night before, and of course, "When can we go again?" It was December 10, 1931, and Marco was very sure that his son was now a disciple of the sport of boxing.

The family went to a late Mass at Our Lady of Good Voyage, and as was the custom, they congregated outside afterward to talk with some of the other parishioners. Marco was looking to see if he could spot Father Bruno, who had not performed the late service, but usually made a point of visiting with the parishioners after every Mass. At last he spotted the young priest as he walked from the rectory.

"Good morning, Father, how are you doing?

A smile came across the face of the priest. "Marco, it's so good to see you, I missed you last Sunday."

"I didn't make it up last weekend, but I assure you that I attended Mass in Boston."

Marco was ill at ease when talking to his priest, because he wasn't sure if Father Bruno knew of his work, and if he did, how he felt about it. If it was a problem, the young priest never let on that it was. Marco knew the priest wanted to visit with some others, so he got right to the point.

"Father, I understand that you instruct some of the boys in the parish in the sport of boxing."

"Yes, yes I do. Each Saturday morning, we get together at the YMCA and work out for two or three hours. However, I have heard of your prowess with the fisticuffs, and I must tell you that you cannot join our group." Both men laughed. People have long memories, Marco thought.

"No, Father it is not me, but my son Johnny I ask for."

"I would be happy to instruct your son, but he would be the only boy of his age, and he could not box with the others. They are twice his age or more."

"That would be fine. He would love to be in the gym even if he were to watch the older boys box."

"Have him at the Y by nine on Saturday; it should be fun to have him there."

Of course, not having a sparring partner was never a problem because as soon as Tony heard of the boxing lessons, he wanted to do it also. Wherever Johnny went, Tony was sure to follow. From that point on, the main event each Saturday morning was Silina versus Silina. The older boys would circle the ring and watch the two boys do battle. Of course, they wore headgear and sixteen-ounce gloves, so there was never any real damage done, but the enthusiasm they demonstrated met with loud approval each week.

Our Lady of Good Voyage Church,
which was located a short walk from the Silina home.

When Marco next saw Pete, he asked if it would be possible to get an additional ticket for the fights. Pete knew that this would not be a problem. The group of six was expanded to include Father Bruno, who never inquired of the source of the tickets, and Marco never offered the information.

As concerned as some were of his work, none could deny that things were working out well, and this went beyond the money alone. When he had been away for long periods, Marco worried of the effect of this on his family. Mary was a rock, and he knew she would be all right, but Johnny and Margaret were young, and he hated being away from them. Now he was home almost as much as he was when he was fishing. Transportation was always a problem, and he knew he could get home more often if he had a car. He had looked at a couple of secondhand cars and found that he could actually afford to buy one but decided against it. Pete had told him that the last thing you wanted to do in this life was to draw attention to yourself. While this was true in Boston, it was even more so in Gloucester. While no one openly talked about it, people strongly suspected that Marco was into something outside the law. There was no telling where this would go if he were to flaunt his good fortune with the purchase of a car while his neighbors struggled to feed themselves.

The next year of so went along quite smoothly, and Marco didn't experience anything close to the wild chase he had earlier with the federal agents. The closest call he has was spring of 1932 when he spotted a car following him from a safe distance as he headed for the rendezvous location for a pickup of Canadian whiskey. He made a couple of unlikely turns, and when the following car followed suit, he was convinced that it was in fact the feds. He decided that to follow the plan for the pickup would be unwise and instead drove past the meeting place and made his way back to Boston deadheaded. When he arrived with an empty truck, he had some explaining to do with Pete, but the determination was made that he had done the right thing. He was relieved; however, that situation never repeated itself, because right decision or not, Pete didn't like to see empty trucks pull into the warehouses.

Things also continued to go smoothly in Gloucester. Several months earlier, Mike had come to Marco inquiring about working with him. It had become increasingly difficult for him to find work, and he decided that if Marco could get him in, that he would jump at the chance. Marco went to Pete and vouched for Mike's toughness and loyalty. A month later, when an opening occurred, Mike got the job. He was put on Marco's crew so their days off coincided, and transportation to and from Gloucester was no longer an issue.

The Silina household was indeed a happy place. Lots of good food, family gatherings, trips to Boston for the fights, the battle of the Silina boys each Saturday morning at the YMCA, and enough for an occasional gift for Mary and Rose. The only cloud in their lives was the fact that one brother fished and the other smuggled whiskey.

CHAPTER EIGHT

The Days of Wine and 3.2 Beer

"Hey, Marco, look at this," said Pete as he looked up from the early edition of the *Record American* newspaper.

"Look at what? Do you forget that I do not read the language?"

"Oh yeah, well, the fuckin' president is changin' the law, and it is goin' to be legal to sell watered-down beer and wine."

"How about the whiskey and gin and the other hard stuff?"

"It doesn't say, but this shit is not good. I'll talk to Don Belamonte and see what he says."

That fuckin president was, of course, Franklin Delano Roosevelt; and what he did was make an amendment to the Volstead Act, which legalized the sale of 3.2 beer and light wines. This simple act was the beginning of the end of Prohibition and the windfall industry it created for organized crime. This took place in March of 1933, and eight months later in December, Prohibition was repealed altogether.

There was a meeting at the Causeway Street warehouse at the end of the month, and the workers were told that beyond the disposal of the current inventory and closing of warehouses, there would be no more work. This was tough to hear, but it was nothing that they hadn't expected. As the men filed heads down out of the warehouse, Marco heard Pete call out to him. "Hold up, Marco, we need to talk."

"Wait for me, Mike, I'll be out soon." Mike nodded and headed for his truck.

"What is it?" asked Marco after the last of the men had left the building.

"Don Belamonte would like to talk to you, he may have something for you."

"Doing what?"

"He didn't say, and I didn't ask. What do you want me to tell him?"

Marco hesitated. He wanted work, but there was a limit to what he would do. The Don knew this, but could he be sure that he would not receive an offer that he must turn down? Don Belamonte liked him, but Dons only hear no from their consigliere and even then it is in the form of a recommendation.

"Tell him that I would be honored to meet with him."

"Come for espresso tomorrow morning, and I will give you the meeting place."

Marco had an idea when and where the meeting would take place, but the Don did not give advance notice of his whereabouts, even to people he trusted. He did guess right, however. When he gained access to the club, he walked toward the table where Pete was seated. Pete looked up and waved for Marco to follow him. He was led to the same plush office where he had last met with the Don. Again, Pete was excused from the office.

It was obvious to Marco that for some reason, Don Belamonte had taken a liking to him. Men of his status may never get to be in the presence of the Don, but he was having his second private audience with the man. He was even more surprised when the Don initiated some small talk.

"How have the fights been that you have seen?"

"The fighters may not be great, but the fights are. These men fight like their lives are at stake."

"In a way they are. They know that they will never be champions, but if they put on a good show, there will be another payday."

"It has been great fun. I thank you for your generosity"

"I am pleased to do this for you. Now tell me who it is that you take along, Pete tells me he gives you many tickets."

"There is my brother and me, our sons, a cousin, my friend Mike, and Father Bruno."

"Father Bruno, does he know where the tickets come from?"

"He doesn't ask, but I suspect he does." Both men had a good laugh at this.

"So this priest loves to watch the fighting?

"He more than loves it, he fought as an amateur and now coaches the young men in the parish. He is my son Johnny's coach."

"How old is your son, will we be seeing him at the Garden some time soon?"

"Ha, not soon, he will be seven years old next week."

"My Joey is six also, maybe some day they can enjoy a fight at the Garden together." How prophetic.

When Marco arrived home that weekend, he was greeted by Santino who could hardly wait to discuss the future with his brother.

"Now that the Prohibition is over, you will be needing work, and there are some good jobs to be had."

"Is that so?" replied Marco, displaying far less enthusiasm than was expected by his brother.

"Yes, the frozen food company is becoming far more successful than they have been in the past, and they are hiring more people all the time."

"I will not be working in a factory," started Marco.

"No," interrupted Santino, "many of the men who have fished in the past are taking these jobs, and I know I can get you on a boat, maybe even my boat. We will go to sea together again, my brother." As he said this, a broad grin came across is face.

Marco knew that there was not going to be a good time to tell his brother of his decision, so he might as well do it now.

"I will not be needing work in Gloucester. I will continue to go to Boston."

"And do what?" asked Santino, while already knowing the answer. "I have not heard of new jobs there."

"I will continue to work for the same people as before. They like my work, and they have asked me to stay."

"I have yet to hear what it is you will do, will you be working with the whores, or will it be the drugs? This is a dirty business, and no good will come of it."

"It is not about that. I will have a territory and run the numbers business for them.

There is nothing wrong with that. I know there was a time when you would make a bet or two."

"Making a bet at the club with the local bookie is not like it is with the people you work for. Nobody in Gloucester is going to break my legs if I can't pay. As the boss, will you have people to do this dirty work, or will you do it yourself?"

"I've had enough. My decision had been made, and I don't need to hear any more from you, my brother."

"That is fine with me because I no longer have a brother. The brother I had was a Silina and a fisherman. I don't know who it is standing before me."

From that point, the two men spoke to one another only when required. Santino insisted on separate accounting of their income, refusing to take any money earned outside of Gloucester.

This made things very odd for the others in the family. Over the past several years, Mary and Rose had become as close as sisters, and the children were very close as well. To hell with these two stubborn men. They will have to deal with their differences, but all the Silinas will sit at the same table for Sunday dinner.

CHAPTER NINE

"Come On, Tony, I'll Show You the Way."

It was September 4, 1934, and the first day of school for the city of Gloucester public schools. Tony Silina could not have been more excited. He was the first to rise, and if school were to start at 6:00 AM, he would have been there on time. Two years earlier, his sister Anna had started school; and last fall, Johnny had done the same. Both of them loved school, and came home each day with stories of what they had done and of their new friends. This was a difficult time for Tony because he had to see his sister and his best friend go off without him each day. That would all end today. Today, he would leave the house with them, make new friends, and have stories to share each evening.

This all seemed very good until they got to the schoolyard in front of the schoolhouse. It was a gray day, and the bare light bulbs that shone through the large glass windows suddenly gave the building a very foreboding look. Johnny looked over at his cousin and could see the concern in his eyes.

Johnny put his arm on the young boy's shoulder and said, "Come on, Tony, I'll show you the way." These two boys would grow up together and become fine young men. They would be good students, popular with their classmates, and fine athletes. With all this, one thing would never change. Tony would always be happiest when he turned and saw Johnny coming his way.

School was a blessing in another way. Things had changed at home, and it had a very different feel than it had even a year ago. There were family squabbles even then, but they were always over minor differences and always quickly resolved and forgotten. When his father and uncle had argued last winter, Johnny had not understood the severity for the disagreement and had assumed that this too would fade away. It took a few weeks, but he finally realized that this was something new to the Silina household. There was a tension that hung over the house; and there were times, when both men were present, that it seemed as if emotions were about to boil over. Sunday's command performance dinners, which were at one time the highlight of the week, were now something to finish as quickly as possible. School served as a refuge from this and took on a special importance for Johnny.

Johnny also noticed a change in his mother. She and Rose were very close, but they had to be guarded when in the presence of either of the men. Mary and Rose worked extremely hard to provide for the needs of the family, and their rewards had always been the smiles, laughter, and the warm feeling which up to now had been commonplace in their home. Part of Mary's sadness was a result of what she saw in the children. Margaret and Annette were not yet in school, but she sensed a difference in their behavior, and there was no question in her mind the three oldest seemed only too happy whenever leaving the house for hours, be it for school or play. She decided to talk to Marco about it after a Sunday Mass. She feared that this was a mistake, but felt it was too important to avoid. They were in the kitchen, she at the stove and Marco seated at the kitchen table, sampling the meatballs she had just finished frying. She removed her apron and took a seat across from her husband.

"Marco, we must talk."

"Talk about what?" he asked as he looked over at her.

"There are many things, there is this thing with you and Santino, there is the job, and also the children."

"What about the children?" he asked as if to say, I have no interest in talking about the job or my brother.

"You do not see what is happening, our home was a good place, a place they wanted to be, but that has changed. What about the children? The children have changed."

"And this is my fault? Is Rose having this same talk with Santino?"

"I have no way of knowing what she is doing. Is this your fault? The fault is shared with you and him, but the biggest blame lies at your feet."

"And what is it you ask me to do? Am I to give up what I am doing to make him happy?"

"No, you do it for the children, and you do it for me."

"What do you expect me to do after that? This job pays good money, what am I supposed to do after that?"

"Have you moved so far from us that you forget why we came to America? Santino is not without fault. But he has not forgotten who he is."

"I too have not forgotten. I am the man in this house, and I will decide where it is that I will work. We will not talk of this again." Mary had spoken her mind, but she knew that her husband was not going to give up his work in Boston.

Johnny was truly torn. He loved his mother, and he hated to see her sad, but he loved his father also. Sure he seemed angry more often then the past, but he was not alone. His uncle, if anything, was worse and seemed more determined by his actions to keep the misunderstanding from being resolved. Johnny was only seven years old, but the only thing he could do was to continue to respect both of his parents and pray that things would get better.

It had been almost three years since Johnny and Tony had been enrolled in Father Bruno's boxing program, which by now had grown from six combatants to over a dozen. All of the new recruits were closer in age to the Silina boys, which was yet another blessing. As enthusiastic as the two boys were about boxing, they were weary of beating up one another every week. They made a pact to box only with the other boys from that day on. They did, however, take on all other comers, and it did not take long for the word to get around that there was another generation of Silinas who were not to be fucked with.

It was not long before all the boys tired of fighting one another, and Father Bruno saw a need to expand the program. He started to call surrounding parishes to inquire of any interest they may have in starting a boxing league. He was overwhelmed by the excitement that his idea generated; and by February 1935, at the age of seven and eight, Tony and Johnny got to test their mettle in a real boxing match. Father Bruno's boys were much more advanced than the others and won six of the eight matches. No one won more convincingly than the Silinas. They were having the time of their lives and couldn't wait for the next match, which would take place one month later.

As good as things were going at school and with the boxing program, the problems at home continued to mount. There was the Saturday when Marco did not return home; and in spite of the fact that both households had, by now, installed telephones, there was no call from him. Mary was concerned, but knew that there was probably a good reason for his failure to call, and he probably would show up before Sunday dinner. After Mass, the congregation made their way out front to the church's courtyard for the Sunday ritual of catching up with neighbors. Father Bruno came out of the rectory and made his way directly to Santino. He greeted him with a handshake and a nervous smile.

"Can I talk to you alone for a minute?"

Santino was immediately alarmed. "What is the matter?"

"Let's move over there," he said, pointing to a spot closer to the rectory.

"It's about my brother is it not?" Suddenly, everything that had gone wrong between him and Marco didn't matter. He was now only concerned for his welfare.

"I read in this morning's paper that Marco was arrested on Friday night." Santino saw red. It was Sunday, April 21, 1935, and now things had finally reached rock bottom.

"Thank you, Father, I must go now and talk to Mary and Rose."

CHAPTER TEN

The Wedge Goes Deeper

It had been over five years since he had seen Joseph Pino, but Marco had certainly expected that he would have seen him last night. He and four members of his crew had spent Friday night in the tank at the police precinct in Hyde Park. It had been twelve hours since his arrest, and he expected he would be back on the street by now. This was his first arrest for booking, but he was familiar with the drill. Every once in a while, someone wants to see their name in the papers. Some politician, or police captain looking for reelection or to gain favor with his superiors, makes a sweep, racks up some arrest, and then calls the *Record American* and *Boston Globe* with the story. It makes the front page the next day and is picked up in the out-of-town papers the following day. It was the Sunday edition of the *Gloucester Daily Times* that brought the arrest to the attention of Father Bruno. Of course, there is no attempt to notify the papers of the releases that take would place in the next couple of days.

Marco was now hoping that he might be out by noon and be in Gloucester before dinner. Instead, it was noon on Sunday before he was released. Mr. Pino explained that the Boston Police had decided to have some fun and that he had spent a day and a half trying to find out where they were being held. As it turned out, they were being held in East Boston, South Boston, Dorchester, and Roxbury in addition to Hyde Park. Maybe word of all this had not reached Gloucester. Even if it hadn't, he had no idea how he would explain his absence on Saturday. He was not the same man who came from Gaeta ten years earlier, but he still hated the idea of lying to his family.

Lying was never an option. He knew as soon as he walked up the front walk that this was going to get ugly. He was immediately confronted by Santino, who wasted no time before starting his tongue-lashing.

"What more can you do to this family? This morning, your actions were all that people could talk about at church. These are our neighbors, the people I work with.

You bring shame to the Silina name, and I want no part of you. I wish I never again would have to look upon you."

"When will you understand? These things mean nothing, I am in and out in a day or two, pay a small fine, and it is over with. This is my first arrest, but it will not be the last. If you do what I do, you have to understand that it is part of the job. I am truly sorry if I caused you shame, but I myself feel none. Now I must talk to Mary." He walked past his brother and through the front door. He did not know what to expect, but he knew it would not be good. Mary heard him come into the kitchen but did not look up from what she was doing. He walked to her and put his hand on her shoulder.

"I am sorry for what has happened. I never wanted to embarrass you with our neighbors. Can you forgive me?"

"You say you are sorry, but will you do anything to change? No, tomorrow you will leave and go back to do the very thing that hurts me. You have told me that you no longer want to talk about what you do for work. I no longer want to talk of it either."

Never once did she stop and look at him, and he did not have an answer to what she had said.

"I am sorry," he repeated, and he left the room to look for the children.

He found Margaret and Johnny in the backyard, and they both ran up to greet him. Johnny knew what had happened; he knew that his uncle was terribly angry, and that his mother had not smiled since returning from church. He knew all of this, but he also knew how much he loved his father.

Sunday night's dinner was very somber. Santino refused to attend and had asked Rose and the children do the same.

"What is happening is between you and Marco, and I am sorry, but I will not do anything to hurt Mary and the children." said Rose. "The wounds that you feel may never be well, but I am going to do whatever I can to hold the family together."

There was very little said at dinner, and when it was over, Marco hugged all of the children and left for Boston. When things were cleaned up and the children were in bed, Mary hugged Rose and thanked her for what she had done that night.

CHAPTER ELEVEN

Life Goes On

No one could expect that life would get back to normal after that weekend. The men of the house had irreparable differences, and neither was interested in resolving them. Things would fall into a pattern. As usual, Marco came home by noon on Saturday and would depart either late Sunday or first thing on Monday morning. What happened during that period only varied from earlier visits where it involved activities with his brother. For the most part, that translated into family dinners. This required a compromise which Mary and Rose not only suggested but insisted upon. Before all this had occurred, the location of the weekend meals would alternate between households, Saturdays at one and Sundays at the other. This, the women had insisted, would not change. When Rose hosted the dinner, only Santino would attend the meal with the roles reversing the following night. There was always a plate prepared for the absentee Silina. At first, there was an uneasy feel with this arrangement, but before too long, this became the norm; and it was accepted that things would never be as before. The development that was most important to Johnny was that things were slowly getting back to normal with his parents. Once again, he would see them smiling and joking with each other, and it was apparent that both were willing to put what happened behind them.

If Johnny was happy with things at home, he was ecstatic about his life beyond that. Father Bruno's parish boxing competition had taken off, and there were matches arranged at least twice a month. Sacred Heart, Holy Family, Saint Ann's, Saint Joachim, and Saint Anthony's Chapel were all represented. He had also discovered baseball and fell in love with it as well as boxing. If not great, he was at worst, a very good student; and the girls would whisper about how cute he was.

There was always one constant: whatever he got involved in, you could be sure Tony was never far behind. As it turned out, they both did well in whatever it was they did. In boxing, Johnny was clearly the best at his age in the city and never lost a match while Tony might well have been the second best. Tony clearly showed early promise in baseball, as well, and possessed a strong throwing arm the powerful body of a catcher. Johnny, being slender and lithe, was born to be a middle infielder. The young ladies also found Tony to be cute and he had a way of always making them laugh. The place where Tony took a back seat to no one was in the classroom, where he really excelled. Tony was an extremely bright young man.

Marco continued to get tickets for the boxing matches with the only difference being that Santino no longer would attend, although he would allow Tony to do so. It was not apparent early, but as time went on, Johnny noticed that his father was taking far more interest not only in the fight but who won and in what manner. It would be a few years yet before he understand the significance of this.

Santino was moving on with his life. When the brothers had their falling out at the end of Prohibition, they split the family savings equally. That included the money from the sale of their boat in Italy, and when combined with Marco's extra earnings during Prohibition, it came to a tidy sum. In the fall of 1936, Santino became the captain of his own fishing vessel. Both Mary and Rose thought that this might be a good time for the men to reconcile but agreed that both were too stubborn to make the first step. Of course, any reconciliation would require Marco to return to Gloucester and fishing, and Mary was not prepared to broach that matter again.

Smooth seas are not commonplace in New England, and this seemed to hold true with the Silina family also, and on February 1, 1937, after almost two years of calm, Marco was arrested for the second time. This time, he was released in less than six hours; and if not for the local newspaper, it would have gone unnoticed in Gloucester. This time there was no confrontation with Santino. A confrontation would require conversation, and the two men had hardly spoken a word to one another in two years. Besides, all that was required to say had already been said.

Mary was all at once angry, sad, and embarrassed; but after some early tension, she seemed to get over it in a relatively short period. Maybe this was now just part of their life. Some men come home and tell their wives that they got a ticket for speeding while her husband tells her that he was arrested for booking. Thankfully, the arrest took place on a Monday and didn't make the Gloucester papers until Wednesday; and by Sunday Mass, it was old news.

The arrest did cause one notable problem outside the Silina home, which did caused quite a stir. When Johnny went to school on Thursday morning, he was greeted by a few young hecklers.

"Hey, Silina I hear your old man is behind bars again. What did he do this time, rob a bank?" He turned to see who was responsible for the jibes and saw three boys who seemed to be enjoying making him the butt of the insults.

"Maybe him and your old lady can hit the road and be the Italian Bonnie and Clyde." More forced laughter. The boy doing all the talking was buoyant by the fact that he was at least a year older than Johnny in addition to being taller and heavier than him. The other two were no bigger than Johnny. He knew all three only by sight and had never exchanged a word with any of them until this moment. He also recognized them as bullies who found enjoyment in harassing others in his class. He walked toward the boys and got in the face of the one responsible for the insults.

"I want you to take that back right now."

"Yeah, I'll take it back, but not until the feds gun them down." Johnny took a step back.

"You better put them up." He warned as he put his own fist up.

"You little shit, you better get out of here while you can still walk."

Johnny flicked a light left hand jab to the older boy's face as a message that he wasn't going anywhere.

"I'm going to kill you, you little prick!" shouted the older boy as he lunged forward.

Johnny slid to his left to sidestep his adversary and hit the other boy with a left hand to the ear. When he turned back to locate Johnny, he was met with another left which missed its mark, but still stung his shoulder. This was immediately followed by a straight right to the nose. The air was filled with the sound of breaking cartilage and blood spewing from a broken nose. His two friends looked as if they may want to jump Johnny from behind, but they saw this other block of muscle eyeing them, and he seemed quite ready to jump into the fray. The boy with the big mouth was bent at the waist with one hand on his face in an effort to stem the bleeding and the other held up in front of him to indicate that he was done.

"I don't hear you. Do you have something to say to me?"

"I'm sorry, I'm sorry. I take it back."

"Good." Johnny then gave the older boy a kick in the balls for good measure.

It must be a Silina tradition. Tony came over and slapped his cousin on the back and said. "I had you covered, cus'.

Within an hour, Johnny was summoned to the principal's office where he found a very angry Mary Silina waiting for him.

"This is unacceptable behavior and will not be tolerated on school grounds. If this were not a public institution I would expel you this very minute. Since I can't do that, I am suspending you for the balance of this week and all of next. I had better not see you in this office ever again. Do you understand Mr. Silina?"

"Yes, sir." These were the only words he uttered. It was clear to him that the principal was not interested in hearing what happened, and it was best to just shut up and get out of that office.

There was not a word said by either mother or son during the cold walk home. When they arrived, Mary calmly took off her coat, turned to her son and said, "Johnny, you are a good boy. You have never given me one minute of unhappiness. Please tell me what happened this morning."

Johnny never loved his mother more. He explained what had taken place, and when he finished, he waited while Mary thought about what she had heard.

"I understand what you did and why you did it. Do you understand that it was wrong? Do you not remember to turn the other cheek?"

"Yes, Mom, I'm very sorry."

"Now go to your room until the others return from school. You might want to think about what you could have done that might have kept you out of trouble."

Johnny did as his mother suggested, and after two hours, he determined that he couldn't think of an alternative to what he had done.

It was about that time that he heard someone at the front door and, several minutes later, his mother calling for him to come to the living room. When he got there, he was surprised to see Father Bruno waiting for him.

"I've been talking to your mother, and she told me what happened this morning. To tell you the truth, I came here to tell you that I will no longer be coaching you to box." The air suddenly seemed to leave his body, and he could not respond to what he had just heard.

Father Bruno continued. "I don't teach you to fight so that you can beat others in the schoolyard, however, your mother has explained what took place, and I am now inclined to give you a second chance. You must understand there will not be a third chance."

"Yes, Father, I'm very sorry." It seemed as if that's all he could think to say this morning. It wasn't much, but he meant every word of it. All five of them.

"Before going to the YMCA on Saturday, you will go to confession, and have many Acts of Contrition to say before you put on the gloves."

As Johnny went back to his room for further meditation, all he could think was, *Thank God he didn't hear about the kick to the nuts.*

When Johnny finally returned to school, he found the he had gained a new status. He was still the cute boy and the nice kid, but he now was looked up to by everyone who ever got pushed around in the schoolyard, or playground. He also picked up a nickname. It seemed as if his friends thought that everything he did had smoothness to it, and they started to call him Silk. Johnny did nothing to discourage this.

Even the principal seemed to look at him differently. Since the incident in the schoolyard had taken place, he had heard the entire story behind it and came to realize that he might have treated the boy too harshly. He, of course, would never admit that to anyone and most assuredly not to Johnny.

Johnny found out one other thing. He no longer had to fight. Even if he saw someone being mistreated, a sideward glance from him was all that was needed to end any harassment. A few months later, another supposed tough guy decided to try Tony on for size, which turned out to be a huge mistake. Tony too had now earned his bones and the new status that went with it.

CHAPTER TWELVE

Back to Normal
Whatever That May Be

As it turned out, except for the schoolyard fight, Marco's second arrest didn't cause nearly as much of a stir in the community as did the first. The Silinas were viewed as a good, God-fearing family; and in a way, Marco Silina was somewhat of a local celebrity who brought a bit of notoriety to their town. Furthermore, Marco never missed Mass on Sundays.

Marco, on the other hand, was beginning to have some misgivings about some of the things he saw going on in Boston. Peter, who had been his boss when he was running booze, was now deep into the loan-sharking end of the business. Prohibition was over, but the Great Depression still had the American people in a stranglehold. People borrowed money for any number of reasons, ranging from paying their rent to covering gambling debts. Santino had been right when he had asked Marco about strong arming bettors who were slow to pay. That usually didn't amount to much more then a finger in their face and a threat of more serious repercussions. The debts were never too big, and the money almost always followed soon after. Did it ever go further? Of course, if the word got out that you were soft, nobody would pay. Loan sharking was different. Usury would be a mild way of describing the interest charged the unfortunate souls who borrowed from these people.

Marco became painfully aware of this when Tom, who used to ride shotgun for him on the truck, came to see him at the betting room. Tom looked terrible. He had obviously received a severe beating in the past few days.

"What the hell happened to you?"

"Marco, I've gotten myself into a mess." He went on to tell Marco of the problems encountered by him and his family since the steady work Prohibition had provided had come to an end.

"I didn't borrow that much, but I also didn't understand how much I had to repay. Every week, I pay what I can, and now I owe more then when I started. If I don't do better, they promise that next week, they will not go so easy on me."

"Who says this to you?"

"The people who work for Pete, they did this. I thought you might talk to Pete on my behalf. Marco, I cannot pay the number that they gave me for next Friday."

"I will talk to Pete tonight, come back here to see me tomorrow. Go now, I will do what I can."

Marco watched his friend walk from the room and wondered if Pete had forgotten that it was Tom riding shotgun the night of that car chase in Vermont.

"No, I didn't forget, but it doesn't matter. He got a nice bonus for that night, and he has nothing else due him."

"Pete, it isn't like he is not trying to pay. He gives you something every week."

"Something is not enough. He knows what he must do. If not, he gets no special treatment."

"I know how this works, he has probably already repaid more than he borrowed. He will never be out of your debt."

"That may be true, but until he is, he will make the number every week, or else."

"What is it he owes you, you prick?"

"Watch what you say, Silina, don't forget who you are talking to."

"I haven't forgotten, just give me the number." He winced when he heard what it was. He reached into his pocket and pulled a large roll of bills and counted out three hundred dollars. Both men knew the money was not Marco's but rather proceeds from today's action, and Marco knew he must replace it before morning.

"This is a big mistake, Silina, are you going into business for yourself?"

"I have no stomach for this business, but unlike you, I don't turn my back on a friend."

The first thing Marco did the next morning was to go to the safe and return the three hundred from yesterday's receipts. It wasn't long before Tom arrived. The two men went into Marco's small office and closed the door behind them. Marco then told Tom what had taken place the previous night.

"You are in my debt now, and I expect to get repaid.

"Of course, tell me what you require?

"Think first then answer. How much can you pay every week?"

"Would ten dollars be enough?"

"You come here every week with ten dollars. Don't let me down."

There was no interest charged and in thirty weeks, Tom was off the cuff.

This entire episode would never be forgotten by Tom, but it left a far larger impression on Marco than it did on his friend. The problem was as he had realized many years ago. The door swing much more freely in than out, and try as he may, he could not imagine making a break without making a rupture.

CHAPTER THIRTEEN

A Time to Grow

While Marco wrestled with his dilemma in Boston, the remainder of the Silinas seemed to thrive in Gloucester. If there was an exception to this, it would have been Mary. Things could never seem whole for her while her husband was in Boston, and his relationship with Santino continued to be estranged. Johnny may have been the only one in the family aware of her feelings since he was always watching for any changers in her demeanor. In a way, this made him angry at his father, but it did not alter the fact that he cared very deeply for him. Marco tried to ensure the timing and duration of his visits by purchasing a car. He remained conscious of the fact that he didn't want to attract attention to himself, and for that reason, he purchased a ten-year-old Ford. It was not much to look at but served the purpose.

Aside from some weekend uneasiness, Johnny and Tony continued as they had in the past. They were very popular at school, and the academics came easy for them. They continued to enjoy Father Bruno's boxing program, and both were always the best in their age and size class; and while they tried to convince the good Father to allow them to move up in class, he steadfastly refused to allow it. Baseball was their latest interest, and both looked forward to the day that they were eligible to play for their church in the CYO League. The year that Tony turned twelve, his father thought it was time to get the two boys involved in the family business and employed them to assist in the cleanup of the boat after returning from a trip. The work was hard, and the pay was small, but they loved being on the boat; and Santino would smile proudly when he heard them talk of the day when they would be old enough to go out as part of the crew. He couldn't help thinking back nearly thirty years earlier when he and Marco would dream of the same thing.

—

When Johnny went back for his first day school in the fall of 1940, he was stopped in his tracks when he saw a classmate, Tina Collins, for the first time in three months. Could this have happened in just three months? Tina and he had started school together in 1933 and were now entering the eighth grade. In that time, while they may have not been friends, they were always friendly. Tina was now taller than she had been when he had last seen her, had definitely transformed from a girl into a young woman, and her cute appearance had moved much closer to beautiful. Add all this to the blue eyes and blonde hair she had always had and the changes were a showstopper. With all this came a self-assurance she had never previously displayed.

"Hi, Johnny, how was your summer?"

"Not too bad, but it may have been too long."

"What do you mean too long? Didn't you always say that you loved summer vacation and wished it would never end?"

Johnny, who never lacked confidence, came back quickly.

"That might have been true once, but now I'm happy to be here."

Tina now realized what he was getting at and momentarily slipped back to the less-self-assured Tina of the previous spring. Tina felt the same spark that Johnny had, and from that day forward, they were a matched pair. Tony's reaction to all of this was simple. "That's great, Johnny, I'll find a girl, and we can all hang out." True to his word, Tony hooked up with Tina's best friend, Ellen, within a week. Tony never had a problem with confidence either.

When Marco came home at the end of the first week in December, he had an announcement to make.

"When you boys go to school next Friday, you tell your teachers you will not be at school on Tuesday." This, of course, caught Mary's attention, and she asked what he meant with this statement.

"The boys will be up very late on Monday night, and it may be best if they rest up on Tuesday." The boys were puzzled and waited for an explanation, and when it came, they were caught up in a frenzy. On Monday, December 16, 1940, Joe Louis, the heavyweight boxing champion of the world, was fighting at the Boston Garden; and Marco had his usual allotment of tickets. He had never received tickets for fights at the Garden, much less a championship fight, but Don Belamonte knew of the great interest Marco and his family had for boxing and saw to it that he got the tickets. This was the time referred to in Joe Louis's career as the Bum of the Month Club. The champ was touring the country and taking on all comers, and he in fact didn't miss a month. There were no real contenders among the opposition, but it didn't matter because the fans wanted to say that they had seen the Brown Bomber in action. Beside which, nobody could beat him anyway.

The anticipation that followed was overwhelming, and it did not end with Tony and Johnny. Even Santino was excited, but when urged by Rose to accept his brother's offer of a ticket, he could not relent; but nonetheless, he was very pleased to watch his own son's smiling face.

Given the magnitude of the event, Father Bruno was not sure there was a ticket for him; and after Mass on Sunday, he approached the Silina gathering in the church courtyard with more than a little trepidation. When Marco saw him coming, he gave a moment's thought to letting the good Father sweat a bit but then decided that a man of the cloth deserved better treatment. He put his left arm around the shoulder of the priest and, with his right hand, he place a ticket into Father Bruno's hand. "Mike will pick you and the boys up at two o'clock next Monday, and I'll meet you in Boston when you arrive. We can all have spaghetti and some good sausage before we go to the Garden."

Monday finally arrived, and the truck departed the city limits of Gloucester just prior to 2:00 PM. It would have been earlier if possible, but the boys did have classes to attend. They pulled up in front of the Patrano home two hours later, and everyone in the truck assumed that Lena Patrano would be preparing dinner for the men.

"Tonight is a special occasion and will be treated as such. Johnny, have you ever eaten in a restaurant?"

"No, Father, I haven't"

"And you, Tony?"

"No, sir, never. My mother is a very good cook, and so is Aunt Mary."

Marco laughed. "And so too is Mrs. Patrano, but tonight, we six men and Mrs. Patrano will eat at the restaurant Angelina's. This should be a night to remember always."

Angelina's was located on the ground level of a storefront on Hanover Street, and while it was clean and orderly, it was obvious that ambiance was not a concept which Angelina embraced. It was also obvious that this was not Marco's first visit to the establishment. The waiters and the bartender all acknowledged his arrival, and the manager made a point to come quickly to the table to greet his group.

"Welcome to Angelina's. I hope you bring with you a big appetite. Marco, which of these two handsome young men is your son?"

"I would be pleased with either, but it is this one here." He said as he ruffled the hair of the boy to his left.

The looks on the faces of the two boys were priceless. A few hours ago, they were in their classrooms, wondering if the final few minutes of the school day would ever be clicked off the clock, which seemed stuck on 1:42 PM. Now they were in the middle of a day that would be, in fact, remembered for their entire lives. More so for Johnny, for a reason he was not yet aware.

He was not yet fourteen, but not too young to notice two things as the evening progressed. First was the waitress assigned to their table. She was young, beautiful, and paying far too much attention to his father. He didn't fully understand what was going on, but he wouldn't forget it either.

The meal too was unforgettable. Each of the seven guests was accustomed to voluminous Italian meals, but tonight surpassed anything they had ever experienced. Everything, of course, was family style; and the offerings seemed endless. And when it was over, Angelina, who had been busy preparing the feast, came from the kitchen to meet her guests and accept the accolades. Johnny had never met either of his grandmothers, but Angelina looked as he had imagined them. She had a broad handsome face, which seemed to be entirely taken up with a smile. She wasn't nearly as tall as his mother and somewhat heavier. This, he reasoned, must be what Grandmother Silina looks like.

It was a short walk to the Boston Garden, and they arrived just as the first round of the first preliminary bout was ending. The fighters in the prelims were at least as good if not superior to the headliners they were used to at the Arena; and while that was great, these matches seemed to be a gauntlet of sorts, which had to be navigated in order to get to the reason for the evening. In spite of the importance of the event, the seats they had for this championship fight were better than they had ever had at the Arena. They were situated in the first row of the first balcony and were right in the center of the building. They looked straight down to the ring and were completely unobstructed.

The undercard was almost complete when Johnny noticed three men and two boys walking down the center aisle at floor level, leading to ringside. There they were seated in front row ringside seats which had been unoccupied to this point. Marco leaned over to his son and whispered, "That man there, the one with a hat and topcoat, he is Mr. Belamonte, the man who I work for and our benefactor."

Johnny wasn't sure what his father meant by *benefactor*, but he knew the man was important. People in the ringside area looked his way and nodded a greeting if they happened to catch his eye.

"The men on either side also work for Mr. Belamonte, and the two to his side are his sons, Carl and Joey." What Marco didn't say was that the men to the sides were not there to enjoy the fight but rather as bodyguards.

What Johnny didn't know was the part the three Belamonte's would eventually play in his life.

The semifinal event finally ended, but before the main event got started, there seemed to be a never-ending parade of ex-champions, aspiring fighters, and politicians who had to be introduced. Finally, it was time for round one of the heavyweight championship match between Joe Louis and Al McCoy. McCoy, of course, was no match for Louis, and the fight was over after five rounds when a game Al McCoy fell victim to a swollen left eye, which left him defenseless to a fighter the caliber of the champ.

Less than three hours later, the truck was back in Gloucester. Mike and Father Bruno were amazed that the two Silina boys were still wide awake and talking about the evening. They had had a very long and exhausting day, but neither seemed ready to have it come to an end.

This event served to further enhance the celebrity of Tony and Johnny. When they arrived at school on Wednesday, they were immediately surrounded by their friends who couldn't wait to hear of every detail that took place at the fight.

There was yet another development emanating from his visit to the Garden. Boxing took on new meanings for Johnny. First, he had his first real sports hero in Joe Louis. He was very impressed with the dignity and grace demonstrated by the champ on Monday night. Beyond that, for the first time, he thought that he may want to box as a professional.

CHAPTER FOURTEEN

Life Can Never Be the Same

Boston Post
May 2, 1941
Boston Cop Killed in Shoot Out

Last evening, just after 10:00 PM, Boston patrolman Thomas Kelley was shot and killed when he got caught in the crossfire of a shoot-out on Prince Street in the North End on Boston. When questioned by police, Frank Turco, owner of the Cantina restaurant, told them that Officer Kelley had been in his establishment and departed a few seconds prior to the sound of the first gunshot. Police theorize that Kelley was not the target of the attack but rather a victim of bad luck and timing and found himself in the rain of bullets being exchanged by rival mafia families.

When interviewed early this morning, both Police Chief Collins and Mayor Tobin promised immediate action and the quick apprehension of the people responsible.

Officer Kelley, a ten-year veteran of the Boston Police Force, was a resident of Charlestown and leaves behind his wife, Kathy, and two daughters, Mary, four, and Elizabeth, two. Details of the funeral ceremonies are expected later today.

The death and ensuing investigation of Officer Kelley's death dominated the news for the next several weeks, and while there were many suspects, there was no hard evidence to support an arrest in the case. The large majority of the people living in the North End were good, God-fearing Italians; but they understood the code of silence and the repercussions of aiding the police in their investigation.

With each passing day, the mayor became more frustrated with the lack of progress being made and the fact that there didn't even appear to be the hint of an arrest. There was almost daily dialog between Chief Collins and himself, but in the first week of June, he summoned Collins to his office.

"Mayor, you know I want to catch these bastards as much as anyone. For God's sake, they killed one of my own."

"I know that, Michael, but people are outraged, I'm outraged, is there anything to hang our hat on?"

"Nobody's talking, and everyone has an alibi. It seems as if Thursdays are family nights for this scum. Brothers, sisters, mothers, they all saw someone on May first."

"Listen, Chief, I've had enough, what can we do to rattle their cage? I'll support anything within the law."

"Well now, Mayor Tobin, I may have an idea."

The chief's plan was simple; it was what would become known as the shotgun effect, meaning if you can't get one person with a silver bullet, then get a bunch of them with a shotgun. This did not mean an arrest for murder or even that the people responsible would be apprehended for any crime whatsoever. What it did mean was that some bad guys would get arrested and charged with something. It took the chief a week to put his plan together. He wanted to hit as many places as possible in a short period because he knew that word would spread fast, and targets would close down as soon as it got to them. He would concentrate on numbers and the prostitution. He picked Friday the thirteenth, not because of luck, good or bad, but because Friday was payday and the busiest day of the week in these businesses.

Timing is everything, and if it weren't an extremely heavy betting day, Marco would not have been at a betting room. He was planning on leaving for home early the next morning and wanted to see that the take for the day was secured at each of the locations. The plan was good and went off swiftly. One second, Marco heard some commotion coming from the outer street front, and within seconds, the door to the back room burst open. There was something very different about this raid than the two previously experienced by Marco. On those occasions, there was a little tongue in cheek feel to the mannerisms of the police. This time, they were all business, pushing and shoving those, including Marco who were slow in his reactions to their orders.

"If any of you fucking wops move, I'll blow your fucking heads off," said the sergeant, sounding as if he meant every word of it.

"No need for this, Sergeant, we are going nowhere."

Marco's comment was answered by a gun barrel across the face. He did not lose his feet but did stumble back into a wall. In a reflex action born of poor judgment, Marco caught his balance and moved toward the officer. Before he could reach the sergeant, he was restrained by two offices and one clear-thinking member of his crew.

"Well, we'll just add resisting arrest to the charges," said a smiling sergeant.

Nothing happened during the booking process that made Marco feel any better about what he was experiencing. Every step, from the drive to the Charlestown precinct, booking and printing had all the earmarks of trouble and Marco was more than a little worried.

It was twelve hours from his booking before he saw a lawyer. When he did, it was not Mr. Pino but rather a young lawyer from his firm by the name of Thomas Polo.

"I apologize for the delay, Mr. Silina, but we have never seen anything like this before. There were more than a hundred arrests, and the bookings were all over Boston. We had no idea when or where we would find you."

What Marco didn't realize was that he was considered a big fish by the Boston Police and they took special care to hide his whereabouts.

"When can I see Mr. Pino?"

"He will be busy for the rest of the day, but he wants to see you and a few others at his office tomorrow afternoon."

Marco asked for an address, and the young lawyer handed him a business card.

"I do not read the language, what is the address?"

"One twenty Endicott Street. Be there by 3:00 PM."

There would be no visit to Gloucester this weekend, and his next visit did not promise to be pleasant.

The meeting on Sunday did nothing but heighten Marco's anxiety concerning the actions taken by the Boston Police Department. There were eight men present at the meeting; there was Joseph Pino, two associates, Marco, and four other men who held similar positions to his. Mr. Pino pointed out that while there were over a hundred arrests made, most of them would be dealt with by heavy fines since they involved peons who knew nothing of what happened beyond the four walls where they worked. The five at this meeting were viewed in a far different manner. They were a couple of levels closer to the bosses that the police were after, and if that was as close as they could get, then so be it. Pino took great pains to explain the severity of what had happened in the past few days. In his experience, which was considerable, he had never seen a sweep as swift, well planned, or intensive as this. He went on to say that he and his entire office would leave no stone unturned in an effort to get these charges resolved without going to trial. He was quick to point out that if the intent of what happened was to bring them to trial, there was little he could do. The last issue he addressed was the importance of not cooperating with the police.

"You will, almost certainly, be offered some sort of a deal if you offer information, which will aid in the police making additional arrests. The police will make it sound like a good idea to do so. I promise you that to do so would not benefit you in the long run." Marco wondered for a minute if this message was in fact the real purpose of this meeting. Either way, there was little doubt in his mind what he would do during questioning.

When the meeting came to a close, Pino asked Marco to stay for a few additional minutes.

"The reason I have asked you to stay is that I think your situation may be a bit more serious than the others."

"Why is that? My job is no different then the others."

"There is a difference, Marco. You all have a few arrests for booking numbers, but in addition to that, you had that assault charge back when we first met, and Friday, they also charged you with resisting arrest."

"What does this all mean? Am I going to jail?"

"That might be the case, but I want you to know that if that happens, your family will be looked after. Of course, we would expect that you will not, in anyway, cooperate with the authorities."

If he didn't know it before, he now understood that of all those arrested, he was in the most trouble, with the most to lose; and that was the reason for the stronger message he was now receiving.

"I understand" was all he said as he left the office.

CHAPTER FIFTEEN

Life Can Never Be the Same
Part Two

Marco and the others had arraignment hearings on the following Friday, and all pleaded not guilty. Marco, of course, was the only one charged with resisting arrest in addition to gaming. It was ruled that all would be held over for trial, and a trial date of August 18, 1941, was set for Marco.

Marco headed to Gloucester on Saturday morning and arrived home by noontime. He had called home the previous week to explain that he could not make it home because of the job, but beyond that, there was little to explain. Everyone had seen the newspaper accounts of the arrest, but no one attached any more importance to it than the earlier ones.

In spite of his years of experience in working outside the law, Marco was quite naive about what would transpire in the future and, because of this, made the decision not to share the information regarding his impending trail. Instead, he hoped that somehow things would get resolved before trial, and it would all just go away. He did know two things for certain: First, Santino would be madder than ever with the news since he was the only person in Gloucester who would never see any arrest as old news; second, there was Mary who he knew would make another plea for him to come home for good.

"Marco, I cannot understand why you continue to do this work. There is plenty of work in Gloucester, we have money put away, you could buy a boat, or if you were to ask, I am sure that your brother would make you a partner on his."

This was not a frivolous comment on her part since Santino, Rose, and she had already discussed this possibility.

"Mary, I must be honest with you. I have recently been giving thought to doing what you ask, but it is not that simple." He had been trying to see a way out since the incident involving Pete and Tom, but the answer continued to elude him.

"Give me one more year, maybe in that time, I can find a way, but you must promise me that nothing of this is said to Santino." Marco was thinking that if the charges got dropped for some reason, that he may be able to convince Pete that it would be best for everyone if he were to leave the business. This, of course, would be after everyone knew that he had kept his mouth shut.

"This would make me very happy, we would have a wonderful life if we could put all that has happened behind us."

"Yes, and maybe my brother and I can once again break bread together."

This, of course, all blew up early the following week when the Gloucester papers were full with the news of Marco's indictment and impending trial. Santino was out on a fishing trip when the news broke, and Rose and Mary tried to think of a way to lessen to some degree the fallout from the news. This was not easy to do since they themselves were furious with Marco, and Mary felt particularly betrayed because of the discussion she and her husband had just a few days earlier. It was decided that there was no good way to break the news, so they planned to sit down and get it over with as soon as he arrived home on Friday.

Santino returned to the Gloucester pier mid afternoon and was a couple of hours putting his boat up for the weekend. He noticed others walking past him, and while some nodded and waved to him, none stopped to say hello or inquire of his trip. Santino had long since become accepted as a good man, one who could be counted upon for help if the need arose, and he found what was happening to be a bit strange. When he got home, he fully understood what had been going on. What happened upon hearing the news completely caught the two women off guard. There was no yelling, no slamming the table, no condemnation of his brother. Instead, he leaned back in his chair, put his hands over his face, and quietly stated.

"I knew it would come to this. What can we do to help him?"

Both women were completely in shock. They were not prepared to respond to what they had just heard.

Rose heard herself say, "Does he deserve our help? He has embraced this life of his." She stopped. The last thing she wanted to do was hurt her dearest friend.

Mary answered her question for her, "You are right, he could have come back here a long time ago. He has made his own bed."

—

Now both Rose and Santino were not sure of what they were hearing. Mary had always been completely loyal to her husband; but they, of course, had no way of knowing how hurt she was because of his promise to her.

"He has made mistakes, many mistakes, but he is my brother, and I will not turn my back on him. What happens after that, I have no way of knowing, but for now, we will do for him whatever we can."

"What can we do?" asked his wife.

"We can start by calling him and make sure he comes here tomorrow. Mary, you can tell him we will have a Silina family meeting."

CHAPTER SIXTEEN

Dealing with Adversity

It was a good thing that school had let out for the summer. The last thing Silk wanted to do was face everyone there. It was Saturday morning, and he hadn't been out of the house in two days. He knew he had to face the music sooner or later and decided that he had better deal with it now, furthermore he really didn't want to see his father, who he was really pissed at. He decided to head to the Y for boxing and then go to Cramer's drugstore on the chance he would bump into Tina. He didn't dare call her at home for fear that one of her parents would answer. He had no idea how that would go. He and Tony headed for the Y with the idea that if anyone had anything to say, they could deal with it in the ring and kick their ass under the careful supervision of Father Bruno. Silk's fears proved to be unfounded. The other guys all came to him to shake his hand or dispense a friendly punch to the arm. The message was clear, he was their friend, and what his father did was of no concern to them.

When they finished with boxing, the two cousins left the Y and headed toward home. A block later, Silk turned right at the corner.

"Where you goin?" inquired Tony.

"Cramer's, I'm hoping I bump onto Tina there."

"You won't."

"How do you know?"

"Her parents don't want her to see you, she won't get out of the house this weekend. Ellen told me."

"When the hell were you going to tell me?"

"Not at all if I could avoid it, hell, you might decide to kill the messenger."

Silk was really pissed now; but with all that Tony, as usual, was able to get a smile out of him.

"Don't worry, Silk, this shit will pass, it always does."
Tony, as usual, was wise beyond his years.

Marco arrived late that morning and wasted no time getting from the car and into the house. He went directly to the kitchen where he knew Mary would be preparing lunch. She heard him coming but didn't turn toward him. He stood at the kitchen door. He had thought about this moment and what he would say as he drove to Gloucester, but somehow, he couldn't formulate the words.

"Mary, I am sorry, we need to talk."

"We talked last week, and you said nothing to me. I have to hear all this from my priest. I am so ashamed, and tomorrow we must go to Mass and face all those people."

"I know now that I should have told you, but I had no idea that this would happen. You must believe me. I didn't want to hurt you."

"I am done talking of this. Rose and Santino will be home soon. We will eat, and then maybe you can tell us what is happening."

A few minutes later, Johnny came home; and when he saw his father, there was an uncomfortable silence. Johnny had been angry with his father for days now, but seeing made him sad. Not for himself but for Marco who looked like a man who had just lost his best friend.

"Johnny, I would like to talk to you and Margaret. Can you go to her room and ask her to come to the parlor?"

Johnny heard himself say "OK." He did as his father asked, and he and Margaret went to the parlor where their father was waiting.

Marco was seated on a parlor chair, and his children sat on the sofa, facing him.

"I am in trouble, and I have brought that trouble into this home. I know this is hard for the both of you, and my heart aches for you. I won't ask forgiveness, but I want you to know that I am sorry."

Johnny suddenly realized that he was angrier for his mother than himself.

"And what about Ma? You are not here to see her cry. When you come home, you think nothing has changed, but it has."

Margaret who seldom raised her voice over anything chimed in loudly, "We went for groceries yesterday, and she spoke to no one, and no one spoke to her. When we returned home, she sat and cried in the kitchen."

"Your mother has made her feelings known to me, and I have told her that I am trying to work things out so that I can return home for good. And I promise you also that if this trouble gets taken care of, I will do that."

This comment somehow eluded Johnny, but Margaret picked up on it.

"What do you mean, if the trouble gets taken care of? Are you going to jail?"

Johnny's head snapped from his sister to his father's. "What?"

"Yes, I could be going to jail."

Johnny got up, left, and didn't return for lunch.

The family meeting did not resolve much regarding his defense and how the family could support him, but it did considerably more for Marco and his state of mind. He knew Mary and his two children were upset with him, and Rose was cool toward him; but Santino, while not outwardly exuberant, was clearly focused solely on helping him. He felt, given time, he could earn back the trust of the others.

"I will be spending more time here until the trial," he announced.

"Mr. Pino, my lawyer, told me that it would be best if I stayed away from Boston as much as possible before the trial. Except for meetings about the defense, I will remain here."

"Good," responded his brother. "When you return from the meetings, we can gather here, and you can tell us what was discussed and how we can help."

That pretty much concluded the meeting, but all four of them remained for over an hour longer. This was the first time he and his brother had really talked in a long time, and in spite of his troubles, Marco had a good feeling inside of him.

He also knew that he had made many bad choices in the past, and none was worse than not returning to Gloucester when work became available. He knew that his choices were selfish, and that he stayed in Boston not only for the money but because he had come to like the life and he had put that before his family.

I can fix all that, he thought. *If only I can escape jail.*

The next morning, the nine Silinas arrived early for the nine o'clock Mass at Our Lady of Good Voyage. They took a row of seats in the front of the church and awaited the reaction of the rest of the parishioners. It was as they expected. As people saw them, they nodded a greeting but said nothing. After Mass, they stood in the church's courtyard as was their practice every week. The only other person to join them was Father Bruno who talked to them and no one else.

The summer passed quickly and, except for a few meetings, Marco was in Gloucester all that time. One of the strategies that Joseph Pino had was that Marco should be very visible at home. Bring a sense of normalcy to his life with the idea that possibly, some of his neighbors may be able to serve as character witnesses.

Marco really embraced this idea. The last thing he wanted to be was a prisoner in his own home. Whenever possible, he went on fishing trips on Santino's boat. When he did, he was always an extra hand so that another crew would not lose work. When a meeting made fishing impossible, he would go to the pier to lend others a hand. Every Saturday, he volunteered his time helping Father Bruno with his boxing program and even refereeing a match now and then; and two nights a week, he would attend an Our Lady of Good Voyage CYO baseball game. Johnny, or Silk as others referred to him, was the only fourteen-year-old starting for the team of boys who were seventeen and under. Although he was an aspiring shortstop, he was stationed in right field. Johnny saw little of Tina during this time, but this would come to an end in the fall. Unless Mr. Collins transferred his daughter to a private school, there was no way to control her whereabouts while classes were in session.

As Tony had so eloquently put it, "This shit will pass, it always does."

CHAPTER SEVENTEEN

A Time to Try All Men

August 18 finally arrived, and opening statement began promptly at 10:00 AM. Joseph Pino had told the family that the best way to support Marco was to be present in court every day. Santino made arrangements for someone to captain his boat in his absence, and he Rose, Mary, Margaret, and Johnny were in attendance.

Johnny was more than a little shocked when he noticed that the attractive waitress from Angelina's restaurant was also in attendance and seated in the rear of the courtroom.

This was the first time any of them had laid eyes on Mr. Pino. What they saw was a tall man, impeccably dressed, who's every move and word displayed the confidence of a man of great experience. Santino, for one, immediately felt better about his brother's fate; however, as the day progressed, these good feelings began to dissipate. The district attorney marched a steady stream of witnesses to the stand. The witness pool was made up primarily of the patrolmen involved in Marco's arrest, and all told stories so similar that one had to believe they were heavily rehearsed. Yes, Marco Silina was known in the North End as a gaming boss; yes, he was present that evening and, without question, was the man in charge; and yes, he attempted to attack the arresting officer. Mr. Pino cross-examined every witness but got no one to contradict the veracity of the testimony. On Wednesday afternoon, the prosecution rested its case. At that point, Joseph Pino made the obligatory request that the judge dismiss the charges on the grounds that the prosecution had failed to present enough evidence to warrant continuing. His request was quickly denied.

The defense in the case of the Commonwealth of Massachusetts versus Marco Silina started and ended on Thursday. Mr. Pino did call some character witnesses, but there were few he dared put on the stand. His star witness was Father Bruno, who was quite effective. He talked of Marco's involvement in the community during the sixteen years since he and his family had settled in Gloucester and of his considerable support of Our Lady of Good Voyage.

By that afternoon, all the witnesses had been called, and the defense rested its case. Both sides would make their closing remarks on Friday morning, and then the case would go to the jury. The district attorney (DA) asked for a meeting with the defendant at this time, and he and an assistant district attorney (ADA) met with Joseph Pino and Marco in a small courthouse conference room. The DA would have preferred that this meeting take place without Mr. Pino being present, but there was no chance of that happening. Normally, the presence of the defense attorney in this type of meeting serves both sides well. They usually have a better sense of what the jury is going to do and can recommend the best course of action for the defendant. The DA was very sure that what was best for Marco was not the first priority of his counsel.

"Mr. Silina, do you understand the graveness of your situation?"

Marco looked at Pino and then back at the DA. "Yes, I believe so."

"Well, just in case Mr. Pino hasn't done so, let me tell you what will take place in the next few days. Tomorrow morning, Mr. Pino and my ADA, Mr. Michaels, will make closing arguments to the jury. I'm sure you know how eloquent a speaker Mr. Pino is, but I promise that Mr. Michaels is also a spellbinder."

Marco wasn't sure what a *spellbinder* was, but sensed it wasn't good.

"By lunchtime, the case will be turned over to the jury, and if I'm any judge at all about how these things go, you will be found guilty and sentenced to jail by this time next week." Marco looked over to Pino who remained calm and responded for his client, "There is no way you can predict what a jury will do. They know Mr. Silina is not a hardened criminal. I'd be willing to bet that there is not a man on that jury who hasn't, at one time, placed a bet with a bookmaker."

"This is a jury that is fed up with crime on their streets and is ready to make someone pay, and yes, Mr. Silina, your attorney is willing to make a bet that you will be paying for."

Mr. Silina, I have a deal for you. I am prepared to walk into that courtroom tomorrow morning and drop all charges against you if you will meet with us this afternoon and tell us everything you know about Dominic Belamonte and his organization."

"I know nothing of Mr. Belamonte."

"You let me be the judge of that. You know more then you realize. Mr. Silina, by this time next week, you could be headed to Norfolk Prison or home to your family in Gloucester. I saw your family in court this week, and I have inquired of them. You have a fine family."

Marco looked at the DA without changing the expression on his face. He wondered if this man thought him stupid. Did he think that he did not understand the consequences of what he is asking?

"I need to talk to my lawyer in private." The DA and his assistant left the room.

"Marco, do I have to tell you how big a mistake he is asking of you?"

"You made that very clear months ago, and I knew before even then, but I need one thing from you."

"What is that?"

"If I am found guilty, I will go quietly to prison, but when I return from prison I am done with this life and I will be back with my family. Tell Mr. Belamonte that I am very grateful for all he has done for me, but I can no longer put my family second. The same is true if I am found innocent. I keep my mouth shut, and I walk away from all of this."

"Consider it done. I will tell the DA that you cannot help him."

"Can you speak for Mr. Belamonte on this matter?"

"In this case, I can speak on his behalf."

The district attorney could not have been more accurate if he had a crystal ball.

The next afternoon, the case went to the jury, and late Monday of the next week, they came in with a guilty verdict on both charges. On Friday, August 29, 1941, Marco was sentenced to four years to be served at Norfolk Prison. If nothing else, Marco's right to a swift trial had been adhered to.

He was granted a few minutes with his family before being taken away.

"I am so ashamed for what I have put you through. I will do my time and, if you will have me when I am finished, I will return to Gloucester. I promise I will spend the rest of my life making this up to you."

Santino was the only one to respond, "Speaking for myself, I look forward to that day." As Johnny turned to leave, he saw the waitress from Angelina's for the only time since the beginning of the trial. She was again in the rear of the courtroom and she was sobbing into her hankie. Either his father was a great tipper, or he was banging this broad. There was no longer any doubt in his mind about what he was up to while away in Boston. He also knew that his mother and everybody else in the family could never learn of this.

Four days later, Silk started his freshman year. This was at a new school with a large majority of students he did not know. He didn't know what might happen, but he expected the worst. As he walked through the front door of the high school, he couldn't help thinking that today, he might get his ass kicked. In a ring or schoolyard and against anyone near his size, he felt confident of the outcome. However, today he was a tall, slender, freshman who weighted only 145 pounds, and there was the possibility that he might come up against someone three years older and fifty pounds heavier. The thing was that he had made up his mind that if someone, anyone gave him a line of shit, he was going to fight. All this without his backup, Tony, who still had a year to go at the junior high school.

Much to his surprise, he barely caused a ripple in the morning's activities. It seemed as if the upper classmen had bigger fish to fry and weren't even going to acknowledge the existence of a nobody freshman. When he found his homeroom, he was greeted by familiar faces from junior high and the neighborhood and began to feel better about things. It was time to look forward and try to put the past out of his thoughts.

Then on December 7, 1941, the Japanese bombed American forces at Pearl Harbor. This event made everything else at the time seem unimportant. Two days later, war was declared with Japan, followed three days later with Germany and Italy. The news of this hit Gloucester particularly hard since over 20 percent of its people were of Italian descent. Suddenly, seniors were not talking about which college they would attend but rather which branch of the service they would enter. Some of the more zealous students requested but were denied early graduation in order to get more quickly into the fray. Silk was only fourteen and not yet halfway into his freshman year of high school, but he knew his time would come to face the same decisions. Being young and naïve, neither he nor his fellow students could ever imagine just how horrendous war really was.

It was now less than a year since school let out in the previous spring. Silk had been very excited about the idea of entering high school in the fall, but everything changed with the events since June 13. The entire family had been consumed with the events surrounding his father's arrest, trial, and now his incarceration. Even having his father at home that summer was a change which, strangely enough, took adjusting to. To further complicate things, Mr. Collins had done an amazing job of keeping Tina on a short leash. If it weren't for CYO baseball, boxing, Tony's never-ending good humor, and the counseling of Father Bruno, he could not have coped with it. Now the country was at war.

There was one other thing which got its start during that time and had gotten more serious as things progressed over the summer. At first, he felt anger for his father, then indifference, and finally resentment. He wasn't angry for himself, but rather his mother who, as the summer progressed, had become more and more melancholy. The smiles and laughter he had grown to know were seldom seen, and the days since the trial had been marked by long periods of sobbing. He knew there was talk of his father returning home after prison, but he hadn't heard his mother say this; and personally, he didn't care if he ever saw his father again. In fact, the seed of an idea was planted in his mind that might make the split with his father more permanent.

CHAPTER EIGHTEEN

Fresh Starts

If there was an upside to Marco's imprisonment, it was that the remaining family once again functioned as a unit. This is how it had been before the hard times in the thirties when all the Silinas worked for the good of the others. The thing that pleased Silk most was that over time, Mary reverted to being herself. There were two very significant differences that did take place. First, Marco was not there, and second were the monthly trips to Norfolk to visit him. At first, it was only Santino who went; then Mary joined him and, on occasion, either Rose or Margaret would make the trip. In four years, Silk never once visited his father.

Silk was finding high school to be everything he has expected. It did require some adjustment since he was no longer the biggest wheel on campus, although he did get a laugh over the fact that Tony now filled that role at the junior high, and he made a point of telling Tony to enjoy it while it lasted.

Although he had never played the game, he went out for the freshmen football team. The coaches soon found out three things about Silk. He was the fastest player on the team, had great hands, and did not know the meaning of fear. He immediately earned starter status as a wide receiver on offence and safety on defense.

His love life, while not great, was considerably improved compared to the summer. Try as he may, Mr. Collins could not control Tina's activities during school hours. He and Tina were in the same freshmen English class and shared the same lunch period, and they were quietly conspiring a way to get to the freshman dance in the spring. If he changed his name to *Cilina*, they would also share the same homeroom.

To say his plate was full would not be accurate. Overflowing would be the word, but that was exactly what made him tick. Freshmen football, boxing, Tina time, schoolwork, fill-in with indoor track, and freshman baseball later. Beyond that, he kept a watch on his mother's moods, tried not to think of his father and where he was; and when he needed a few laughs, he would get Tony and head to Cramer's drugstore for a root beer float. Tony was having a great time as the man at school, and he and Ellen were still seeing one another, but he missed the time he had with Silk when they were in the same school.

"It doesn't seem right, Tina, Ellen, and you are together in high school, and I get left behind."

"Who are you kidding; you have it made where you are. Tony Silina, big man on campus. Enjoy it while you can because next year, it's going to be Tony, who?"

"What the hell are you talking about? You seem to be doing OK."

"Yeah, but don't forget, I'm Silk and trust me, you'll be Tony who? Another thing, don't forget, next year, you're a freshman, and Ellen will be a sophomore. She may not even talk to you."

"Well, that's OK, lover boy, because I'll still like my chances better than what you'll be looking at. I don't think you'll be getting much in English class."

"You little prick; I may have to kick your ass."

"Hey, watch what you say, I've already passed you in weight class, you skinny shit."

With that, Tony turned and did a mock runaway. Weight or no weight, he knew he was no match for Silk.

Silk, Silk, Silk, will I do it now or give some more thought? He kept going over it in his mind. Mentally and emotionally, he had made the break from his father, and the idea of changing his name was something that occupied more and more of his thoughts. If everything else had eluded his father's attention, this certainly would deliver the message and really piss him off.

Then on the first Saturday in October, something happened to make him delay his decision on whether or not to go through with the change. Late morning, a black, late-model Cadillac pulled up to the front of the house. Silk and Tony were returning home from boxing and watched as a short, stocky man wearing a dark suit walked up to Silk's front door and rang the bell. He had no way of knowing that the bell wasn't working, and even if it were, there was no one home. Mary and Margaret had gone food shopping, and Silk was still coming up the street. He rang a second and then a third time before he realized that the bell wasn't working. Now a bit angry, he started pounding on the door. This brought Santino to his front door.

"There is no one at home. Can I help you?"

"I have come to see Mrs. Silina; do you know where she is?"

"She left only a few minutes ago, and I think she will not return soon. Is there something I can do for you?" Santino began to get very suspicious. A big car and a man in a dark business suit was not something he ever saw on a Saturday in Gloucester.

"Who are you?" asked the suit.

"I am Mary's brother-in-law, Santino, and who are you?"

"I'm an acquaintance of Marco Silina, you must be his brother."

"Do you have a name?"

"Yes, my name is Carl."

"And, Carl, what do you want with my sister-in-law."

"I've got something for her. Maybe you can give it to her when she returns."

With that, he reached into his coat pocket and retrieved a brown envelope. He handed it to Santino while telling him there would be an envelope delivered every month. Silk and Tony had stopped walking when they reached the front gate and stood listening. Much to Carl's surprise, Santino tore open the envelope and looked inside. It contained cash, but he had no idea how much.

Carl never expected what happened next. With his right hand, Santino grabbed the collar of the other man and, with his left; he shoved the envelope into his face.

"This is dirty money, and you are garbage. If I ever see either of you again, I'll break your fucking neck."

Carl thought a second about retaliating, but remembering the stories about the fighting skill of Marco, he decided against it. This man seemed every bit as volatile as his brother. Santino had no way of knowing the magnitude of what has just taken place. The young man, half running to his car, was Carl Belamonte, the oldest son of Dominic Belamonte.

The two boys laughed as they watched the man jump into his car and speed away. Maybe being a Silina is not so bad after all, thought Silk.

When Mary returned home, Santino told her what had happened. He had realized while he waited that, while the money was dirty, it was not his money; and maybe he should not have interceded. He and Silk both heard her answer.

"If I were here, I would have done the same."

"Ma, you would have to be a lot bigger to have done the same."

It was good to hear his mother laugh.

The next several months passed without incident and, as it always had been, school and athletics dominated Silk's time and interest. Football turned out to be more fun than he expected, but it still ranked behind both boxing and baseball in interest. The biggest star on the football team was the quarterback, Manny Perry. While not gifted with great speed, he was big, strong, tough, and possessed a cannon of a throwing arm. Much of the game plan was to have three guys run downfield, and Manny would find one of them for a long gainer. Silk, with his speed and hands, was frequently Manny's favorite target. The Gloucester freshmen football team finished a very respectable season and fantasized about what they could accomplish when they would become seniors. He and Manny had become good friends. It was easy to like Manny; he had almost as much of a sense of humor as Tony, a handsome face, and didn't have a mean bone in his body. Well, at least when off the football field. When on it he went all out on every play.

When football was done, there was a void to be filled before spring and the baseball season. Manny and some of the others were going to play basketball, which Silk had never played; and unlike football, you couldn't play basketball simply because you could run fast and catch a ball. Silk decided that indoor track would be a good fit. He ran the fifty-yard dash and loved competing with the fastest boys in the North Shore. He won all but two of his races and never finished worse than second, and the best thing about it was that with good coaching, he was two-tenths of a second faster by the end of the season.

Finally the Ides of March and baseball season. While he enjoyed every sport, there was none that came close to baseball for Silk. The first day for tryouts was March 16, and the first game would be played in Newburyport three weeks later. Tryouts started at 2:00 PM, and after the coach spent a few minutes explaining how he was going to run things, he asked the players to go onto the field and the position they want to play. Three boys went to the shortstop position, Manny, Silk, and one other. The third player looked at Manny and moved over to second base.

"Hey, runt, you better follow him, you look more like a second baseman."

"No, big man, I'm a shortstop. There's a spot for you over there," Silk responded pointing to his right and the third base bag.

"We'll see, runt," said Manny while flashing a broad smile.

That Friday, Silk was at his locker between classes and saw Manny approaching.

"Hey, runt, I want you to meet our new third baseman." Manny was alone. "I just had English with coach, and he told me you were his shortstop." Manny gave him a friendly poke to the shoulder and kept walking.

"See you at lunch."

They played sixteen games that spring, winning thirteen; and when the season ended, there was no doubt who was the best freshmen player in the entire league.

—

Silk was the man. This carried over to the summer when he starred for Gloucester's Post 3 American Legion baseball team.

There were just a few days left in the school year; exams were over, and everyone was coasting and waiting for grades to be released. Silk was headed to what was now his favorite class, English. As soon as he saw Tina, he knew something was wrong.

"Have you seen the *Boston Post* this morning?" she asked.

"No, what's up?"

"It's a mess. You had better get a copy and get home. I mean now!"

Silk didn't even ask to be excused or return to homeroom for his jacket.

He walked out of school and headed to Cramer's for a copy of the *Post*. He sat at the soda fountain and stared at the front page.

Arrest Made in Cop Killing
June 3, 1942

Late last evening, after an investigation which spanned thirteen months, arrests were made for the murder of Boston Patrolman Thomas Kelley. Three men, all from the North End, were apprehended as they left a club frequented by known criminals and alleged members of the Boston underworld. The men have been identified as Julio Carmella, Thomas Allersaro, and Dominic Pelissia. Information as to where the men are being held was not released by the Boston Police. In a statement made by the arresting officer, Captain Donald Richards, it was indicated that the three men would be charged with first-degree murder, and a date for their indictment hearing would be announced shortly. Cont on page 3.

The report of the arrest dominated the entire front page with related stories continuing throughout the paper. What was bad was that the newspaper account revisited the bookmaking sweep of the previous June and featured in this article was none other than Marco Silina. What was worse was that while they never actually said it, the article did nothing to indicate that the cases were not related. It was a clear case of guilt by association and would leave one to believe the Marco Silina was part of their organization.

Silk raced home to find that Margaret had arrived before him. She was sitting at the kitchen table, reading the article to her mother who was crying almost out of control. Silk went to console his mother and realized that Margaret was also sobbing heavily.

CHAPTER NINETEEN

Johnny Silk?

Silk waited a few weeks before talking to his mother about the name change he wanted to make. He wanted his mother to get past the emotion of the newspaper reports before he brought it up. He really didn't know what the process entailed, but being a minor, he was pretty sure that he would need her consent.

"Ma, can we talk for a few minutes?"

"When have you needed permission to talk to me? So talk."

"This is different; could you put down the knife and sit at the table?"

"This sounds serious; maybe I'll need the knife." With that, she smiled, put the knife to rest on the kitchen counter, and sat down.

"What is it that is so important?"

"I have given this a lot of thought. You know how angry I have been at Dad, and that I have refused to visit him in prison. What you don't know is that I am so angry for what he has put you through that I don't care if I ever see him again."

Mary interrupted. "He is you're your father, and you should have more compassion for him. We all knew about his business, and we did nothing to change that. We all accepted the benefits, the money, the food and clothing, and the visits to Boston to watch the boxing." That stung, but it was true.

"Johnny, it is not his fault for what appeared in the paper. I admit I was very hurt, but it was not his doing."

"I overheard the two of you talking many times, I know you asked him to leave the life in Boston behind and return home. I will never understand why you and Uncle Santino are so quick to forgive what he has done."

"He is my husband, and he shares the same blood with Santino. He needed help, and that is what brothers do. That is what Silinas do."

"That's fine because I will no longer be a Silina. I'm going to change my name."

"I don't believe what I am hearing. All of your life, you have seemed older than your age, and now you speak like a child. I will not let you do this."

"I don't need your consent. I can do it without you." This wasn't really a lie, he reasoned, since he didn't he didn't know what was required.

"Then do what you want but, you'd better talk to your uncle first."

I can only imagine how that will go, he thought.

Silk saw no point in putting off the inevitable and was waiting at the pier when his uncle returned home on Friday afternoon.

"You want to do what? What are you thinking?"

"I don't want you to be angry, but I want to distance myself from my father. It is him not me that has dishonored our family and the Silina name."

"Regardless of what your father has done, I still walk around Gloucester with my head high. We are not responsible for what he has done, and the shame is not ours."

"Then why is it that my mother is unhappy, why is it that I come home to find her crying?"

"You change your name, and it will be you who will make her unhappy, her name is Silina too."

"No, not really, her name was DeSimone before she married. I will take the name DeSimone. That will please her."

"Do what you want, but you will no longer be my nephew."

"I am not worried, you forgave my father, and you will forgive me also."

As soon as he said that, he wished he hadn't. Defying his uncle was bad enough, but to challenge him was far from being smart.

"I have talked to Uncle Santino. He was not pleased with me, but he said to do what I want."

"Not pleased? Was that all that he said?"

"There was more, a lot more. I believe he has disowned me, but you know Uncle Santino, he is quick to anger, but he is softhearted, and he will get over it."

"What name will you take? I hope at least it will be Italian."

He decided not to tell her his first idea was John Silk and went directly to plan B.

"DeSimone, John DeSimone. What do you think?"

"Well, I guess that is OK." Her voice was noncommittal, but Johnny looked into her eyes and saw something he had not seen in a long while. She was very pleased.

As it turned out, her approval was required, and because she didn't read the language, the change of name approval form was read to her by a city hall employee. That same employee witnessed her signature. Mary had to smile when the form was read to her because when the new name was read to her, it was John Silk DeSimone.

Silk wanted word of the name change to get spread as fast as possible; so he told the town crier, Tony, to get to work. By the time that school opened that September, only the teachers had to be brought up to date.

The name change did nothing to soften Mr. Collins's position on Silk, but he didn't expect it would. What it did accomplish was that *DeSimone* and *Collins* was close enough in the alphabet to get them into the same homeroom. They now had that in addition to English and lunch. This along with the fact that Tony was now once again in the same school made the coming year look very promising.

In a strange way, going into the sophomore year was like going into another school. The good news was that he was no longer a lowly freshman, but the bad news was that he was now competing athletically against guys who were older, bigger, and far more experienced than himself. Football was, of course, the best example of this; and Silk found himself limited exclusively to special teams. His speed and good hands made him a natural for returning punts and kickoffs. Manny was the second string quarterback, but his size and reckless abandon earned him a starter's position at linebacker. Of course, now that he was playing varsity football, games were played on Saturday, which meant that boxing had to be put on hold during the fall. Those three months made Silk realize how much he really loved competing in the square ring.

Indoor track was somewhat better, and although he managed to win only two races for the season, he did earn some valuable points for the team with one second-place finish and a fistful of thirds. Again, he finished the season with better times then when it started.

When baseball started, Silk took a backseat to no one. He was the second best hitter on the team, but it was his play at shortstop that caught everyone's eyes. Great range, great hands, and a rifle arm earned him a spot on the league's all-star team as a sophomore.

At home, things got back to normal quicker than he expected. Once again, Tony played a big part in how things transpired. As always, he seemed to have a sense of what would be the right thing to say and when to say it. Soon after the name change and the boys got back to school, Tony started filling his father's ears about how much Johnny was helping him make friends and teaching him the ropes in high school. This went on for a few weeks, and while his father knew what was going on, he let himself be converted. Santino loved Silk almost as a son, and while he never brought up the name change, he managed to put the entire thing behind him. One Saturday morning, as Silk was leaving for a football game, he met his uncle on the front porch. It was awkward for a second, and then his uncle spoke to him for the first time in weeks.

"I'm coming to the game today, so you better play good. You don't want embarrass your uncle, do you, Silk? It was the first and only time he ever called him *Silk*.

Silk was not too young to understand what had just taken place, and he wondered if he would ever be man enough to do what his uncle has just done.

Silk really looked up to his uncle, and having lost his father he really didn't want to lose him too.

CHAPTER TWENTY

No Need to Plan, That Will Be Done for Us

Generally speaking, when students enter their junior year of high school, they begin to think far more seriously about what they will do after graduation. There were times many years ago when the Silina boys would talk of the day that they would carry on the family tradition and go to sea to earn a living. This dream was shared with countless boys in Gloucester and was followed by many. Others saw that it was a very hard life and one that was not always that rewarding. More and more students, men and women, began to look at college as the next step in their plans for the future. This changed to a great extent in the early 1940s.

When Silk started his junior year in the fall of 1943, war was raging in Europe, the Pacific, and Russia. Although the German forces in Africa had been defeated in May, the news from the front was not always good. It sort of became a forgone conclusion that your draft notice would come right on the heels of your diploma. Your plans, at least for the foreseeable future, were clearly in the hands of Uncle Sam.

Some, the smart ones like Tony, were far more pragmatic. He saw this as an unfortunate turn of events, but only of a temporary nature. This meant that while some upperclassmen put their plans on hold, Tony as a sophomore was already looking into scholarship opportunities.

Silk was caught in between. While he wasn't in his cousin's class academically, he was a very good student, and there was no reason to believe that this would not carry over into college. On the other hand, he knew that his number would come up quickly, and he couldn't see beyond that. Even without the military, his first preference would be a baseball contract over college, and he wanted to hang onto that dream.

"Come on, Silk I don't want to show up late for the first day of practice."

"You don't really think you're going to make the team do you?"

"Make it! Hell, I was the star of freshmen football. I'm not just going to make the team, I'm going to start."

"Bullshit, you're in with the big boys now. You'll be lucky if you don't get killed."

When he didn't have a practice conflict, Silk had caught a couple of freshmen games last fall, and Tony was good. He knew he would have no trouble making the team, but he was full of himself if he really thought he would start.

"Come on, DeSimone, get up and get in the huddle."

"What the hell had just happened? One second I catch a pass, and the next second I get hit by a truck." Silk looked up and saw Tony standing over him; hell he didn't even go down.

"You OK, Silk?"

"Yeah, I'm OK."

"Good, then get your sorry ass off the fucking ground."

It soon became clear. If you were on offense, you had better know where Tony Silina was. He was as crazy as Manny, only faster, and the offense was grateful that Manny was now starting at quarterback and they weren't on defense together. Come game days, they were on the field together, and it got quite dangerous for opposing players.

Silk got a lot more playing time, starting at both wide receiver and safety; and while a senior wideout, Fred Macaulay, was the receiver of choice for the coach, Manny made sure the his buddy got his fair share of catches. The team finished with six wins and three loses, and it began to look as if their senior season might well turn out as expected. Most of their freshmen team was still intact, and of course, there was the addition of Truck Silina, who was clearly the alter ego of his best friend, Tony.

Silk continued his steady improvement in track. His times were again improved, and it was amazing what a tenth of a second can do in a sprint event. He was asked by the coach if he would like to compete in the 220 in addition to the 100, and he jumped at the chance. Track was an altogether different sport than the others he competed in. In boxing, football, and baseball, you're always pretty much in the action; but in track, you'd spend more time watching than competing. If Silk was competing in a dual meet, even with the addition of the 220, after stretching and warming up, he would run about thirty-five seconds and be done for the day. You would think that a person with Silk's energy level would find this to be insufferable, but that was far from true. Track is a sport that when not immersed in your own event(s), you are caught up in what your teammates are doing, and you find yourself more in the role of a fan than that of a competitor. It is a sport where the outcome may come down to the final event, and if a teammate can get a third-place finish and the one point that goes with it, the meet is yours.

When spring rolled around, Silk's thoughts were normally dominated by baseball; but this year, he had been working on the seed of an idea, and it's time had come. First thing on a Saturday morning, he got out of bed, put on a freshly pressed shirt and his best slacks. He then went a calling, but not on a girl.

"Mr. Collins, there's a young man out here asking to see you. His name is John DeSimone.

Larry Collins owned the largest insurance agency in Gloucester. The business had been started by his father shortly after the turn of the century and, in the past twenty years, had grown to its present size mainly on back of Larry Collins.

At first, the name almost eluded him since for years, his daughter always seemed to be talking to him about—at first the boy Johnny and now Silk.

He took a second and then told the messenger to have Mr. DeSimone wait five minutes and send him in. Larry needed a few minutes to think about this. When Silk was finally shown in, Larry Collins was a little taken aback. He realized that he hadn't really seen this young man in several years. He was taller and while still slender, appeared to be a wiry 170 pounds. He noticed that the young man had dressed appropriately for the occasion, and he couldn't help being a little impressed.

"Please have a seat. What can I do for you, Mr. DeSimone?"

"You can call me John."

Smart, he avoided calling himself Johnny, or even worse, Silk.

"OK, John what can I do for you?"

"Mr. Collins, I thought that the time had come for us to talk about things."

Larry never said, "Call me Larry." Not that he even thought for a second that that would happen.

"Tina and I have known each other since grade school and have always been friends—"

"Did she put you up to this?"

"No, sir, she has no idea that I'm here. In fact, if I had mentioned it to her, I'm sure she would have told me not to do it."

"Smart girl."

"Mr. Collins, I'm only asking that you have and open mind and let me tell you what's on my mind"

This kid might have a future in insurance, he thought.

"Before you do that, John, let me tell you what's on my mind. I don't want my daughter hanging around with the son of a gangster, and I don't like you coming in here and telling me that I'm wrong to think that way."

Silk found himself beginning to lose it, Larry was goading him in an attempt to have him lose his temper. He paused a second in order to collect his thoughts.

"Mr. Collins, nobody is angrier with my father then me, but he is not a bad person, and he's not a gangster. He is a person who made some bad decisions. He didn't hang out with gangsters. He lived with relatives in Boston and was back here with us every weekend. There are men right here in Gloucester doing exactly what he did, but here the police choose to look the other way."

In spite of himself Collins continued to be impressed with the young man sitting across from him.

"Let's cut through the minutiae, what is it that you want?"

Silk knew this was the fork in the road. He had to get it right or he was lost.

"Give me a fair chance. Good or bad, I'm not Marco, I'm John. Have you ever heard anyone say anything really bad about me? I'm a good student, I go to Mass every Sunday and holy days, and I have never treated Tina with anything but the highest respect." Then Silk did something out of instinct that every good salesman ought to be taught. Make your pitch and shut up. Generally if you speak next, you lose.

"Listen, Mrs. Collins is not crazy about the idea of you and Tina either. Let me talk to her this weekend. Come by here on Monday after school, and we'll talk some more. I don't want you to mention this to Tina because there'll be hell to pay if the answer is no."

"You have my word."

Silk left without an answer but couldn't help being encouraged.

Usually, the weekends passed quickly, but this was an exception. When Monday finally arrived, Silk once again put a bit more thought into getting dressed since he would be going directly from school to Mr. Collins's office.

Classes dragged as had the weekend, and it didn't help that he saw Tina several times during the day and could not divulge to her what was going on.

When classes let out, he went directly to the Collins Insurance Agency.

As it turned out, he had to wait more than twenty minute before he got in to see him. He wondered about this and came to the conclusion that it was one of three things. Either Larry was having him cool his heels to show who was in control, the news was bad and he was in no hurry to tell him, or hell, maybe he's actually busy.

Finally, he was shown in and was happy to note that Larry's desk was covered with papers, and he in fact looked quite busy.

"John, I'm really buried today so let's make this fast. The Collins test part two. Mrs. Collin's would like to meet you and was wondering if you could come for dinner on Saturday?"

"Yes, that would be great. What time would I come?"

"How about six, we usually dine at seven."

"I can see how busy you are. Thanks for everything. I'll see you on Saturday."

Silk couldn't get out of there fast enough for fear that Larry would change his mind.

"So you go on trial on Saturday? I wouldn't want to be in your shoes for all the tea in China. You're smooth, Silk, but I'll bet you fuck this up."

"You know, Tony, sometimes, you can be a real asshole. The way I look at it is that I can't make it any worse then it already was."

"That's true, if you fuck up, you can go back to trying to cop a feel in homeroom."

"I should have known I wouldn't get any encouragement from you."

"You're right, but don't forget to bring some chocolates for Mrs. C."

"Thanks, Tony, you must have inside info that she's a diabetic."

Silk decided that he needed to give this some thought, and that if he did, he could pull it off.

He left his house promptly at 5:45 on Saturday afternoon, and to this point, he felt that he had not yet fucked up. That morning, he had gotten a haircut, which was a bit closer than usual. As proud as he was of his ancestry, he didn't want to come off to Mrs. C. as a slick-looking Italian. His dress was similar to what he had worn to Larry's office, but he added his best (of two) sport jackets. He had spent twenty minutes shining his shoes and, of course, carried a box of chocolates for Mrs. C.

He got to the Collins house five minutes early and decided to wait on the corner rather than arrive early. He kept looking at the watch he had borrowed from his uncle and was amazed at how long a period of five minutes could be.

At exactly 6:00 PM, the doorbell rang at the Collins' home. It was a very nice home that had once belonged to the owner of a large Gloucester fishing fleet. Admiral Cody, as he was affectionately called by his close friends, passed away twenty years earlier; and Larry had put himself into heavy debt in order to purchase it from the estate. He had never, for one moment, regretted that decision.

—

It was Larry who answered the door and, much to his surprise, he was greeted with a smile and a firm handshake.

"You're right on time, come on in."

Well that went well, he thought.

When Silk entered the foyer, he was suddenly stuck with the size of the home and its grand appearance. The rooms that he could see as he followed Larry to the living room where very large, with high ceilings and elegantly furnished. It was difficult to comprehend that this huge home was occupied by only three people. The entire Silina family, plus one DeSimone, lived in a house one half the size.

Now for Collins' test part two, he thought.

Mrs. C., who had been sitting on the living room sofa got up, smiled and extended a hand to Silk who, at this point, wasn't sure what he should do with it. *Certainly not the firm shake he just exchanged with Larry. What would Tony advise?* he wondered. *No doubt, he would say kiss the lady's hand.* That settles it; he took her hand gently in his and introduced himself.

"Hello, Mrs. Collins, I'm John DeSimone."

"Hello, John, welcome to our home. Have a seat here," she said as she pointed to living room chair.

Well, thought Silk, *if this is what Tina will look like in twenty years, that would be fine.* Mrs. C looked to be nothing more than an older version of her daughter.

The balance of the evening went smoothly. He was pleased that Mrs. C., although she asked of his mother, never broached the subject of his father. Silk attributed this to two things—the first being that Larry had covered that with her and the other being that she simply had too much class to do so. Dinner was very good while being quite different from what he was accustomed to. To start with, they had a woman serving the meal, and he wondered if this happened every night or only when they had guests. Dinner started with clear beef soup, which he would discover at a much later date was a consommé. The main course was a tenderloin of beef, which Silk had never had before tonight but immediately loved; and then for some reason, they served a lemon sherbet, which he assumed was dessert and the end of the dinner. They then brought out salads, which answered Silk question regarding the two dressings on the dinner table. Finally, the woman served individual plates containing sliced fresh fruit and assorted cheeses. *What, no cannoli?* It was a bit strange but very good, and while he never saw the volume of food that he was used to, he certainly was more than satisfied. They then returned to the living room where Larry poured himself an after-dinner drink while the others had coffee.

Silk had no idea how and when the evening would end but found that Mrs. C. was quite skilled at working that detail.

About an hour later, Silk found himself at the front door, thanking the Collins family for the wonderful dinner. Mrs. C. must have sensed something in his demeanor and spoke next.

"We enjoyed your company, John, and I hope to see you more often."

Silk wondered if *more often* meant in comparison to never, but he felt better when behind her, he saw a broad smile covering Tina's pretty face. As he walked home, he realized that he had just spent over three hours in her company but came away not knowing Mrs. Collins's first name. *We'll,* he thought, *I guess it's Mrs. C and Mr. Collins.*

That spring brought more than just baseball. There was the junior prom with Tina, cookouts at the Collins's, and two to three games a week. *It doesn't get any better than this,* he thought.

The baseball season was a huge success. Gloucester won their league title; Silk was among the league leaders in every offensive category and was selected second team all scholastic. To make things even better, Tony made the team and was the starting catcher. Tony loved the game as much as Silk, and while his skills didn't match those of his cousin, no one was better at blocking home plate and creating bone-bruising collisions.

The summer of 1944 may have been the best of his life. It seemed as if something good was always going on. He was playing his third season of baseball for Post 3, bowling and going to movies with Tina, Ellen, and Tony, cookouts with the Collins, warm family gathering on Sundays, and working at the pier to support the good life.

Better yet, there was no news coming by way of the *Boston Globe, Boston Post,* and the *Record American.* He was about to enter his senior year, and it was hard to believe that this time next year, he could be in the jungle of some remote Pacific island.

Chapter Twenty-One

A Mixed Bag

September arrived all too soon. While Silk enjoyed school, this was a summer he didn't want to end. It seemed as if he and his family had cleared a final hurdle and were finally enjoying a level of contentment that they hadn't experienced in a while. Occasionally, he would see his mother sitting quietly in the kitchen, and he realized that in spite of everything that had happened in the past several years, she still cared deeply for her husband and missed him dearly.

Each year, like all towns, families were moving in or moving on. Gloucester probably saw less then most, because peoples' livelihoods were tied to the city, but it did occur. Unfortunately, two of the football team's best linemen were no longer living in Gloucester; and to make things worse, they both played on both sides of the ball. This alone was enough to put the great season they had looked forward to in jeopardy, but what happened in the last week of practice drove a stake into the heart of the team. On the last Saturday, before the season was to start, the team held a live scrimmage. This was not an unusual event. The coach had been doing it for years, and it was heavily attended. The first time the number one offence got the ball, they marched down the field with ease. On the tenth play of the drive, Manny missed on a handoff; and rather than accepting it as a broken play, he decided to attempt to make something of it. And given his courage and ability, he managed to do so. As he approached the goal line he had two options, one being to run out of bounds and two was to hurdle the last defender and go ass over teakettle into the end zone. If you knew Manny Perry, you would know that there was only one option. A huge cheer went up from the students and faculty in the stands, and even Silk got caught up in the moment as he raced to the end zone to congratulate his teammate. Before he got there, he realized that rather than springing to his feet as usually was the case, he remained on the ground writhing in pain. Manny had broken his right collarbone, bringing his season to an end and, with it, any hope for an undefeated season. He was replaced by a sophomore Lenny Cramer, who had quarterbacked a good freshmen team the previous season, but clearly wasn't ready to replace Manny Perry, who was the best player in the league and a serious candidate to be the all-scholastic quarterback in Eastern Massachusetts.

The season that held so much promise became a disaster for the Gloucester High Fishermen. The season opened the following Saturday with a crushing 33 to 0 loss to Lynn Classical, and that was only the beginning. The offence, which had been built around a big strong-armed senior quarterback, was now in the hands of an inexperienced player whose offensive line had been decimated by summer relocations. The defense was no better off since it had lost the same two linemen along with Manny. Silk was rendered ineffective, because there was no longer, the go-deep-and-I'll-find you ability that Manny brought to the team. Clearly, the best player still standing, both on offence and defense, was Tony Silina; and that was not nearly enough. The opposing defenses packed the line of scrimmage to stop Tony's bull-like runs up the middle, and when Lenny Cramer tried to pass, he got run over by what resembled a jailbreak.

After a 27 to 0 second week loss to Newburyport, the team had a meeting and resolved that they would not quit or place blame but rather take whatever the season held for them. What it brought them was a 6 to 0 win against Swampscott the following Saturday. In the fourth quarter of that game, Tony ran the ball on eight consecutive plays covering sixty yard before doing a Manny-like dive into the end zone for the game's only score. Fortunately, unlike Manny, he was able to jump to his feet to celebrate. That was it for the season as they lost three of their last five games to Salem, Amesbury, and Peabody by a combined score of 71 to 0 to go along with two scoreless ties against Marblehead and Beverly. If there was a highlight to the season beyond the play of Tony, it was when Manny made a cameo appearance in the Thanksgiving Day game and was able to earn his football letter for his senior year.

As he ran onto the field for the final snap of the game, Silk went to him and said, "Please Manny, take a knee."

"Don't worry, my mother didn't have any stupid kids."

Thanksgiving seemed a little more festive than usual. It was probably so because the disastrous football season was over and hopefully, better things lay ahead.

Later that afternoon, Tony and Silk sat on the back porch for a little break before the sugar deluge known as dessert was to be served.

"You know, Tony, I'm a little worried about Manny."

"Yeah, me too. If he had played this year, I think he might have gotten a football scholarship. He deserves a chance at college, for all his bullshit, he's a good student."

"I know that, I have French and algebra with him, and he does well in both, but that's not it."

"You lost me, what are you worried about?"

"We graduate in six months, and we get drafted and get sent overseas. You know Manny, I think the son of a bitch will be a hero and get his head shot off."

Tony pondered that for a second before responding, "Even worse, he could come home a hero and bust our chops for the next fifty years."

"You know, Tony, you could be right for a change."

The following day, everyone returned to school. The football season was something to put in the past only to be brought up at class reunions as the record they posted which nobody ever wanted to surpass. Once football was put behind him, the good times experienced that summer seemed to resume and continued throughout his senior year. Tony joined the track team and competed in the shot put. He was a bit upset with himself because he realized that barring injury, both Silk and Manny were going to earn nine varsity letters; and because he did not compete in track as a sophomore, he would only earn eight.

Maybe they'll give me a letter for graduating first in my class, he thought.

Silk continued with steady improvement in his times and posted the second best time in the fifty of anyone in the league.

By this time, Tony had gotten his driver's license, and dating took on an entirely different slant. The boys discovered a drive-in movie, in Lynn, Massachusetts, which was a reasonable commute from Gloucester. The Lynn Open Air Theater became a frequent destination for their Saturday-night dates. Obviously, Larry and Mrs. C never really comprehended the repercussions of this, or they most certainly would have put an end to it. One Saturday night, after the guys had dropped off the girls, they headed home on a ride that was strangely quiet. As usual it was Tony who broke the silence.

"I don't know about you, Silk, but I think I'm about to expire from a terminal case of lovers nuts. Jesus Christ, I have to get laid, or I'm going to explode."

"You think that you're the only one? Thank God we're going double, if not I would have gone for second base a long time ago."

"Well, maybe it's time you got your license, and we can go in two cars."

"Oh good, Tony. You know, for a smart guy, you say some really stupid things. And besides, every time I think about going for it, I think of Larry and Mrs. C and how good they've been to me, and I back off."

"Well, you know the first time is the hardest. After the first cut of the cake, no one's going to miss another piece."

"Let me write that down so I won't forget it when Larry comes after me with a shot gun."

"Ellen's dad doesn't have a shotgun."

"Get me home, I'm tired."

"OK, but I'm going to come up with a plan."

"Good, but do it on your own time."

As they walked to Mass the next morning, Tony pulled Silk aside and shared the plan he had come up with the previous night as he was applying ice to his aching balls.

"Silk, I know these two cheerleaders from Newburyport. I talked to them a few minutes at the track meet last month. They gave me their phone number and said they would like to meet you."

"I suppose you get first choice on who gets who."

"Hell no, you can have first dibs, they're twins, for Christ's sake."

"And what do we tell Ellen and Tina when we leave for Newburyport on Saturday?"

"I'll think about that." After about two minutes of much-appreciated quiet, Tony had the answer.

"Wednesdays would be good."

Silk didn't offer a reply, and Tony took that as a no.

Manny had earned his eighth varsity letter playing basketball that winter, which was no easy task for a player who still couldn't raise his shooting hand over his head. He adjusted by developing a decent inside game with his left hand and becoming a tenacious one-armed defender and rebounder. When spring arrived, the question was how does one play third base when you can't raise your throwing hand over your head? He, of course, got all the sympathy he expected from Tony.

"Well, you could always become a pinch runner, but the problem is that we don't have anyone that's slower than you. Do they give letters for coaching third base? You could wave everyone home with your good arm." Tony, of course, was being a nut buster and knew that when the time came, Manny would find a way.

"Side arm. I've been throwing a rubber ball in our cellar for the last month, and I'm sure I can get a baseball to first base." He could, and he did.

Silk could do it all, and he did. The senior season of baseball was diametrically opposed to that of the football. The team won, and Silk excelled in every phase of the game.

———

As the season progressed, each game took on extra meaning to all the players on both teams because it was general knowledge that there were major league scouts in attendance. They were there to look a Silk, but who knows who may have a great day and catch their eyes.

Then one Tuesday, in early May, something happened which made everything seem far less important. On May 8, 1945, the headlines in the morning papers read:

Germany Surrenders, War in Europe is Over

This seemed to change everything. At times, it seemed as if the war would go on forever, and now all that remained was defeating the Japanese and the Second World War would be over. The future of young men either already in the military or soon to be suddenly became less clouded and much more promising.

Even after such wonderful news, simple things such as a high school baseball season remained important to those involved. The Gloucester High Fishermen had set a goal for themselves, and they were determined to achieve it.

Their team repeated its success as league champions, and John DeSimone was selected first team all scholastic.

When the season came to a close, scouts started to make calls to the Silina household. Several teams were interested, and while Silk was flattered he couldn't get too excited because he knew that Uncle Sam was only one mail delivery away.

The scouts were of one opinion: sign now and worry about the draft later. Two years is not a lifetime, and you'll only be twenty when you get out.

Toward the end of June, Silk made his decision.

"I'm signing with the Red Sox."

"Good," responded his mother. "This way you can live at home."

"No, Ma, it doesn't work that way. I will be assigned to one of their farm teams."

"Farm team? What are you saying?"

"I'll explain that later, Aunt Mary," said Tony. "But first, let's hear about the money."

"They will pay me seventy-five dollars a week for the season, but they are giving me a four-thousand-dollar bonus to sign with them."

Mary had to sit down. *Four thousand dollars to play a game?* she thought.

The next week, Silk was on a bus headed to Durham, North Carolina, to play for the Sox Class C team in the Carolina League. The legendary Durham Bulls.

CHAPTER TWENTY-TWO

"What's Up, Sam?"

Silk was not ready for what he found in Durham on many levels. For one thing, it was a much larger city than he expected with a population in excess of 200,000. Somehow, he imagined something quite different. The fans were very passionate, and that enthusiasm frequently spilled over off the playing field in a way that offered interesting opportunities for lonely guys away from home for the first time in their lives. Durham was also the home of North Carolina College and Duke University, and while the institutions were not in session, the city had the year-round feel of a college town.

The idea of playing baseball every day had always appealed to Silk, but the reality of playing a road game and piling onto a bus for a long restless drive to yet another town and another game soon took much of the luster off that illusion. Then there was the competition itself. Every game, he would face a pitcher who was better than he had ever faced in high school. While his play in the field was outstanding, his batting average hovered in the .240 range. Add this to a heavy dose of home sickness, and you had a young man wondering if he had made the right decision.

If there was one thing that lifted his spirits it was the letters he received from Tina and Tony. Tina would tell him the things he wanted to hear and share both her excitement and apprehension about entering college in the fall. She was staying close to home, and being enrolled at Endicott College meant that they could see each other every weekend during the winter.

Tony, on the other hand, was like a town crier with a sense of humor.

"Hey, it finally happened. Manny got his draft notice."

Two weeks later.

"Would you believe his fucking luck? Because of his bad arm, Manny is 4-F."

Two weeks later.

"Manny's going to college. Mr. Babson got him a full scholarship to his college in Wellesley. With all his bullshit, I forgot he had a brain."

One week later.

"Hey, Silk, did you know that you are the only male virgin living at 55 Taylor Street in Gloucester, Mass.?

One week later.

"Hey, Virg, still nothing from Uncle Sam."

On August 6, the war in the Pacific took an unexpected turn when the United States bombed Hiroshima, Japan, with a new and devastating weapon called the atomic bomb. Three days later, the bombing of Nagasaki took place, and on the 15th of August, Japan announced it surrender. World War II was over.

"Hey, Silk, there's a phone call for you. He said he's Tony."
Oh fuck, thought Silk, *it's not Tony, its uncle Sam.*
Silk picked up the phone, composed himself and asked, "Hi, Tony, did I get my draft notice?"
"No, Silk, that isn't it, but I've got a couple of theories about that."
"I'll bet you do. What would they be?"
"Well first, there's the name change. You know, Silina to DeSimone. I think you threw them off. If that's not it, I think the Sox pulled some strings and got you exempt. What do you think of that?"
"OK, Einstein, you think the Red Sox have a favor to call in, and they used it for me while Ted Williams was flying combat missions?"
"Listen, Silk, I'm trying to keep it light here. The real reason I called is that your dad was released from prison, and he's back here in Gloucester."
"He's moved in to stay?"
"Yes."
"Thanks for the heads-up. I need some time to think about this." He hung up the phone. This was really going to be a problem.

When Silk got word on his father, there was about three weeks left to the season; and whether it was the news that gave him a jolt or the fact that he was finally catching up with the pitching, he caught fire at the plate.

The players were asked to stay around Durham for a couple of days after the close of the season for a small team breakup gathering and some coach evaluations. Silk was told that the organization was pleased with his play but was not yet sure where he would be assigned next spring. The war was over, and players would be returning at every level of play, which would impact where he might end up.

Silk smiled at this and said, "With Pesky coming back, I guess it won't be Boston."

"That's a pretty good guess," replied the coach, returning the smile.

Silk arrived back in Boston on the 18th of September, but rather than going home to Gloucester, he headed to the home of Dominic and Lena Patrano and arranged for room and board just as his father had done over fifteen years earlier. They had now come full circle. Who could know where it would lead them next?

Marco Silina was released from Norfolk on August 22nd, and unlike most men walking out of prison after four years of incarceration, he knew exactly what he would do for the rest of his life. During his entire prison term, there was one constant. Each month, without fail, Santino would make the trip from Gloucester to Norfolk to visit his brother. At first, the conversations always focused on the same things. Santino would ask how things were going for Marco, and Marco would inquire about how the family was doing.

This changed as Marco's sentence came closer to its conclusion. They talked then of the future.

"We will work out a partnership, and we will fish as we planned when we came to this country," offered Santino.

"That is very generous of you, Santino, you have put in so much work for such a long period of time. Don't forget, I still have some money, and as soon as possible, we will purchase a second boat and double our income."

"With God's blessing, we will make it happen."

"I need only one other thing to make me a happy man. I need to make things right with my son."

"In due time, Marco, in due time."

When Marco walked out of prison on the twenty-second, there were two people there waiting for him. One, of course, was his brother; the other his wife, Mary. How he loved this woman could not be put into words. How he ever could have betrayed her trust, he would never know. What he did know was that he had ended that transgression when his lover had first visited him after his imprisonment. He thanked God that no one in the family had ever learned of his affair.

CHAPTER TWENTY-THREE

A Second Career

September 20th was a Thursday, which was perfect for Silk's purposes. His plan was to visit his mother, and being a Thursday, he knew his father would be at sea. The second part of his plan was to see Tina. He had called her on Wednesday to tell her that he would be there by midafternoon on the next day, and they could go to dinner. He had also called his mother and told her that he would arrive on Thursday morning. He knew that would be enough to get the ball rolling for a lunch that would suit a king. It had been almost three months since his last real home-cooked meal. On Thursday morning, he dropped off Dominic at work and headed for home. In spite of everything that had transpired, his family was in Gloucester and that made it home.

"You look so skinny, don't those Red Sox feed you?"

He knew that was coming. It wasn't the lack of food that had caused him to lose ten pounds but rather the heavy schedule of games and the oppressive summer heat in the Carolinas.

"Ma, you know I only like your food. Have you ever heard of grits? Those Southerners eat that stuff like we eat pasta."

"Gee, grits, is that something under your shoes?"

"Good guess, Ma, that's close enough."

She must have been up at dawn to make his favorite. The ravioli would have been enough for him, but not in her mind. Lunch consisted of escarole soup, ravioli, Italian hot sausage, and was topped off with fresh fruit and sharp provolone cheese. After this, his dinner date with Tina could present some challenges; but even with that in mind, he knew that not accepting seconds on the ravs would disappoint his mother.

With lunch finished, he knew he had to face the inevitable.

"So, Johnny, when are you coming home?"

"I am home, and I plan to return every week."

"Don't get smart with me, Mr. DeSimone, you know what I mean. *This is your home.*"

Silk took *Mr. DeSimone* to mean that she was not to be trifled with.

"He is your father, he has made many mistakes, but he had paid for them, and he feels sorrow for what he has done. I have forgiven him, Santino and Rose, even Margaret is happy that he has returned. It is only you that keeps the family divided."

"Ma, I'm not angry at him for what he did. My anger comes from what he did to you. I saw you cry, saw the sadness. I saw too much to ever forgive him."

She would never hear from him everything that he had seen.

Just then and just in time, he heard someone burst through the front door. It was Tony; and while he always was happy to see him, today was as much a relief as it was a pleasure.

"Hey, the war's over. It looks like you dodged a bullet. In more ways than one.

I guess like everything else around here, I'll be the first one drafted."

"What the hell are you raving about now?"

"Don't make me elaborate in front of your mother."

"Why don't you two boys talk Johnny, I'm not done with you."

"I know, Ma."

Silk knew that she didn't necessarily mean later, but more likely at every ensuing visit. Silk and Tony spent the next hour catching up, which meant Tony talked and Silk listened. It was amazing how often Tony was able to bring the conversation back to Newburyport cheerleaders.

It was then that both Margaret and Annette arrived home, which brought emotions once again to the breaking point. At around three, Johnny's visit ended with round of embraces and a promise to return the following week.

He would be late getting to see Tina, but it couldn't be avoided. He called ahead to give her a best guess of his new arrival time.

Beverly was in the Cape Ann League, so Silk had been in the city several times for games, but he has no idea where Endicott College was located. Fortunately, Tina's directions to the college were idiotproof, and Silk found the campus without much difficulty. As he drove up to the road leading to Tina's dormitory, he could not help but be impressed with what he saw. Beautifully landscaped grounds, wooded areas, handsome buildings were all in view of the seacoast that bordered the campus.

As he pulled up in front of the dorm, he saw Tina and three other girls engaged in what appeared to be a humorous conversation. She had not recognized the car, but when it stopped in front of her building, she spotted him and ran to it.

"Silk, I thought you'd never get here. It seemed like forever." They threw their arms around each other and held on in a warm embrace.

"Geez you look great, I didn't think you could get any prettier."

Silk didn't know if it was appropriate or not, but he decided to find out. He put his hand to the nape of her neck and moved her face to him and gave her a long kiss. She returned his kiss with her own, and all seemed good in the world of Silk DeSimone.

"I'd better introduce you to my friends before they go into heat." She later told Silk that she had timed the meeting with her friends at the dorm to coincide with his arrival in order to show him off.

Tina's three friends were all pretty.

"Silk, I'd like to meet my closest friends on campus. Sandra, Chris, and my roommate Betsy." During Tina's two years at Endicott, Betsy became her best friend; but at this moment, she was undressing Silk with her eyes. He was hoping that he was the only one to realize it.

After some polite conversation, they made their escape. They went to a small restaurant, which was located right on the water in Beverly. It specialized in seafood and was a favorite of Endicott students. Dinner consisted of a bowl of New England clam chowder and steamers. They spent almost two hours catching up after being apart for over two months. When they got back to the car, Tina announced that she knew of a place they could go to do some additional catching up. After a couple of missed turns, they finally arrived at a spot which was secluded while still having a beautiful view of a landscape which was once farmland.

"Now tell me, Tina, how did you know about this place?"

"Betsy told me about it this morning. I think if we looked, we could find a couple of trees with her name carved on them."

They spent the next hour here during which, Silk made a couple of aborted attempts you get beyond first base.

"We had better get back. This is just too tough," announced Tina.

"Listen, this is a bridge we are going to have to cross at some point, but if you're not ready, I'm not going to press you."

"I'm clearly not ready, and I don't know when I will be. I'm sorry, but let's go now."

The first five minutes of the drive back to campus was very quiet, but after that, they slid back to talk of their next date and settled on same time next Thursday. Silk kissed her at the front door of her dorm and made a special effort to go for gentle, rather than passionate.

The drive back to Boston was more than a little painful.

I'm going to have to do a Newburyport road trip with Tony, he thought.

It was 10:00 AM the following Monday, and the phone was on the sixth ring before it was picked up by Mrs. Driscoll, the housekeeper and cook at the rectory of Our Lady of Good Voyage. Mrs. Driscoll was not only an employee but also the unofficial historian for the parish since her thirty years of employment at the church gave her seniority over everyone, including Pastor Scolari who was a comparative newcomer of twenty-three years.

She was a bit winded by the time she got to the phone but managed to maintain the polite decorum she never seemed to lose.

"Our Lady's rectory, how may I help you?"

"Mrs. Driscoll, this is John DeSimone, is Father Bruno available?"

"Oh hello, John, I didn't know you were home. Father just returned from his morning rounds at the hospital. Let me see if I can get him for you."

Silk heard her first few footsteps as she hurried off to locate Father Bruno.

"Silk, I heard you were back, why didn't you come by? I would really like to have a talk with you. It may be time to forgive and forget."

"I'm not sure I'm ready for either, Father, but I promise I'll come by to see you soon."

"I'll look for you the next time you come home. What can I do for you today?"

"Well, Father, I've decided that I'd like to try boxing professionally. It's a long winter, and I have to work at something, and since I know the church would frown on your handling me, I was wondering if you might know of someone who could."

"Are you sure you want to do this? You know I love boxing, but professional boxing is a very dirty business."

"I know that, Father, but I thought you might be able to set me off in the right direction. There must be some decent people involved in the sport."

"They are few and far between, and those I knew are no longer in the game. I'll tell you what I will do, and I'll do so conditionally."

"What would that be, Father?"

"I'll put you in touch with an old friend of mine from the seminary, Father Pasquale. Father shares the same passion as I for the game, and being assigned to a parish in the North End has kept him much closer to what's going on than me. The condition is this, if Father Joe cannot, in good conscience, recommend someone, you will find employment doing something else. You must promise me that."

"Father, you have my word."

CHAPTER TWENTY-FOUR

Boxing, the Good, the Bad, and It's Not All Bad

Father Pasquale was assigned to Sacred Heart Church in the North End of Boston, which is known to be the first Roman Catholic Church built by Italian immigrants in New England. Silk did not know what to expect when he met the priest but was not disappointed when he did. He was about the same age and size as Father Bruno and, like him, would never be mistaken as anything but Italian. He greeted Silk with a warm smile and a firm handshake.

"So you're Silk, Tom has told me so much about you that I feel that I know you."

This was the first time that Silk had ever heard his priest being called anything except Father Bruno and was caught a bit off guard.

"Well, I don't know what he said, but he speaks highly of you. He said you met in the seminary."

"That's not entirely correct, we met once prior to that, and I'm glad to hear that he is a good enough friend not to have mentioned it. We first met in the ring during a Golden Gloves tournament over twenty years ago, and he kicked my butt. A year later, we both entered St. John's Seminary."

"No, he never mentioned that, and as a matter of fact, this is the first time I've heard that he fought in the Golden Gloves."

"That doesn't surprise me. He not only fought, but he won the middleweight title."

"I'm going to see him soon. I'll get the details from him."

"Do that and ask him why he's not leveling with his parishioners." He laughed. "OK now, let's get to why you're here. You want to fight professionally, and you want a good person to handle and train you. Does that cover it?"

"That's it, and if you have no one, I've got to find a job in a hardware store or something."

"It's a short list, but I know a couple of people who I can recommend. I took the liberty of talking to both on your behalf. One, Tim Duffy, said he can't take on a new fighter at this time and that leaves Carmen Bucci. He would be my first choice anyway because he has a smaller stable of fighters, and he can give you more time."

"Have you talked to him?"

"Yes, and he wants to meet you tomorrow at his gym. If, I know Carmen you had better go prepared to enter the ring. That will be your interview."

"How can I repay you?"

"There are several ways. If you see that you are outclassed, give up boxing sooner than later. I will see you at Mass on Sundays, and most important, listen to Father Tom when you next meet him."

"I understand, and I'll let you know how it goes with Carmen Bucci."

Silk left Sacred Heart feeling that he had, if noting else, made a new friend.

Sacred Heart Church is located at 12 North Square across the street from The Paul Revere House.

Bucci's Gym was on Fleet Street, which like everything in the North End, was a short walk from the Patranos. The meeting was for one o'clock, and Silk was ten minutes early, which didn't impress Carmen, who didn't acknowledge his arrival until ten past the hour. *Just setting ground rules*, thought Silk.

Carmen was not much for small talk, and the first words out of his mouth after waving Silk over to him were "What makes you think you can fight?"

"I've been boxing a long time, and I've always been good at it."

"Who have you fought?"

"Nobody you'd know."

"Yeah, I'll bet. Listen, kid, if it wasn't that Father Pasquale asked a favor, you wouldn't be here. Did you bring any gear?"

"Yes."

"Well, get in it, loosen up, and be out here in twenty minutes."

Father Pasquale was right on about the interview, he thought.

Twenty minutes later, Silk found himself in the ring, and standing across from him was a guy who looked as if he was the veteran of fifty matches. He had no idea if this guy was good or just some punching bag, trying to hold onto a dream.

A bell sounded, and Silk moved to the center of the ring as did his adversary. The other guy was more than a little good, or at least Silk hoped so, because they boxed a fairly even three rounds.

"Grab a shower and come out to see me," ordered Carmen

"At least he didn't tell me to shower and get out," Silk mused.

"Do you know who that was in the ring with you?" asked Carmen.

"No, but I hope he is someone, because he was all that I could handle."

"His name is Tom Upley, and he's one of my best middleweights. You did OK in there, kid. What do you weigh?"

"Right now, I'm about 160, but my normal weight is about ten pounds heavier."

"That's good, because I see you as a light heavy. Go home, eat plenty of speget, and do about five miles of roadwork a day. Bulk up, I want you to fight at about 170. Come back and see me the middle of next month. Understand?"

"I understand, and thanks, Mr. Bucci for taking me on."

"Ya, ya, and it's Carmen, and don't thank me, thank Father Joe."

Spaghetti, running, and a few trips to mom's kitchen, and I'll be ready by the fifteenth. This was the easy part; the tough part was that he had promised to see Father Bruno on his next visit to Gloucester, and he was not looking forward to that in the least. He called ahead, and on Thursday, he arrived in Gloucester early so that he could meet with Father Bruno before going to see his family.

They began with some small talk about his meetings with Father Pasquale and Carman Bucci, and Silk told him what he had learned about the Golden Gloves. Not surprisingly, Father Bruno dismissed this as ancient history.

Finally they got around to the purpose of the meeting.

"John, I've known you a very long time, but more than that I know you as well as anyone could without being family. You are someone I would be proud to call a brother, but in this case, I feel you are wrong in carrying this anger as long as you have."

"Father, let me make it clear where I stand in this matter. I knew for years what my father did for a living. I enjoyed the benefits of this. There was food on the table, a roof over my head, and clothes on my back. I never asked questions about where the tickets to the boxing matches came from. Because of this, I cannot hold a grudge against my father, but the time came when he knew the life he was leading caused my mother pain, when honest work was available here at home, and he still chose to stay in Boston."

"All that is true, John, but your mother has forgiven him for those mistakes, and it is time for you to do the same."

"There is more to it than that, and if truth be told, my mother would not be so quick to forgive. You don't know everything, and if you did, you would understand."

"Marco and I have spent many hours, outside of the confessional, talking of things, of which he is not proud. He is very repentant for those indiscretions, but there is no way to change the past."

"Father, this conversation must never leave this room, but I need to know if we are talking about the same thing."

"What would that be, John?"

"The woman or women he knew in Boston."

"There was only one woman. How do you know of this?"

"That doesn't matter, but what does is that you know about this and still want me to forgive and forget. I'm afraid that I'm not a good-enough Catholic to do that. Tell me, please, that he never told my mother about this."

"I'm not sure that the church would approve, but I advised him not to do so."

"Well, we agree on one thing, but I'm sorry, Father, because we'll never agree on the other."

"Never is a long time. Time heals, and given time, you may surprise yourself."

Silk got up from his chair, signaling an end of the discussion, and Father Bruno walked him to the front door.

The balance of the day was more pleasant than the start. His mother did, for a moment, broach the matter of his meeting with Father Bruno, but Silk managed to move the conversation in another direction. Lunch was, as usual, great and then the two of them did something he never recalled doing before. They went to the living room and talked for close to two hours. When he left at mid afternoon, Silk felt an emotion that he couldn't fully understand. His visit with his mother left him feeling a void that his meeting with Father Bruno failed to create.

Then it was off to Endicott, a drive, dinner, heavy petting, and another painful ride home.

"Why the hell didn't you tell me that you were a baseball player?"

"I didn't know it was important. What difference does it make?"

"The difference is that this is not a hobby for me, this is how I make a buck. I can't waste my time training you and then have you take off for six months."

"Well, if it makes you feel any better, it's not a hobby for me either. I think I can make us both a lot of money."

"Yeah, until the Sox call you up, and then it's tough shit Bucci."

"I hit .265 in C ball last summer, and Pesky will be back from the Navy this spring. The Sox won't be calling me real soon."

"OK, DeSimone, let me tell you what all this bullshit comes down to. We train for a month then you fight every three weeks or until you get killed, whatever comes first. This way, you get six bouts before you leave in March. If you do good, I'll see you next fall. If you don't, have a nice life."

What Silk discovered in the next month was that if things hadn't panned out for Father Bruno with the church, he could have done quite well as a fight trainer. There was virtually nothing that Carmen could tell him that he didn't already know. Of course, he did his best to keep this revelation from Carmen and appeared to hang on every word uttered by his new best friend. The difference came in the training outside the ring. The roadwork continued on a daily basis, and with it came work on the light and heavy bags, rope work, and sessions with the medicine ball. Sparring became a reward for enduring the drudgery of the grunt work. After two weeks of this, Silk realized he had been working at this for a month and had yet to see a penny.

His first payday came on November 16, against another first-timer named Tommy Holt. This was not at the Boston Garden, or even the Arena, but rather the Mechanics Building. They were the first bout on the undercard of a couple of journeymen middleweights who were going nowhere. By the time the main event started, there were barely a thousand people in attendance. When the DeSimone-Holt bout got underway, you could have thrown a grenade from the ring and not hurt a soul.

An interesting aspect of the bout was that the winner would go home undefeated, and the loser may as well just go home.

Carmen gave Silk instructions that at first seemed strange but in fact made sense.

"Listen to me, Silk. You're going to beat this guy, but I don't want you to knock him out."

"You didn't put money on this guy to finish, did you Carmen?"

"Don't be a wise ass. You knock this guy out in thirty seconds, and what good does it do? We need you in the ring and getting some rounds under your belt. Understand?"

"Now I know why I pay you all this money." Three rounds, a unanimous decision, and Silk DeSimone was an undefeated professional boxer. Tommy Holt went home, but didn't retire. He was a real gamer and fought another twenty bouts before retiring four years latter with a record of 11-9-1.

Both Manny and Tony came into Boston to see the fight. Tony, from Gloucester in the family car, and Manny, from Wellesley in a 1938 Ford his parents bought for him when he got the scholarship to Babson.

After the fight, the three friends headed to the North End for pizza.

"Jesus, Silk, I gave up a trip to Newburyport to come here tonight, and you can't put this stiff away?" Silk attempted to explain Carmen's strategy, but neither of his friends were listening.

"You know, Tony has a point," added Manny. "You were punching like a pussy in there tonight." The tone was set for the night, and Silk knew they would not let up. He loved every minute of it. Friday fight nights became a regular event for the balance of the winter.

True to his word, Carmen had Silk fighting three weeks later. This time, his opponent was a Tommy Holt at the other end of his career. Jeff Simms came in with a record of 10-9-3. And even though he presented more of a challenge than Holt, because of his experience, Carmen's instructions remained the same. No knockout.

Silk followed the instructions, almost. In the third round, a very frustrated Jeff Simms head butted Silk while in a clinch. Silk knew it was intentional and lost it. Thirty seconds later, the referee had counted out Simms, and Silk was 2-0-0. The small crowd was suddenly a bit excited and quite impressed by the unexpected show of skill that they had just witnessed. Carmen was not pleased.

"You know what happened out there? You lost your poise. You can get away with that against a stiff like this, but if you do it against a real fighter, you'll get your ass kicked."

Well, at least I know that he knows that these guys are stiffs, he thought. *And I won't get crap with my pizza tonight.* He should have known better. Tony's opening line, when he came into the locker room, was delivered without the trace of a smile.

"I hope that guy didn't hurt himself when he fell down."

"I can't win," Silk answered, smiling.

The next nine weeks were more of the same. Each match was against a guy a little better than the last, but still chopped liver, and Carmen's instructions went unchanged. On February 8, Silk fought his fifth three-rounder, giving him just short of fifteen rounds of experience and a record of 5-0-0.

The last match before heading to spring training was scheduled at the Boston Arena on 1st of March. It was his first scheduled six-rounder, and his opponent, Mark Webber, was definitely a couple of cuts better than his last opponent.

"This fight will tell us a lot. Webber can fight, he can hit with both hands, and he can take a punch. If you win this one, you might be worth the time I've given you. And by the way, if you can knock this guy out, do it. You might not get a second chance."

Silk didn't knock him out. Mark Webber proved to be a real tough guy who could take a punch. As a matter of fact, he took several punches every round, and left the ring a bloodied loser of a unanimous decision. Silk would leave for spring training at 6-0-0. As he climbed out of the ring and head up the aisle to the dressing room, he caught a glimpse of four familiar figures hastily leaving the Arena. Marco, Santino, and the good Fathers, Bruno and Pasquale had witnessed the fight.

"Did you know they were coming?"

"Of course I knew, I didn't have a car tonight. Manny had to come up to get me."

"Why didn't you come in with them?"

"Did you ever hear the phrase *guilt by association*? It was one thing not to tell you the enemy was on the way, it's another thing to arrive with them."

"Yeah," added Manny, "and how could we pass up pizza and the critique of the fight?"

"That's right," chimed in Tony. "Please tell me that you weren't trying to knock out this stiff."

"This guy has had nearly fifty fights, and he never even been knocked down. You might as well know the facts."

"The fact is that he must have been fighting pussy punches like you."

"You too, Manny?"

That brought an end to Silk's first year of boxing, and he learned an important lesson. Yes, boxing can be a dirty business, but if you surround yourself with good people like Carmen Bucci, and Fathers Bruno and Pasquale, it's not all bad.

CHAPTER TWENTY-FIVE

A Second Season

Silk left for spring training on the Monday following the Webber fight. He was very pleased when he had received a letter from the Sox, informing him that he was moving up to the class B Roanoke Red Sox in the Piedmont League. Evidently, his strong finish at Durham had not gone unnoticed. The Sox were putting a class B team in Lynn that season. And at first, he had hoped to be assigned there but, on further reflection, reasoned that it would not be a good idea. There would be too many distractions, Carmen would want him to continue to take matches, and there would be nightly critiques from Tony and Manny.

Silk had been told to report on the sixth, so he had a couple of days to move around and get a feel for the city. Again, he discovered a larger city than he had expected, and while there was no Duke University, Roanoke was proud to be the home of Hollins College, the oldest women's college in the country. Originally, the city was named Big Lick, but late in the nineteenth century, it became the junction for the Shenandoah Valley Railroad, and the name was changed to Roanoke after the river it abuts. It seemed to Silk that this was opposite to the way that namings normally occurred, but who was he to judge? As a result, Roanoke's history has a lasting link to the railroad industry in the South.

When he reported to the park on Wednesday, he was surprised to see that most of the players either had been with Roanoke the previous year or were players returning from the military. Only he and a bonus baby pitcher named Curt Manning were new to class B baseball. It also quickly became obvious that, barring a fuckup on his part, he was expected to be the team's shortstop.

The team's manager was a career minor league infielder named Eddie Popowski, who in his long minor league career was known to be an outstanding defensive second baseman. Silk saw it as positive that his manager was an infielder who might help him with the defensive part of his game and wondered if this was part the reason that he had been assigned here rather than Lynn. Whatever the case, Silk took an immediate liking to his new manager who clearly had a passion for the game. It seemed as if the only thing he liked better than playing the game was teaching others how it should be played.

Every day was a new learning experience in aspects of the game, which to this point in his career, had never received much emphasis. Cutoff plays, rundowns, covering on pickoffs and steals, bunting drills, and the proper execution of double plays, including the phantom touching of second base.

Silk started fast on offence during the intersquad games, which meant one of two things. Either he was picking up where he had left off from last year, or the Roanoke Red Sox had a bad pitching staff. Whatever the case, when opening day arrived, Silk found himself batting leadoff.

With players returning from the service, the average age of his teammates was much higher than his first year in the minors, and going out for a few beers after the games was a regular occurrence. Silk had enjoyed an occasional beer in both high school and during the previous season, and he usually joined the other guys in hoisting a couple. As with everything else, he was very disciplined and never overdid the drinking. He did it more because of team chemistry than anything else.

Winning became the rule rather than the exception, and it was evident early in the season that the Sox were one of the better teams in the Piedmont League. Silk wondered if things could get any better. The team was winning, he was performing well both a bat and in the field, playing for Eddie Popowski was a blast, and the news from home continued to be good.

"Silk, I couldn't wait to tell you." Tony's voice which, when excited, often would wake the dead, seemed to reach a new level, causing Silk to move the receiver a few inches from his ear.

"I applied to Boston College and just got word that I've been accepted, and they gave me a free ride. Do you believe it, a full academic scholarship to BC?"

"Of course, I believe it, you finished first in your class, you were class president and a good guy. I'd be surprised if you didn't get it. Congratulations, Tony, you earned it."

That conversation took place in mid-June and was, without question, the highlight of the news that would come out of Gloucester that summer.

The low point was reached about two months later when he received a letter from Tina.

Dear Silk,

I can't tell you how long I've agonized over this decision or how difficult it has been, putting it into words. I have reached a point where I find myself looking for more that what we have in our relationship. It has been over a year since you first left to play baseball in Durham, and in that time, we have had very little time together. Your life is quite full with baseball and boxing while I have little to look forward to each day. Silk, if you were overseas with the military, I wouldn't be writing this letter, but you're not. You're absences are by choice. One of those choices is not to live in Gloucester when you are at home. I know why you chose to do so, but it is just one more thing that results in our not having time together.

Silk, I want you to know that I have not met anyone else, and this decision is my own and has not been influenced by my parents. You will always have a special place in my heart.

Sincerely,
Tina.

Silk, who had been standing when he opened the letter, found he was sitting on the floor by the mailbox when he finished. He didn't recall sliding down the wall to get there, but he was aware that he felt as if he had been kicked in the stomach. His mind jumped back to recent letters he had received from Tina.

"Did I miss something?" he heard himself say. "Was she trying to tell me something?"

After a minute, he got to his feet and went to the phone and dialed the Collin's number. Mrs. C answered the phone after several rings, and Silk could only imagine there was a lot of "No you answer it" going on.

"Hello, Mrs. C," Silk realized that this was the first time he had called her this to her face, but he didn't know how else to address her. "This is Silk. Is Tina there? I'd like to talk to her."

"I'm sorry, John, but she's not at home."

"Will she be home if I call later?"

"Probably not, I don't think she wants to talk to you right now. She is having a difficult time with all this."

"So am I and would think that after all the time we've known each, she could give me a few minutes on the phone." Silk's voice got a bit louder than he intended. He knew that if he displayed the anger he was feeling, he would never get to talk to Tina.

"I'm not sure I care for your tone, John, and I think this conversation is over."

He heard the phone click and go dead. His first thought was to call right back, but then realized that doing so would not serve his best interest. Instead, he called Tony. His father answered.

"This is Silk, is Tony there?"

"Johnny, this is your father, how are you, son?"

Silk suddenly realized that he had not heard his father's voice in five years and felt a moment of guilt because of it.

"I'm good, Dad, how are you doing?"

"It could be better, you know how that goes?"

Silk wanted to change the subject and asked again.

"Is Tony there? I really need to talk to him."

"He's here somewhere. I'll get him for you. It was nice hearing your voice."

More guilt. A few seconds passed, and Tony came to the phone.

"I'll bet you were surprised to hear your father's voice. He's here, going over some things with my dad, and he just picked up."

"Yeah, I could do without another surprise right now."

"Why, what up?"

Silk told Tony about the letter and made the mistake of not moving the receiver from his ear.

"The bitch did what?" Tony shouted in disbelief. "She sent you a Dear John."

"Well, actually it was a Dear Silk, but yeah, that's pretty much it. I was wondering if you knew anything about what's going on?"

"Are you kidding me? I know I kid about your not killing the messenger, but this is important shit. I'd never keep something like this from you. You know that, don't you?"

"I know, I know, but you have to know that I'm in shock here. Do me a favor and keep your eyes open and let me know if she is fucking around with somebody else. And whatever you do, be a little subtle. I don't want you parking in front of her house all night. Understand?"

"If I see her with a guy, do you want me to kick his ass?"

"No, it's not like that, I just have to know."

"Listen, Silk, I'm sorry about this. I know how much you liked her."

"Yeah, thanks, give me a call if you find out anything."

"Count on it, buddy."

The Sox played and won that night, and as usual, Silk joined the guys for beers after the game. At first, he felt that he would hang one on; but after the usual two, he left the bar. He was not alone.

Much to his surprise, Silk's play continued to be good in spite of the breakup. Of course, his newfound relationship with Connie might have had something to do with that, but whatever the case, he was able to keep his mind off Tina.

Connie was, in fact, like a tonic for what ailed him. She was an attractive, if not beautiful, young woman, with blonde hair and a slender figure. Silk was sure that he was more than likely the latest ballplayer du jour for her, but that didn't alter the fact that she was fun to be around and didn't have the sexual inhibitions harbored by Tina.

Given the benefit of 20/20 hindsight, Silk should have called Tony and told him to forget his detective work because he didn't need the call he received a few weeks later.

"She is seeing a guy. I got it out of Ellen who felt guilty about it because she knew about it for a couple of months."

Silk didn't say anything and knew by doing so, Tony would continue without any input on his part.

"The guy is an associate professor at Endicott."

"Great, that means this all started while I was around."

"Yeah, and I'll bet she's fucking the guy too."

"Thanks, Tony, I needed that. Do yourself a favor and don't major in diplomacy at BC."

In a way, this was a relief for him. Now he wouldn't be holding out hope that he and Tina would get back together, and he could start to put this whole episode behind him.

The balance of the summer was really good, considering what had happened at home. The Roanoke Red Sox, like the parent team in Boston, won the league title; Silk was selected Rookie of the Year for the Piedmont League; and he and Connie were rolling in the hay on a regular basis. If there were any negatives at all, they were that he probably would not be playing for Eddie Popowski again, and Johnny Pesky was back from the navy and tearing up American League pitching.

CHAPTER TWENTY-SIX

Back to Boston
Round Two

"Silk, it's so nice to see you back at Mass, how was your summer?"

"Great, Father, but it's always nice to come home, and of course, to attend Sacred Heart and hear another one of your fire-and-brimstone sermons."

"You know we have a social get-together every Sunday night at the parish hall. You might want to come by and meet a few of our nice Italian young ladies."

Silk almost forgot who he was talking to and said, *I'm not in the market for a nice girl right now.* Instead, he caught himself and replied, "You must have been talking to Father Bruno, you guys must have some sort of Catholicism grapevine going on or something."

"We talk, but we don't gossip, and we try to help our parishioners during difficult times."

"Well, Father Pasquale, if I have a free Sunday when my face doesn't look like chopped liver, I may take you up on your offer." He had no intention of doing so.

Carmen Bucci was even less subtle than the good father.

"You look like a piece of shit. You lost weight again, and I'll bet that you didn't run a foot all summer."

Silk was tempted to explain the ninety feet between bases, but thought better of it. He knew that no matter how he looked or how much he had worked out, Carmen was going to bust his balls.

"Are you ready for this, Mr. Baseball? Two weeks to get into shape and then a fight every three weeks. If you don't get killed, we can get in seven or eight bouts before spring. I really don't know why I'm wasting my time on you."

"I'm glad to see you too, Carmen."

Silk looked around as he arrived the next morning for his first workout of the year. The appearance of Bucci's Gym had always amazed him. Carmen had one of the best stable of fighters in the east, he was considered the finest trainer in Boston, and the gym that bore his name was a dump. Paint peeled off the walls and ceiling; the lighting was poor mainly because of burnt-out bulbs, locker doors didn't lock because of being punched by frustrated boxers, and showers that sparingly dispensed water, which was lukewarm at best. With all this, men—both boxers and professional businessmen—angled for the privilege of boasting that they worked out at Bucci's Gym.

"Hey, DeSimone, you're five minutes late. I ain't got all day. You know the routine, light bag, heavy bag, and ropes. Did you do five miles before you got here?"

Music to my ears, thought Silk.

Silk was in great shape, but baseball and boxing were two different things, and the first two weeks of training were very painful. If they weren't, Carmen would see to it that they became so. Carmen insisted on emphasing punching technique because he was concerned with what he called Silk's lack of punching power.

"You know, Carmen, I don't mind working on this stuff, but I have pretty good power in both hands."

"Six fights and you KO one stiff, you call that a punch."

"You told me to carry those guys, you said, don't knock them out."

"I told you to knock out the last guy, and you didn't."

"Nobody ever knocked that guy out."

"That's OK if you want to be a nobody, but if you want to be somebody, you better be able to punch."

"How's it going in Bucci's torture chamber, has he broken you yet?" Tony was making his Wednesday prefight call.

"Yeah, a couple of times, but he doesn't know it. I won't give the prick the satisfaction. I think he wants to punish me because boxing isn't my life."

"Is he still planning to have you fight every three weeks? You know that's all right if you're in there with punching bags, but if he plans on moving you up in class, you could come out of this with cotton for brains."

126

"Don't think for a second that that would make old Carmen sad, and he's one of the good guys in this business. The guy I'm going in with on Friday has a pretty good record, but he did lose to Webber a year ago, whatever that means."

"Well, Manny and I will be there. I'm bringing a couple of guys from BC with me. Who knows about these college guys, if you don't get your ass kicked, they may start a fan club."

"I don't do autographs. Make sure they understand."

Silk was back at the Boston Arena for his first match of the year. He took this as a good sign; at least his six-month absence didn't mean starting over at the Mechanics Building. The fight was scheduled for six rounds, and Carmen didn't tell him to carry the guy, so he knew he had better put him away, or next week would be hell. The third bout on the card featuring Frank Pinto and Silk DeSimone was over at 1:19 of the third round. When Carmen climbed in the ring after Pinto was counted out, he uttered the kindest words Silk had ever heard from his mouth.

"That's better," he said as he threw him a towel. Silk's new fan club of two insisted on buying the pizza, which for them was a bargain. They were convinced they were in the company of a future champion and the cost of a few pizzas gave them bragging rights back on campus.

Except for the elimination of the weekly trips to Endicott, Silk's routine was pretty similar to that of the previous winter. His Thursday trips to Gloucester were a fixture, and on the weeks he had a Friday fight, he often extended his stay with an overnight. Of course, the issue of reconciliation with his father intensified as Mary, Father Bruno, and now even Father Pasquale never seemed to waste an opportunity to broach the matter as frequently as possible. In spite of their efforts, Silk could not get past the matter of the waitress at Angelina's.

Silk considered dropping by to see Tina at Endicott to give him some closure to their relationship but realized it could serve no purpose, and truth be known, with the help of Connie back in Roanoke, he had gotten over her far better than he expected. Of course, it didn't hurt that just when it was needed most, Tony struck gold. It seemed that there were a number of small women's colleges and junior colleges in close proximity to Boston College's Chestnut Hill campus.

"Silk, you won't believe it. These girls think BC men are good catches, and they are hot to trot. I mean, they have parties and dances and are more than willing to jump into bed. If you don't get your face bloodied up, you could pass for a flaming *Eagle*. You lie and your fan club will swear to it."

"Where do I sign up? I'm surrounded by Italian virgins in the North End, and if that's not bad enough, their old men have guns. It's been a long time since Roanoke"

"I'll see you Friday at the fight. I'll have a plan for Saturday. You know, it may be time to find a place of your own. Living with the Patranos has to be cramping your style."

"I just told you, I have no style to be cramped, but you're right, the time has come to move on. It's too bad because Lena is a great cook."

The routine was now set. Carmen would bust his balls in the gym; he would visit his mom once a week, fight every three weeks, and get laid on a regular basis. The only problem was food. Without Lena's table, he was down to one good *(free)* meal a week; and being a male brought up in an Italian home, he couldn't boil water. Of course, there were plenty of good places to eat in the North End, but the free meals went the way of the buggy whip.

The winter flew by; Silk was enjoying a celebrity status in the North End since Father Pasquale never missed a chance to brag about his young parishioner. He even gained the interest of several parents who felt he might be a good catch for their daughters. Silk's attitude on this was "You keep them locked up for now and maybe we can deal later."

Carmen, true to his word, had him fight seven matches, all of which he won. His punching power was still a concern of his trainer. None of the fights went the distance, but five of the wins were TKOs, which led Carmen to only one conclusion.

"Kid, you can really fight, but if you ever have to put someone away, I'm not sure you can do it."

That spring, Silk left Boston for Scranton, Pennsylvania, where he was to play for the Red Sox Class A representative in the Eastern League.

CHAPTER TWENTY-SEVEN

Silk DeSimone
Fast Track One
Fast Track Two

Silk's two careers seemed to mirror one another. The summer of '47 was another good one for Silk. It marked three consecutive years of movement through the Red Sox farm system and the third season of steady improvement. Johnny Pesky continued to shine up in Boston, but Silk was convinced that he was the top shortstop prospect in the Sox minor league system.

That fall he returned to Boston and a regimen that Carmen had laid out for him. The drill was pretty much the same with regard to training, but the level of competition he had lined up for Silk was definitely a cut above what it had been in year two. This was fine with Silk, who saw no benefit in all this work, if he couldn't compete at a higher level. The Boston College contingency grew to the point where there were four to five carloads making the trip to the arena for the fights. This made Carmen about as happy as a man coming home and finding his wife shacked up with his best friend, and he didn't mince words in voicing his displeasure on the matter. Silk promised to keep a lid on it but did so without much conviction.

Silk won his first three fights rather easily although he scored only one knockout. The Monday following the third fight, he was back in the gym; and after yet another cold shower, Carmen asked that they have a talk.

"What are you doing next Saturday night?" inquired Carmen.

Silk saw this as a loaded question and proceeded with caution.

"I'm really not sure. Why, what's up?"

"Good, then you're free for the night."

"Yeah, I guess I am," answered Silk, kicking himself and knowing the plans he had were going down the tubes.

"There's a good card at the Garden, and the main event is Walt Farley and Willie Taylor. They're ranked light heavies, and I want you to get a look at them."

"If you're paying, I'll be there." *What the hell, I won't get laid, but it should be a good take.*

"You forget who you're talking to? I'm a big shot in this game. I get freebies."

Carmen must have been a big shot because the seats were only about ten rows back from ringside. There was a very good crowd although not nearly the standing-room-only mob he had witnessed at the Louis fight a half-dozen years ago.

The first bout started at seven, and it didn't surprise Silk that Carmen insisted that they be seated prior to the first bell. He certainly couldn't understand what he might learn from two featherweights with less experience than him. He also knew better than to point this out to his manager.

The bouts got progressively better, and Silk began to see the merit of being in attendance. The semifinal bout was about ten minutes from starting when Silk became aware of people stirring around him. He turned to see what was causing the commotion and was struck by a strangely familiar sight. Four men slowly worked their way down the aisle to four vacant ringside seats. It took Silk a minute to put it all together. One of the men, the youngest of the four, was the man who came to his front door some years ago. The very same man who got his ass kicked by his uncle Santino. Now it came back in a flash; the elder man of the four was, of course, Dominic Belamonte, the Don of the Boston Mafia. *Farley and Taylor must be better than I thought to bring this guy out; either that or he has a vested interest in the fight. Farley is a prohibited favorite, so maybe he's going in the tank.*

Silk couldn't have been more wrong. A few minutes later, it all came into focus. The semifinal combatants were being introduced, and suddenly, the name Joey Belamonte rang into his consciousness.

"Son of a bitch," he said aloud. "That's Belamonte's kid. I didn't know he was a fighter."

"No shit, that's a surprise. Do you ever pick up a paper to read about anything but fucking baseball?"

"How come I've never seen him on a card?

"Because he isn't on any arena cards. All of his fights are at the Garden."

At the moment, Silk was six feet tall and weighed in at about 168. Joey was announced at 174 and looked to be about five ten. He was built more like Tony than himself. He was also introduced with a record of 24-0-0, with twenty-two knockouts. This was to be a ten-round fight, but it didn't take long to realize that there was no way it would go the limit. Belamonte moved around the ring well, but it was not outstanding boxing skills that had got him to this point. Simply stated, this prick could punch. Silk could almost hear Carmen moaning in envy. Less than fifteen minutes into the fight, it was over.

Belamonte climbed out of the ring and headed for the locker room amid the cheers of a crowd that was either adoring or putting on a show for the Don. His father and the others followed.

I guess I was wrong about Farley taking a tank, thought Silk.

True to his code, as a boxing junkie, Carmen stayed for the main event, but it was clear to Silk that the purpose of the evening was for him to get a look at Joey Belamonte. Whatever the motive, it worked. The following Monday, Silk arrived at the gym with a new sense of urgency. He now knew the enemy, and if he expected to compete at that level, he had better get far more intense than he had been in the past.

Silk had three more fights before the end of his third year in the ring, winning them all while scoring two knockouts. Carmen intensified his focus on the basics of the trade. He and Silk both knew, if he were to meet Belamonte in the ring, he had better outbox him because he definitely wasn't going to out punch him.

Belamonte had only one more bout before Silk was to head for spring training, and Silk asked Tony and Manny to attend the fight with him. His scheduled ten-rounder went six before he put his opponent away.

"Well, what do you think?" Silk asked over pizza.

"Do you have medical insurance?" Tony shot back without hesitation.

"Forget medical, I'd get some life insurance."

It was clear the these two assholes had rehearsed this skit earlier in the day, and he simply shook his head and repeated the question.

"Are you finished? Can I get a straight answer?"

"The guy is good, but I think I can take him," responded Tony without missing a beat.

"You know," added Manny, "I think you're right. You always had a better punch than Silk."

Silk gave up and concentrated on his anchovy pizza.

When his friends dropped him off at his apartment, Tony finally relented and got serious.

"All shittin' aside, the guy is good, but my money is on you."

"Mine too," added Manny.

CHAPTER TWENTY-EIGHT

Moving Up
and
Going South

After playing a summer in the cooler climates of Pennsylvania, Silk once again found himself assigned in the Deep South. He was pleased that he had made it to AA, but at the same time, he wished that the Sox had an AA team in Vermont.

Instead, it was the AA Birmingham Barons of the American Association. It was about the same size as the towns he had previously played in, and all told if it weren't for the heat, it wouldn't have been half bad.

He wasn't in town long before he discovered that there was a second baseball team located there. It was a Negro League team, distastefully named the Birmingham Black Barons. Out of curiosity, Silk made it a point to attend several of their games. Jackie Robinson had broken the major league color barrier the previous season, and his success insured the fact the other Negro players would soon follow. What he saw was astounding. If the two Birmingham teams were merged into one, many of his teammates would not have made the team. He might well be one of those left out in the cold.

Well, he thought, *I may as well deal with it, because I'm sure the Sox have scouts looking at these guys right now.*

The season was an all-around success. The team played well, especially at home at Richwood Field, and won the Dixie Series Championship. Silk hit very well, excelled at shortstop, and discovered Bobbi, the Birmingham equivalent of Connie in Roanoke and Doris in Scranton. There was, however, one cloud looming on the horizon. Some changes had taken place prior to the 1948 season with the parent team, which created some questions in his mind regarding his future. The Sox had made a major deal with the St. Louis Browns, which resulted in their securing the services of a new shortstop. Vern Stephens was a power hitter, who was good enough defensively to cause the Sox to move Pesky from shortstop to third base. Both Pesky and Stephens had outstanding seasons, leaving Silk to wonder if his days with the Sox were numbered. He decided to put it out of his mind and file it under the heading of Don't Worry about Things over Which You Have No Control. If there was one positive thing with all this, it was that he would be moved to the AAA for the '49 season.

Silk arrived home on a Wednesday, so he had the weekend free before having to report in to Bucci's torture chamber on Monday. He made good use of the time by visiting his mother on Thursday and partying at BC on Friday and Saturday. He had no way of knowing that this would be the extent of his partying for several months to come. He and Manny slept on the floor of Tony's dorm room on both of those nights, and Sunday morning was the first real chance for the three friends to catch up.

"What are you going to be when you grow up?" Silk asked his cousin over a breakfast of Wheaties and coffee.

"When I graduate, I'm going back to school," he responded nonchalantly. "I'm going to enroll in BC Law School." This caught Silk a bit off guard, but he suddenly felt a great sense of pride for his lifelong friend. There was never any doubt in his mind that Tony would be a success, but now, success was beginning to become more defined. Silk tried to come back with a wiseass remark, but was at a loss for words.

"That's great, Tony" was all he could come up with. On the other hand, Tony was never left wanting for a wise crack.

"I was thinking, maybe you should come back to school. With this Stephens guy being around, you may be out of work soon. You know he had about 45 homers and 175 RBI this season." Silk knew only too well that the correct numbers were 29 and 137 but decided to let it pass. He knew that Tony knew the correct stats.

"How about you, Manny?" he asked, turning his head from his nut-busting cousin.

"It's a little early to tell. I'm just starting my sophomore year, but Babson, being what it is, I should have plenty of options."

"Yeah, options are good," injected Tony.

I swear if I didn't love this guy, I'd have to kill him, he thought.

Silk decided to kick-start the training and was up early Monday morning and had five miles in before breakfast. He walked in the gym a little before eight and wasn't surprised to see that nothing had changed. There was a certain comfort in that fact. He then spotted Carmen coming toward him, and he was immediately struck with a strange difference in Carmen's face. Suddenly, it occurred to him what it was. Carmen Bucci was smiling. In the three years he had known the man, he had no recollection of ever seeing a smile on his face.

"We gotta talk, let's go to the office." Wow, now an invitation to Carmen's inner sanctum, the place where business was done.

"What's up?" was all that Silk could muster. His curiosity was killing him.

"Willie Albert has retired and vacated his title." Albert had been the reigning New England light heavyweight champion of the past half-dozen years.

"There was a lot of pressure put on him to give a shot to Belamonte, and he didn't want any part of it. He decided to retire instead of taking the fight. I think Joey's old man told him, fight or retire or else."

"So what does all this mean to me?"

Carmen went to his battered desk and retrieved a letter from it and handed it to Silk. It bore the letterhead of the New England Boxing Commission and stated that eight fighters had been selected to compete in an elimination series to determine the crowning of a new champion. Silk DeSimone was one of the eight names.

"I've never heard of most of these guys, what do you know about them?"

"Enough to know that the list should have only three names on it and the other five are just to draw the thing out and put some money in the right pockets."

"How is it going to work? When does it start?" These were just two of the questions buzzing through Silk's mind.

"Sit down, and I'll fill you in."

The six combatants other than him and Belamonte were Jeff Tanner, Billy Maxwell, Tommy Washington, Chris Jackson, Tim Donaldson, and Miller Greene, with Chris Jackson being the class of the group.

"The first match is in less than a month. There will be a total of seven matches with the championship being held at the Garden on December 18. The matches haven't been announced yet, but I'm trying to get you a later date so you'll have some extra time to get ready. Don't forget, the championship fight will be fifteen rounds, and that's a whole new ballgame."

This may have been the longest speech he had ever heard from Carman, who was visibly pumped.

"I hope you realize what all this means. If you win this thing, you may be ranked in the top ten in your class. You'll also make more money in the next couple of months than the Sox have paid you in the past two years, and maybe, just maybe, I can recoup some of my losses on you."

Silk wondered how many times he had heard that before today. Try as he may, he couldn't recall how or when Carmen had ever spent a dime since he had known him. Did he have a time clock running on the time they spent working together, was it the occasional time when there was warm water in the shower? Or maybe it was wear and tear on the equipment that hadn't been new for a very long time. Whatever it was, he let it pass.

"I guess I'd better get started," he said with all the resolve he could muster.

"One more thing, the women. I know you're a good-lookin' guy, and the girls think you're somethin', but chicks are poison to fighters. You gotta promise me that no fuckin' around until this is over with. You hear me?"

"Women are the last thing on my mind," he lied.

Silk really didn't need any prodding from the task master. He wanted this as badly as Carmen. He put extra time in on everything from roadwork to the rounds he sparred. He broke the news to Tony regarding his moratorium on women. For recreation, he decided to accept Father Pasquale's open invitation to the Sunday social at the parish hall. Since he couldn't get laid, he might as well meet some nice girls. He extended an invitation to Tony and Manny to join him, but wasn't surprised to hear their response.

"We'll see you after the fights."

A week later, Carmen approached Silk with a letter in hand.

"They finalized the schedule of the fights, and I guess I don't have the pull I thought I had. You're fighting Tommy Washington on the first week. The fight's on the second, at the Garden. It'll be your first main event."

"I can't believe you didn't get me a later date. Why the hell do I pay you the big bucks anyway?" He turned and walked away as Carmen assaulted him with a barrage of expletives.

Well, at least his routine was set. Work Monday through Friday, fight or attend fights on Saturday, and play nice Italian catholic boy on Sunday. It was better than a stick in the eye, but not much.

As it turned out, the Sunday social wasn't all that bad. There was only unspiked punch and coffee to drink, so with beer being taboo for him, he didn't feel deprived in any way. He knew many of the people from church and the neighborhood, and he was treated like a local celebrity, which was nice after being treated like crap all week at the gym.

There were also some very attractive young Italian girls who seemed eager to meet him, but an irate Italian father was the last thing he needed right now.

The three weeks leading up to the fight came and went in a flash. While Tommy Washington was not one of the top boxers in the group, he was better than the guys he had fought in the past and the fight was taken on short notice. What made things worse was that after a closer look at the format, it was apparent that Belamonte was given an easier road to the championship match. He would fight the stiffs, while Silk and Chris Jackson were on a collision course with one another. In any case, the winner of that bout was liable to enter the ring with Belamonte a little beat-up. None of this surprised any of the people involved.

The night of October 2 arrived; and Silk, for the first time in his professional life, boxing or baseball, felt as if he was in the big leagues. The Boston Garden was miles from pristine, but when compared with the Mechanics Building or the Boston Arena it seemed special. Everything about it was several cuts above any of his previous venues. Carmen noticed the fact that Silk was somewhat in awe of his surroundings and brought him back to earth with his usual subtlety.

"If you don't get your head out of your ass soon, Washington will hand it to you."

The crashing sound was Silk coming too quickly back to earth.

The fighters were instructed to be in the ring at 9:45 to allow time for introductions and announcements. Carmen made sure that Washington was left to wait, and he and his fighter climbed through the ropes ten minutes late. Silk stood with his back to the announcer, as instructed by Carmen, to show further distain for his opponent. With all this one-upsmanship, Silk remained totally focused; and rather than seeing faces in the crowd, he saw instead a sea of humanity. When the bell sounded starting the fight, Silk came out of his corner and was surprised to see a left-handed fighter standing before him. He knew this must be some sort of a ploy because he was confident that Carmen wouldn't have overlooked such a detail. To everyone's amazement Silk immediately turned southpawed also. No one was more surprised than Tommy Washington who actually looked dumbfounded. He looked that way for only a second before he hit the canvas under a barrage of right jabs and a left hook to the bridge of his nose. He somehow managed to get to his feet, but his broken nose was bleeding beyond repair, and the referee called a halt to the fight at twenty-two seconds of the first round. As Silk left the ring, some faces came into focus. Mr. Belamonte was at his usual ringside seats along with Carl and two hard types. Joey was nowhere in sight. He then spotted his two friends and the BC contingent. He couldn't very well have missed them because of their outlandish behavior. Silk couldn't help but smile but didn't give any indication that he knew them. He did not see Fathers Bruno and Pasquale, Santino, or his father, but he was sure they were there.

"Where the hell did you get that southpaw shit?"

"What, do you think that you're the first trainer I ever had? I came to you a well-trained fighting machine." Carmen and Silk were back in the locker room.

"Try not to say too much when the press gets in here. I don't want them to know that you're an arrogant asshole."

"That's fine with me. Let's get them out of here so I can get in the shower. I heard a rumor that they have hot water."

It would be six weeks before his next bout, and much to his amazement, Carman gave him the next week off. Silk made a point of getting to Gloucester to see the family. He arrived on Tuesday and slept in his old bed for two nights before returning to the North End on Thursday night. While taking a walk to the pier on Wednesday, he spotted Tina with a guy he guessed was the professor. She spotted him also and quickly ushered her guy in the other direction, no doubt in fear that Silk would have an unscheduled bout in his honor. She could not have been more wrong. For the first time since receiving her Dear Silk letter, he was sure that he was over her.

That Saturday, he, along with Carmen, Tony, and Manny was back at the Garden for the Jackson-Donaldson bout. It went pretty much as expected: Jackson by a KO in eight rounds. Jackson showed experience, poise, and confidence. He was by far the most experienced fighter in the competition, having fought in excess of fifty bouts with one of his only five losses coming at the hands of the retiring ex-champ in a split decision three years earlier.

The four of them went out to eat after the fight, and Carman asked no one in particular what they had seen tonight. Silk was amazed when Tony resisted the temptation of being a wiseass and responded authoritatively, "I saw the second best boxer and the second best puncher in the competition."

"Where did you find this guy, Silk? He actually knows what he's talking about."

"I don't know this guy, I thought he was with you."

Silk knew that Tony was right on about Jackson, and that he'd better be on his game when they met next month.

It was another two weeks before Joey Belamonte finally fought his first bout, and the outcome was no surprise. What was a surprise was the fact that it went nine rounds before he could put Maxwell away. This guy had a jaw reminiscent of Mark Webber, the guy he had failed to put away a couple of years ago.

Silk and the other three turned down seats at ringside and watched the bout from good seats in the front row of the balcony. They did so, at Carmen's insistence, to avoid being seen by the same Belamonte contingent of four who showed for Silk's initial bout. Silk wasn't sure that all this covert stuff was necessary, but he wasn't about to piss off his manager over something so trivial.

The four finalist were now set. Jeff Tanner had defeated Miller Greene a week earlier. Next up, DeSimone versus Jackson to be followed by Tanner and Belamonte.

Both Silk and Jackson had over a month to prepare for their bout, so there was no advantage gained by either in that regard. In fact, the only discernable difference between the fighters was in the area of experience, where Jackson had a clear edge. Silk had a lot of respect for Jackson, but even with that, he had to look past their bout and train for the final match of the competition. He realized that if he got to that point, he would not only have to deal with Belamonte, but also the possibility of having to go fifteen rounds. He trained for the Jackson bout as if it too was a fifteen-rounder.

Carmen was inwardly pleased with Silk's approach to the fight, but outwardly, he maintained his usual caustic demeanor.

"You sparred today like a guy who got laid last night. Didn't I tell you to cut out that crap?"

"If I was any more celibate, I'd be in a seminary. Did you ever think that the ten miles I'm doing every morning might have something to do with it?"

"Did I tell you to go to ten miles? You did that on your own, and if you don't mind getting your ass kicked by Belamonte, you can stop anytime. It won't matter anyway, if you don't fight better than you did today, it'll be Jackson who will be kicking your ass."

"I'm sure you're right. In fact, when was the last time you were wrong?"

That was a rhetorical question, but Silk knew it would not go unanswered.

Other than going from five to ten miles of roadwork, Silk's routine remained the same for this match as it had been for Tommy Washington.

The same held true with his activities away from the gym. To his amazement, he started to look forward to the Sunday night socials. He wasn't sure if it was because it was that good or the fact that the rest of his social life sucked so badly. The girls were pretty, and he enjoyed the dancing and a night out with the absence of complications. Visits to Boston College were taboo, but he did see Tony and Manny at the fights on Saturdays. He knew that they both attended the fights out of friendship and at great personal sacrifice.

November 13 finally arrived and not a day too soon. For once, Silk and Carmen were in agreement regarding training. Both were concerned that Silk may have over trained and left his best fight in the gym. Two weeks earlier, the workouts had been brisk and sharp, but they turned sluggish toward the end. When the bell sounded marking the start of the bout, the concerns turned into reality. It was Jackson who was sharp, and it was he who was clearly taking the fight to Silk, whose sole goal at this point was to somehow get it together before he lost the bout. After two rounds, Silk sat in his corner, listening to Carmen who was calmer than might be expected and doing his best to get his fighter on track. Round three was much of the same with the exception that a second or two before it ended, Jackson caught Silk with a hard right to the cheekbone and almost sent him to the canvas. The bell sounded, and Silk made it back to his corner on rubbery legs.

Carmen jumped into the ring and splashed Silks face with cold water from a huge sponge and then applied a cold compress to the back of his neck. It was a full twenty seconds into the break before he looked at Silk's face and then his eyes. What he saw caught him completely off guard. He never expected to see fear, for he knew his fighter too well for that. He did expect maybe confusion, disbelief, or even disillusionment. What he didn't expect was anger and what he had no way of knowing was that in all his years of boxing, this was the first time Silk had ever been hurt in the ring. That made him angry as did the fact that Carmen had allowed him to over train for the fight that he himself had been a part of that; and maybe, just maybe, he had looked past Jackson and on to the Belamonte fight. Neither man said a word to the other before the bell for round four sounded.

Jackson came out of his corner and straight at Silk, wanting to finish him while he was still shaky. Before he could get off a punch, he was met with a straight left jab to the face. All of a sudden he seemed a little in shock and unprepared for what followed, which was a series of blows to the head and body. His experience then kicked in, and he quickly realized that it was time to clutch and hold in order to weather the assault. He didn't know it then, but the fight was over. Silk spent the next four rounds punishing Jackson before he was unable to answer the bell for the ninth round.

The Garden was alive. The crowd knew that they had been treated to a great fight by two really game boxers. As Silk left the ring and headed to the locker room, he spotted the two priests and the two Salina brothers, sitting in floor level seats, about fifteen rows back from the ring. They made no attempt to hide their presence and were yelling in approval at what they had just witnessed. Silk hesitated then smiled and waved at the group. There was a racket from above; and Silk looked up to the first balcony to see Tony, Manny, and the BC mob, yelling and banging on several large drums. When they got to the locker room, Carmen turned to Silk and said, "We were lucky tonight. We made some mistakes, and we got away with it."

"We both learned something tonight. We won't make the same mistake again."

A minute later, the boxing beat writers were at the locker room door. They seemed as excited as many of the fans, and for the first time, Silk sensed that they saw him as a legitimate contender. After three years and twenty-one wins, they acted as if they had just discovered him. Most of them had in fact predicted a Jackson-Belamonte championship match-up. While most of the questions were directed at Silk, all were answered by Carmen. Finally, one of the writers asked, "Well, what do you think, DeSimone?"

"I don't think, and I don't talk. You'll have to ask my manager."

As he said this, he looked past the writer and saw Manny and Tony, observing the spectacle and sporting huge smiles. The writer was relentless and fired yet another question at the young boxer.

"How do the Red Sox feel about your boxing in the off-season?"

"It ain't like that," shot back Carmen. "I give him permission to play ball in the summer."

Silk was sure that Carmen really believed what he had just uttered.

"After tonight, do you think your boy will be favored in the Belamonte fight?"

"I didn't know that Belamonte was in the final yet."

With that, Carmen brought the proceedings to an abrupt end and showed the writers the door.

After a shower, it was time to kick back and relax for at least a few hours. The BC crowd had taken on a life of its own, so the R & R was limited to his two buddies. Pizza never tasted so good, and Silk even allowed himself a few beers.

With the next fight scheduled over a month away, Carmen told Silk to stay away from the gym until Thursday. Silk welcomed the break and spent three days at home in Gloucester, visiting the family.

On Saturday, his two friends, along with Carmen, joined him at the Garden for the Belamonte-Tanner card. It got so that Silk enjoyed the predictable, ceremonial type entrance of the Belamonte group. The Don, the two goons, and Carl, the idiot son. Always after the semifinal bout and always the grand entrance.

This, in fact, was more enjoyable and only slightly shorter in length, than the fight itself. Any sweat worked up by Belamonte had probably been done in the locker room prior to the fight. It was all over at 1:10 of the third round. Any doubt about his punching power, after his nine rounds with Maxwell, was put to rest. This guy was the real deal.

CHAPTER TWENTY-NINE

Idiot Son
Part Two

For the next four weeks prior to the championship match, Carman and Silk struck a good balance in his training routine. The only constant was the ten-mile daily roadwork; beyond that, the daily sessions, while brisk, were shorter in duration. To Silk's amazement, Carmen insisted that Thursday be an off day and that he go to Gloucester and get his mind off the training routine.

Silk had a surprise for Carmen also.

"I have an idea for a sparring partner for the fight. I've had twenty-one bouts and I've never been in there with anyone who punches like this guy."

"Do I know the guy?"

"Oh, you know him, it's my cousin Tony."

"What, you have to be shittin' me. If he could fight like he mouths off, he'd be a world champ."

"Listen, with that mouth, he'd have been dead a long time ago if he couldn't fight."

"Who's next, that Manny kid?"

"He's good too."

The sparring went on for three rounds, and when it was over, Carmen was a believer. Tony was very similar to Chris Jackson. He wasn't the boxer that his cousin was, but he was a heavier puncher.

"You interested in this game? I think you could do good as a heavyweight."

"Sorry, Carmen, I like my face just the way it is. If we do business in the future, I'll probably be trying to keep you out of jail."

The timing wasn't great for Tony. His first semester was coming to a close, and he had finals, but they were able to adjust the training routine to best accommodate his schedule; and while boxing was not in his long term plans, his love for the sport was rekindled.

On a whim, Silk asked his two friends if they'd like to join him at the Sunday night social at the parish house, and he was not at all surprised when they accepted.

"What took you so long?" queried Manny. "You keeping all those Italian virgins to yourself?"

"No, I'm trying to keep all those Italians virgins so you guys won't be waking up with your balls in your mouths. These are Sicilians we're fuckin with, and they don't like anyone screwing with the cherries."

Silk had to admit his friends were on their best behavior and seemed to have a great time. Father Pasquale had seen the boys with Silk; and of course, he knew Tony's father from the fights. He was pleased to see that Silk enjoyed the socials enough to invite his friends.

He made a point of introducing the young men around and it was then that Tony met Theresa "Terry" Giuliani. From this point forward, partying at BC and at surrounding campuses was no longer what Tony wanted to do on weekends. He would become a regular Sunday night participant. Manny was in halfway; he would party on Saturday and socialize on Sunday.

It was a Friday night, about a week from the night of the fight, and Silk and Tony were leaving Bucci's Gym after a good workout. Both were feeling confident, and you could hear it in their voices and lighthearted chatter. They didn't get more than twenty five yards or so before being approached by a hulk of a guy dressed in a bad suit with a face to match.

"You DeSimone?"

"Who's asking?"

"Mr. Belamonte wants to talk with you. He's in the car over there."

Silk glanced at the late-model Cadillac and saw the figure of a man much younger than Dominic Belamonte.

"What the hell are you talking about, that's not Mr. Belamonte?"

"It's Carl Belamonte, remember him, the idiot son that came to the house in Gloucester?" interjected Tony.

"You're right, he's always tagging behind his father."

"What does he want with me?"

"He wants to talk to you alone in the car."

"If he wants to talk to me, tell him to get out of the car, and he'll talk to me and my friend."

"He's not going to like this. You better get in the car."

"See you around." Silk and Tony turned in unison and started to walk away.

"Wait, I'll tell him," said the bad suit as he turned and walked to the car.

They watched as the two men talked through the lowered window of the car.

The door opened, and a very angry-looking Carl Belamonte walked toward them.

"You're going to have to learn a little respect, DeSimone."

"You're going to have to earn it, Belamonte."

The comeback seemed to confuse him, and he moved on. He got right to the point.

"You're fightin' my brother Joey next week, and I got a proposition for you."

"Let me guess, you want me to tank the fight. Am I right?"

Again, Carl wasn't ready for the response and paused before moving on.

"There's some good money to be made, and with the purse, you can have a big payday."

Tony could hardly contain himself. He couldn't believe what he was hearing and the depth of this man's stupidity.

"Listen, Carl, your brother's a big favorite. If you get him to tank it, we can all make some real money."

"Who's this asshole?"

"I'm his lawyer, and I handle all his light work. Like if you want to hit him, you have to go through me. Asshole."

Carl might have been the idiot son, but he was the idiot son of Don Belamonte, and no one ever called him an asshole. At least, not to his face. He charged Tony and let fly a roundhouse right hand, which Tony deftly ducked under as he delivered an uppercut to the flabby skin just below Carl's breastbone. The loud hissing sound they heard was the air leaving his lungs. He immediately fell to the sidewalk, gasping for air. The bad suit came rushing to his aid. The man must have weighed three hundred pounds, and it didn't take Tony long to assess the situation. It called for the famous Silina kick to the balls, which he delivered with precision. The hulk joined his boss on the sidewalk.

"Now you've done it. You really know how to make enemies in high places."

"You're welcome, you'd do the same for me."

The next day, Silk told Carmen what had happened.

"What do you think Mr. Belamonte will do?"

"He won't do nothing because the son is not about to tell his old man that he got his ass kicked on a street in the North End, but you better watch your back with Carl."

—

CHAPTER THIRTY

Fight Night

The calendar read December 18, and the day of the Belamonte-DeSimone championship fight had arrived. It was being treated as a much larger event than Silk ever imagined. Carmen, on the other hand, wasn't at all surprised.

"You got two local Italian boys, both undefeated, fighting for a title, and word is that the winner will be ranked in the top ten light heavies in the world. And it don't hurt that Joey's old man is a mob boss."

The Garden was sold out, and the crowd came early and was loud even during the prelims. Silk knew he would have a pretty good following. A couple of busloads were coming in from BC, and he had heard from Father Bruno that a convoy was heading in from Gloucester. Even with that, Belamonte was expected to be a huge crowd favorite. He was born and bred in the North End, and the Belamonte name commanded a lot of respect and loyalty—or else.

The locker room was all business, and the only a small group of people were granted access. Carmen was occupied taping Silk's hands; the cut man was looking after his gear; and Tony, now a member of the DeSimone team, would be in his corner during the fight. The only other people allowed in, and only for a short visit, were Manny and the good Fathers Bruno and Pasquale.

Silk made a point of mentioning that it was Father Bruno who had taught him the trick of quickly going southpaw when necessary. He could tell by the look on his face that the comment meant a lot to his longtime friend and coach.

"Ten minutes. Get out there in ten minutes" was the word from the ringside messenger. Silk knew that he had twenty minutes before he would be directed by Carmen to exit the locker room.

When he finally made his way down the aisle toward the ring, he was amazed by the roar of approval his arrival prompted. His fans would be outnumbered, but they would not be out shouted. He was, however, not surprised that in spite of his tardy arrival that he was still left waiting for his opponent. There was no chance that the Belamontes would get upstaged in their own backyard.

A couple of minutes later, Belamonte entered the ring to a deafening chorus of cheers from the North End contingent. Silk made it a point not to look his way or in any way acknowledge his arrival. At that point, Silk went through a transformation he had never experienced prior to that moment. It was as if his mind was blocking out everything that was going on around him. Words and sounds seemed to be coming from the other end of a tunnel and it was as if he was standing alone in this cavernous arena. There was the usual parade of local dignitaries and boxers, both current and retired, being introduced to the crowd; but it was all lost on him. Silk was in a zone, focused on only one thing. There was nothing happening that night other than the boxing match, which would start sometime after all this nonsense was over with. Finally, the ring was cleared, and the combatants were brought to the center of the ring for the referee's instructions. If the referee had anything to say other than the regular prefight stuff, Silk would not have heard it. Belamonte and DeSimone stood at center ring, glared at one another, touched gloves and returned to their corners to await the bell which would start the first round. When, a few seconds later, the bell sounded, it suddenly brought Silk back from the place he had been; and he heard the roar of the crowd and saw Joey Belamonte coming out of his corner and directly across the ring. This was it; after all this time and all the grueling training, the fight was underway. Silk slid to his left. Joey's plan was to move straight ahead and Silk's was to avoid a slugfest.

The first round was typical of so many other opening rounds. Each of the fighters wanted to get a feel of the other man in the ring while not wanting to risk too much. Tonight, this was also an indication of the respect each of the fighters had for the other. With about thirty seconds left in the round, Joey decided to try and steal the round with a late flurry; but this strategy was flawed, as Silk answered his move with several right jabs. They were not heavy punches, but in a round almost devoid of any real action, they may have been enough to win the round. On the other hand, Belamonte was always moving forward and, as the aggressor, he would garner favor from the judges.

While the first round did not have much action, it clearly defined the fight plan of each of the camps. Belamonte would move forward, try to maneuver DeSimone into a corner, and create as much infighting as possible. DeSimone, on the other hand, would offer a moving target and pile up points with his clearly faster hands.

The fans were being treated to a good fight, and while there was no toe-to-toe action, there was an abundance of effort being made by each fighter to provide a good show. At least, as it pertained to their fight strategy. If either boxer held an edge over the first half of the bout it was Belamonte, primarily because he was taking the fight to DeSimone. Silk sensed this and was a bit surprised when, between each round, he was urged by Carmen to continue to stick to their plan of moving and counterpunching. When they got past the eleventh round, it appeared to Silk that his trainer knew what he was doing. Belamonte began to slow down a bit and become an easier target. Joey had trained hard, but it appeared that he never expected the fight to go the distance. What edge he had built up in the early rounds began the slip away, and by the end of round fourteen, the fight was too close to call. As Carmen spoke the words, Silk couldn't help but wonder how many times fighters had heard these exact words, going into the final round of a fight.

"You win this round big, and the fight is yours. Do you hear?"

Silk nodded and looked across the ring to Belamonte's corner. He couldn't hear the words, but he knew what was being said. The bell for the final round sounded, but this, time both fighters circled from their corners and moved cautiously to the left. Three minutes is an eternity in the ring, and there was no need to rush into anything; you just had to win the round. They then moved together and began to feel their way in a manner not dissimilar to the first round, except that neither fighter planned on waiting for the final thirty seconds before opening up. Less than a half minute into the round, the two fighters engaged in a flurry of punches; and when it broke off, it was Belamonte backing off for the first time in the fight. Silk sensed that this was the time to throw caution out the window and press the advantage. He moved after Belamonte and hit him with a series of jabs and followed up with a hard straight right, which caught his opponent flush on the left cheekbone. Belamonte was hurt, and he staggered back, trying to buy some time; but Silk was all over him, first with a left and then a right, which caught Belamonte on the same cheekbone. Joey was on his way down; the only thing between him and canvas were the ring ropes which he was hanging onto while he was sliding to the canvas. He was done, and for Silk, it was as if he and Joey were suspended in time. What Silk did next was something he would never understand. He threw yet another right hand which landed on Belamonte's left temple. His head swung to his right, and perspiration sprayed from his long black hair. He was now on the canvas. The Garden erupted; even those who were supporters of Joey Belamonte roared their approval and appreciation for what they had witnessed. While all this was going on, Joey's seconds had helped him to his feet and got him to his corner. Silk finally turned and started over to congratulate his opponent for his performance. Before he got there, he saw Joey slump down and almost slip from his stool to the canvas. He was caught by one of his seconds, but it was clear that the young man was in trouble. What followed next was chaotic; the ring doctor, who had been in Joey's corner prior to his passing out, was now joined by emergency medics who were on site, Don Belamonte along with Carl and several of Boston's finest. Silk could not get near the corner. The police used their bodies and the nightsticks to create a barrier across the middle of the ring. Within minutes, Joey was placed on a stretcher and removed from the ring and into a waiting ambulance. The Belamontes were right on the heels of the ambulance attendants, and the "family" followed quickly in their footsteps.

Silk went directly to the locker room to throw on some clothes.

"Where did they take him?"

"Mass General," replied Carmen. "Your not goin' over there are you?"

"Why wouldn't I?"

"Because you could be the fighter that dies tonight."

"I'm going with you," added Tony.

"Somehow, I don't see you as the guy that will keep a lid on things."

"No, I'm the guy who has your back."

"Let's go."

The traffic leaving the Garden was heavy, and the short drive to the Massachusetts General Hospital took nearly an hour.

"We would have been better off walking," lamented Silk as they entered the hospital. They two young men went to the information desk and made an inquiry as to the whereabouts of Joey Belamonte.

"There's no indication that he's been admitted. Let me try the emergency room for you," responded the elderly woman working the desk. She was probably someone's grandmother and, based on her eagerness to assist them, a good one at that. It's funny how the mind works; but amid all the emotions he was feeling, it occurred to Silk, probably for the first time ever, that he had never met his grandparents.

"Yes, he's been in the emergency room for over an hour," she said, putting down the phone and pointing to the sign at the entrance to a corridor. "Follow the red line on the floor and it'll get you there."

When they arrived, they found a scene that looked like a mob convention. There were more overweight men wearing dark suits and fedora hats than one might expect to see in a lifetime.

Tony's first thought was to suggest they get their collective asses out of there, but he knew his cousin too well to think that the suggestion would be heeded.

Silk was not unaware of the situation, but the Don and Carl were nowhere in sight, and he guessed that the goons in the room would not place him in street clothes.

"Let's go to the desk and act as if we're here for treatment," said Silk. "Then we can sit and wait like the rest of the regular people."

"Good idea, cus', now you're thinking like me."

They should have gotten their story straight before going to the desk because the first minute was a little like a Bud Abbott and Lou Costello routine. Who's got what and what's got who? Finally, Silk decided to shut up since he knew there was no chance of Tony doing so.

"Yeah, he slipped in the kitchen and hit his face on the table. I don't think he lost consciousness, but I wasn't in the room when it happened, so I can't be sure."

Silk had enough bruises on his face to make the story plausible, and the boys where told to take a seat; it would be a while.

"All that with a straight face. You're going to be a great lawyer."

A short time later the Don, with Carl in tow, came into the waiting room, and he was immediately surrounded by his underlings. They could see him talking to them, but hadn't a clue what was being said. One of the things he said must have been for them to leave because, as if one, they started to do so. It was then that Carl spotted Silk and Tony.

"Geez, look over there. It's that DeSimone shit. I'll get a few of the guys and take care if him right now."

"This is not the time or the place. It will hold for a while."

The two men left the emergency room for places unknown. The Don looked straight ahead while Carl glared at the cousins all the way to the door.

Silk saw a nurse leaving the treatment area and intercepted her on her way to the service desk.

"Hi, I'm a friend of Joey Belamonte," he lied, "what you can tell me about his condition?"

"Didn't his father just come out here to tell you about that?"

"Well, he and I don't get along, so I didn't listen in on what he said." He lied again.

"You know, I don't really believe you, but what's the harm. The young man is in critical condition and has been sent up to the intensive care unit, and you didn't hear that from me."

Silk quickly glanced at her name tag. June English.

"Thank you, June, this means a lot to me. Really thanks a lot."

They found a sign and, this time, followed the green line to ICU. When they arrived, they found that there was no way they would be admitted to the waiting room at this time of night and decided to head home. Tony was on Christmas break and decided to spend the night at his cousin's apartment.

CHAPTER THIRTY-ONE

The Vigil

They got up early the next morning and made the 7:00 AM Mass at Sacred Heart. Father Pasquale delivered the service, and after Mass, they waited to talk to him. The morning papers had the fight results, but went to press too early to have any word on what happened at the hospital. Rumors were rampant and covered everything from Joey's death to Silk's murder. Silk knew the latter to be premature and hoped the former to be also.

"We're going to the Mass General now. I'll let you know if there's anything new to report. And, Father, when this is behind us, there's something I need to talk to you about."

They arrived at the hospital before nine and went to the information desk where they identified themselves as cousins of Mr. Belamonte and were told that his condition was unchanged from the previous night. They went from there to the visitor's lounge of the ICU. It was, as expected, crowded with men in dark suits. What did catch Silk off guard was the presence of two women, both of whom were sobbing to the point of being almost out of control. One of the women was middle-aged and the other young enough to be her daughter. Silk guessed the older woman was probably Joey's mother and suddenly wished he were somewhere else; anywhere else. He then spotted the Don himself approaching and his desire to be elsewhere increased by several multiples.

"I would like you to leave and give my family some privacy."

Since the room was filled with mobsters; Silk wasn't sure what family he was referring to, but wasn't about to asked the Don or clarification.

"Sure." was all he said before he and Tony left the room. "What now?" asked Tony as they reached the corridor?

"You might as well head home and fill the family in on what's going on. I'm going to see Father Pasquale, there's something I need to talk to him about."

"I'll be back tomorrow. I'll be at your place by ten."

"Listen, Tony, I think it's best if I go to the hospital alone. They may back off if I do."

"I'm coming anyway, even if I have to sit in the lobby."

"Fair enough, cus', I'll see you in the morning."

It was early afternoon before Silk caught up with the priest who delivered his second Mass of the day at noon. They met in his office in the rectory.

"How can I help you, Silk?"

"Father, it's about what happened last night—"

The priest interrupted, "What happened last night was an accident and was God's will. There is nothing you did that you should feel guilty about although it is natural to feel that way."

"There's more to it than that, Father. I was in the ring, I was feeling emotions, and I was reacting to them in a way that does leave me feeling guilty."

"Tell me about it, and I'll try to help you with it."

"Father, I had him on the ropes, I knew he was done and I had won the fight. I could have let him slip to the floor, and it would have been over. Instead, I hit him again, hard. I'm sure it was that last punch that hurt him so badly, and even if it wasn't, it didn't change my intent. Father, I wanted to hurt him."

"Silk, I've known you long enough to know the type of person you are, and I know what happened last night was in the heat of battle. The emotions you felt have probably been shared by thousands of others in similar situations. The simple fact that we are here now, talking about it, speaks volumes about the type of person you are."

"What do you suggest I do? It's all I can think about."

"I suggest you give it time. Pray to God for forgiveness for any wrongdoing you feel in your heart, and if at anytime you feel the need to talk, you know where to find me."

Father Pasquale kept the visit going for another half hour, talking about anything but boxing. Silk left the rectory feeling better, if for nothing else, knowing he had a friend to confide in.

The next morning, Tony arrived at ten and drove his cousin to the Massachusetts General and took a seat in the lobby while Silk headed up to the ICU. When he got to the glassed door and looked in, he saw a smaller gathering than the previous morning but no sign of the two women. He decided against going in only to be sent away again and found a bench in the corridor, a short distance from the ICU waiting room. A few minutes passed when two dark suits walked past, gave him long look, and then entered the waiting room. He fully expected to see someone coming out of the waiting room with yet another invitation to leave. The door did open about ten minutes later, but rather than a dark suit, Silk saw an attractive young woman, a starched gray uniform, and a familiar face. It took him a second to place the face before he realized it belonged to Serena Tessi, one of the pretty girls from the Sunday Socials.

"Serena," he called to her in a low voice. "I didn't know you worked here. Do you work in intensive care?

"Yes, I do, and I'm surprised to see you here today. I heard you were asked to leave yesterday."

"That was yesterday. I'm keeping my head down today, and it seems to be working. What can you tell me about Joey Belamonte?"

"I wasn't here when they brought him in on Saturday, but I've been assigned to him since yesterday. His condition is critical, but he is stable, and all of his vital signs seem good. He's still in a coma, and that's never good."

"Listen, I have no chance on getting any updates, can you help me out with that?"

"Normally, this type of information is given only to immediate members of the family, but I'll make an exception in this case. Just keep it to yourself."

"Thanks a lot Serena, if there's any change, I'll be right here. If they throw me out, you can reach me at this number." Silk quickly jotted down his phone number and handed it to her. Serena took the slip of paper, smiled, and was on her way. At that moment, Silk felt something and was pretty sure it was more than gratitude.

Silk went down to the lobby to collect Tony and head to the hospital cafeteria for some lunch. He gave him an update on what he had heard and whom he had heard if from.

"Serena Tessi, I remember her. Pretty chick, nice body and she seemed to have a head on her shoulders. If it wasn't for Terry, I might have made a run at her."

"Well, as of now, consider her out of bounds."

"Got ya, cus'. Nice girl, try not to fuck it up."

"I knew I could count on you to come up with some words of wisdom."

The balance of the day passed without any events, and they left the hospital in time to catch a late dinner. Serena called Silk later that night to tell him that there was nothing new. Knowing that the plan was that she would call if there was something new to report, told him that she, too, might be interested. Silk felt good for the first time since this all started.

Tuesday was more of the same. A long day with really no new developments. By this time, the suits had become used to seeing Silk, sitting in the corridor and paid him little attention. When he was spotted by Carl, without incident, he was sure that the Don had given the hands-off order.

Serena called again after she arrived home, with little to report, but that didn't seem to matter to either of them.

On Wednesday morning, Silk arrived at the ICU at about ten and discovered a flurry of activity in the area. Several minutes passed before he spotted Serena, who seemed to be at the center of the action. She spotted him and gave him a sign that indicated she would get to him in a minute.

"I'm sorry, I couldn't get free to give you a call, but it's been crazy here since I got in. The good news is that Belamonte regained consciousness last night, and the staff has been evaluating his condition through the evening. It appears as if he's in good shape, and he's being transferred to a private room as we speak."

"That's great news. I began to think that the longer it went on, the less chance there was for a good outcome."

"That's true, but it has been only a few days and, in cases like this, it could go even longer and still turn out OK. The important thing is that his vital signs remained good for the entire time he was in the coma."

"Do you know where they're taking him?"

"I can find out, but it may be a good idea to stay clear of these guys. They're not nice people."

"I know about these people, but I need closure on this thing. I'll explain it to you sometime." He said this knowing he didn't intend to ever to tell her the full story.

Eighth floor, room 42 was the word he got from Serena. Before he went there, he headed to the lobby to bring Tony up to speed on what was going on. Tony insisted on going along with him and somehow convinced him that it was a good idea. As expected, when they arrived on the eighth floor, there was a large gathering in the corridor by the door numbered 42. The two new arrivals were met with several long looks. None were as long and ugly as the look from Carl as he moved past the others and into his brother's room.

Common sense should have told them to leave right then, and much to Silk's surprise, that's exactly what Tony suggested.

"Let's give it a while. Don't ask me why, but I want to see this through," responded Silk.

It wasn't ten minutes later that the door to room 42 opened, and the idiot brother came out and walked toward the two outsiders.

"My father wants to see you, follow me."

There was no *please*, but then again, Dons don't say *please*.

Silk was suddenly aware of a strange taste in his mouth, which he had never experienced prior to that moment. He would come to learn later that it was the taste of fear, a mere chemical reaction of the body in a time of imminent danger.

He had no idea what the elder Belamonte had in mind but guessed it may be a recommendation to get out of town, or worse. When he entered the room, he spotted Mrs. Belamonte and the same young woman he had seen the morning following the fight. He took this as a good sign since he doubted they would bump him off in front of Mama. He figured he was good until a later time and another place. He turned his attention to the hospital bed occupied by Joey. Two things immediately struck him: First, Joey, while obviously conscious, looked like hell; and second, his face was fixed with a broad smile.

"Hi, champ. You here looking for a rematch already?"

"There won't be any rematch, I'm hanging them up."

A puzzled look showed on Joey's face, and several heads turned to look at Silk.

They were surprised to hear the revelation coming from the young man, but probably the most shocked person present in the room was Silk himself. He must have been entertaining this thought in his mind over the past few days, but it was the first time it entered his conscious mind.

"What are you talking about? You have a future in this game." He heard Joey say.

"There are some things more important than boxing. I never want to go through this again."

"Jesus, they told me I can't fight again because my next fight could be my last, but I still want to give it a go. You can't quit."

"Watch you mouth, Joey," chimed in his mother in reference to the Lord's name being taken in vain.

"Listen, Joey, I'm glad to see you doing so well, but you need some rest. Is it OK if I come back in a couple of days and spent a little more time?"

"That will be Christmas Eve. You should be with your family."

Maybe Mrs. Belamonte was right, he thought.

"I'll be in touch." He then shook Joey's hand, turned, and left the room without another word being said by him or any of the Belamonte family members.

For the first time in several days, Silk felt good with a clear and focused mind. He collected Tony and headed for the front door. On the way, he filled his friend in on Joey's condition and then dropped two bombs.

"Tell my mother that I'll be home for the holiday and to get my room set up for Friday night. You can also tell our fathers that I've fought my last fight. I'm heading over to tell Carmen now."

"Oh shit, do you have any other news? You're not getting married or anything this afternoon, are you?"

"Thanks for everything, buddy, I'll see you on Christmas Eve."

He watched his cousin leave the building and headed for the ICU. He wanted to thank Serena for her help and ask if she would be attending the Sunday social this week.

CHAPTER THIRTY-TWO

Moving On with Plan B

There were few things in his life that he dreaded more than what lay before him today. His first confession, maybe. Telling his mother of his name change, maybe. His first *real confession*, maybe. Whatever it was, he was sure that it didn't prompt the stream of expletives he was going to hear from Carmen. For all his bluster and exaggerations about expenses, Carmen did in fact invest a lot of time and energy to get them to where they were last Saturday night.

When he entered the gym, he was greeted with shouts of congratulations from the fighters who were in attendance and the smiling face of his manager.

"Hey, champ, I just got the good news about Belamonte. I know that takes a load off your mind."

"Yeah, I guess good news travels fast, I saw him about an hour ago. He didn't look great, but the doctors feel good about his condition."

"Let's go in my office, the phones been ringing off the hook. We've got a lot to talk about."

"You're what! Are you fucking crazy? After all the time and money I've put into you, you're quitting just when we can get some real fucking purses?"

Silk had decided not to waste any time in getting to the reason for his visit. He now questioned his wisdom in doing so.

"You useless prick, if I had a fucking gun, I'd shoot you. What, did one of those goddamn priest friends of yours put this bug in your fucking ear?"

Silk knew all these questions were rhetorical and decided the best thing to do was let the man vent until he ran out of breath. It took longer than he expected, and his closing words were not a question, but rather a statement.

"Get the fuck out of my gym, and never show your fucking face here again."

"I'll see you next week, we can talk then."

"I'll have a gun by then. Show your ass in here, and I'll shoot your balls off. If in fact you had any fucking balls."

The walls in the gym were paper thin and as Silk made his exit, he felt the following eyes of every person in the gym. "Well, that could have gone worse," he mused. "He could have had a gun."

With all that was going on, Silk had done zero Christmas shopping and had only one day to get it done. This would be his first Christmas at home in four years, and he was looking forward to it more with each gift he picked out. On each of the past three years, Tony would pick up the family's gifts from Silk a couple of days prior to the holiday and deliver Silk's at the same time. He was really looking forward to opening them together on Christmas morning.

Silk pulled up in front of the house, and within a few minutes, it was the site of a mob scene. If he was a celebrity at the Sunday socials, he was a superstar to his family and friends in Gloucester. The word of his imminent arrival had gotten around, and people came out of the woodwork to say hello. While Silk enjoyed seeing old friends and neighbors, he was anxious to get past this and get to his family visit. There was the issue with his father, but he had made up his mind that the visit came first, and any problems he had with Marco would be put on the back burner. He wouldn't look beyond the next two days.

After a nice visit, Mary and Rose excused themselves and returned to the kitchen; Anna, Margaret, and Annette, like good Italian daughters, followed to help with the dinner preparation. This left the men to talk. The two brothers were outwardly proud of what Silk has accomplished, but the talk quickly turned to Silk's decision to retire from boxing. He explained to them what had happened on Saturday night and went on to mention the anger he had felt during his fight with Chris Jackson a month earlier. Marco was the first to speak.

"John, although you no longer share my name, I am your father, and other than my Mary, I know you better than anyone else in this world. I know that you are a good, God-fearing man, and I know you would never do harm to another. But if in your heart you feel this is right, than you must do it." This was probably the longest speech of his father's life, but Silk knew it was from the heart. The other two Silinas in the room echoed Marco's feelings, and from that moment, the talk was no different from most of the other households in

Gloucester. Talk centered around the holidays, the family, and the omnipresent subject of the Silina residence; the fishing.

The meaning of Christmas was never in question in the Silina home. They were Catholics, they were Italian, and they were very religious; but food played a major role in their celebration of the day. By 7:00 PM, the entire family was seated at the dining room table. Everything was served family style, and it was a dining marathon. The table was covered with platters and bowls containing fried baccala', escarole soup, fried eel, shrimp scampi, fried smelts, spaghetti with clam sauce, baked sea bass, cannoli and good Italian red table wine.

After dinner and cleanup, the nine family members headed for Our Lady of Good Voyage for the midnight Mass.

When Silk's head hit the pillow, he almost immediately fell into a deep and peaceful sleep. It was the best day he had in a long time.

He awoke on Christmas morning to the aroma of strong coffee, and when he made his way to the kitchen, he found his aunt Rose preparing his favorite breakfast of banana pancakes and Italian omelets.

The balance of the morning was taken up with the opening of gifts, happy laughter, stories of Christmas past, and strong coffee. Silk looked around the room at the faces of those he loved and realized that he had made a mistake to have stayed away so long.

Father Bruno arrived after he had served at the 11:00 AM Mass. He was clearly more than their parish priest; he was a valued friend. Every year he would be presented with a family gift, and every year he would protest but couldn't mask his joy for their thoughtfulness. This year's gift was a new rod and reel.

"We felt it was time that you found time for a new hobby," offered Mary.

Christmas lunch was the last meal of the dining marathon and, because of the prodigious amounts of food consumed prior to that, didn't start until 3:00 PM.

It was a wonderful day and much to his mother's joy, Silk decided to stay the night.

On Sunday, they all attended Mass, and after returning home, Silk prepared to leave for Boston.

"Why don't you stay the day?" asked Mary. Tony answered the question for him.

"He has to get back for the Sunday social at Sacred Heart.

Mary was puzzled, but that expression turned to a smile when Silk added.

I'll be back next weekend." Beyond his mother, he also observed the smile covering his father's face.

The next two months passed quickly as Silk fell into pattern which filled his time. Dominic Patrano got him a job unloading fish at Commonwealth Pier.

The very job he got for Santino twenty-five years earlier. He got in a workout a few afternoons a week, visited home on weekends, saw Serena whenever her hospital schedule allowed. He managed to hold off his mother when she urged, "Bring the girl here for dinner, it is time we meet her." One development which caught him completely off guard was when he got a call from Joey Belamonte, asking if he would join him and his father for dinner. He accepted, and this became a fairly regular event. Every couple of weeks, the three would meet at the Don's hangout, La Ristorante Roma, which was located on Richmond Street in the North End. On one occasion, he was invited to the Belamonte home for dinner, although calling their living arrangements a home is a bit misleading. The family occupied all three apartments of a three-floor walk-up located on Hanover Street. The Don's daughter and her husband, Vincent, lived on the ground floor, Joey and Carl shared the second-floor apartment, and Mr. Belamonte occupied the third floor with his wife Stella. The entire family was at dinner that evening, including Carl who looked as if he would have preferred to be almost anywhere else. Mrs. Belamonte prepared a meal fit for a Don and seemed quite happy to cook for the man who had nearly killed her son.

The only other significant events which took place prior to his leaving for spring training were conversations he had with his father, Carmen Bucci, and then Joey Belamonte.

On a Saturday afternoon in late February, Silk and his father walked to the pier to have a look at the newest family fishing vessel, which he had never seen. Marco put on a pot of coffee, and the two men sat and had their first real conversation in many years. It was the father that broached the subject of their estranged relationship.

"John, don't you think this has gone long enough? What do I have to do to earn your forgiveness?"

"That's a good question, what is it I must forgive?"

"I don't understand, we know what I was guilty of, and I paid dearly for my mistakes. You, my son, are the only one who cannot accept this."

"That's the problem; you don't know what it is that I can't forgive. It is the affair with the woman from Angelina's restaurant that I can't forgive."

Marco was clearly caught off guard.

"How do you know of this, was it Father Bruno?"

"Not that it matters, but no, it wasn't Father, I figured it out myself. I was angry about the other stuff because of how much it hurt Ma, but she forgave you for that, and so could I. The woman, neither of us could forgive you for that."

"I can never ask her forgiveness, it would hurt her to much."

"We agree on that at least."

"Maybe if we give it more time."

"Maybe, but I don't know."

"Can I say just one more thing on a different matter?"

"What's that?"

"I know that you have been spending some time with the Belamonte family. Don't get involved with them. They are trouble."

"I can handle them."

They sat awhile, and finally, Marco suggested they return home. Silk decided to stay a bit longer. He had forgotten how much he enjoyed the gentle swaying of the boat, and memories of Tony and him working summers at the pier came back to him in waves.

His next visit was Carmen. Originally, he had intended for this conversation to take place at an earlier date, but he kept putting it off. Rather than returning home after finishing work, Silk stopped at a sandwich shop and ordered two large Italian subs, two cannoli, and two coffees. He knew that Carmen always had hot coffee on hand but also knew it was undrinkable. He arrived at about six, and the place was pretty quiet. When he walked through the door, Carmen spotted him and started in.

"If it ain't the ball player. What brings Joe DiMaggio to this dump?"

"Hi, Carmen, I come with a peace offering," he said, holding up the two bags containing their dinner or possibly, his new body garnish.

"You think you can pay me off with some food? What you got in there anyway?

"Two large from Maria's, cannoli, and coffee light with three sugars."

Carmen's face lit up and Silk saw what he always suspected but never really knew to be true. Carmen was more than a manager, he was a friend.

They got the heavy stuff out of the way first before breaking bread.

Silk, expressing his regret for the decision and Carmen, saying he knew the second they carried Joey from the ring that it was over.

"I saw it in your eyes. It didn't make me happy, but I knew." Then he added, "How about your cousin? Do you think he wants to give it a go?"

The question was rhetorical, and they shared a good laugh.

They stayed and talked for over two hours. Silk was surprised to find out that Carman was quite a Sox fan and amazed at how much he knew of his minor league accomplishments.

A few days before heading to spring training, he had lunch with Joey. Joey was there for lunch, but Silk had an agenda. He waited until they has finished and ordered coffee before getting to the point.

"Joey, if we're going to be friends, there is something I have to tell you."

He went on to tell Joey what had gone on in his mind in the final seconds of their fight.

"I knew you were going down, I knew that the knockdown would give me the fight, and I hit you anyway. I could have killed you."

A smile came to Joey's face.

"I'm an Italian, I grew up in the North End, my name is Belamonte. You know what that means? Believe me when I say this. If I get to my feet, I get the hometown decision. And by the way, I would have smacked you too."

They had espresso and never talked of it again.

CHAPTER THIRTY-THREE

Another Turn in the Road

Silk arrived in Louisville to find something very different than he had experienced in his previous stops through the Sox minor league system. Louisville was a bigger city than the others with about three quarters of a million residents. It also offered more points of interest for a newcomer like himself, all of which helped him to push boxing and missing Serena from the forefront of his mind. He and Serena had promised to write, but they agreed that any break in their relationship would not be communicated by the written word. He cared a lot for Serena, so there would be no chance of him either writing such a letter or running with the local talent in Louisville.

Silk found there was plenty to fill his free time other than women. There were several college campuses to wander through, many historical points of interest, and of course the Ohio River, which ran through the city. Louisville made up only a small part of the Ohio route, which spanned six states and nearly a thousand miles. As it ran through Louisville, the Ohio passed through the McAlpine Locks and Dams, which created a beautiful waterfall that Silk found strangely therapeutic. Even more strange, he found a new pastime: fishing. Numerous species of sport fish were in plentiful supply, and he became the first member of his family to fish without having a boat beneath him.

All of that became minuscule and mundane as May approached, and Silk became aware that he was in the midst of something both mystical and magical. Not only was the Kentucky Derby about to take place, but it was the seventy-fifth anniversary of the event. The owner of the Louisville Colonels was, all at once, the owner of a baseball team, a huge supporter of horse racing in general and the Derby in particular, and a rich and generous man. If his players wished to see the Derby, he would procure the tickets. Even tickets as hot as those for

—

the Diamond Jubilee celebration of the Kentucky Derby at beautiful Churchill Downs. Silk and his teammates had never witnessed so much overindulgence in their lives, and they enjoyed every second of it. Their senses were awash with the grandeur of it all. Beautiful women impeccably dressed, the sounds of chatter mixed with music, the colorful silks of the different stables, and the majestic beauty of the thoroughbreds being paraded before them.

There were a dozen players in Silk's group, and they decided to place a bet. They pooled their money, made their selection, and cheered like hell as Ponder, a sixteen-to-one shot crossed the finish line and won the seventy-fifth running of the Kentucky Derby. A great day was made even better as each of them left Churchill Downs with over four hundred dollars in winnings.

Then, of course, there was the real reason for being in Louisville in the first place. This was AAA baseball and the final test, be it a major one, for any player with aspirations of reaching the big leagues. Being a step closer to the big leagues, Silk found everything somewhat better than the lower minors. The food, lodging, travel, and playing conditions all showed improvements over what he had experienced in the past four years. The most noticeable difference, however, was the competition. The Sox had three class D teams, four class C, two Bs, and one each at A and AA. This meant that three hundred players were competing to be on the only team at the AAA level, and the competition was fierce.

He started a little slow in April, but by May, he was catching up with the pitching; and in June, his bat was as torrid as the weather. When the players were selected for the all-star game, he was named as a bench player. The game was scheduled for July 20, and while he tried to stay focused on the regular games, he was clearly excited about competing in the all-star game. In the next-to-last series before the all-star break, that all changed.

The Colonels were hosting the Columbus Red Birds, the AAA farm team of the St. Louis Cardinals. It was an unusually cool Sunday afternoon, which was fine with Silk because the heat in July could sap your strength and make for a long nine innings. The Derby was a distant memory by this time; and that, combined with a nice day and a hot baseball team, produced a larger crowd the usual. The Colonels were leading 3 to 1 in the top of the fourth inning, but the Birds had the bases loaded with two outs. The next batter swung at the first pitch and hit flair into short left field. Silk streaked back and, with every succeeding step, felt more confident that he could make the catch. Unfortunately, the Colonels' left fielder, Bobby Gibson, had the exact same thought. Both players were calling for the ball, but couldn't hear one another over the shouting fans. An instant later, the two bodies came together with a force that defied description. The sickening sound of damaged bones and ligaments could not be heard over the crowd noise but were certainly felt by the two players. The ball lay next to them, but neither could move to retrieve it. All but the batter scored, and he stood at second base, in shock at what he had just witnessed.

Neither player lost consciousness, but both were writhing in pain as they lay on the outfield grass. Silk's ribs were killing him, and he was also aware of sharp pain in his right shoulder. Both players were put on stretchers and taken by ambulances to the hospital. Louisville lost the game 11 to 3.

"How's Gibbie, is he OK?"

"Gibbie?"

Silk realized that the ambulance attendant had no way of knowing who Bobby Gibson was and then continued.

"The other player, how is he?"

"Oh, he's in the other ambulance, I don't know for sure, but I think he's doing OK. You're banged up, but your vital signs look fine. As soon as we get you to emergency, we'll get you something for the pain."

There was plenty of pain, but it was the injuries that concerned Silk. He felt better after being laid out by Tony on the football field than he did right now.

Both ambulances arrived at the Jewish Hospital emergency entrance within seconds of one another. Silk was rolled in first and this, combined with his refusing any painkillers, got him to x-ray first. Once they started rolling him around the x-ray table, he began to question the wisdom of declining the medications offered earlier.

As he was being rolled back to emergency, Silk passed his teammate as he was being rolled to x-ray. The meds hadn't taken affect yet because Gibson still seemed in a lot of pain. The two players exchanged waves as they passed in the corridor.

Silk finally got admitted and assigned a room. He wondered when he would hear word on his injuries and, while waiting, decided to accept the meds he had earlier declined. The meds did their job, and within an hour, Silk found comfort in a sound sleep.

He awoke a few hours later to the muffled sound of familiar voices. He located their source and saw his manager Len Dunlop and the team owner Kenneth Bell. They smiled when they saw he was awake, and he took it as a sign that neither he or Gibbie were going to die.

"Hi," he managed. "Have you seen Gibbie? How's he doing."

Later, when he thought about his concern for Bobby, he realized that some of it was because he was a friend, but a certain portion was that he didn't want to be part of ending another career, as had been the case with Joey.

"We just came from there. He's sleeping, but he seems to be fine," responded Len.

"It appears that you guys collided shoulders, your right and his left, any other injuries seem to be the result of you getting tangled up," added Bell.

It wasn't until the next morning that he received any definitive word. The words sent Silk into an immediate state of depression. The attending physician was a Dr. Riseberg, who was an excellent doctor, with a bedside manner which didn't come close to his medical skills.

"Your shoulder is very severely injured and will require surgery and several months of rehabilitation before you have normal use of your arm."

"What do you mean normal? I'm a baseball player. That's normal to me."

"Be grateful that you will have a normal life, but I'm really sorry, but throwing a baseball is not going to be part of it."

He found out later that Bobby had a severe shoulder separation and could be expected to return to baseball for the following season.

For that much, Silk was sincerely grateful.

CHAPTER THIRTY-FOUR

Starting Over

Jewish Hospital had a very good reputation, and the Red Sox advised that he stay right there for the surgery required to his shoulder. He was also informed that Mr. Personality, Dr. Riseberg, was one of the best in his field with this type of procedure. *Well,* thought Silk, *at least I'll know he won't be candy coating any information he gives me.*

It is really remarkable how a doctor comes into the room and administers the anesthesia; you drift off to a wonderful place within seconds, and then seconds later, you're awake in the recovery room. At least, it seemed that way to Silk; but in reality, the surgery took four hours. Major reconstruction of the shoulder was required, and while Silk had no idea how it went, he did know that his shoulder hurt like hell. He asked for and received immediate relief when Florence Nightingale arrived with some drugs.

It was two hours later when Dr. Riseberg showed his face.
Must have been attending his Dale Carnegie class, thought Silk.
"How are you feeling?"
That's nice, the course must be helping, mused Silk. The drugs seemed to make everything a bit humorous to him.
"I'm doing great, how are you?"
"Not bad, and as a matter of fact, you are doing great, the surgery went quite well."
Before Silk could ask, the doctor added, "That doesn't mean that baseball is in your future, but you will be able to play toss with your kids."

Silk spent the next week at Jewish, and when Dr. Riseberg was confident that there would be no complications with the surgery, he consented to Silk heading back to Boston to begin rehab at Massachusetts General.

The Red Sox showed some compassion and allowed Silk to fly from Kentucky to Boston. He arrived at Logan Airport a couple of days after he was to play in the all-star game.

He was met at the airport by Tony, who had strict instructions from his aunt to get him to Gloucester—with no detours. It was a Friday, and the Sox team doctor had arranged for his rehab to begin on Monday, so Silk went along with the plan. He would return to Boston on Sunday afternoon and see Serena that night.

"I thought Manny would be with you? Is he dumping me now that I'm a has-been?"

"Yeah, in fact I was thinking of doing the same thing, but I didn't think that would fly at home. Manny wanted to be here, but when he graduated last month, he had three or four investment firms making him offers, which he turned down. He finally decided to go with Eagle Frozen Foods. Now he's a working stiff and loving it, but he didn't think he could ask for a vacation day in his second week there."

"That's great. Is he coming up for air soon so we can get together?"

"We're set for dinner on Wednesday. Our main man insists on buying."

"Who am I to argue with the man?"

As it turned out, going to Gloucester was a tonic. Silk had been feeling bad for himself, and being around family made him realize that he had a great support system working in his favor. He had not been in Gloucester during the summer in years and had forgotten how great it could be. Aside from a few light exercises prescribed to keep his shoulder from freezing, he had nothing to do but start the healing process. That being not the physical, but rather that of the heart and mind.

Seeing Serena served only to reinforce what he had felt at home. She had already been working the system at Massachusetts General on his behalf.

"I have some good friends in physical therapy, and they're going to give you the VIP treatment for as long as it takes to get you fixed up. The Mass General is the best place for you, and with me in your corner, you'll get the best treatment possible."

"I don't doubt that, but what I need to know is how often I'll get to see you."

"You'll get to see me every day."

"Perfect."

Things were, in fact, perfect because it was this night that they first slept together. It was an act which required the tenderness of both lovers. First,

Silk guiding Serena through her first experience with lovemaking, and Serena helping him with the awkwardness resulting from his healing shoulder. With all that he had been through in the past several months, Silk was now ready to look to the future. A future with Serena made everything, once again, seem full of promise.

Silk had a plan for the following week that went beyond rehab and seeing Serena. He had a lot of time to reflect on things in recent days, and one thing he knew was that he had to start thinking about what he was going to do with the rest of his life. That afternoon, he walked to the Suffolk University admission office to discuss starting classes in September.

If Sunday was a cure for the heart, then Wednesday night was a tonic for the mind. It was like old times for Silk and his two closest friends. Manny couldn't stop talking about his new job with Eagle Frozen Foods. Babson was a great business school, and he had good offers from companies in the financial community, but he felt Eagle was a better fit for him.

"Eagle is located on the North Shore, is a growing company, and I can be assured that I won't have to accept a transfer to God knows where in order to advance.

It all boils down to the fact that I want to stay in Gloucester and close to my family."

"That sounds good, but when I graduate law school, I'm going with a big Boston firm. I love Gloucester too, but the big bucks are in the big cities."

"Yeah, and Terry's a Boston girl at heart," injected his cousin.

"Are you kidding? She'd follow me anywhere, the girl's crazy about me."

"Or just crazy," added Manny.

"I guess the next question is for you, cus', where do you go from here?"

"I thought you guys would never stop talking about yourselves. I'm starting at Suffolk in the fall. I'm going to live in either Boston or Gloucester, and I think I've found the girl I'm going to marry."

As if he had not heard a word of this and, sporting a big shit-eating grin, Tony asked, "How's the veal here?"

"Anyone we know?" inquired Manny as he and Tony shared a good laugh.

"One more thing, I think it's time to put Silk behind me. From now, on it's John DeSimone."

CHAPTER THIRTY-FIVE

Plan B Takes Shape

August was a grind. Therapy, which had started slowly, soon became more intense. Even with that, John became impatient and urged the therapist to move faster. They humored him but would not alter the prescribed plan for treatment.

What made things worse was that he had too much time on his hands. He spent a couple of hours a day at the hospital, visited Carman at the gym a couple of times; but beyond that, there was nothing much to do. Manny was working full-time, Tony had a summer job working on one of the family boats, and Serena had a work schedule that bordered on ridiculous.

He filled his days as best he could and spent a few nights at Fenway Park, watching the Sox.

He was relieved when September arrived and classes began at Suffolk. Now with classes, study, and therapy, his schedule became as full as the others; and his time again had purpose. He was still getting treatments every morning, so he selected all afternoon classes. This left nights and weekends for study, friends, family, and of course, Serena.

John was at Lucia's, his favorite hangout for morning coffee and biscotti.

"Hey, stranger, where have you been hiding?"

John looked up from his Saturday morning *Globe* and found the source of the familiar voice.

"Hey, Joey. I'm not hiding, hell, how can you hide out from a Belamonte in the North End?"

"Listen, I'm sorry about what happened last summer. Fuck, you gut worse luck than me. Hell, you're what we call a two-time loser."

"Things could be worse. Who knows, I could have spent another five years in the bush leagues before I got even a cup of coffee in the bigs."

John realized that for the first time, he had verbalized the rationale he had been working in his mind for weeks. Now that he heard it aloud, he knew that he didn't believe it for a second. He also understood that to say anything different would sound like self-pity. So that was his story, and he was sticking to it.

"Yeah, maybe, but you were burning it up down there. I think you had a shot."

"Well, that's ancient history now. It doesn't do any good to look back. It's over."

"I guess so. Listen, the old man would love to see you. When can you come to the house for dinner?"

"It better be soon. If he hears you calling him 'the old man,' he'll kick your ass out of town. How about some day next week? Thursday?"

"Sounds good, see you then." Their families were very different in many ways, but in one way, they were the same. You never had to check before inviting a friend to dinner.

Dinner on Thursday night was very similar to John's first visit to the Belamonte home. The menu was different, while still being superb, but the participants were the same, and Carl continued to make no effort to mask his dislike for John. He seemed to disapprove of everything and showed complete disdain when John explained that he had dropped Silk in favor of his birth name, John.

After dinner, the men moved to the living room while Stella and her daughter took care of cleaning up. There were stogies and anisette available, and even though John wasn't a fan of either, he accepted both.

"So tell me, John, how are you keeping yourself busy?" asked the Don.

John couldn't help but be taken aback by where he found himself. He was seated across this small room from one of the top mob bosses on the East Coast, a man who had impacted his life more than he could ever imagine, and they were making small talk after dinner.

"My time is pretty much taken up with classes at Suffolk, studies, physical therapy, and of course, visiting with friends."

That last part seemed to please Mr. Belamonte and brought an almost indiscernible smile to his lips. Joey smiled, Carl grimaced, and Vincent missed the point altogether. John was keenly aware of Carl's feelings toward him and was now taking pleasure in pissing him off.

"I understand that you have a special friend in the young Serena Tessi. Is this not true?"

That caught John a bit off guard, and he could only manage a simple response of, "Yes, it is."

"She is a good girl from a fine family. Her father, Mario, is my barber. It might be a good idea if you made of point of visiting with them."

Was this the purpose of tonight's dinner? The barber goes to the Don, seeking a favor. Carl sensed his discomfort, and now, he smiled.

"I told him that you are a fine young man, one who I would be proud to call a son of my own." The smile disappeared from Carl's face and was replaced with a scowl.

"Even so, a visit would be a good idea." Message received.

"Serena and I have been talking about having Thanksgiving with her family," he lied. "We'll make it a point to do that."

"Mario would like that."

Joey felt the need to move the conversation in another direction.

"So what's the scoop on the therapy, how much longer do you have to go?"

"It looks as if I have another six or seven weeks, hopefully no later than the middle of November. They really do a great job at the Mass General."

"That's good, that will give you more time for studies and your friends, of course."

John wondered if the Don was now also trying to piss off his eldest son.

"Not really, when the therapy is finished, I really need to get a job. I have some money put away, but not enough to get me through four years of school."

"Maybe I can help you with that. Give me a few days. If I come up with something, I'll have Joey look you up." Yup, he's really trying to fuck with Carl's head.

"Sounds good to me," said John. *This could get awkward*, he thought. Just then, the Belamonte women arrived with coffee and spumoni, fresh fruit, and cheese. Thank God for small favors.

The next morning, John finished his treatment and headed over to ICU to see Serena. He didn't do this often because he didn't want to bother her while she was at work, but on this day, he made an exception.

"Something came up at dinner last night that I thought you might find interesting."

"I'm always interested in your visits with your mob friends," she said, half-jokingly.

"Well, it seems as if I'm not the only one who's connected. The Don delivered a message to me from your father."

"You're kidding. What do you mean?"

"You must know that he cuts Mr. Belamonte's hair."

"That doesn't mean he's connected."

"No, but it does mean he can ask a favor from the big man. I can't be sure, but I think that we had dinner last night because your father wants to formally meet me. I lied and said we were planning on having Thanksgiving with your parents, and now we have to have our stories straight and make it happen."

Serena couldn't help herself, something about this seemed very comical, and she couldn't help but laugh.

"I sort of have to provide you with an alibi, huh? That's mob talk, you know."

"Call it what you want as long as your father buys it."

"Buy it? You have to be kidding. There is no way he'll buy it, but he'll like it anyway."

John must have been becoming a creature of habit because the following Saturday, Joey found him yet again at the same café, drinking coffee, and reading the *Globe*.

"You better change your routine, if Carl decides he wants to pop you one, he'll know just where to find you."

"Hi, Joey, have a seat. Let me buy you an espresso," he said, getting up to pull another chair to the table.

"What is it with you and Carl? He hates your fucking guts."

"It's a long story, and if I told you, he'd hate me even more. Let's just leave it alone."

"OK with me. That's not why I looked you up anyway. This is a business meeting.

You were talking the other night about work, and I think we have something for you—"

John interrupted, "Listen, Joey, no offense, but I'm not sure that's a good idea."

He was happy he was not having this conversation with Mr. Belamonte because he knew what he had just said would not go well with a mob boss. He also didn't know how he would take the news secondhand, but he had to risk it.

"No, no, it's not like that, this is on the up-and-up. It's clean," responded his friend.

"What is it like? Has he got me a job cutting hair at Tessi's shop?"

"That was funny the other night, wasn't it? You gotta believe me, I was as surprised as you with that one."

"I don't know why, but I'll take your word on that. So what's up with the job?"

"We're opening a new club on the North Shore, in Danvers, and we'd like you to run it for us. What s do you think?"

"I think that I don't know shit about running a club, and I think I could lose a lot of your family money doing it."

"There's not that much to it. Grand opening is two weeks before New Year's, so you can work at another club and learn the ropes before then?"

"Sounds good, but can I have a couple of days to think about it?"

Joey reached into his jacket pocket and retrieved a pen. He then got a napkin, wrote something on it, and handed it to John.

"That's what you make every week. Plus a nice bonus at the end of the year."

John looked at the figure on the napkin and asked.

"When did you say I start?"

He then thought, *these Belamontes really know how to corrupt us Silinas.*

As it turned out, the deal was even better than he thought. The club was open 6:00 PM to 2:00 AM from Wednesday through Saturday, and while the hours were long, he could arrange for second semester classes that would work very well.

"You're doing what? Are you fucking crazy? I always gave you credit for having more brains than that. Didn't what happened to your father teach you anything about getting mixed up with these people?" To say that Tony was incensed would be an understatement.

"The difference is that what my father did was against the law. Smuggling booze and running numbers were illegal. Managing a nightclub is not, and if I don't like what's going on, I can walk. I'm going into this with my eyes wide open. I can handle it."

"Maybe you can, but I don't want to be around when you break this to your mother."

He wasn't around, and it didn't go well. Somehow, it never occurred to John that he would have to have this conversation with his parents, and if it had, he might have done differently. They were angry; they ranted and raved and questioned his judgment. But in the end, he was their child, and they ultimately accepted his decision.

Serena, on the other hand, had no knowledge of the history between the Silinas and the Belamontes. As a matter of fact, she wasn't aware that John, being called DeSimone, was anything more than a name he took for the ring.

"You just have to promise me two things," she asked.

"What's that?"

"First, the day you graduate, you walk away from the nightclub. Second, you don't go near the cocktail waitresses."

"Hey, you're talking about fringe benefits here."

"No, I'm talking about you not waking up with your balls in your mouth."

"Well, if you put it that way."

End of conversation. Her dad had friends in high places.

Chapter Thirty-Six

It Was a Very Good Year

The next year was marked with several significant events, none of which were bad. The first of these was Thanksgiving at the Tessis. Of course, this was preceded by a conversation with John's mother. Mary Silina took the news that her son would not be home for the holiday with mixed emotions. While she would miss his presence, she took the news of her son meeting Serena's parents as a sign that he may be getting ready to settling down. "So can I expect to meet her soon? Christmas dinner maybe?"

"Maybe before then. I'll work out a day and let you know."

"I'll work it out. It will be the second Sunday after Thanksgiving."

"Sounds good to me," answered John, as he prayed that Serena's work schedule would allow it to happen. As it turned out, it did.

John was asked to arrive for Thanksgiving at 10:00 AM. Thanksgiving to the Tessis didn't mean dinner; it meant Thanksgiving Day. If the Tessis were impressed by promptness, he got off to a good start. Reminiscent of his first visit to Tina's home, he arrived early and waited until precisely ten o'clock to ring the front doorbell. The door was answered by Mario Tessi, who greeted him with a smile, a firm handshake, and a sincere sounding, "I'm Mario, welcome to the Tessi home."

Mario was tall and slender with Italian good looks.

Serena must favor her father, he thought.

"Thanks for inviting me. I've been looking forward to meeting you and Mrs. Tessi."

"Come, I'll introduce you."

He led John to the kitchen where Serena and her mother were preparing for dinner.

"This is my wife, Gloria. Gloria, this is John DeSimone." Gloria was a knockout. If this is what Serena will look like in thirty years, John was prepared to buy a ring tomorrow.

"Pleased to meet you, Mrs. Tessi, and thank you for inviting me to your home today."

"Oh, we are pleased that you could come, and please call me Gloria."

I never got this far with Mrs. C. Never, he thought.

"Let's leave the women to their work, come with me to the courtyard."

When they got to the courtyard, they were greeted by two neighbors who were warming up at the bocce court. Let the games begin. The day went something like this: bocce, wine, dinner, grappa and cigars, dessert and anisette, poker and more wine. Twelve hours after arriving, John left with handshakes, hugs, and the feeling that he was onto something really great.

A couple weeks later, it was Serena's turn to pass muster, and she did it beautifully. She insisted on arriving early and went directly to the kitchen and put on an apron.

"What can I do to help?" she asked.

Mary was caught a little off guard, but Margaret didn't miss a beat.

"You can fry the veal cutlets. Here, let me get you a fry pan."

So while John had made points with Mr. Tessi by expertly rolling a bocce ball, Serena did the same by showing she knew her way around a kitchen.

The only thing that she found a bit overwhelming was the size of the dinner gathering. What was once a family gathering of nine had now, with the addition of Anna's husband Hal and herself, grown to eleven. This was more people at the table than she was accustomed to, but the ease at which it was handled told her that it was a regular occurrence at the Silina household.

"Well, what do you think? Do you think they liked me?"

"No, I think they loved you. When I said good night to my mother, she whispered to me, 'Don't screw this up, or you answer to me.' You have it made with the Silinas. Do you think your parents would mind if I dropped in to say hello?"

"You learn fast, maybe you have a future in politics. Come on in, they'll love it."

"Mayor DeSimone, that has a nice ring to it."

The club, Night Life, opened as planned, in the middle of December. The past several weeks were a blur for John as he had to balance semester finals at Suffolk, family commitments, and getting up to speed on club management. It wasn't a complicated business, but there were a lot of details which required attention. Not the least of which was making sure the profits didn't leave each night in the pockets of the bartenders. For the most part, the customers were young men and women looking to have a good time. They drank, they danced, and with luck, met someone to their liking. There was an occasional disturbance, but there were "staff" to deal with that. If there was one downside, it was that Carl showed up each morning to pick up the receipts and cash register tapes from the previous night's business and then make the bank deposit. It didn't take long for John to realize that there were more than table linens being laundered here, but he thought the best thing to do in this case was to employ the "three monkeys' rule" and play dumb.

To everyone's amazement, including his own, he really not only liked the business but actually had a flare for it. While he never saw the "books," he did know the cost and sales, before Carl's involvement, and the club was turning a profit.

The winter passed quickly. John was able to front-load his schedule at Suffolk so that he didn't have classes beyond Wednesday, which gave him some level of normalcy. Serena's schedule, as always, was all over the place; but they managed to find time for each other. The summer was like the proverbial "light at the end of the tunnel" and held the promise of better things to come.

June meant the end of his freshman year at Suffolk, but that was of little consequence to him in the light of Tony's graduation from Boston College. Tony, for all his playing the part of the court jester, was a dedicated student and finished in the top five percent of his graduating class. John got Saturday night off, and the party in Gloucester lasted all weekend. It was somewhat of a reunion for Tony, Manny, and him since they were so busy with work, classes, and significant others that their usual get-togethers had been curtailed. The gang of three was now six, with addition of Serena, Terry, and Ellen. Yes, that Ellen.

True to his word, Tony had applied and been accepted to Boston College Law School.

The following couple of months were almost like a vacation for John. With therapy behind him and no classes, he had only a four-day work week to deal with.

He was able to dedicate some extra time during this period to learning more about the bar business, which he continued to enjoy. When September arrived, he was more than ready to return to Suffolk for his second year.

The fall may well be the best of the four distinctively different seasons in Boston. Wedged between the summers, which can be oppressively hot, and the winters, which always seemed to be excessively harsh, were the two glorious months of September and October. The only redeeming factor with the emergence of November was that it served as a segue into the holiday season.

Thanksgiving called for a return visit to the Tessis. There had been several dinners with Serena's parents in the past twelve months, so this year's visit did not carry the stress that John had experienced the previous year. There were only two minor changes from last Thanksgiving, neither of which bothered him. This year, Gloria invited her sister, Tina, and her husband, Peter Vilonia, to dinner (no doubt, to get the family stamp of approval). The bocce brought with it something new also. Betting on the results had always been part of the tradition, but it had been suspended the previous holiday to avoid giving Serena's boyfriend a bad impression of the family. *They should only know*, thought John. Regardless of all that, winning Tina Vilonia's approval was not a problem; and Peter, who was the boxing fan in the family, was in awe of Serena's young man.

Serena accepted Mary's invitation to join the Silinas' Christmas Eve dinner.

This meant a late-night return trip to Boston since she had to be home for Christmas morning. As was the case with John, she had visited with his family several times during the past year, and she had long since received the approval of the entire family, plus Father Bruno. This was her first experience with the traditional Christmas Eve seafood extravaganza served by many, but not all Italians, on this occasion. Despite this, she was still able to take her place in the kitchen and assist in preparing the meal. She also insisted on staying for the midnight Mass portion of the celebration and, although she had plenty banked already, this decision won her countless additional family points.

It was almost three in the morning when she and John arrived at her front door.

"I'm going back to Gloucester first thing in the morning, so I'd like to give you your Christmas gift now, if you'll accept it."

Accept it? she thought. Then she realized what he was saying.

He reached into his coat pocket and retrieved a jeweler's box, which contained a solitaire diamond ring.

"I love you, Serena Tessi, and I want to spend the rest of my life with you. Will you marry me?" She answered by throwing her arms around his neck and kissing him hotly. He returned her kiss, and when they finally came up for air, he stated, "I'll take that as a yes."

"Yes, that is a yes. I can't wait for tomorrow to tell my parents. I'm going to wake them up now and tell them."

"Let them sleep. I stopped by the shop the other day and asked your father for your hand in marriage. I'm sure he's told your mother by now. In fact, I know he has."

"OK then, I'll wake them up and kill them."

They both laughed and then sat on the front stoop of the house and talked for another hour.

The next morning, he returned to Gloucester as planned and told his family of the previous night's developments.

"And you couldn't have done that here so we could see her face?"

"Yeah, and what if she said no? How stupid would I look then?"

"Did I bring up an idiot? There was no way she was going to say no. Come here, you, and give your mother a kiss, you did good."

The next week was hectic. New Year's Eve was the biggest night of the year in the club business, and although he had been planning it for weeks, there were still plenty of last-minute details to see to. He was shocked when, a few days before the big night, Joey showed up at the club in the company of the Don himself. He had never been at the club before, not even for the opening, and John couldn't imagine what brought him here today.

"John, good to see you, how were your holidays?"

"Good, Mr. Belamonte, well I guess you can say they were great."

"I know, I had a trim yesterday, and Mario told me the news. Congratulations, you're a lucky guy. Serena is a wonderful young lady."

"Thank you, I couldn't agree with you more, but that's not what brought you here. When the boss shows up in person, you think that maybe you're getting canned or something."

"If we were dumping you, we would have sent my big brother. It would have made his day." Joey and John shared a laugh but stopped when the Don didn't join them.

"When you accepted our offer to work for us, Joey mentioned a bonus for doing a good job. We came here to deliver your bonus. Come, follow me," he said as he headed toward the door. Parked at the front door was sparkling new 1951 Cadillac De Ville Coupe.

"I hope you like midnight blue. Good luck." And with that, he handed John the keys to his car.

"I don't know what to say. To tell you the truth, I forgot what Joey had said about the bonus. This is unbelievable. Thank you, I can't tell you how much I appreciate this."

"I am pleased that I could do this for you. Now do me a favor."

Oh shit, here it comes, he thought.

"Sure, what can I do for you?" he said

"Give Joey the keys to that shit box you've been driving so he can dump it for you."

"Here you go," he said, reaching into his pocket and handing the keys to his friend. "Be careful, sometimes it gets stuck in reverse."

They left in separate cars as quickly as they arrived, and John wondered how he would explain his new car to the family. He didn't think a gift from the Don would go over very well. "Well, first things first," he said to no one but himself. "Time to see what this baby can do." He jumped into his Caddie and heated north on Route 1.

New Year's Eve arrived, and business wise, it was everything that was expected and more. The place was mobbed far beyond the legal seating limit, and the booze was flowing as if it were rolling downhill. Everyone seemed obsessed with a goal of being the first in their party to become inebriated. The music was good, the dance floor was packed, and the party was in high swing; but like anytime you get too many strangers drinking too much alcohol, trouble is always only a second away.

A couple of hours before the New Year was to be rung in, there was a loud commotion in a far corner of the seating area, and two of the club's finest rushed over to put a lid on any real trouble. John watched from his vantage point beside the bar. From there, he could be on alert for potential trouble and keep an eye on the bartenders and the cash registers. To his surprise, one of his bouncers broke away from the disturbance and headed his way.

"What the fuck is going on, Tom? You need to be over there, not here."

"Matt's trying to cool these guys off, but they're packing and not trying to hide it. The big prick says he's from Providence, and he's made."

John headed over to the trouble with his muscle in tow. As he approached, he saw two hard cases with their lady friends who seemed quite impressed by the mano a mano show being displayed by their dates. There were also two younger couples who were now aware of what was going on and appeared to be scared shitless.

"What's goin on, Matt?" he asked as he approached the scene.

"It looks like these people," he answered, motioning toward the younger couples, "were dancing, and when they came back to their table, it was taken by these people."

"Listen, the place is mobbed, we see a table, and we take it. End of story. Tell these shits to go find another table."

"That's not how it works. This is their table, and if you wait a couple of minutes, we'll find something for you and your friends."

"That's OK," interjected one of the younger guys. "We'll wait for another table."

"Just a minute, I'll handle this," instructed John.

"I don't know who the fuck you are, but let me tell you who I am. I'm Jimmie Georgio, and I work for Angelo Parise in Providence."

"If that's true, you must know who owns this place."

At this point, Jimmie the Sausage, as he was labeled because of the prodigious amount of the hot Italian variety he could consume at one sitting, had had enough of this discussion. He extended the huge forefinger of his right hand and proceeded to poke John, with all the force he could muster, on the chest.

"Listen, you motherfucker, I don't care who owns this place, and if you don't get the fuck out of my face, I'm going to kick your ass."

"Good idea, let's take this outside. After you, you fat slob."

"You sure you want to do this? If we go out there, I'm going to have to kill your ass."

"Let's go, fatso."

A minute later, all eleven of them were in the parking lot. If their verbal confrontation hadn't been drowned out by the blaring music and the shouting revelers, the entire club might have joined them.

Jimmie made a show of removing his suit jacket, folding it, and handing it to his date.

"Anytime soon?" needled John.

"Yeah now!" shouted Jimmie as he lunged at his antagonist and unloaded a right-hand roundhouse swing. John ducked, and the big man's momentum carried him past John. As he did, John hit him in the kidney area with a sharp left hand. He knew that had to hurt, and he moved forward, waiting for the big man to turn his way. When he did, it was all but over. John didn't bother with technique; he just threw right hand after right hand, driving his adversary backward until he landed flat on his back. Jimmie really didn't want to get up, but he made a show of it. All of a sudden, John was once again a Silina. He walked toward the prone mobster and unloaded a heavy kick to the balls.

He then walked over to the second guy and asked, "Want some?"

"No."

"Then, get him in a car and get the fuck out of here, now."

It took more than a few minutes to load Jimmie into the car, but they moved as quickly as possible and then sped south on Route 1 toward Providence.

Those that remained walked back into the club.

"Sorry for the commotion," he apologized to the four younger customers. "Matt, see that they get compted for the night."

Somehow, John knew he hadn't heard the last of this.

When he got to the club on Wednesday afternoon, he discovered Carl sitting at the bar. Carl looked up and smiled, and John saw this as a bad omen.

"Hey, tough guy, I hear you had some excitement here the other night. Do you know who that was that you punched out?" he then proceeded to answer his own question. "That was Jimmie Georgio from the Parise family in Providence."

Carl was on a roll and clearly enjoying it, so John decided to shut up and let him drop his load.

"Don Parise called my old man this morning, and he is really pissed. One of his men, his made men, comes to my father's club and gets jumped by the manager and a couple of bouncers. This is not the way it happens, asshole. You stop in to see my father at ten tomorrow morning. Don't be late."

He didn't wait for a response but instead headed for the exit, again, sporting a wide smile.

John knocked on the door to the Don's apartment at five before ten the following morning. Mrs. Belamonte came to the door and greeted him with a smile and sincere, "Good morning, John, Dominic is waiting in the living room." She led him there and excused herself.

The Don looked up from some paperwork and motioned him toward a chair. There was not going to be any small talk. He got right to the point.

He talked in an even tone, never raising his voice or showing anger. There was never a question in his mind as to whether or not he had John's full attention.

"I had a call the other day from my friend in Providence. He is a very angry man. Do you understand the gravity of what happened the other night?"

John didn't know if the question was rhetorical or not but didn't take any chances.

"Yes, sir, I understand,"

"Angelo Parise and I have coexisted in the area for many, many years, and we have done so because we have always respected each other and the code that we live by. There is always a delicate balance of power here, and an incident like this can throw this out of whack. When that happens, there can be serious repercussions. People get angry, they let that anger blind them, and sometimes, people die.

Oh fuck, is Carl in a closet somewhere? he wondered. *No they'd never do it here,* he rationalized as he quietly allowed himself to breathe again.

"If Jimmie Georgio had his way today, you would be a very dead young man.

My friendship with Angelo Parise has earned you a reprieve this time, but it ends right here. Do you hear what I'm saying? Do you understand?"

"Yes, sir, I understand." This, he was sure, required a response.

"Now tell me why you and your boys felt you needed to jump Georgio?"

"He was being a real problem, he wouldn't back off, and he threatened me, but I want to make it clear, the fight was between him and me. There was no one else involved. I simply kicked his ass."

"I understand that was not the only thing you kicked. Jimmie spent the holiday in bed and iced down."

"I guess I got carried away."

"Georgio is a fool, but he's a made fool. Learn from this, John."

With that, he turned his attention back his paperwork and John took this as a signal to leave.

Not too bad, he thought. *I'm still alive, and he didn't take the Caddie back.*

"Beat a man senseless and then kick him in the balls. Where did I hear that before?" wondered the Don.

John left the Belamonte home and headed for his car.

As he did, he said to himself in a tone that only he could hear, "Christ, I've gotta be crazy working for these fuckers. They could kill my ass and then go to bed and sleep like a baby."

CHAPTER THIRTY-SEVEN

Back in Good Graces, or Not

John gave the idea of walking away from this job and the Belamontes all together, a lot of thought, but the money was good, and the work schedule worked too well with his classes at Suffolk to pull the trigger. The irony of how similar this situation was to his father's twenty years earlier was not lost on him. He reasoned that the only explanation was that both Silinas shared a genetic blind spot when it came to the Belamontes.

"All I have to do is keep my nose clean and my temper in check, and I'll be fine," he reasoned. "If I do that, I'll stay out of trouble."

The reasoning seemed sound; he had worked at the club for over a year, and he had never come close to personally getting involved in a confrontation. If there was a problem, he would stay clear and leave it for Matt and his guys to settle. He also heard from Joey that the Sausage man had been told to stay clear of the club.

Even with all that, he couldn't help but realize how quickly things can turn with these people. One day you're treated like family, and the next you're put on warning. He made the decision to keep the meeting to himself. He saw no purpose in having everyone in his life thrown into a state of panic.

It shouldn't be forgotten that the Silinas and the Tessis are Italians and do not believe in long engagements. So it didn't come as a surprise that it took only a couple of weeks after their engagement that the inquiries commenced.

"So have you set a date yet?

"Are you planning a June wedding?"

"Have you talked to Father Bruno?"

"Have you visited with Father Pasquale?"

—

"When are we going to meet the family?"

After a week or two of this, Serena and John made an announcement, be it not a popular one.

"We will be married in June, but not this year. It will be a year from this June."

This decision was not met with great enthusiasm, particularly by Mr. Tessi, and John wondered if he would be asked to have yet another conversation with Mr. Belamonte. To his relief, that did not occur.

They chose to wait the additional year so that John could complete his third year at Suffolk, and because they knew that if they suggested waiting until he graduated, Mr. Tessi might very well purchase a shotgun.

They did mend some fences by suggesting dinners in Boston and Gloucester so that their families could meet one another and do some bonding.

This turned out to be a stroke of genius because they immediately liked one another.

The next several months were uneventful. March came and went, and John realized that not going off to spring training was less painful than it had been twelve months earlier. In fact, given his feelings for Serena, he wondered if he could handle a six-month separation. Things were back to normal at the club, which translated to "No Sausage, no problem." He was having some difficulty with his grades at Suffolk. He was trying to balance, work, classes, a fiancé, friends, and family, and something had to suffer. He would get passing grades, but he would disappear from the dean's list. He longed for spring and the reduced workload that it would bring.

Aside from New Year's Eve, the biggest grossing night of the year was July 4th, and by now, John had learned how to maximize the opportunities and profits that the holidays offered. He promoted the club's events in local and Boston papers, sent personal invitations to high-roller regulars and even to many of the sports celebrities who quite often frequented the club. When the Fourth finally came, all the planning and hard work paid off; he had customers hanging from the rafters. He had prepared for this by setting up a satellite bar and putting in more tables than the fire marshal would ever approve. Everyone was upbeat; the waitresses were making great tips, the bartenders were raking it in, and everyone felt sure that they would earn the bonus John had promised if they exceeded the prior year's sales by 25 percent.

At about ten o'clock, he went to his office to get a replacement drawer for one of the cash registers. He had made it a practice of changing drawers, and getting cash register readings, randomly during the evening. He was in the process of doing this when Matt came into the office.

"We may have some trouble out there, boss."

He liked Matt and enjoyed yanking his chain, which Matt would set himself up for so often that it seemed as if he enjoyed being the butt of a joke.

"Now let me think," said John holding a finger to his right temple. "We have trouble out there, I pay you to handle the trouble, and you're in here telling me that we have trouble."

He then moved the finger from his temple to the corner of his smiling mouth.

"Now tell me what's wrong with this picture?"

"You don't understand, boss, Jimmie Georgio just showed up with his friends."

The smile disappeared from John's face. It was replaced with a look that Matt had only seen once since he had known John. That was last New Year's Eve.

John put the cash drawer back into the safe, spun the dial, and headed for the door.

"The prick was told to stay away from here. He's here looking to put my ass in a sling."

As they approached the Georgio party, John observed Tom, Matt's second in command setting up yet another table in the already-packed seating area. *Smart boy, that Tom*, he thought.

The guy with Jimmy was not the one who accompanied him on New Year's Eve, and John surmised that this guy was brought to provide some extra muscle. The two bimbos were definitely from a much more recent vintage.

"Is this the best you can do, asshole?"

"Good to see you too, Jimmie. I was told you wouldn't be coming by."

"You know how it is. I pretty much do what I want to do."

"Not here, you don't. If you're here to have a good time fine. If you're here to make trouble, I'll have your ass hauled out of here. Have a seat here and consider yourself my guest for the evening."

Three things occurred so quickly, that they seemed as one. First, John thought, *Well, I handled that well.*

Second, Jimmie flipped the table over and shouted, "This is what I think of this fucking table." And finally, Matt, Tom, and two of their coworkers grabbed the two guests from Providence and did, in fact, haul their considerable asses out of the building. John took the hands of their two lovelies and followed.

Thinking there was going to be a rematch, several of the regulars followed the procession to the parking lot. Jimmie may not be the sharpest knife in the draw, but he was smart enough not to want a repeat of the ass kicking he took six months earlier. He settled instead for threats.

"You've made a big mistake, DeSimone, this is not over. I'm going to kill your ass. Hear me, you're a dead man."

"Not if I see you first, Sausage man. If someone here is going to die, it's going to be you. I've had enough of your bullshit."

John was driving home before he had the time to work his way through the process and get it clear in his mind as to what the fallout might be for what had transpired tonight. He mentally took himself through several scenarios before he came up with one that was plausible. He reasoned that there was little chance that Jimmie went to Don Parise and told him of the first confrontation. There is no way he wanted his boss to know he got his ass kicked in a club in Boston. The Don would have made inquiries about Jimmie's wounds and injuries and discovered on his own what had taken place. John also knew that Jimmie had been told by his boss to stay away from the club, and given that, there was no way he would carry this story back to Providence. It wasn't until he was home and enjoying a good glass of wine before he concluded, "I think I'm in the clear."

As was his practice John arrived at the club about two hours before opening the following day. He was surprised to see that one of the bartenders, Jay, was already prepping for the evening.

"Carl let me in, he's in the office," said the bartender, reading his boss's mind.

John found Carl at the desk, safe opened, going through the receipts from the previous night.

"Big night, I think this might beat last New Year's. It's amazing that you can do all this business and still have time to throw Jimmie Georgio out on his ass again."

Fucking Jay's got a fucking big mouth, he thought.

"Well, to be completely accurate, the bouncers threw him out, but I guess that's academic," he answered.

Carl didn't quite grasp what he had just heard but pushed on.

"The old man isn't going to be happy about this. You know that I have to tell him," he said, while halfheartedly suppressing a smile.

"Why doesn't that surprise me? Let me see the sales numbers when your done, I need to figure out the staff bonuses from last night."

Rather than a summons to the Don's home, John, instead, received a phone call from the man. The conversation was short and to the point and for the most part, one-sided.

"I looked into what happened the other night and, from what hear, I believe the situation was has handled as well as can be expected. I have not heard from Mr. Parise, so it appears that he is OK also. I think he shares my feeling about Jimmie. We both believe he is a fool. He was told to stay away and chose to do differently.

I will make sure that he is told, once again, to stay away from the club.

If I were to give you one bit of advice, it would be to be careful not to threaten to kill someone in public. Do we need to discuss this any further?"

"No, sir."

How is that for one-sided?

Actually, it all worked out fairly well. He had dodged the bullet again, and it was unlikely that he would ever see Jimmie at the club again. Of course, if he were ever to see the Sausage Man again, he may have to dodge a few real bullets.

On a Saturday, ten days following the altercation, the club was having a bang out night. In an effort to capitalize from the momentum generated by the Fourth, John had booked in some real hot entertainment and was getting the hoped for results. When 2:00 AM arrived, the registers were still ringing up big-time sales, and John decided to push the envelope and go for another hour. If the cops showed, he would pay his fine on the spot, in cash, and still be ahead of the game.

It was after 4:00 AM before the place was cleaned up, and John decided to spend the night on a couch in his office. The next morning, he got up before noon and returned to his apartment shortly after 1:00 PM. He saw a few of his neighbors returning from Mass and received some very disapproving glances. Not only did he look like hell, but he obviously had also missed Mass. He waved and smiled weakly as he ducked into his front door. He would be seeing Serena that evening when she finished her shift at Massachusetts General, so he decided to catch a little more sleep before getting ready to see her.

Mondays in the summer were great. It was really the start of two full days with no work, no classes, no nothing. By ten that morning, he found himself sitting at Lucia's having an espresso. He looked up from the sports and saw Joey approaching.

"DeSimone, you are really a creature of habit aren't you?"

"Yeah, I guess you're right. With all those Providence goombars after my ass, I'd better be harder to find."

"This is no joke, John, I'm sure you're on their short list for what happened, and if you come to the top, your ass has had it."

"What the hell are you talking about, what happened, what short list?"

"Where the fuck have you been, you're telling me you don't know? The Sausage man took one in the head last Saturday night, and help me remember this, didn't you threaten to kill his ass a couple of weeks ago?"

"Hey, that's bullshit, I was at the club Saturday night. We didn't close until three."

"John, these people aren't going to talk to witnesses. That bullshit is for the cops. Besides, Saturday night means anytime before the sun comes up on Sunday. Did anyone see you come home Saturday night?"

"I slept at the club. I didn't come home until Sunday morning."

"You're fucked."

CHAPTER THIRTY-EIGHT

Frying Pan to Fire

At that very moment, there was a meeting going on at the home of Angelo Parise in Providence, Rhode Island. There were four men in attendance: Don Parise, his consigliere, Sal Tangille, and two of his captains, Ralphie Bagglio and Tony Vincentia. They had been meeting for over two hours, and both patience and tempers were wearing thin. Vincentia and Bagglio were men who allowed their emotions to dictate their actions, and right now, they were ready to put a hit on "that fucking club guy in Boston." The only thing that was stopping them was that the Don had supreme confidence in Sal Tangille and the counsel he provided, and at this moment, Sal was convinced that John DeSimone was not responsible for Georgio's death. The reasons for his position were simple.

"Last January, when Jimmie first had trouble with this man, you asked me to find out more about him. What I found out was that he a very tough guy with a short fuse, and he was always ready to settle a dispute with his hands. I also found out that he gave up boxing because he almost killed Joey Belamonte in the ring. If Jimmie Georgio had been beaten to death, I would say he is your man. Jimmie was executed with a .22 shot to the back of the head. I feel confident in saying that DeSimone did not pull the trigger."

"Then who did?" shouted Bagglio.

"That I don't know, but if pushed for an opinion, I would say it was someone in the Belamonte family."

"I agree," chimed the Don. "And since we don't know who, I'll give you a name, and we will settle accounts. How does Rico Generice sound?"

The Boston Globe
Wednesday, July 25, 1951

The body of Rico Generice, 49, a resident of Fleet Street in the North End section of Boston was discovered last evening in a secluded marsh area in Medford. The body was discovered just before dark by Todd Greene and his son, Joseph, who were catching frogs.

Mr. Generice was reputed to be a member of the Belamonte crime family, and while it is being speculated that his death is in retaliation for the murder of Jimmie "the Sausage" Georgio earlier this month, police would not comment on the matter. Speculation, based on the condition of the body, is that Mr. Generice was killed elsewhere over the weekend, and his body was disposed of in the marsh to avoid early discovery. Cont. marsh murder, page 21.

John was back at Lucia's, reading of Generice's murder and could hardly contain himself. It was clear to him the this was in retaliation of Jimmie's murder, and while he was sorry for Rico, whoever he was, he was sure that he was no longer on the Parise short list of people who were to pay for Jimmie's death.

Whatever state of euphoria John was feeling was short-lived. Two weeks later, he was at the club, getting ready to open. He was in the office setting up the cash register boxes when Matt came to the door.

"Someone here to see you, boss."

"Ill be right out, who is it?"

"The Boston police, they said it was important."

John stuffed the cash boxes back into the safe, spun the dial, and went to see his guest.

When John entered the room, he was surprised to see four plainclothes officers. It was not unusual to have the police come by, looking for a donation, or a favor of some kind, but they were usually uniformed local cops. He was caught further off guard when one of the officers flashed a wide smile and a robust handshake.

"Silk DeSimone, I'm Detective Donovan from Boston Homicide. I was a huge fan of yours, in fact I was at the Garden the night you KOed that Belamonte kid. It was the best fight I've ever seen."

A second officer turned to the other two, and added his two cents' worth.

"Yeah, and if he didn't get banged up in the minors, he'd be playing for Sox right now."

He then turned to John and extended a hand.

"Detective Quinn, glad to meet you."

"Same here, what can I do for you?"

Donovan answered, "Just routine, these gentlemen are Detectives Lacy and Battles of the Providence Police, and they would like to ask you a few questions. Just routine stuff."

"If you consider murder routine," cut in Battles, obviously annoyed by the manner with which the Boston officers were conducting themselves.

"Murder, what the hell are you talking about?" blurted John.

Lacy spoke for the first time. He was the senior of the two Providence detectives; he wanted to put a lid on his young partner.

"We received an anonymous call yesterday stating that you and a recent murder victim, James Georgio, have had some major run-ins. The last of which as recently as a few weeks ago. Is that true?"

"Jimmie was a troublemaker and caused some real problems here, but any trouble we had never got any farther than the parking lot. He was killed in Providence, wasn't he? Hell, I've never even been in Rhode Island, never mind Providence."

"Did you threaten to kill him?" asked Lacy.

"He threatened me, and I threatened him, that stuff happens all the time. You get hot, and you say stupid things. It doesn't mean anything."

"It does when someone ends up dead," retorted Battles.

"Do you own a gun, Mr. DeSimone?" asked Lacy.

"No, I've never owned a gun."

"It's unusual that there isn't a gun of some sort in this type of place. Would you like to answer that question again?"

"There is a gun, but I don't own it."

"What caliber is it?"

"I don't know."

"Where is the gun now, Mr. DeSimone?"

"It's in a locked drawer in the office safe."

"Let's go see it."

The five men went to the office, and John dialed up the combination. It took him two tries. He was more than a little nervous. He then reached into his pant pocket, retrieved the club keys and opened the draw containing the gun. When he pulled open the draw he couldn't believe what he saw, or to be more accurate what he didn't see. The draw contained only a slip of paper.

"It's not here, it's gone."

"Surprise, surprise. Where do you suppose it is?" said the young detective, his voice dripping with sarcasm.

"Do you have a permit for the gun?" asked Battles.

John reached into the draw for the slip of paper which he always kept with the gun. The permit was issued for a .22-caliber handgun.

"You better come with us for additional questioning and arrange for someone to bring your car back to Boston. You won't be returning here today."

"Come on, you can't be serious. I never did anything. I couldn't kill another person. This is crazy."

To say that these pleas were falling on deaf ears would be an understatement; John was ushered to an unmarked police car and driven to the Sudbury Street Police Precinct in Boston.

That same afternoon, there was a meeting at the home of Dominic Belamonte. Although there were more people in attendance, the agenda was similar to that of the meeting at Angelo Parise's a week or so earlier. There were eight men present, the Don, his two sons, four captains, and his consigliere, Michael Orlando. The discussion centered on how and when they should retaliate for the shooting of Rico Generice or whether to end it right here. The Don spoke, "It pains me that we are here today to resolve a problem that never should have occurred. Jimmie Georgio is dead, our good friend Rico Generice is dead. It is clear that Don Parise believes that someone in our family is responsible for Georgio's death. What troubles me is that we would have no reason to hit Jimmie. Sure, he was a fool and a pain in the ass, but he was in good standing in the Parise family and a good soldier."

The Don seldom made long speeches in meetings with his inner circle. His usual tact was to listen, sort out what he heard, and make a decision. The simple fact that he went on as long as he did left little doubt in anyone's mind that he was a very angry man. There was a pause; Michael Orlando was carefully contemplating his next words.

"Most of us here know both Angelo Parise and Sal Tangille very well. Neither of them are hotheads or impulsive. The decision to hit Rico was not one made lightly. I'm sure they would have considered the possibility that someone in their own family was responsible for Jimmie's death, but the fact is that in spite of all his antics, he was well liked within the organization. He was a party guy, and he was very generous with both his money and his women. Right or wrong, they placed the responsibility for his murder at our feet."

Dante Socio, one of the captains, was next to speak.

"Right or wrong. What if they were wrong? Rico Generice was a good man and a good soldier. I think they were wrong, and we owe them one."

Joey then spoke up with the voice of caution.

"Right or wrong, they believe they were right. We hit them now, and they hit us next week. Where does it end?"

What Joey said made sense, and the Don nodded in agreement. That he had said it at all didn't make Dante happy. If Joey was not the boss's son, he would have come back at him. Instead he just thought to himself. *Who asked you, you little shit. You haven't even earned your bones.*

This went on for another thirty minutes, and the Don had heard enough.

"It ends here and now. Michael, I want you to contact Sal Tangille and set up a meet with Don Parise. I want it to end, but I also don't want to look weak. Make this happen as soon as possible. One other thing, I want everyone here to keep your eyes and ears open. If someone in this family hit Jimmie Georgio, I want to know who it was. This was stupid, and I don't want stupid people working for me."

The meeting was over, and everyone got up to leave. Joey was stopped by the voice of his father.

"Joey, stay for a minute, I have something to discuss with you."

The others turned and looked back. *"What is this about?"* was a thought shared by more than one of the group. They were not about to ask and moved on as if the thought had never entered their minds.

"Something about this troubles me," started the Don. "Your brother was strangely quiet today. Usually, he says too much, but today not a word."

'I'm not too sure I understand your concern."

"I think you do. I don't need for you to look out for Carl, I need to know if he was involved in this mess. Was he home the night that Georgio was hit?"

"To tell you the truth, I wasn't home that night. I spent the night with Maria, and I didn't get home until morning. He was in bed when I got there."

"Did Carl have trouble with Georgio, was there bad blood?"

"Jimmy was a pain in the ass. None of us liked him, but there is no reason to think that Carl would take him out."

"I trust your judgment, but let's be on the safe side. Talk to Carl and make sure he has an alibi. Ironclad, as the police like to say."

John was taken to the interrogation room where he spent the next three hours answering the same questions over and over again. Things not only didn't get better, they got worse.

"Did anyone see you when you arrived home on the morning of the fifteenth?"

"We had a late night on Saturday, so I spent the night at the club."

"Was that black Cadillac back at the club yours?"

"It dark blue, yes it's mine."

"Nice car, did you know that a dark-colored, late-model Cadillac was seen leaving the scene of the murder on Sunday morning, just before sunrise?"

"I want a lawyer."

"No problem, while we wait for him to get here, we'll book you for the murder of James Georgio."

Because he didn't know what else to do, he called Joey Belamonte and asked him to send a lawyer.

John had no sooner got off the phone, when he was asked to wave extradition. He did so without knowing the motives of detectives Lacy and Battles, which was to immediately hustle him out of the building and into a car with Rhode Island tags. They were taking him to Providence, which meant it would take hours for Joey and a lawyer to track him down. That was the bad news; the good news, if that's what you'd call it, was that for the first time in hours, he had time to calm down and collect his thoughts. It took almost two hours to negotiate the trip to the District 2 police station in Providence, and during that time, several things suddenly became crystal clear. He asked himself and then answered a series of questions, some of which were asked of him in the interrogation room by Officers Lacy and Battles.

"Who was it that had history with Jimmie Georgio?"

"Who had access to the gun in the club safe?"

"Who had opportunity?"

"Who drives a dark-colored, late-model Cadillac?"

And one they didn't ask.

"Mr. DeSimone, who hates your ass more than anyone else on this fucking planet?"

CHAPTER THIRTY-NINE

Good News? Not Really

Little did the Providence police know how much their ploy to delay John receiving counsel helped him. He now had time to work out in his mind how he would bullshit his way through his meeting with Joey and the lawyer. He knew for sure he wouldn't open with, "Oh, by the way, I just figured it out. It was your brother Carl who hit Georgio and framed my ass for it."

He could call in Lacy and Battles and share his revelation with them, and bagging a Belamonte would also earn them more recognition than a lowly club manager.

That would work until word got out that he dropped the dime on Carl, and in no time, he would be a free, but dead man.

How many times would the Silina men find themselves in this same predicament?

"Up and at 'em, DeSimone, you've got company." Johnny had managed to doze off and momentarily escape his dilemma with the gift of sleep. The guard's voice was a rude awakening.

"Jesus, John, I'm sorry it took so long to get here. These mental midgets love to play this game. Somehow it gives them the idea that they're smarter than us."

"Fuck you, grease ball," added the officer as he locked the cell door and departed.

"What time is it anyway?" asked John.

"John, you are something else, I know that I couldn't sleep if I were in your shoes." "It's after 4:00 AM," answered the third person in the cell.

"My name is Thomas DeBella, and I work for the law officers of Pino and Pino."

Now that has a familiar ring to it, thought John.

"John, you work for my father. We will take care of this, and everything that goes along with it. You have a blank check. You understand?"

John nodded and returned his attention to the lawyer.

DeBella was short and thin, with unmistakably Italian features. If the suit he threw on for the idiocy of tracking down his client was any indication, he was doing very well with Pino and Pino.

"Thanks for coming. The cops have the wrong guy, but they have him right by the balls."

"OK, let's start from the beginning, tell me everything that has taken place since the cops got to the club."

They talked for more than two hours. John had to navigate this territory very carefully because he didn't want to share the epiphany he had during the trip from Boston.

When they were finished, DeBella tried, without much success, to put John at ease; however, he did say one thing that solved a problem that needed to be addressed.

"John, we are not licensed to practice in Rhode Island, so we will be working with a local firm. We are familiar with several excellent firms."

That was just the opening that John was hoping for and he jumped on it.

"I've been thinking about this. I'm looking for three things in a law firm: first, an excellent track record, second, they must have no previous mob connections, and finally, they have to be WASP. All three, do I make myself clear?"

DeBella smiled and answered, "That could be a tall order in Rhode Island."

John had already been allowed one phone call and didn't want to run the risk of not being granted a second, so before letting DeBella go, he gave him a phone number with specific instructions.

"This is my cousin Tony's number. Call, fill him in, and tell him to get down here as soon as he can. Tell him not to say anything to anybody until we talk."

DeBella had his instructions also.

"Don't talk to anyone, no one, without your counsel being in the room."

"I've probably talked too much already," admitted John.

By the time he was alone, it was nearly six o'clock on Thursday morning. John went back to his cot and lay down. He really didn't expect to sleep but instead wanted to go over everything in his mind. He couldn't help but wonder if he could actually be tried for Jimmie's murder. "Fuck, if you can go to trial, you could also lose. What about my mother? This will kill her. This makes my father look like an altar boy. Oh shit, I've got to get word to Serena."

Lunch arrived at ten after noon, and Tony arrived along with the guard bearing a luncheon of shit on a shingle and Kool-Aid. In all these years he had spent growing up with his best friend, it was the first he had ever seem Tony enter a room, or in this case a cell, when he didn't have a smile on his face. He felt a sadness in this because he knew that Tony was in pain, and that he was the cause of the pain. He also knew he was exhausted and starving, but it was not the time to sleep, and he certainly wasn't about to eat that crap that the guard had just delivered. He and Tony had a lot to cover, and while he knew that DeBella had hit the high points with him, he wanted to start from the beginning to make sure Tony got a full account of what had taken place since yesterday. When he was done, Tony asked a question that had been bouncing around his own head since he had put things together the previous night.

"Do you think the Don and Joey know what happened and are going to do whatever necessary to protect Carl?"

"I don't know what they know, but if it comes down to me or Carl, well, blood is thicker than water. What I do know is that they can't be trusted."

"Do you think it was them who dropped a dime on you?"

"My money would be on Carl, I would guess he's in this alone."

"Well, let's return the favor. I'll make a call and see if we can get them to like Carl for the hit. I have to think he's a bigger fish than you."

"Let's wait on that, maybe I can get out of this mess without going that route. I don't want to beat this rap and end up with a bullet in the back of my head."

"I hear what you're saying, but there's one other thing that's bothering me."

"What's that?

"Didn't you say they are getting you counsel? Given that they could be looking to cover Carl's ass, that might not be a great idea."

"You're right, why don't you ask a couple of your law professors at BC if they could recommend any good Rhode Island firms.

"Good idea, I'll get the names of a couple of firms that are not connected."

"Great, so you understand the plan."

"I've got it. I'll be back tomorrow to let you know how it went."

"One more thing, don't ever come back here without food. I don't care how many guards you have to bribe."

Tony looked at lunch, smiled, and nodded.

It was the first time he had seen Tony smile since he arrived.

The plan called for Tony to head straight for Gloucester in an effort to break the news to the family before they saw it in the paper or heard it on the news. It would already be too late to get to Serena because word of mouth would already have spread the news through the North End. It was late afternoon when Tony walked through the front door. His mother and Aunt Mary were in the backyard, having coffee and enjoying the warmth of an August afternoon.

Rose was the first to see her son come through the screen door, leading from her kitchen to the backyard. She, like John earlier in the day, was struck at the fact that her son was not his usual smiling self. She sensed trouble, but never in a lifetime could have guessed what it might be.

Tony had hoped that Margaret and Annette would be here as well. In that way, he could tell them what happened and answer their questions only once, in addition to having their support in comforting their mothers. He knew that his uncle and father would not return home until tomorrow, and he needed to be here for that also.

"My John is in jail? What are you saying, what does this mean?"

"It means that a terrible mistake has been made, and we will get it straightened out.

Innocent people are arrested all the time and, in many cases, never even go to trial. The police are anxious to make arrest and often make mistakes. We will be getting the best lawyers available to handle this for John, and if it goes to trial, he will be found not guilty."

"Just as his father was found not guilty? The police made mistakes, the courts, the juries, they all made mistakes, and innocent people go to jail."

Tony didn't think it was a good time to remind her that her husband wasn't exactly innocent; hopefully, his uncle would take care of that himself.

The questions that followed were as he expected, filled with anguish and emotion, but he remained patient and calmly answered each one, sometimes more than once. This went on for at least an hour and predictably, just as it looked as if it was done, Margaret and Annette returned home from work. The two girls were nearly as close as were their brothers, and while they didn't work with one another, they always arrived home together. It had become a ritual that they would meet for coffee and have a quiet visit before heading home. They both had steady boyfriends, and their coffee talks often turned out to be strategic planning sessions on getting the boys to take next big step.

Tony now had to go through the entire thing again and, to make it worse, his mother and aunt felt a need to assist him in doing so.

Dinner that night was more like a wake; there was some quiet conversation, but the usual friendly banter and laughter was understandably absent.

First thing Friday morning, Tony headed to the North End home of Gloria and Mario Tessi. Given Serena's work schedule, he had no idea if she would be there or at the Massachusetts General. Gloria answered the door. Tony had met Mrs. Tessi at a family dinner but introduced himself anyway. She hesitated a moment as if she didn't know what to do but then recovered and invited him in. As it turned out, Serena was home, having called in sick that morning. She was glad to see Tony, knowing that he could bring her up to date on what was going on with John.

"First off, you have to know that this is all a terrible mistake. John would never be involved in anything like this."

"I know that, Tony," said Serena, as her mother nodded in agreement. "But what is going on, why has he been arrested?"

Tony went on to explain that there was enough circumstantial evidence to make an arrest, but there was nothing conclusive, and that there may not even be enough to get an indictment. Tony wasn't sure that Mrs. Tessi was following all of this, but given the fact that she had lived most of her life in the North End, he guessed she did. Of course, he never mentioned their theory on Carl's involvement, but he shared all that he could in order to give Serena some level of comfort. Before leaving, he got Serena's schedule for the next week and promised to call her at home every day with any new developments.

Tony made only one stop before arriving at the Prairie Avenue police station in Providence. When he arrived, he had three monster meatball subs and six Coca-Colas in-tow enough for himself, John, and the desk sergeant.

There wasn't anything new going on, but John was interested in how everyone was dealing with the mess he was in. Tony summed it up in very few words.

"The women in the family are scared and worried, the Tessi women are worried and supportive, but tonight, the Silina men could set off some fireworks."

Tony was at the pier when the two family boats arrived within minutes of each other. By now, the news of John's arrest was all over town, and Tony wanted to be the person delivering the message.

"Leave the cleanup for the crew, we have family business," said Tony in an effort to get his father and uncle headed home quickly and with as little conversation as possible.

"What's going on? Is everyone OK?" asked Santino.

"Not here, and yes, everyone's OK." Sort of, he thought.

Tony ushered them into a waiting car and moved as quickly as possible from the pier.

Tony had already asked the women to allow him to talk to the men in private. He explained that it would be easier for him explain everything that had taken place if there were as few people as possible present. The three men adjourned to his parent's apartment. The real reason for the private meeting was that he wanted to share the "Carl" theory with his father and uncle and have as few people as possible hear it.

"I don't know this Carl at all, he was a young man when I went to work for his father, and I never had any dealings with him," stated Marco.

"I met him once. That was here shortly after you were sent to jail. I threw his fat ass off our front porch," added Santino.

"I remember that," said Tony. "And that may have been the high point of his dealings with the Silina family."

Tony went on to tell them of Carl's failed attempt to fix the fight between his brother and Tony.

"He hated both of us, he hated us that day and every day since."

Santino could hardly contain himself.

"Then we must go to the police with this. It is clear that he is responsible for all of this."

"Not yet, Dad," said Tony as he went on to explain John's concern with doing so at this time.

"He is right," added Marco. "I faced the same dilemma when I went on trial. I went to jail rather than put others in danger."

Tony and his father looked at Marco. That was the first they had heard of that having happened.

There was one other thing decided that night. John's lawyer, whoever it turned out to be, would not be retained by the Belamonte family but rather the Silinas. Any relationship that ever existed with the Belamontes, Silinas, or DeSimones, would not survive that day.

CHAPTER FORTY

The Trial

Tony had asked three faculty members at Boston College to give him a list of three Rhode Island law firms that they would recommend to defend his cousin. There was one firm that appeared on all three lists and, as luck would have it, they agreed to take the case. Clark, Kenney, and Clark was a small firm with both a squeaky clean reputation and an excellent trial record.

John delivered the news to the Belamontes, through Joey, that he would not be accepting their generous offer to finance his defense and at the same time making it clear that he was severing all working relationships with them.

This, of course, did not sit well with Joey, and the news was received by his father as a personal affront.

An indictment hearing was scheduled for the last week in August, and any hope of the case being thrown out was quickly squelched. While the district attorney's case was built on circumstantial evidence, there was enough of it to warrant a trial. To make things worse, John was ordered to be held without bail and remanded to be held in custody at the Providence Jail House until trial. He was given a trial date of October 22, 1951.

The next two months were torture for John, for many reasons. The visits from his family in general and his mother in particular were extremely painful. The sadness he had seen in her eyes when his father was in trouble was now being caused by him. The anger he felt for his father was now directed at himself. "How could I ever let his happen?" was a question he asked himself countless times. His incarceration was completely foreign to him. His parents had always trusted his judgment and had given him a long leash. Now he was confined to an eight-by-ten cell behind a locked iron-barred door. And then there was all the time he had to think, and the one thought he couldn't get past was the possibility that he would spend the rest of his life right where he was. Then of course, there was Serena. They were to be married in the spring, and now that seemed to be a million years away. Serena was unshakable in her belief of his innocence and that he would be cleared of this crime. If John tried to broach the subject of what if, she would not hear of it. She gave him hope when, possibly, there was no good reason for it. The only respite he got from all this guilt and depression was when Tony and Manny visited. It wasn't the laugh-a-minute routine which usually marked their get-togethers, but these two guys had a gift for taking John out of the present and, for a short period, putting him in a better place.

The three lawyers assigned to John's trial by Clark, Kenney, and Clark included a partner, Thomas Kenney, and two associates Lisa Downes and Peter Taylor. John took an immediate liking to his trial team and looked forward to meetings with them because they could very well prove to be the key to getting his life back. That and the fact that all three seemed quite capable, believed in his innocence, and demonstrated a positive attitude.

It was at one of the earlier meetings that John decided to share his suspicions about Carl Belamonte's involvement in Jimmie Georgio's murder. He also shared his concern about what might happen to him if it became known that he dropped the dime on Carl. They agreed that, given the circumstances, an anonymous call was the best way to go. They agreed that the call would be made from a Providence public phone, by Lisa, and that no attempt would be made to avoid the call from being traced.

To their credit, the Providence Police actually followed up on the lead. After all, they did have an indictment and a good case against DeSimone and could have very well ignored the call altogether. Battles and Lacy called the Boston Police and arranged to have Carl Belamonte brought in for questioning.

"Did you know the victim, Mr. Georgio?"

"Yeah, I would see him around once in a while, ya, know, to say hello."

"Did you ever have a beef with Mr. Georgio?"

"No, I'd just see him around."

"Did you ever have access to the .22-caliber gun at the Night Life club?"

"I don't know about any gun."

"Do you own a late-model Cadillac?"

"Yeah."

"What color?"

"Black."

"Where were you on the night that Jimmie Georgio was murdered?"

"I was playing poker with some friends at Gus Abruzzi's place. We played all night. We finished at five thirty, six, and I went home."

"Can you write down the names of the other men who were playing that night?"

"Sure, give me some paper and a pencil."

"Do you know John DeSimone?"

"Yeah, good kid, too bad about what happened to him."

"Don't go far, we may want to talk to you again."

"I ain't goin' nowhere, I ain't hard to find."

On the way out, the two Providence cops stopped by to see detective Donavan to ask a favor.

"No problem, I'll follow up on the alibi, but I'll tell you now it'll hold up."

"I know," responded Battles. "But we have to close the loop."

As they left the station house, Lacy looked over to his partner and asked, "Gut feeling, what do you think?"

"Carl Belamonte is a piece of crap, but we'll never pin this on him. What do you think, Casa Del Roma for dinner?"

October 22 finally arrived. The trial was held in Providence at the Superior Court of Rhode Island and presided over by the Honorable Judge Richard Celona. John sat for two long days in a courtroom while Thomas Kenney and the state's district attorney, Gilbert Kelly, went through the jury selection process. In the end, Mr. Kenney seemed pleased with people that made the final cut, and on Wednesday, October 24, the prosecution and defense made their opening statements to the jury. Now the time had come for the state to present its case.

What followed for the remainder of the day was a parade of witnesses, all former employees of his from the club. If the DA wanted to establish the fact that John and James Georgio were not buddies, he hit a home run. The details of the New Year's and July 4th confrontations were repeated by one witness after another. Beyond the impact that this would have on the outcome of the trial, this was really uncomfortable for John. He knew that none of these people wanted to testify in this manner, but short of perjuring themselves, they had no choice. In cross-examination, his counsel did the best they could in damage control.

"Would you consider John DeSimone to be a good person?"

"Describe, in your own words the events leading up to the confrontations between Mr. Georgio and Mr. DeSimone on New Year's Eve and July Fourth."

"Did Mr. DeSimone try to settle the disputes peacefully?"

"Is it not a fact that it was Mr. Georgio who first threatened Mr. DeSimone?"

By the end of day one of testimony, motive had clearly been established by the state.

As the prosecution worked its way through the second day of questioning witnesses, John could not help but be struck at how drawn out these testimonies could be. How many times the same questions could be asked in a slightly different way. It started with Detective Battles and continued with Detective Lacy. Both were asked the same questions, first about the interview at the club, the missing .22, the Cadillac seen leaving the murder scene, and finally the interrogation at police headquarters. The DA went on ad nauseam, and John wondered if this tactic was having the same effect on the jury as it was having on him. He glanced at the jury box, but could not get a read. Now someone from the coroner's department was called to establish the time of death, pretty clear-cut, so why was this guy on the stand for an hour? Was there any doubt that Jimmie was murdered by a shot in the head? Of course, ballistics had to confirm that the murder weapon was a .22-caliber handgun, and there were no matches on file with the markings found on the bullet.

"Could that bullet have come from the .22-caliber gun missing from the club safe?"

"Yes, that is possible."

It was pretty much a given that John had no real alibi. His story that he had spent the night on a couch in his office, while true, did not resonate with the jury.

However, when the prosecution called two North End residents to confirm that John had in fact been seen returning home on the Sunday in question, after twelve o'clock Mass, there was little doubt that John could not account for his whereabouts. When the prosecution rested its case after three days of testimony, there could be no doubt that they had established motive, opportunity, access to the weapon as well as the lack of any alibi.

As a matter of procedure, the defense asked that the case be dismissed due to the fact that the state had failed to meet its burden of proof sufficiently enough to warrant continuing. To absolutely no one's surprise the motion was denied.

The defense would present its case starting on Monday, October 29.

As John got up to be taken back to the jailhouse he looked around the courtroom. He spotted his father and uncle. They had been there the entire week, and he felt sure he would see them again on Monday. Aside from the cost of his defense, the family was incurring the additional cost required to cover their being here. Could he feel any worse? He also spotted Thomas DeBella, the lawyer with Pino and Pino. It was the first time he had seen him in attendance. The simple fact that he was there confirmed the continued interest of the Belamonte family.

The next day, he had a visit from Tony and Manny. They tried to keep the banter light, but they all knew that the past three days had not gone well, and unless his defense team pulled off something big, John could actually be convicted of first-degree murder.

"Listen, Mr. Lawyer man, I have a little legal work for you. When you come back next week, I want you to bring the paperwork so that I can give you power of attorney for my assets."

"What are you talking about?"

"I thought I'd be able to take care of this after the trial, but it's looking like that won't be possible. Whatever money I have will be the first money used to cover my defense. You can find my bankbook in my top bureau drawer. There's a fair amount in the bank from my signing bonus, the fights, and the money I've been pulling down at the club."

Tony threw his arms around his cousin. He was sobbing shamelessly.

"How can this be happening? It's like a nightmare."

"If it is, you can wake me up at any time."

Manny couldn't speak, but the tears streaming down his face spoke volumes.

At 10:00 o'clock on Monday morning, court was in session, and the defense in the case of the State of Rhode Island vs. John DeSimone began presenting its case, be that as it may. The evidence presented by the prosecution was circumstantial, but nonetheless convincing. The defense strategy was simple: call an endless list of witnesses who would testify to the character of the defendant. The defense team of Thomas Kenney, Lisa Downes, and Peter Taylor left no stone unturned; they went as far back as teachers and coaches from Gloucester High School. Each attorney took a turn every few witnesses as a tactic to keep the questioning fresh and the jurors involved. It was impressive; after all, John was a good guy, a leader, a boy who stood up to the bullies in defense of his classmates. He was an honor student and a terrific athlete. His strongest and most effective witnesses were Father Bruno, Carmen Bucci, and Father Pasquale.

Father Bruno: "John was a superb athlete and a wonderful boxer. He approached boxing the same way he did everything else, whether it was academics, athletics, or his church, with respect, honor, and decency."

Carmen Bucci: "John was the best fighter and finest young man I ever managed. He was a world-class contender and could have made a small fortune in the ring, but he gave it all up because he seriously hurt somebody in the ring."

Father Pasquale: "I met John as a favor to my friend, Father Bruno. Since then, we have become far more than priest and parishioner. As was the case with John and Father

Bruno, we have become friends and confidants. To think that John is capable of this crime is ludicrous."

This went on for two full days, and when Tuesday night arrived, John was feeling better about his chances. He was meeting with his lawyers, and he asked if Tony could sit in since they had some business to attend to after the conference.

Tony was feeling better also and that fact was reflective in his voice and in the return of his sense of humor.

"You people did a nice job out there. You convinced me that he's innocent. Where do I vote?"

These people had never met Tony and his comments were met with blank stares.

"What?" Thomas asked rhetorically.

"Keep your mouth shut, Tony, or these people will never give you a job."

More looks, now confused.

"Boston College, law student," clarified John.

"Boston College Law School, class of 1940," smiled Thomas.

John decided to put old home week on hold and asked, "What's next? What are you going to do tomorrow?"

"Well, I see two options. We did have two good days this week, so we can close and turn it over to the jury, or"—he paused—"or we can put you on the stand."

"OK, so what do think? What are the pros and cons?"

"Well, the upside is that we are on a good roll and, if you handle it well, we can reinforce everything that they have heard the past two days. The downside is that putting the defendant on the stand can be viewed as a last-resort panic move."

Tony couldn't help himself, "Wouldn't putting John on the stand give the DA and opportunity to revisit all that testimony from last week?"

"I was going there," answered Thomas, not knowing whether to be annoyed or impressed.

"That would be the main reason for my recommending not taking the stand."

"Hey, I pay you for advice, I guess I'd be stupid to ignore it. Case closed as they say."

The Clark, Kenney, and Clark contingent departed, leaving John and Tony to see to family business.

—

"You know, John, I had no idea how much money you had squirreled away. It must have been all those free pizzas from the BC fan club."

"Yeah, that must be it. I'm sure it has nothing to do with the fact that I've been busting my ass while you were sitting on yours in a classroom for the past five years."

"You might be right. When you're right, you're right. Now are you sure you want to do this? Things are looking a lot better then last week. You might actually get a chance to spend this dough."

"It really doesn't matter. I can't let the family go into hock when I can do something about it. No, I'm sure."

John signed the paperwork, the friends embraced, and John was left alone to ponder what might happen in the next couple of days.

Court was called into session promptly at 10:00 AM the following morning, and Judge Celona asked the defense to call its next witness. There were still six names remaining on the witness list which the defense had submitted.

"The defense wishes to rest its case at this time, Your Honor."

"All right, court is now adjourned until 10:00 AM tomorrow morning. I will expect both sides will be prepared to present their summations to the jury at that time."

Some of the jurors look annoyed as if to question why they were dragged in here for two-minutes of dialog. Others realized that they would be given the case for deliberation the next afternoon and probably have this thing wrapped up before the weekend. Judge Celona then reminded the members of the jury that once the summations were completed and the case turned over to them that they would be sequestered until a verdict was reached. This was received with a predictable lack of enthusiasm.

John suddenly realized the quick adjournment would result in a quick return to his cell and a long day of agonizing over what the next few days might bring. Before he was moved, his lawyers asked if they might have a few minutes with him.

"Is there anything you can think of that might be helpful in our preparing for our summation?"

"You know, Tom, if there was something we haven't talked about in the past couple of months, I can't imagine what it could be."

"You're right, but I wanted to touch base before moving ahead. One other thing, would you like me to talk to the DA and see if we could plea this down?"

"What are you talking about?" asked John, now understanding what this meeting was all about.

"Well, that means we go to the—" started Thomas who was then cut short mid sentence.

"I know what a plea is all about, what I don't know is why you would ask me about copping to a plea. I didn't murder Jimmie Georgio, and I'm not going to say I did, even if it means I spend the rest of my life in prison."

"That's easy to say now, John, but if that jury comes back in with a guilty verdict, you might realize how long a lifetime really is."

"You three better get busy on that summation. I'll see you in the morning."

Tony and Mammy came by the jailhouse that afternoon to visit their friend. This was the perfect tonic for what was ailing John. The first thing he did was to tell the other two about the question posed by Kenney.

"What do you guys think? Did I do the right thing or am I being stupid about this?"

"First of all, you have to realize that Tom is doing his job. He is required to make you aware of your options, and failure to do so would be negligent on his part."

"That said, innocent or not, if you're going down for the crime, go for a plea."

"I understand what you're saying, Tony, But it's not going to happen. Besides, we're going to win. This time next week, I'll be back to work at the club."

The tension was eased with that comment, and the three friends shared a good laugh.

The summation by the defense was simple. Thomas Kenney spent some time talking about the evidence presented by the prosecution. The "circumstantial evidence." he pointed out disdainfully.

"A late-model Cadillac was seen leaving the scene of the crime. How many late-model Cadillacs do you suppose there are in New England?"

"John was seen arriving home early Sunday afternoon. He slept at the club. There are several witnesses who attested to the fact that this was not an uncommon practice for John."

"The .22-caliber handgun at the club Night Life was lost or stolen. Mr. Georgio was murdered with a bullet from a .22, but the weapon was never found. If Mr. DeSimone planned to murder Mr. Georgio, why in the world would he not do so with a weapon that couldn't be traced? Let's not forget that the .22 is the weapon of choice in mob killings, and Mr. Georgio was known to be a member of the Rhode Island Mafia."

—

"The two men were known to be antagonists, but Mr. Georgio was a twice convicted felon, and Mr. DeSimone is an ex-athlete, a college student, and a young man of good standing in the community, whether it be the North End or his hometown of Gloucester, Massachusetts."

With that, Thomas segued into the long list of character witnesses the defense had presented to the jury. During all this time John, as instructed, had his eyes on his lawyer or making contact with members of the jury. John was more than a little pleased with his counsel; in fact, he was ecstatic.

Thomas Kenney finished; hands firmly placed on the wooden railing of the jury box, explaining reasonable doubt to its members. He thanked the jurors, turned, and returned to the defense table. He could not help, but think, *How could there not be reasonable doubt?*

The voice of Judge Celona rung out.

"We will adjourn for lunch until two o'clock, at which time the state will present it's closing argument to the jury."

Thomas had lunch sent in and he, along with Lisa, Peter, and John critiqued the morning's proceedings.

"I think it went very well," started Tom. "We had an opportunity to revisit all the positive testimony from the beginning of the week, and the jurors seemed quite attentive. What was your read, Peter?" Peter had been instructed to observe Thomas's interaction with the jury while Lisa was doing the same with John.

"I believe you had their full attention, there were several nods of affirmation, and I really didn't observe any negative body language at all. Saving the reasonable doubt for the end was very effective. It was almost as if a light went on in some of their eyes."

"Good, I felt the same, but sometimes you can't be sure while presenting. How about you, Lisa? What did you see?

"John did a great job, his timing was close to perfect. He watched you making points and looked at the jurors for their reaction. I think our jury selection was right on, the chemistry seemed very good."

"What was your assessment from where you sat, John?"

"Well, I'm not as experienced with all this as you people, but I have to believe that if we don't get killed this afternoon, we may be OK."

"I think you're right. I have a good feeling," said Thomas as he reached for a sandwich. "Bon appétit."

District Attorney Kelly was a very skilled lawyer and a polished speaker. He was organized and deliberate in his approach and led the jury back through the testimony and witnesses the prosecution had presented the previous week. He closed by pointing out that while the defense called many fine people to the stand, they did nothing to negate the fact that the defendant had motive, opportunity, no alibi, and had conveniently misplaced the .22-caliber gun under his care.

When he was done, the possible outcome of the trial was once again too close to call. Judge Celona gave his instructions to the jury and told them to go to the hotel for the evening and return in the morning to begin deliberations.

John was returned to the Providence jailhouse where he declined the offer of dinner and, after recapping the events of the day at least a dozen times in his head, entered into a long and fitful night's sleep.

The next morning was the continuation of what would be a weeklong string of events leading to the conclusion of the trial.

As an athlete, John had frequently found himself in pressurized situations and had always responded well to the situation, and while the stakes had never been nearly as high, he found himself settling down as the day progressed. Tom had gone over the pros and cons of a quick verdict, and John felt the longer the wait, the better it would be for him.

Friday came and went with no word from the jury room. Any hope by the members of the jury for a quick verdict vanished when the jury foreman opened deliberation by polling the members. They were clearly split.

After eight hours, with little movement in either direction, they adjourned and were returned to their hotel where they would be sequestered for the weekend.

Monday was endless; John thought that a weekend in a fleabag Providence hotel would bring the jury back to deliberations with a renewed determination to reach a verdict. He couldn't have been more wrong.

"Tom, what's going on in there? Is there any indication of what's happening?"

"There seldom is and with a sequestered jury, you can be sure there won't be a leak. I still think the longer it goes, the better it is for us."

John couldn't help but think, what's this *us* bullshit? If *we* lose it's me going to prison, alone. He let it pass. Monday came to an end, and good or bad, there was still no verdict.

Tuesday brought with it some movement, not by the jury, but rather from District Attorney Kelly. Following lunch, the DA requested a meeting with Thomas Kenney; he had a proposal.

After some light banter and lawyer talk designed to determine who had the bigger balls, Kelly got to the point.

"My office is prepared to make a one-time offer which, if not accepted, will be off the table at 5:00 PM. We will reduce the charges from murder one to murder two. We will recommend that sentencing be ten to fifteen years, and your client will be eligible for parole after seven."

"That's very generous of you, but I've already had this conversation with my client, and he will never cop to a murder charge. He's a young man, so the years may fly, but murder won't. Make it manslaughter one, and I'll bring it to him."

Kelly got up, and Tom thought for sure that he would simply walk out the door.

"You have a deal. I'll be at my office waiting for your call."

"It's a good offer, John, and if I were in your shoes, I'd accept it."

"Murder one or manslaughter one, either way he wins. Murder one or man one, either way I lose. Either way, I go to prison, and either way, I look as if I murdered Georgio. Sorry, but no deal. I'll take my chances with the jury."

"I don't agree, but I'll make the call."

A few hours later, John and his lawyers were summoned by the judge to hear from the jury. The jury foreman stood and addressed the bench.

"Judge, we have been deliberating for three days, and I believe we are hopelessly split in our judgment. I don't believe we can deliver a verdict in the case."

At this moment, John looked like a genius. He and Tom had talked about the possibility of a hung jury, and aside from a finding of not guilty, this was the next best thing. The district attorney's office would have to think long and hard about retrying the case. This was their best chance for a conviction, and a new trial would be costly and probably would not have a positive result. John glanced over at Tom Kenney who masked his feelings very well while not moving his eyes from the judge. He knew that the ball was in Celona's court, so to speak, and the next minute or less was critical to his case.

For several seconds, which seemed frozen in time, the judge sat expressionless and stared at the jury box. He finally spoke.

"I don't care if this takes the rest of our collective lives, but I will not accept a hung jury and a mistrial. You all will return to the jury room and call me only after you have reached a verdict." With this, he rose and left the bench.

Thomas Kenney requested and was granted permission to consult with his client before he was returned to the jailhouse. They were given the use of a conference room directly outside the courtroom.

"John, you don't realize how close you just came to walking out of here a free man. I really believe that the judge considered declaring a mistrial."

"Well, if he did, he certainly did an about-face pretty fast. I mean, don't come back without a verdict."

"You have to understand, John, the judge wants a verdict, and he doesn't want to run the risk that he will be spending a month on this same case in a year. He has to play the hard ass, but trust me, if the jury is still hung in two days, all bets are off, and so will you be. Sit tight, time is on our side."

The following afternoon, they received a call to return to the courtroom; a verdict had been reached.

At 4:00 PM on Wednesday, November 7, the foreman of the jury was asked to announce the verdict to all those present.

The jury foreman was middle-aged man by the name of Nicholas Spada, and he appeared quite nervous as he stood to read the verdict.

"We, the jury in the case of the State of Rhode Island vs. John DeSimone, finds for the prosecution. We find Mr. DeSimone guilty as charged of first-degree murder."

There was the usual stir in the courtroom as people from both sides of the issue voiced their opinion. John felt his knees go weak, but he remained standing. He looked around the courtroom and spotted his father working his way in his direction. He also saw Thomas De Bella of Pino and Pino as he headed for the exit.

Once again, Thomas Kenney requested time with his client and he, his two associates, and Marco Silina met with John in the same conference room they had used the previous afternoon.

"What just happened out there? They go from hopelessly hung to finding me guilty in twenty-four hours?"

"John, I have no answer for that. I have never seen anything like it in all my years of practicing law. Sentencing is one week from today, I intend to ask the judge that given what has just happened that he is lenient in his sentencing."

"How about an appeal? How soon can we file for one?" asked Marco.

"I'm sorry, Mr. Silina, but you can't appeal a verdict in the Superior Court of Rhode Island unless the presiding judge makes an important mistake in the law. Our best hope is to push for leniency."

On November 13, 1951, John DeSimone was sentenced to twenty-five years to life for what Judge Richard Celona called the cold-blooded murder of Mr. James Georgio.

CHAPTER FORTY-ONE

Hard Time

John spent the next week back at the Providence Jail House while the state processed him through the system. There was little doubt where he would end up since the state only had one maximum-security prison, which was located in Cranston. The state demonstrated a lack of imagination in the naming of the facility, and the best they could do was to come up with was Maximum Security Prison.

On November 21, John, along with seven other men, was moved by bus from Providence to Cranston.

Upon arrival, the eight men were moved from the bus to a processing room in leg irons. This seemed to be an unnecessary precaution since the men were already behind locked gates and being ushered into the prison by four heavily armed guards. He would come to realize, as time passed, that this was simply part of the intimidation and dehumanization goal of the prison system.

Once the processing was completed, the newly inducted prisoners were marched, bedding and new prison attire in hand, to a large conference room. There was a large table in the center of the room but no chairs. The eight prisoners and four guards stood waiting for almost twenty minutes until a second door opened and a very large red-headed man entered the room.

"I'm Warden Crandall, and I want to spend the next several minutes familiarizing each of you with our rules here at Maximum Security." Nelson Crandall was a lifer in the Rhode Island penal system, a fact that he was quite proud of and eager to point out. He wanted not to be seen as a reformer but rather a hard-ass and had no problem pulling that off.

"The rules are quite simple, and if you observe them, your stay here can be quite tolerable. If you choose to be a problem, I will do everything in my power to make your life a living hell. Am I making myself clear?"

John made himself a promise, that being that this man would never see his face again. Being here was bad enough, but he didn't have to make it worse. True to his word the warden took only a few minutes to deliver his message.

There were two facilities at Maximum Security. The original facility opened over seventy years earlier and was followed nearly fifty years later with a new addition known as *"steel city"*. Three of the new prisoners were assigned to the older facility and the other four along with John were moved to steel city.

What happened next was like a scene from and old Cagney movie.

Five new guys to the prison block were marched, gear in hand, down a corridor lined by prison cells on each side and were greeted with catcalls from every direction, and the message was clear. "Your ass is mine."

John was brought to his cell. The door slid open, and he walked in. There was already another man assigned to the cell, and he was one of the few inmates who was not at the cell bars, shouting at the new arrivals. The occupant was young, maybe younger than John, average in size, and clearly scared to death.

John knew it was important to establish a demeanor that exuded toughness and confidence and purposely did nothing that would even acknowledge the other man's existence in the cell. He threw his gear on the unoccupied bunk and walked to the cells bars where he stood quietly, looking down on the corridor he had just walked. The last week had been a nightmare filled with disbelief in the verdict he had received, denial as it related the hopelessness of his situation, realization of its gravity and finally, somewhere along the line, he had become a very angry young man. Other than exercising some bad judgment, he had done nothing wrong, and if his parole efforts failed, he would be incarcerated in this hellhole until he was at least fifty years old.

The other man was first to speak. He could not care less about demeanor. What was important to him was whether or not his new cellmate intended to ass fuck him like the guy who had been transferred out last month.

"Hi, I'm Dave, Dave Ryan. Looks like we'll be cellmates for a while."

"I'm John," he answered without turning to look at the other man. "I guess this is a place of rules, so here's mine. If I try to fuck you, you have my permission to kill me. If you so much as touch me I'll kill you. Understood?"

"Yes, understood," replied Dave repressing the urge to hug his new cellmate.

"Good morning, Joey told me that you wanted to see me, what's up?" Don Belamonte looked up from his morning paper and waved his eldest to a chair opposite him at the kitchen table.

"Carl, there had been something eating at me for a while now, and I want to clear it up right here, right now."

"Sure, how can I help?"

"They convicted John DeSimone for the Georgio murder, and I'm convinced that they got the wrong guy. John can be quick to use his hands, but not a gun. He did not do this thing."

"Who did it? Jimmie was well liked in Providence, and if someone down there did it, Don Parise would have taken care of it by now."

"That is what's troubling me, someone down there did not do it. If that were the case, the Don would not have hit Rico. He believes we are responsible for Georgio's murder, and I think he is right, but John is not the guilty one."

"Then who is, no one else had a beef with Jimmie?"

"No, but you had a beef with John, you hated his guts. Someone would have to be blind not to see that."

"Do you think I hit Jimmie?"

"I really don't know, but if I ever find out that you did, I will be very disappointed and it will not go well between us."

"I did not do this, you have to believe me."

"I pray you did not, you can go now."

Carl got up and headed for the door, hoping that his father could not see the wobbliness in his walk.

What was I thinking, how could I fuck up so bad? was all he could think as he left his father's house.

Everyone deserves a break once in a while, and John got one when someone at Maximum Security unearthed the fact that he had completed a couple of years of college and assigned him to work in the prison's library. Without a doubt this was the best of all the jobs available at Maximum Security.

John was assigned to work for a prison trustee by the name of Bill Wexler, who was in fact a librarian in a prior life. Seven years earlier, Bill returned home from work early, suffering from flu symptoms and discovered his wife and best friend in bed and in a torrid exchange of carnal knowledge. Upon this discovery, Bill went directly to his gun cabinet, retrieved his 12 gauge shotgun and blew wife and friend into their next life, wherever that may have been. Bill, who had a sly sense of humor, liked to joke. "To this day, I regret having to shoot Dave."

If Bill was trying to make a new friend, he did so when at their initial meeting, he said to John, "I followed your trial every day in the papers, and I'm telling you, you got fucked over."

Bill could never say the same in his case because after offing spouse and best friend, he promptly called the police and reported his crime.

The library was surprisingly busy, but there was plenty of time left after doing the grunt work to pursue other interests. John discovered a passion for reading and began reading mystery novels, but soon switched to a prisoner's favorite: law books.

As therapeutic as the library might have been, it was nothing more than an oasis of sanity in a desert of madness. A madness he had to deal with every day.

It took no more than a couple of weeks for the madness to find him, and it came in the form of a psychotic named Donnie Hollis. Hollis was freshly released from a month of solitary confinement; prior to which he had been Dave Ryan's cellmate. John and Dave were at dinner mess, and suddenly Dave stopped talking mid sentence and seemed to shrivel up in his seat. Then for the first time, John heard the booming voice of Donnie Hollis.

"So there they are, my bitch and his new squeeze. How's it going for you lovebirds?"

John turned in the direction of the voice and, for a second, was taken aback. This guy was big, ugly, covered with tattoos, and sporting a Mohawk haircut, which John had seen only in movies. When Hollis got to where they were seated, he stopped only long enough to share his feelings with John, "Davey was my bitch, now you'll have to take his place."

John knew only two things for sure: first, this asshole is not just making conversation; and second, someone might be dead before this was over.

It had been two weeks since his incarceration at Maximum, which brought to a close a moratorium which he had established. He had sent word through his attorney that he preferred not to see visitors during that period.

His father was the first to come, and it was now evident that all but one of their issues were now long forgotten. Aside from his father's affair, there was nothing that he could have done which would have hurt his mother as much as he had done himself. It was strange that here he was now, having a conversation with his father about the perils of prison life and how to deal with them.

"No matter what, let the sick bastards know what a bad ass you are. Act first and hurt them before they hurt you. Never show fear. Fear to them means weakness. Am I making myself clear?"

"I understand. I've already heard about this crap, and I knew I was going to have to deal with it. Now I know that it has to be dealt with soon."

In spite of its serious nature, John couldn't help but laugh later in the day about the counseling he had received from his father. This was not your typical father-son, birds-and-bee conversation. Although it was the first they had ever had.

Tony was the next to visit, and he was so distraught that you would have thought that the conviction had happened just a day earlier.

"Listen to me, Tony, my dad told me what's going on with you. You're cutting classes, moping around, and you look as if you haven't eaten in a weeks. Shit, man, I've got enough baggage to carry around without thinking that I fucked up your life too."

"I'll be okay, it hasn't helped that I couldn't get in to see you, see how your doing. No shit, I'm going to be OK."

"You're my rock man, you have to put on a good front and help the family get on with their lives."

"That's easier said than done, John, it's like they've lost a loved one, and you don't get over that easily, but I hear you. I'll do what I can."

"Have you seen Serena, how's she doing?"

"She's a mess. She calls me every other day, she wants to get down to see you, but I've been putting her off until I could get here. I told her that it might be best if I saw how you were doing before she came to see you."

"Can you bring her down? I have to see if I can help her in any way."

"I have to get back to classes, how about this Saturday?"

"I'll check my calendar, but I think I'm available."

The two friends managed a smile.

Each day, the inmates got some yard time. This was without a doubt the highlight of their existence and the first privilege taken away for those involved in any minor violation of the prison rules. It was also the time and place that inmate bosses got the opportunity to exhibit their authority. For goons like Donnie Hollis, it's a time to intimidate, extort, and to put the fear of God into those too weak to defend themselves. The yard time hour was over, and the inmates were being herded up and returned to their work details. John found himself only a few inmates removed from where Hollis was walking. Once again, he heard Hollis before he saw him. A practice which he knew had to be reversed.

"Hey, guinea boy, your time is coming soon. Your sweet ass is all mine."

John looked over to Hollis and responded with a simple, "Go fuck yourself, you fucking fag."

Hollis tried to move toward John, but the yard guards got between them, and a confrontation never materialized.

Visitor's day finally arrived, and John greeted it with mixed emotions. On the one hand, he really missed Serena, and he wanted badly to see her; on the other hand, he knew she was terribly hurt, and there was no way he could help her. When he got to the visitors' area, Serena was already seated on the other side of a glassed partition. They could not touch and were required to talk face-to-face using telephone receivers. She looked better than he had feared she would, and her face lit up when she saw him.

"I've missed you so much, how are you doing? It looks like a terrible place."

"I miss you too, I'm sorry I've made such a mess out of all this, but it's important to me that you know that I didn't kill that guy. I could never have done that."

"John, you don't have worry about that, no one believes you capable of killing anyone. My father is very angry with you, but I don't think even he thinks you are guilty."

"I can understand the way he feels, he sees you being hurt, and I'm responsible for that happening. I was angry for years with my father for hurting my mother in the same way."

"Somehow, this will all get straightened out, I'll bet you'll be home for next Thanksgiving. You and he will play bocce, and all will be forgotten."

"I wish you were right, but that's not going to happen. There is no possibility of an appeal, and the police are not looking for anyone else. For them the case is closed."

"Then what can we do? There must be something?"

"Yes, there is something that you can do. You have to get on with your life, a life that doesn't include me."

"What are you talking about? I have no intention of going on without you, how can you even think that?"

"Listen, Serena, the best I can hope for is to get out of here in twenty-five years, that's the best I can hope for. I've made a mess of your life, but I won't ruin it. I don't want you to come back here. If you come, I won't see you."

Serena was sobbing uncontrollably. She tried to speak, but the words would not come.

"I love you, Serena, someday, you will see that this is the right thing to do."

John got up and left the area; he wished he were dead.

John had been angry when he arrived at Maximum, but after his splitting up with Serena, his anger moved to another level. That evening, he and the other inmates from his section were being marched to the mess hall. With his new mantra of not getting caught by surprise he was walking head up and looking around. This time, he saw Hollis before he heard him. Hollis and his group were returning from mess and heading in his direction, and when he spotted John, his face lit up. As he got closer, he delivered his usual message.

"OK, wop, any day now."

John's response was short and to the point.

"How about right now, asshole?"

Hollis had a puzzled look on his face not knowing what was meant by "right now."

It didn't take long for him to find out. John let fly with straight right hand, which caught Hollis directly on his left cheekbone. He was knocked backward but remained on his feet. John rushed forward and grabbed the front of the other inmate's shirt with his left hand and then pummeled him with right hand after right hand. A few seconds later, he felt arms around his neck and shoulders, pulling him away from a very bloody Donnie Hollis. As he was being pulled back, he let fly with his left foot, but the Salina trademark kick to the balls missed its mark.

John spent Christmas of 1951 in solitary confinement where he was held for a month. Donnie Hollis was in the prison infirmary for the holidays where he was treated for facial cuts, broken nose, jaw, and cheekbone, concussion, and serious loss of face in the prison community.

Solitary proved to be every bit as bad as he had expected. He saw no one except the guards who delivered his meals or took him from his cell every afternoon for a thirty-minute walk in a courtyard that measured thirty by thirty feet. He played mind games to keep alert. He added endless columns of numbers in his head, recited the forty-eight states, and then added their capitals; it didn't matter if he got it all right but only that he continued with the mental gymnastics. He kept fit physically by exercising on his cell floor for hours a day. There were no windows in the cell, and if it weren't for the meals and walks, he would not have been able to keep track of the days he had spent there.

It was 1952 when John was finally released from solitary and returned to his cell. Dave was clearly pleased to see him return; John being his cellmate bought for him a certain amount of status and security that he had never enjoyed prior to his arrival.

He was quick to fill in the blanks for his friend.

"Hollis was released from the infirmary just a few days ago. Before that, he spent three weeks in Boston, having some serious oral surgery done to his face. His mouth is wired shut, and he can't talk much, but he got word to me that he was going to see you dead."

"Why doesn't that surprise me? Did he give you any idea when this was going to happen or where and how?"

"I'd take this serious, John, this guy is crazy. He's in on a multiple murder conviction, and he's also suspected of a murder since he's been here."

"Don't worry, Dave, I know this guy is sick, and he's got my full attention."

"Yeah, but be careful, he may not be the one to do it. He may call in a favor."

"Good point, thanks."

The next day was Sunday, and there was no work detail. After breakfast mess, John sat in his cell, trying to teach Dave how to play hearts. He had no idea why he was doing this because if everything went by plan, they would have no use for the game anytime soon.

The next major event of the weekend finally arrived. The lunch alarm sounded, and the two cellmates put the cards down and waited for their cell door to open. When they arrived at the mess hall, John looked around, and as best he could tell, Hollis and his posse had not yet arrived. They went through the service line, and then John looked for the right seats for his plan. He found two seats directly on the aisle, leading from the mess entrance and the service line. He directed Dave to take the seat facing the entrance and he took the seat opposite him.

"Keep your eye on the door, when Hollis shows, let me know right away."

"What's up, what are you going to do?"

"You'll know when it happens, just watch that door."

"Can I eat?"

"Can you eat and look at the door?"

"Sure."

"Then eat."

It was less then five minutes before Hollis showed.

"He's here, he just came through the door."

John said nothing; he just turned and looked in Hollis's direction. His reason for doing so was twofold. First, he wanted Hollis to see him, and second, he wanted to time his arrival at their table.

When he turned, Hollis spotted him and made the best effort that he could muster, given his wired jaw, at a half smile and half sinister smirk.

John turned back to Dave and counted, "One thousand one, one thousand two." At one thousand four, he looked back again to find that his timing was almost perfect. With his left hand, he gripped the edge of the cafeteria tray and, as he rose from his seat, swung the tray discus style; catching Hollis squarely in the mouth. His face contorted from the blow and the wiring permanently affixed the smirk on his face.

He put his hands to his face, which was fine with John who followed with a right hand which caught him just below his breast bone. You could almost hear the air as it exited his body. Hollis fell to the floor, and John moved in quickly; he knew the guards would be on him any second now. Two steps and he was where Hollis had landed.

"This one's for Ryan." That's all he said before delivering the Silina trademark with a perfectly placed right foot. He then put his hands on his head and waited for the on-rushing guards. After the obligatory roughing up, John was returned to the same cell in solitary confinement that he had left the day before.

John was caught a bit by surprise when the following morning, a guard came to his cell announcing, "Warden Crandall wants to see you."

What the hell is this about? he thought as he exited the cell.

When he entered the warden's office, John was more than a little impressed. He looked around and saw a setting you might expect befitting a college president rather than a prison warden. Dark wood, nice furnishings, walls lined with hundreds of books, and wood floors adorned with oriental carpeting.

The red-headed warden looked up and, with a nod, directed John to take a seat opposite him.

"Well, DeSimone, you've been here less than two months and you've managed to make quite a name for yourself."

John saw no reason to respond and waited for Crandall to continue.

"When one is sent to prison, he must decide whether he wants to do hard time or easy time. It appears that you have chosen hard time."

John still didn't know if a response was expected but decided to give it a go anyway.

"Well, Warden, if easy time means I have to get ass fucked by some goon, I guess I'll go for hard time. If I don't take care of myself, who will? Guys are getting raped around here all the time, and you and your guards can't or won't do anything about it."

"You're out of line, mister, and furthermore, that stuff is way overblown. It doesn't happen all that often."

"Is that right, well maybe if my head was up my ass, I wouldn't see it either."

"Listen, you little fucking punk, you're in for a long hard stay here, and if Hollis presses charges, it could get a lot longer."

"You think that bothers me, and there's no way Hollis presses charges. Do you think he'll get up in court and admit that a guy forty pounds lighter than him kicked his ass, twice? Even if he does, I don't give a fuck. More time doesn't bother me, I can handle solitary," he lied. "And I can take whatever crap you hand me. You took my life away, what can you do now, take my birthday?"

"Guard, take this insolent little prick back to solitary, and I'll tell you when to let him out. It won't be anytime soon."

The guard grabbed John and half dragged him from the room.

Well that went well, he thought.

John was returned to his cell where he recited states and added numbers until the last week in February.

When John was returned to the regular prison population, he discovered several things, all good.

He found that he had earned hands-off status, and Dave, as his friend, fell into the same category. Hollis, after several more weeks in the hospital, had been moved to the older Maximum Security facility. The most amazing happening was that he retained his job in the prison library. The Warden Crandall decided it would be best if he kept John removed from the general population as much as possible, and as it turned out, he really disliked Hollis even more than he did John.

As a result of his extended stays in solitary confinement, John did not have a visitor for over two months. That ended on the first weekend following his most recent release. First on the scene was his father, who arrived on Saturday afternoon. Once again, the conversation between father and son was of the atypical variety. A father condoning the actions of his son which got the son in serious trouble.

"You were right, Dad, I won't say the remedy was painless, but in the long run, it was the smart thing to do. Everyone gives me a lot of space, and I'm not afraid to drop the soap in the shower."

"That's all good, John, but you can never let your guard down in a place like this. This Hollis guy may have friends who want to put a knife in you back."

"I understand. I won't let that happen. I know who my enemies are."

The two men talked for whatever time remained of the visit. They couldn't avoid talking of how they had managed to hurt the women they loved most; for Marco it was Mary, and for John, both his mother and Serena.

As Marco was about to leave, he leaned forward.

"John, do not give up, there is always hope. You are innocent, and somehow this will turn out for the best."

"I won't give up, don't worry about me," he lied.

The following afternoon, Tony arrived with Manny in tow. For the most part, the conversation was almost as atypical as was the one with Marco on the previous day. John's friends did not drive for nearly three hours to brood with him but rather to lift his spirits in any way they could. Before they got to that, Tony had to get something off his chest.

"John, I've known you all my life, and I don't ever think I was ever as pissed at you as I was the last time I left here. You asked me to bring Serena here to see you and then you dump her. Do you have any idea what the ride back to Boston was like? The poor girl cried for two hours nonstop. I understand what you did and why, but you owed me a heads-up. I almost came right back in to tell you off, but I didn't dare leave her alone."

"I'm sorry, Tony, I gave some thought to cluing you in, but then you would have felt complicit in what I was going to do. I'm sorry, I was trying to do the right thing and I fucked up.'

"I know, but I had to get that off my chest."

Manny saw the need to move on to lighter conversation and did so with "So, John, are you getting much?"

The two friends agreed to return every two weeks; of course, no one said anything about twenty-five years.

When Tony returned for his next visit, he had news that was at best a mixed bag.

"I dropped by the Tessis to see how Serena was doing. I thought her old man might kill me, but instead he asked me in for a talk. Would you believe he actually thanked me for getting Serena home that night?"

"There're a great family, there's no way Mario would kill the messenger, but he might put a contract out on me."

"Well, the news I got from Mr. Tessi was not good. Serena has left home, and she's taken a job somewhere out of state. She's living with Mrs. Tessi's sister."

"Why did she do that, and where did she go?"

"I don't know where she went. Mario wasn't about to share that information, but she left because she was too embarrassed to face people and answer all their questions. And you're right, he does hate you, and if you were to die, he would be there to dance on your grave."

"Well, at least she'll have a chance to start fresh, but you're right, the Tessis must be sick over her leaving, and yours truly is the one to blame."

CHAPTER FORTY-TWO

Ready to Do the Time

With the Hollis thing behind him, John was able to settle into a routine of "easy time," that would have made Warden Crandall proud. He would spend his days in the library with a workload that called for two hours work and six hours of reading every law book he could get his hands on, and with Bill Wexler filling out the book requisitions, there wasn't much he couldn't get.

He had plenty of visitors, including his mother who insisted that she had to see her son, and heaven help anyone who stood in her way. Even the good priests, Fathers Bruno and Pasquale, made a couple of trips together. They would ask that he join them in prayer for his release and laughed with him when he suggested that they pray not to God but rather to Saint Jude, the patron saint of lost causes.

It was just after 10:00 PM, of May 5, 1952. Dominic Belamonte was reading the evening paper and enjoying a glass of red table wine. He heard the door to the apartment being opened by key followed by the voice of his younger son.

"Dad, are you up?"

The Don did not like the sound of his son's voice.

"In here, I'm in the living room."

If the Don didn't like the sound of his son voice, the look on his face as he entered the room caused him to have a sick feeling in the pit of his stomach.

"What is it, what has happened?"

Joey walked to where his father was seated, squatted down, and took one of his father's hands in his own.

"Dad, they just found Carl's body, he's been murdered."

The police had found the body in Public Alley 101 after receiving an anonymous call from a resident who reported hearing a gunshot. This was a frequent occurrence for the police and, after following up, almost always found the source of the noise to be the backfiring of a neighborhood car. This time, the report was accurate. They found the body, which they identified as Carl Belamonte, with a bullet hole in his right temple and a gun at his side.

The Don decided it would be best if he and Joey waited in the apartment for the police to arrive. He also made the decision not to wake his wife. He would let her get her last good night's sleep for a long time.

While they waited, they talked about what had happened and, of course, who might be responsible. The first person to come to mind was Angelo Parise. They had thought that the hit on Rico Generice was in retaliation for the murder of Georgio, but maybe Parise shared the same suspicion as him. That being that it was Carl who did the hit on Jimmie. He would meet with his captains and consigliere to see what they thought or may have heard.

The wait was longer than expected. Two uniformed officers arrived about 1:00 AM, told Mr. Belamonte that there had been a shooting, and that it was believed that the victim was his son, Carl. "We need you to come with us to the city morgue to identify the body." The first thing to come to the Don's mind was that maybe it was a mistake, maybe it wasn't Carl. A half hour later, it was confirmed; Carl was gone. The Don and his son were then escorted to the Sudbury Street Police Precinct where they were introduced to homicide Detectives Keating and Levin. The detectives were well aware of who this person before them was; and while they hated what he stood for, they tried to remember that at this moment, he was a man who had just identified his son's remains. Officer Levin was the first to speak.

"Mr. Belamonte we are sorry for your loss. It is very early in our investigation, but—"The Don was in no mood to listen, "Do you think I'm going to wait around while you go through the motions of trying to find who killed my son? I came here only to find out when I can get his body and put him in the ground."

"I'm sorry if that's what you believe," replied Levin, now feeling less sorry for the man before him. "But I do believe we know the person responsible for his death."

This clearly caught the Don off guard, and before he could mount a response, Levin finished his remarks. "It appears that your son committed suicide."

"What? That's crazy! Carl would never do such a thing. He had no reason to do such a thing. You lazy bastards just want to bury this and put it behind you."

"Mr. Belamonte, we found a suicide note in his coat pocket. We believe it to be in his own handwriting. We have a handwriting expert looking at the note and comparing the signature with the one on your son's driver's license. We will know later today."

Keating then spoke for the first time.

"Your son's body won't be ready for release anytime soon, so if that's all you need from us, we will have the patrolmen return you to your home."

Keating clearly didn't give a shit about the feelings of the two men standing before him.

Later that day, John was busy replacing returned books to their designated place on the library shelves. The quiet of the library was interrupted by the voice of his boss, who was killing time perusing a copy of one of the several New England newspapers that were delivered to the prison library every afternoon.

"Hey, John, a goombar from your old neighborhood got murdered yesterday. His name was Belamonte, did you know him?"

John felt a rush of emotion, the cause of which he wasn't certain, and his voice was shaky when he answered.

"Belamonte, yes, what was his first name?"

Bill looked at the paper and then back at John.

"Carl, Carl Belamonte, did you really know the guy?"

"Yeah, he was the guy who made the hit that I'm in here for. Let me see that paper."

Bill handed him the late edition of the *Boston Record American*.

The Boston Record American

The body of a man identified as Carl Belamonte was discovered late last evening by Boston Police. The police were responding to an anonymous call reporting a gunshot in the Richmond Street area of the North End. Mr. Belamonte is the son of reputed crime boss, Dominic Belamonte. Efforts to reach the elder Mr. Belamonte were unsuccessful. Carl Belamonte appears to be the victim of a gang-style execution. He apparently died from a single gunshot to the head, and the murder weapon was discarded beside his body. The police declined to offer any additional information pending further investigation. Cont. pg. 5. North End Murder.

John now realized the sensation he experienced upon hearing the news. Since his conviction, he had clung to the hope that someone would continue to look at Carl as a suspect and, somehow, get everything turned around. In reality, he knew that wouldn't happen, but it gave him some small measure of hope. He no longer had even that shred of hope.

That all changed the next morning when a prison guard came to the library looking for him.

"Come with me, DeSimone, you have a visitor."

"What's up? It's not visitors' day."

"We make exceptions for lawyers, let's go."

John was led, not to the usual visitor's area, but rather a room reserved for lawyer-client consultations. Thomas Kenney and Lisa Downes were waiting when he arrived. They greeted him with broad smiles, which he thought strange.

Thomas got right to the point.

"Did you hear of the death of Carl Belamonte?"

"Yeah, I read about his murder yesterday. Why, what does that have to do with me?"

"Well, the fact is, Belamonte wasn't murdered, he committed suicide. Furthermore, he left a suicide note confessing to the murder of Jimmie Georgio."

"Jesus, does that mean I get out of this place? What's going to happen now?"

"This is great news, John, but it doesn't ensure anything, what it does is present us with an opportunity for a new trial and a very good chance of getting you out of here. You have to be patient, it won't happen overnight. In fact, it could a long time. Do you understand what I'm saying?"

"As long as there's a light at the end of the tunnel, something to hope for, I'll be OK. That said, don't drag your feet."

CHAPTER FORTY-THREE

Investigations Reopened

Dominic Belamonte believed beyond a doubt that his son had not committed suicide. He commissioned his people to go into the neighborhood and garner whatever information they could on his son's murder. He offered rewards to those offering assistance and a large bounty for whoever gave him a "name."

After a week, they came up with nothing, which brought him to the next step. He summoned his captains, consigliere, and Joey to meet with him in his home.

"This leaves only the man in Providence, who I once called my friend, as someone to gain by my son's death."

Michael Orlando was the only one to speak.

"What reason would he have to do this, and why your son?"

"In retaliation for the death of Georgio, that could be the reason."

"We were in agreement that the death of Rico Generice was to avenge Georgio, why now would that have changed?"

"Because now he is convinced that it was Carl who killed Georgio, and that was the reason for the note. To tell us that he knew that Carl had done it."

"Why would he suspect Carl of the murder?" asked the consigliere.

"Why? He was my son, and I also suspected him."

"What do we do now?" asked Joey. He had lost his brother, and he was no longer interested in being the voice of reason.

"We have no choice, there is no one else that could have murdered Carl. If we do not act, we look weak and invite them to do as they wish."

"Who do we hit?" asked Dante Socio with a renewed interest. Dante was not happy with the lack of action after the Generice hit, and he was eager to deliver a message to the people in Providence.

"They hit Carl, we must hit someone close to Parise," answered the Don.

"He has a son," offered Socio.

"No, not the son. I could not be so cruel," he lied. He would like to hit Parise's son, but to do so might provoke Parise to target Joey.

"Then how about Ralphie Bagglio?" responded Dante, anxious to settle on a name.

"Bagglio is a good choice. It is important we act quickly and do it right. I want to hit Bagglio and no one else. We must deliver the correct message."

On Thursday, May 9, Thomas Kenney petitioned the Superior Court of Rhode Island for a new trial. The petition was based on the discovery of new evidence which cast substantial doubt on the verdict rendered by the court on November 7, 1951.

On the following Monday, the office of District Attorney Kelly filed a brief with the court in opposition to the petition made on the behalf of John DeSimone.

It took the judge almost two weeks to announce his decision, which for John was a good news-bad news scenario. The good news was that he judged that there were grounds for a hearing; the bad news was that he set a hearing date of August 28.

"John, I told you that you'd have to be patient, these things take time."

"I know that, Tom, but three months for a hearing, God only knows how long it will be before we get a new trial. I mean, what the hell, I might be in here for another year or more, and I'm innocent."

"The court's dockets are full. Let's be grateful you'll have a day in court. The only important thing now is that we are granted a new trial."

"Winning would be good too," added John.

"Keep that sense of humor, you'll need it."

The murder of Ralph Bagglio, which took place in front of his home in Warwick, Rhode Island, set off a bloodbath which continued for close to two months. The message was clear to Don Parise: Dominic Belamonte believed that he was in some way responsible for the death of his son Carl. It was also clear that Belamonte believed that his son, in some way, was responsible for the hit on Jimmie Georgio.

"Other than that, what possible reason would I have for killing his son?"

Parise was talking to Sal Tangille, Tony Vincentia, and his other two surviving captains.

He turned to Tangille. "What do we do now?"

"We have lost Jimmie and Ralph. They have lost Rico Generice and Carl. We could call it off right now and not lose face. You could call for a sit-down, assure Don Belamonte that we did not have a hand in his son's death, and call for a truce. The other option is that we seek revenge and set off a chain of events that could go anywhere."

"I understand that, but that was not what I asked. What do we do now?" asked the Don. Tangille hesitated; as consigliere, he was looked to as the voice of reason. He was expected to provide options to men who, by nature, were quick to act on emotion.

"I don't believe we can accept this. They hit Ralph Bagglio, a man close to you, a captain. We can't allow that to happen and not hit back. Whatever happens after that happens."

"We go to the mattresses today and plan the hit." The Don paused and looked this time at Vincentia who knew the meaning of this.

"Tommie Sinncotta, he's a captain, and he is close to Don Belamonte."

The only thing that limited the killing was that both organizations went to the mattresses after the murder of Tommie Sinncotta. With all the made men in hiding, the killing was limited to the street soldiers and, in one case, someone mistaken for one. The peons were killing peons while those higher in rank found safety in hiding.

Wars between countries and organized crime had one similarity and one major difference. War wasn't popular with either, and it was very unprofitable for the criminals—in this case, organized crime. A truce was needed, and a meeting was arranged between the consiglieres from both of the families. Sal Tangille and Michael Orlando, along with one captain from each organization, met at an Italian restaurant in Woburn, Massachusetts. There was little chance that the discussions would fail since there would be no effort to place blame, only to negotiate a cease-fire and get back to business. Make no mistake, however; whatever mutual respect and trust that was once shared between the two families would not survive their war.

Michael Orlando reported back to Don Belamonte as soon as he returned from Woburn.

"It is done. There will be no further hostilities."

"As simple as that. They have taken my son from me, and they believe I will take that to my grave. Someday I will avenge Carl's death. Angelo Parise also has sons."

"Tangille asked that I deliver a message to you. Parise fears that you will not be able to put this behind you. He wanted to say to you one more time that he would never have allowed a hit on Carl. He hopes you understand this."

—

"I understand that Parise is lying, I understand that my son would never commit suicide, and no one but Parise had any reason to see him dead. I'm a patient man, it does not end here."

The news of the Mafia war barely trickled down to Baltimore which had enough issues of its own to fill its papers and newscasts, but Serena was kept abreast of things in her weekly calls home. While her parents shared this information, they had agreed not to inform their daughter of the possibility of John getting a new trial. They felt justified in doing this because they rationalized that her relationship with John had caused her enough pain and ultimately driven Serena from their home.

In Serena's mind, the move to Baltimore had no real long-term implications. Boston was her home, and she had every intention of returning there after her failed relationship with John had become old news. Of course, Carl's death, which her parents positioned as a gang-style murder, and the ensuing fallout were not helping that in any way. Her parents had never deceived her before, and she had no reason to believe that they were doing so now.

In the meantime, aided by a strong letter of recommendation from her supervisor at Massachusetts General, she had landed a nursing position at Johns Hopkins Hospital. It was now early July, and while she enjoyed her job at Johns Hopkins and loved living with her aunt Josie, she hoped to be able to return home before the holidays. Two weeks hence, a quiet fell upon the North End of Boston and Federal Hill in Providence, and Thanksgiving at home was looking like a strong possibility.

As the August 28 hearing date moved closer, the Clark, Kenney, and Clark team of Kenney, Downes, and Taylor worked on a strategy for getting a new trial for their client. They saw having Judge Celona hear their request as a positive. The fact that John had been convicted had little bearing on the judge personally. He had run a good trial and couldn't, in any way, be seen as having an influence on the verdict. Here's where it became a bit tricky. Aside from the new evidence, Belamonte's suicide note, Judge Celona had heard it all. They had to find the correct balance of what and what not to present. Too much could bore, or even anger the judge, and too little may seem as if they didn't place much stock in their earlier defense. There was, however, one thing they wanted to get in that they were not allowed to use in the trial itself. It could be powerful, and could also be seen as irrelevant, but they now had the opportunity to find out.

Since the petition for a new trial, visits by friends took on entirely different tone, and why not, these were his friends and family. Even Tony, who had a much more realistic understanding of what would happen in court, could not harness his enthusiasm.

"So let's talk about what you're going to do when you get out of here." As usual, it was Tony who speaking.

"Would that be before or after I get laid?"

"Don't even worry about that, Manny and I plan to get you set up for a night at the Ritz, a room service steak, and the best piece of ass that money can buy."

"Yeah, and since Perry Mason here is unemployed, that would be my money he's talking about," chipped in Manny.

"How many times do I have to explain this, Manny, we're a team. I'm research and development, and you're finance."

"Translation, you made the calls, I pay the bills."

"I think you've finally got it."

"What happens after the Ritz depends on timing. The way the courts move, this could take a long time, but if I can get out before the New Year, I'll return to Suffolk for the second semester. If not, I'll wait for the fall. Hopefully, with all that, I'll be able to track down Serena and get that part of my life straightened away."

"Listen to this"—it was now Manny's turn to make a suggestion—"you've become somewhat of a folk hero, and Eagle Foods would love to have you come on board with us. You've packed a lot of adversity into twenty-five years, and now you're going to land on your feet. Your name is gold to people who have struggled all their lives to make a go of it. Eagle are good people, this as a great opportunity."

"That sounds great Manny, but whatever I end up doing, it will be with a college degree. I want to have options, and a degree will do that for me."

"I understand all that, but this is not a take-it-or-leave-it offer. When you get your degree, Eagle will remain as an option."

"One step at a time, step one is we get you out of the shit hole."

"Well said, Tony, get me out of this place."

Returning to the Superior Court had a very familiar feel to it for John with one major difference—the last time he was here, it was to be sentenced for first-degree murder. Today, there was a good chance that the day's proceedings could be the first step in having that conviction reversed. Worst case is that there would be closure to the whole thing. If he and his attorneys win, he's a free man. If they lose, he goes back to Maximum Security, knowing that there is no hope, and he can settle in for the long haul. Sort of like those winner-take-all boxing matches that took place fifty years ago, except with much higher stakes.

Since the burden of proof was now on the defense, Thomas Kenney was the first to present to Judge Celona.

"Your Honor, we are here today to correct a wrong that took place in this court last November. This is possible because of new evidence, strong evidence that has come to light."

Mr. Kenney went on to detail the events in the death of Carl Belamonte, and presented into evidence the suicide note found on his body. He stated that he was prepared to present witnesses to verify that the handwriting in the note was that of Mr. Belamonte, and the gun found at his side contained his, and only his, fingerprints. To make this point more powerful, he pointed out that these expert witnesses were employed by the Boston Police department.

He then went to the personal aspect of his presentation. He reminded the judge of the endless stream of character witnesses that had testified on his client's behalf.

"Judge, these people were not only friends and family but included teachers, businessmen, coaches, and even two priests. John DeSimone has, for all his life, been the boy next door. John DeSimone was not capable of the crime for which he was convicted."

Thomas Kenny then paused. He did so to collect his thoughts and for effect. He knew what he was to say next was new to the judge, and he wanted to get it just right.

"Your Honor, in light of this new evidence, there are other events that now take on new importance. After the arrest of my client, but before his trial, the Providence Police received anonymous phone call implicating Carl Belamonte in the murder of James Georgio. The Providence Police Department sent the two detectives assigned to the case to Boston to question Mr. Belamonte. Let me tell you what they should have gleaned from that interview. Mr. Belamonte knew Mr. Georgio, they were, in fact, members of competing crime families. He was Mr. DeSimone's boss at the Night Life club, which gave him access to the gun believed to have been used in the murder. In fact, he was the only person other than my client who knew the combination of the safe where it was kept. There was a dark-colored late-model Cadillac seen leaving the murder scene. Mr. Belamonte drove a 1951 Cadillac Deville Coupe, black. Did he have an alibi? Yes, he was in an all-night poker game with members of his father's crime family. And by the way, he hated John DeSimone with a passion. He was insanely jealous of the way John was treated by his father. You're Honor, Carl Belamonte had motive, opportunity, and an alibi only a father would believe." He finished with his eyes fixed on those of Judge Celona and liked what he believed he saw. He returned to his place at the defendant's table and was seated.

Judge Celona sat quietly at his bench, sorting through what he had just heard.

"Will counsel approach the bench?"

Thomas Kenney and the district attorney got quickly to their feet and did as instructed.

"District Attorney Kelly, did you, prior to today, have any knowledge of Carl Belamonte being questioned in connection with the murder of James Georgio?"

"No, sir, I did not."

"Are the two detectives who allegedly conducted the questioning in court today?"

"Yes, sir, they are," said the DA as he turned and pointed to detectives Lacy and Battles.

"Well, Mr. Kelly, I'm going to call a recess. During which time, I want you to meet with the two detectives and inquire of them, first if there was in fact a meeting with Mr. Belamonte, and if so, what took place at that meeting. I will expect you to return at 11:00 and report your findings to this court. Don't make the mistake of putting a spin on this and misrepresenting the facts. Do I make myself clear?"

"Yes, sir, you have been very clear."

With that, the judge brought his gavel down heavily on the sound block.

"Court is in recess and we will reconvene at 11:00 AM."

District Attorney Kelly along with an ADA and Lacy and Battles went into a conference room. The DA closed and locked the door before being seated. The symbolism of this action was not lost on Battles or Lacy. Without saying a word, the DA made a statement: *Nobody leaves this room until I get the whole story.*

"Well, gentlemen, we all know why we're here. Who would like to start?"

Neither of the detectives made any indication that they were willing to offer anything unsolicited, so Kelly moved ahead.

"Detective Lacy, is it true that one of you received an anonymous telephone call which implicated Carl Belamonte in the murder of James Georgio?"

"Yes, I received the call."

"This was after DeSimone's arrest and prior to his trial?"

"Yes, it was."

Kelly then turned his attention to the other detective.

"Detective Battles, did you and Lacy go to Boston and question Belamonte?"

"Yes, we contacted the Boston Police Department and arranged for them to bring him in for questioning."

"We all heard the counsel for the defense go through a list of things that you may or may not have asked Belamonte. How accurate were they in depicting what actually took place?"

After a short delay, Lacy took the lead. "I'd say that they pretty much aced it."

"Can you please tell me why the hell you didn't come to me with this information?"

This time, it was Battles who responded in an effort to pull their collective asses from the fire. "We had already made an arrest, and we had a good case against DeSimone, and Belamonte had an alibi. We didn't think that we could make it stick with him." Lacy looked over at Battles, who all of a sudden didn't feel real good about what he had just divulged.

"Let me point something out to you two. You are members of the Providence Police Department. I, on the other hand, am the district attorney. The decision as to whether or not to pursue Carl Belamonte for this murder was mine, not yours. We have an hour before we have to go back in there. I'm leaving now, but I want you to stay in this room until 10:50 and then get your asses back to the courtroom."

It was now Lacy's turn to look stupid.

"How do you suppose they knew so much about our line of questioning?" Kelly shook his head and made no effort to mask his distain.

"Well, genius, my guess is that it was defense that made the anonymous call."

Although he didn't have a clue, Battles looked at Lacy as if to say, *You didn't figure that out?*

Meanwhile, in the defense conference room, the mood was quite different.

"I'm no genius, but I have to think what happened just now was really good."

Kenney smiled; he could understand why this young man was held in such high esteem by those who knew him well. He himself had come to like him also.

"You're right, it was very good, but funny things happen in court, particularly when it comes to admitting to a wrongful conviction. That said, I don't think I could have scripted a more positive reaction by Judge Celona to what we introduced. I believe that the DA will resist, but I feel very strongly that Celona will award us a new trial, and don't be surprised if the judge finds an early date for the retrial."

"I have to believe that we'll win the next one," added John.

And 11:00 AM finally arrived. Both sides were present and seated five minutes before the designated time. John glanced over to the prosecution's table in a futile attempt to get a read from the opposition. A more court-savvy Thomas Kenney busied himself going through his notes, looking for nothing in particular.

Promptly at 11:00 AM, the door to the judge's chambers opened, and Judge Celona made his entrance. The court bailiff asked those in attendance to rise, and the judge immediately motioned them to remain seated. Court protocol be damned, the judge was all business.

He immediately looked directly at Gilbert Kelly.

"Have you completed your interview with Detectives Battles and Lacy?"

"Yes, Your Honor, I have."

"Did you find that the new information presented by defense was, in fact, accurate?"

"Yes, sir, the validity of the information was substantiated by the detectives."

"Based on this new information, what is your recommendation regarding a new trial for Mr. DeSimone?"

It was Kelly who now glanced over to the defense table.

"My recommendation is that a new trial not be awarded."

Judge Celona could feel the blood moving quickly to his face as he began to rise to his feet.

The district attorney's next words stopped him midway out of his chair.

"My recommendation is that all charges against John DeSimone be dropped, and that he be released immediately."

The judge's red face was now hosting a suppressed smile. He settled back into his chair.

"So be it. Mr. DeSimone, you are free to go. Mr. Kelly, I want you to send letters to the station commander of both Lacy and Battles. They are to receive an official reprimand, and the letters are to be placed in their personnel files."

After "free to go," John heard nothing. He sat a few seconds, too stunned to move; he then got to his feet and raised his arms in the air. He looked around and saw his father and Tony hugging each other. He worked his way across the room to join them. It was then he realized that the court officers were allowing him to do so; he was a free man.

After a few minutes, the three of them moved back to the defense table.

"What can I say, Thomas, you were worth your weight in gold. I'll be in your debt forever."

"John, if I ever question why I do what I do, I'll remember today."

"Did you ever think this might happen?"

"Yes, when the judge sent the DA to question the detectives, I thought this was possible. I never said anything because you had been disappointed too many times, and I figured I'd wait and see where it went."

"So I can just go now, just walk out of here?"

"Free to go, have a good life, John."

"I'll call home right now and tell your mother that we will have a special guest for dinner." Marco Silina was beaming.

"One other thing, John, I'd like to file a suit on your behalf for wrongful conviction. I think we'd have a strong case."

"I don't know Tom, I think I've had enough of courts and trials."

"I don't think it will ever get to court, I think we'll get a negotiated settlement. The worst we can do is recover your legal fees."

"Would you take the case on a contingency basis?"

"Now I know what you've been doing all those hours in the library. Yes, we'd take the case on contingency."

"What the hell, go for it."

CHAPTER FORTY-FOUR

Moving Home

There were countless reasons for moving home to Gloucester. John could not get enough of his family, and he knew that they felt the same about him. Of course, he no longer worked at the club, so he didn't have to be concerned with the commute. He had decided not to rush back to school since he had originally planned to return for the spring semester. Plus he was almost broke. There were still a few bucks left after his legal expenses, but living at home put a free roof over his head and would allow him to work one of the family boats and replenish his stash.

The only unfinished business he had in Boston was visiting the Tessis and locating Serena.

John waited until the second Sunday after his release to call on the Tessis. He decided against calling ahead, knowing that it would be easier to hang up on him than slamming the door in his face. As he approached the front door, he recalled his first visit to the Tessi home. It was less than three years ago, but it may well have been a hundred. He rang the bell and waited. He had given considerable thought to what he was going to say, but at this moment, those thoughts were a jumbled mess in his head. At first, he wondered how, with all that he's been through, he could be so nervous now? Then it came to him—the stakes were higher.

The door opened, and Gloria stood before him. She had a stunned look on her face and simply stated his name.

"John."

John took her answering the door as a good omen. Angry as she might be, she was too much a lady to slam the door in his face. He was right; furthermore, she asked him in and led him to the living room.

"Make yourself comfortable, John, I'll get Mario."

He then realized the Tessis had planned for this day also, and while they had no way of knowing when it would come, they would be prepared when it did.

A minute later, the Tessis entered the living room, their body language did not give off good vibes. If you could put a phrase to it, it would have been United We Stand. John started to rise to his feet and extend a hand toward Mario but was waved back to his seat with a dismissive movement of a hand.

There was no attempt at small talk; these people who he had been so close to just a year earlier were now acting as if nothing that happened before his arrest took place. If he had not been wrongfully convicted of a crime, he would now be their son-in-law.

"I think you know why I'm here. I would like to know where Serena is living, and if there is some way I can make things right with her."

"This was explained to your cousin Tony when he made a plea on your behalf, long before there was even a chance of your being released. She is living out of state with my wife's sister, and she is starting a new life, a life that does not include you."

"I don't believe that, I know that I hurt her, but I did that so she could get on with her life. If I knew I would get vindicated, I would have asked her to wait."

"Wait for what, so you could get in trouble again?"

"I've never been in trouble with the law before this, what makes you think it will ever happen again?"

"You lived and worked on the edge of an evil world, and you fell into it. You made that mistake once, you are capable of doing it again."

"If you don't help me, I'll find her myself."

"Go right ahead and try, but you get no help from us."

Gloria Tessi spoke for the first time.

"You drove our daughter from our home. Now I want you to leave also, and you need never return."

John left the Tessi home and stood on the front stoop, facing the street. His statement about finding Serena on his own didn't ring true even to himself. Hell, she could be anywhere. There was one thing that he did know for sure, the Tessis were a very close family, and Serena would not stay away forever. When the holidays came, she would be home, and he would see her then. She may never want to see him again, and he could understand that, but he would have to hear that from her.

John went directly from the Tessis to the Sacred Heart church. He hadn't seen Father Pasquale since his release and owed him a visit. He also wanted to solicit help from the priest.

He was greeted at the door of the rectory by a woman, and the image of Mrs. Driscoll from Our Lady of Good Voyage immediately came to mind. *They must get these women from central casting*, he thought.

"Hello, I'm John DeSimone, I'd like to see Father Pasquale.

The face of the woman lit up and a smile came to her face.

"Father was wondering when you would come to visit. Come on in, I'll get Father for you, by the way my name is Mrs. Driscoll."

"I don't believe it!" he said without realizing that he was speaking aloud.

"What is it you don't believe?" inquired Mrs. Driscoll.

"Oh nothing, just thinking out loud."

John was led to yet another living room and another soft chair. It seemed as if Mrs. Driscoll had no sooner left the room when Father Pasquale came charging in.

"Did you think we'd ever see this day? Come here and give me a hug."

Why didn't this happen at the Tessis? he asked himself.

Also, unlike the visit with the Tessis, there was a lot of chatter, reminiscing, and catching up going on. It was great to be back.

The conversation finally got around to Serena.

"Father, I know the Tessis are parishioners, and that you must take that into consideration, but I really need your help in finding Serena."

"The Tessis are part of my parish, and they are fine people, but I don't believe that they are in keeping with the wishes of their daughter when it comes to keeping the two of you apart. That said, I don't know how I can help you. I have no idea where she is living."

"All I need from you, Father, is for you to call me when she returns home. I know Serena, and I know that she will not miss the holidays with her family."

"I would be pleased to help you two reunite. In the meantime, I will ask around with some of her girlfriends in the parish. Maybe one of them will know something."

John left the rectory feeling a lot better. It may be Thanksgiving or it may be Christmas, but he would get to see Serena soon.

John had one more stop to make before calling it a day. He stopped by the Massachusetts General Hospital's Personnel Department but was stonewalled in his effort to solicit any information at all. He made one last stab at ICU and did get to talk to two nurses who had worked with Serena. Neither of them had any idea of her whereabouts.

—

The waiting game had begun, but it was less bothersome because Johnny had plenty to keep his mind occupied. He was working full-time with Santino and his father, and while the work was extremely hard, his love for the ocean was rekindled. Weekends were free, and Manny and Tony were determined to make up for the time lost while he was away, and of course, there were family dinners where Mary and Rose seemed determined to make up for every bad meal he had ever had while at Maximum Security.

The big news events came one week apart from one another in October. On the Fourth, over a beer and pizza, Manny announced that he and Ellen would be getting married in June. At Sunday dinner the following weekend, Margaret shared the news that she and Doug Massina would be married on June 28.

John had every intention in the world of returning to school for the second semester but had to admit to himself that if he were to spend the rest of his life right there in Gloucester, that would be OK also.

It was a couple of weeks before Thanksgiving, and John knew the clock was ticking. The holiday fell on the twenty-seventh that year, which meant that Serena could be back in Boston in ten days or less.

It was 6:00 PM on a Friday night, and Santino, Marco, and John arrived home after a week of fishing. When John walked into the kitchen and saw the look on his mother's face he immediately knew that something was wrong. She handed him a letter that she had been clutching in her hand. He knew what it was before opening the envelope. The Selective Service System printed in the upper left-hand corner of the envelope answered any questions he may have had about its contents. He had skirted the end of the World War II, but had landed in the middle of the Korean War. Johnny sat down in a kitchen chair and opened his mail. He was to report in one week to the Boston Army Base for a physical.

Margaret tried to lift his spirits, "Johnny, your shoulder is all messed up, there's no way that you'll pass the physical."

"Thanks, sis, but you wouldn't like to make a little wager would you?"

Needless to say, there was very little partying going on that weekend.

A Friday physical meant his not going out to sea the next week or cutting a day off one of the boat's catches. Things were good but never so good that they could give up a day of fishing. The worst part of this was that it gave him far too much time to think about what might or might not happen in the next several days. He came to the conclusion that if he could fix things with Serena, the army could have his ass for two years.

On the twenty-first, Johnny was at the Boston Army Base by the appointed time of 8:00 AM. And, for the first time, experienced the army custom of

"Hurry up and wait." There was a roll call, an interview with a civilian clerk, at which time, Johnny shared the history of his shattered right shoulder, some short IQ testing, a box lunch, and finally the physical. There was at least one doctor for every six recruits, but the process managed to stretch out for almost ten hours. The doctor that saw Johnny did not seem at all impressed with the information on his shoulder.

"When did this injury occur?"

"About three years ago."

"I see. Lift your arm like this, move it backward, to the left, to the right. That looks fine to me."

It was late when he left the army base, but as planned, he stopped at Sacred Heart to see what news Father Pasquale may have. He might as well have gone directly home.

Thanksgiving came and went, and Serena didn't show. While Johnny was disappointed, it did give a level of certainty that Serena would be home for Christmas. Hopefully, the United States Army will hurry up and wait long enough for him to be around when that happened. Good old Uncle Sam didn't let him down; on December 12, he received a letter ordering him to report to the Boston Army Base at 8:00 AM on January 12 for induction into the army of the United States of America. Not great news, but it could have been a lot worse.

The next afternoon, the three friends got together for their weekly ritual. Since the announcement of his engagement, Manny had been getting pressure from Ellen to keep Saturday nights exclusively for her. Manny, of course, got ragged on big time when he broke that news. Tony, of course, showed no mercy while at the same time, he was secretly relieved. Terry was suggesting the same of him, and now he could pacify her and deflect all the flack to Manny.

"I don't get it, Manny hurts his shoulder and comes up 4-F, you graduate high school, go to college, and never hear from the army. I get my shoulder busted up, get convicted for a capital crime, and off I go."

Tony, never at a loss for an answer, offered, "First of all, Manny's injury was fresh, and your injury took place years ago. As far as I'm concerned, I have to believe the military saw me as an intellectual asset not to be risked in the field of battle."

"That bullshit and a dime will get you a cup of coffee at the George's. Speaking of dodging bullets, when the hell are you going to pop the question to Terry? You've had her on the string forever."

"I already have. We're waiting until next fall to get married. Terry wanted a June wedding, but I didn't want to steel Manny's thunder."

"Great, I'll send you a plant from Korea."

"Listen, they have some beautiful tea sets over there, you might want to check that out."

"It will be right at the top of my to-do list, right above, keep my ass alive."

John made it a point of being in Boston on the morning of Christmas Eve. He knew it would be a hectic day for Father Pasquale, so he called a week ahead of time and made an appointment with Mrs. Driscoll. She was able to find a half hour for him. He would have lunch at the rectory.

It was over tuna noodle casserole that Johnny got the unexpected news.

"I'm sorry to have to tell you this, but the Tessis went to Gloria's sister for Christmas. I didn't find out about it myself until this morning when Gloria didn't show up for mass."

"These bastards aren't taking any chances are they?" The priest let that pass. "This was my best shot, do you have any idea what I can do now?"

"Well, my son, I believe we are in agreement that Serena will not stay away from home permanently, and when she does return, you'll be the first to know."

"Father, I'm out of here in a couple of weeks. If she does come home I could be thousands of miles away."

"If that should happen, I will speak to her on your behalf. Trust me to do that."

"You've been a good friend, Father, thank you very much, and have a merry Christmas."

Johnny had less than three weeks before he would head to basic training, and he was determined to make the most of the holidays with his family. He would answer when asked, but never mention Serena otherwise. The last thing to be celebrated was his birthday, one week prior to induction.

CHAPTER FORTY-FIVE

Moving On

Induction into the armed forces was, by military standards, fairly fast and dirty. In by eight and on a train to Fort Dix, New Jersey, by noon. There were about the same amount of recruits inducted that day as there were at the physicals; however, John had no idea if any of them were from the original group. One thing he did notice was the age of the other inductees. He doubted that any of them were over nineteen. They were probably high school seniors six months earlier. Some of them would be dead this time next year. What a fucking waste.

The recruits didn't arrive at Fort Dix, soon to become simply Dix, until midmorning of the next day. When they started the trip the previous day, they were a pretty somber group of guys, but twenty plus hours on the train gave them time to relax and get to know one another. There was nothing like a trip into hell to accelerate the bonding process. Johnny felt a bit old to share in the process but enjoyed sitting back and observing the metamorphoses taking place before his eyes.

Basic training began the second your feet hit the ground at Dix. There were drill instructors (DIs) everywhere. They were all shouting at the same time, and for the most part, they were all shouting pretty much the same thing.

"Form up you useless pieces of shit."

"I said move, and I mean now."

"Don't look at me, keep your eyes looking straight ahead."

"What a sorry excuse for soldiers, this may be hopeless."

On and on they went, they knew the drill because it got repeated verbatim with the arrival of each new group of recruits. Hell, someone could slip in eighty recent West Point grads, and these knuckleheads would go through the same act.

The DIs did everything they could for the next several days to keep the newcomers in a constant state of unrest. Time to issue backpacks and shelter halves; no better time than 2:00 AM when they would enter the barracks, screaming everyone out of a sound sleep. Sleep deprivation was a key component in the training plan. It was done in an effort to help you deal with the stresses of combat, which you very likely would be experiencing in a few short months.

Not surprisingly, none of this had any real impact on John. There was nothing that they could do that would in anyway be more traumatic than what he had faced at Maximum. While others moaned about everything, he shrugged it off.

The food was gourmet compared to prison fare, and there was plenty of it.

His eight-by-twelve prison cell made up of stone and steel bars compared to a clean and warm environment, which featured toilet facilities in a separate room.

A DI shouting in your face rather than a prison screw, whacking you with a billy club.

Then, of course, there were the rapes. Maximum would look the other way while the military would likely put you in front of a firing squad.

John's reactions, or lack of same, were not lost on the younger recruits or the DIs. They had no idea of why this was the case. The DIs thought it was because he was older than the others, although that had never been the case in the past. The other recruits simply looked up to him. Both groups viewed him as a leader.

There were two things in basic training that Johnny had never experienced before: one good the other sucked. The good was the firing range. John and his new best friend, his M1 rifle serial number 4817798003, would go to the range at least once a week and fire at targets several hundred yards down range. He and his fellow recruits would fire away until all the ammo was gone. They never returned from the range with ordinance because while the army had a procedure for requisitioning things it appeared as if they had never figured out how to turn it back in. This was fine with the trainees because the firing range was a welcomed escape from the typical training routine.

The other thing new to John was not fun, far from it. Right in the middle of the training period, the troops were sent to the field for a new experience: bivouac. Two weeks of camping out in the field and sleeping in small tents. The tents were made up of two shelter halves. One was yours, the other belonged to your tent buddy. Now in June or July, this would not have been terrible; but in February it, was brutal. Winters at Dix were cold as a witch's tit. To make it even worse, John had come to enjoy his reputation of being unflappable, so bitching was out of the question.

The need for replacement troops in Korea was critical, so basic training was reduced to eight weeks. It was then the recruits got word of where they would be assigned. Not all would be sent immediately into action. Some would be assigned to military installations in the states, others to Germany. The majority was going into the fray, and as luck would have it, John was in that group. Before being sent to their next assignment, the army privates were given two weeks leave. Johnny, like the rest, headed home.

Chapter Forty-Six

Say Hello, Say Good-Bye

Tony was at the Boston Army Base when John arrived. Personally, he felt like shit. In a few weeks, his lifelong friend was being sent thousands of miles away to fight a war, ostensibly to stem the tide of Communism. A dozen years ago, it took the bombing of Pearl Harbor to drag us into a war to stop a maniac named Hitler. That was a righteous war; this was not. He couldn't help but wonder if he would ever see Johnny after his two-week leave.

Tony waited as the soldiers disembarked the train. He finally spotted his cousin, shaking hands with some of the others and began walking toward him.

Johnny turned, saw his cousin, and a wide smile covered his handsome Italian face.

They hugged tightly. They both understood why.

"Hey, you look great in that uniform. You wouldn't happen to have an extra. We could do some serious trolling in those duds."

"You can have this one. I can't wait to get out of it."

"Let's get headed home, if you didn't know different, you'd think it was Christmas. Both of our fathers hired other captains and are taking the week off. They have never done that before."

They started toward the car, and while he knew the answer, he still had to ask.

"Any word of Serena?"

"Sorry, cus', I've been touching base with Father Pasquale, but he hasn't heard a thing."

Johnny quickly changed the subject, "Hey, Tony, nice car. Where does a law student get the money for a Caddie?"

"Listen, I'm doing you a favor, if this thing sat in the driveway for two years, it wouldn't be worth a damn."

"Just make sure the tank is full when I get back."

"OK, but it was on E when you left."

"Tony, Tony, Tony, it's like I never left."

Everyone was there when he arrived: mothers, fathers, sisters, cousins, spouses, fiancés, Manny and Father Bruno. Rose and his mother had been cooking from early morning. There was hugging, kissing, and no absence of tears. They all supported Johnny's desire to get into some civvies. The uniform served as too much a reminder of what brought them here.

That night, when he laid in his bed, he couldn't help but muse, *homecomings are great, but I have to find better reasons for them other than the military and prison.*

He made the most of his two weeks at home. He made a point of spending considerable time, during the first week, with his father and uncle Santino. He knew that they had incurred some extra expenses to be home that week, and he wanted to show his appreciation for their having done so. Their business was doing well, but fishing for a living seldom made anyone wealthy, and there was never a time for frivolous spending.

He did set aside one afternoon during the following week to drive to Sacred Heart to visit with Father Pasquale.

"I know that Tony had been keeping in touch with you and that you have no news on Serena or her whereabouts, but I felt a need to talk to you myself."

"Whatever the reason, I am always happy to see you, but you are right, there is nothing new to report. It appears that the holidays will once again be our best opportunity to see her."

"I've been thinking about that, Father. I'll more than likely be in Korea at that time, so it might be a good idea if you mentioned that to the Tessis. Knowing that I'm on the other side of the world should make them feel safe in having Serena come home for one of the holidays. That would give you the opportunity to talk to her on my behalf."

"That could work, although it may be a little devious for a parish priest."

"God works in strange ways, will you do it?"

"Since you put it that way, how can I say no?"

The following week, Tony drove his best friend back to the Boston Army Base.

"When are you leaving for Korea?"

"In a couple of weeks."

"How long will you be there?"

"The same amount of time as the last time we talked about this—thirteen months."

"I'm sorry, but my head is all fucked up, I can't think about anything else to say."

"Tony can't think of anything to say? I'm overwhelmed. You know it's OK not to say anything."

They finally got to the army base, and he got Johnny's duffel bag out of the trunk.

"Feel free the use the Caddie while I'm gone. As a matter of fact, I put it in your name this week, just in case."

"Johnny, if anything happens to you, I'd torch this car before I'd ever drive it again."

CHAPTER FORTY-SEVEN

A Trip into Hell

It took the United States Army two weeks to get Johnny's butt from Boston, Massachusetts, to Korea. He was sent there as one of the troops required to replace those leaving. These troops fell into three categories: the lucky being rotated out after completing their thirteen-month tour, the less lucky would be the wounded being evacuated with injuries requiring care beyond what could be provided in field hospitals, and the very unfortunate were those whose bodies were being sent home to their loved ones.

Johnny was assigned, with about twenty other replacements, to Company F, Seventeenth Infantry. At first, the veterans treated the new guys in a way that bordered on contemptuous but this was really nothing more than a right of passage that they themselves had experienced. As it was, some of the vets had been in Korea no more than a couple of weeks themselves.

For some reason lost on most of the troops involved, certain pieces of real estate took on importance of enormous proportions. One such example of this was Pork Chop Hill. Less than two weeks after his arrival in Korea, United Nations troops manning the hill were overrun by a Chinese regiment. Recapturing the hill became an immediate priority of the United States infantry. They mounted a counterattack in the early morning of April 17. Companies K and L were assigned this task and suffered very high casualties. They requested and received reinforcements. They continued to experience heavy shelling and requested additional reinforcements. Late that evening, Johnny and Company F Seventeenth Infantry was ordered into the battle. In the first half hour, they lost nineteen men.

The Chinese attacked again in the early hours of April 18, and Company F was in serious trouble. The American troops were dug in and fought bravely against overwhelming odds. Nothing that they had experienced in basic training could have prepared them for what they were facing. Just gut it out and keep firing your weapon. There were boys being hit all around him; there were screams of pain and pleas for medics. Whenever there was a lull in the hostilities, even for a few minutes, Johnny helped those near him in any way possible. While in training, you were instructed to never use your own first aid supplies on another; use theirs only. That bit of training went out the window quickly. John and the others did whatever they could for their fallen brothers.

There was artillery fire, screaming, rifle and automatic weapons being discharged—the sounds were deafening. Johnny then felt a jolt to his shoulder, a sharp pain, a pain severe enough to elicit a scream, a scream louder than he felt he was capable of. Then there as nothing. Only a counterattack by Company E saved the lives of what was left of Johnny and his comrades.

It was later that same day that he regained consciousness. He and the other wounded men had been moved to MASH units somewhere south of the 38th parallel. He was lying on a bunk in what might be described as a hospital emergency room except that it was a large tent. He looked around as best he could. There were doctors, nurses, and orderlies moving around the tent, evaluating the wounded in order to determine who would be treated first based on the seriousness of their injuries. He didn't know that they had already classified him as stable and, as such, he would wait before receiving treatment. He did know that he was not in serious pain; what he didn't know was that this would change as the effects of the morphine injection he had received diminished.

While his wounds were not life threatening, they would require reconstructive surgery that could not be performed at a MASH Unit. Within a few days, he was transported to a hospital in Japan.

On the first full day after his arrival at the US hospital in Japan, surgery was performed on his badly damaged right shoulder. When Johnny regained consciousness, he found himself in what appeared to be a sea of white but was, in reality, the very sterile environment of a recovery room. He was still feeling the effects of the anesthesia and thought every nurse entering the room was Serena.

When the effects of the drugs began to wear thin, his head cleared, and the pain increased. He also realized that Serena was not part of the military nursing staff.

"How are you feeling?" The question came from a doctor who he had not noticed until now.

"If I'm supposed to feel like crap, I'm perfect."

"Well that sounds about right, how's the pain?"

"Is there any morphine in my future? The pain is getting worse every minute."

"We can give you another few days, and then we'll have to wean you off. That stuff is really addictive, and we have to get it out of your system before your next surgery."

"We have to do this again?"

"We found quite a bit of damage in there, private. It looked as if you had extensive damage to that shoulder before this."

"Yeah, I injured it in a previous life. I had it operated on a few years ago."

"With a shoulder like that, you probably should have been classified 4-F."

"Great, where the hell were you a few months ago?"

The doctor wore a nametag that identified him as Captain Floyd. He obviously took Johnny's question as rhetorical and moved on.

"Let's see how the healing process goes. We'll get you on light rehab as soon as possible, and depending on how that goes, we'll schedule your next surgery."

"How long am I going to be here?"

"That depends on how the next surgery goes and how much I can get done. I wouldn't be surprised if there were at least one more operation after that. We want to get this right so you'll have some semblance of normal use of your arm."

Johnny turned his head away from the doctor and fought back tears.

That's more fucking information than I needed, he thought. Then in a voice just louder than a whisper, "When is this all going to end? I've got nowhere to go."

CHAPTER FORTY-EIGHT

The Road Back

Johnny's therapist was a young Negro man who had the body of an NFL defensive end and hands that transitioned effortlessly from the grip of a blacksmith to those of a neurosurgeon. Nate Henry had gone directly from high school graduation to the US Army recruitment office. He had requested training in physical therapy and, after scoring well in his exams, was given the opportunity for training in that field.

Nate was already into his second tour of duty and close to Johnny in age. They quickly become friends. This friendship was tested frequently because Johnny was convinced that there were times that his new friend was trying to kill him.

"Jesus, Nate is the term light rehab lost on you? I need to recover from old injuries, I don't need new ones."

"Hell, private, they told me you were tough. You're nothing but a pussy. Wait until we get to the serious stuff, you'll be begging for mercy."

"We'll see who begs for help after I get on my feet."

"You want to rumble. I'll call my little brother to take care of my light work."

As it turned out, Nate didn't have a little brother; he had five little brothers and two little sisters, and they were all at home in Biloxi, Mississippi, with his parents. His father was a carpenter, and his mother worked at home, doing alterations and repairs on clothing.

Nate would not be classified as radical, but neither was he complacent regarding the complete lack of racial equality he had experienced growing up in Biloxi. He and Johnny would talk about this from time to time, and each time they did Johnny's admiration for the young man increased. One day, they got to talking about going home. Johnny still had close to two years to serve while Nate had almost three to go.

"Did you reenlist to avoid going back to Mississippi?"

"Hell no, I reenlisted because I still have a lot to learn about physical therapy and how better to learn that by inflicting pain on white boys like you? Besides, my family is in Biloxi, that's home."

Johnny knew exactly how he felt. He was receiving a steady stream of mail from home, and while he loved mail call, he was always left with a feeling of emptiness when he was done reading one of his letters.

With each passing day, Johnny felt better. His progress with the therapy, while slow, was on schedule.

Who knows, maybe I've turned the corner, maybe my luck has changed, he thought one afternoon after a particularly good day in the gym.

Captain Floyd came by to see him every few days, and one day, about a month after his surgery, Johnny decided to test his newfound luck.

"Captain, I'd like to ask as favor." Without waiting for the captain to ask the nature of the favor, he moved on.

"My sister is getting married at the end of next month. Is there any chance I could get leave and attend the wedding?"

He was not sure, but he thought he was holding his breath in anticipation of the answer. He didn't have long to wait long.

"I'm sorry, private, I've scheduled your next surgery for the first week in June, and I will need to monitor the results closely in the weeks following the operation. I can't risk your chances for full recovery for anything."

In his disappointment with the captain's response, Johnny missed the comment regarding a full recovery. Things were, in fact, moving along better than anticipated.

One day before Tony was to graduate from law school, Johnny went under the knife in Tokyo. In the days following the operation, he came to understand the reasoning behind Captain Floyd denying his request for a leave. Floyd came by every day to check on his progress and then, based on what he observed, he would then meet with Nate to go over the therapy planned for the day. Again, the therapy was very light on the days immediately following surgery and then increased as Floyd saw fit. By the third week following the surgery, the intensity of the program already exceeded what had been achieved after the first operation. This, of course, elicited a strong reaction from Nate's patient.

"Are you sure that Floyd prescribed this level? You're killing me."

Truth be known, the pain while considerable, was not unbearable. It had become a form of gamesmanship, which both men enjoyed.

"Yeah, this is what he ordered, but he must have thought he was ordering it for a man."

"You better get your little brother over here real fast because when he gets here, I'm going to kick both your asses."

"If you plan to do me any damage, you'd better plan on having a gun."

Johnny decided to leave this alone.

They say that good things happen in threes. Being cleared of a murder conviction would certainly qualify as a good thing, and the day before he was booked in for his third operation, he got word of a second good thing. While certainly not to the extent of his release from jail, this too came as a big surprise.

It seemed as if his actions under fire on Pork Chop Hill had been observed by his squad leader and verified by others in Company F. He was credited with saving the lives of six men and lending aid to two others who did not survive the battle. For this, he was being awarded a silver star. The award itself did not have that much meaning. During his short stay on that godforsaken hill, he had witnessed many acts of heroism, and he was not all that sure he did more than many others. The important thing was that after a long drought, good things were again happening to him.

The third surgery took place on July 1, and the following day, he had a visit from both Captain Floyd and Nate.

"John, the surgeries that were performed on you turned out better than we could have hoped for. I see no reason why you will not recover fully from your wounds. There are at least three reasons that we got these results. One, of course, is the superior skill of your surgeon." This was the first time in over two months that Johnny had seen even an attempt at humor from Floyd. "Another was the effort you put into your rehab, but foremost was the job this guy did for you. You owe Nate big time."

"OK, big guy, thanks a million. What now, round three in your torture chamber?"

Captain Floyd answered the question for him.

"It's just a short visit. Two weeks and we move you to a VA Hospital outside of Boston."

Good things were happening so fast, he was losing track. Prison was one. The medal award was two, full recovery three, now a transfer to Boston would make four—or maybe four was one in round two.

The two weeks passed more quickly than one might expect. There were letters to write, friends to say good-bye to, a small ceremony for the medal award, and the torture chamber. The toughest part would be the last day when he and Nate would say their good-byes. The two men had become close friends in the past three months, and in spite of all their good intentions, it was doubtful that they would ever see one another again.

Johnny left Tokyo on the 14th of July on a military transport headed for Pearl Harbor. After that, there were stops in San Francisco and Atlanta before he reached Otis Air Force base in Barnstable County on Cape Cod on the eighteenth.

From Otis, he was transported by bus to the Veterans Administration Hospital in West Roxbury.

Flying military transports is nothing like traveling commercial. Military aircraft are built for functional purposes, and comfort was not even an afterthought. Johnny wasn't complaining, but by the time he reached the hospital, he only took time for a call to Gloucester before he hit the sack.

The next morning, the Silinas attended the 7:00 AM Mass at Our Lady of Good Voyage, and then five of them piled into a family car and headed directly to West Roxbury. John's parents left Rose, Santino, and Margaret in the hospital lobby to wait their turn to visit. The family had made out a pecking order for visits, and under strong protest, Tony had been relegated to a Monday visit along with Anna and Annette.

There was plenty to talk about: Tony's graduation, the weddings of both Manny and Margaret, and Tony's constant string of job interviews where it appeared that he was interviewing the law firms rather than the other way around.

The family tried to broach Johnny's time in Korea and even his silver metal, but he was having no part of that. They quickly realized that the last thing men returning from combat wanted to discuss was the war. Visiting hours lasted three hours, and Johnny loved every second of it, but when they ended, all he could think of was a nap.

The minute that visiting hours began the next day, Tony came charging into Johnny's room with his two sisters in tow. All three were sporting wide smiles, and Tony was clutching a white envelope in each of his hands. Johnny got to his feet to greet his cousins while cautioned them against being too exuberant with their embraces. He was still feeling the effects of yesterday's visits. All three were speaking at once, which accomplished nothing in the way of communication but did bring a broad grin to his face. They were finally able to work their way through the early excitement and settled into the friendly banter that had marked their childhood.

Tony never once commented on the envelopes he had brought with him. He had, for dramatic effect, placed them on a small table next to where he was seated but never a word as to their contents. If he was trying to heighten his cousin's curiosity, he had certainly succeeded—big time. Johnny knew the game was on and was determined not to bite. He failed.

"OK, what's with the damn envelopes?"

A sly smile appeared on Tony's face; his little ploy had worked, now he would milk it a while longer.

"Listen, there is some news here that I haven't shared with the rest of the family. It all happened on Friday, and I decided I'd wait until now to go public. So when I tell Mom and Dad about this tonight, you girls have to act surprised, agreed?"

Anna answered for the others.

"For God's sake Tony, what the hell is it?"

Tony took one of the envelopes, and for the first time, Johnny noticed the business name and address on the top left-hand corner. Clark, Kenney, and Clark, Attorneys at Law.

"I won't bore you with the details, but Clark, Kenney, and Clark are opening an office in Boston, and I've accepted a position with them. They made a very generous offer and agreed to compensate me while I prepare for the bar exams."

"That's terrific, Tony, they're a good firm, and you get to stay in Boston."

Johnny pressed on because he knew Tony was dying to share the number.

"So what constitutes a very generous offer?"

"Twenty big ones a year and a bonus based on my performance."

Johnny joined Anna and Annette in a group hug and congratulations, which much to their surprise, Tony quickly brought to a close.

"Wait, wait there's more." He now reached for the second envelope, which bore the same identification as the first.

"Here, Johnny, this is for you," he said as he handed it to his cousin.

In all honesty, Johnny had no idea as to the contents of the envelope he was opening. He read the enclosed letter.

Dear Mr. Desimone,

As you know, we filed charges on your behalf against the State of Rhode Island for wrongful arrest and conviction for the murder of one James Georgio.

We have sued the State for the recovery of legal cost and for punitive damages.

We have recently been offered a settlement from the State and ask that you contact us at your earliest convenience to discuss with us how you would like to proceed. The total amount of the settlement offer is $45,000. Clark, Kenney and Clark are waving all applicable fees.

We anxiously await your reply. You may contact us during business hours of 8:00 AM to 6:00 PM, Monday through Friday at 737-1122.

"Tony, get me to a phone, now."

The next month flew by, and with each passing day, Johnny felt better. The only thing that continued to plague him was the continued failure to learn of Serena's whereabouts. If there was any discouragement in this regard, it came in conjunction with some good news. The United States Army had concluded that his wounds were too severe for continued active duty, and when he was released from the hospital, he would do so with his discharge in hand. This news set off a deluge of ideas by Tony on how he saw their future.

"Johnny, I've got some ideas, and I want you to be quiet until I finish before you say anything."

"So why are you stopping?"

"Good, OK. When you get out of here, you enroll for the fall semester at Suffolk. In two years, you get your degree and enroll in law school. I know you spent a lot of time reading law books while you were away, and I know that the law interests you." He wasn't even slowing down to take a breath.

"I'll work for two or three years with Clark, Kenney, and Clark to learn the ropes, and then I'll hang out my own shingle. When you graduate, we get a new shingle.

Silina and DeSimone Attorneys at Law. Now don't say no without thinking it through. We can do this, and it'll be great."

"Two conditions and I'm in."

"What are they?"

"First, we defend no one who is mob connected, and second, the shingle says, Silina and Silina Attorneys at Law."

If success could be measured by the size of a smile, these guys have it made.

"You've got it, cus'."

CHAPTER FORTY-NINE

Mother to Mother

Tony was seated in the Caddie, which was parked across the street from the home of Mario and Gloria Tessi, and he wasn't sure that he believed what he was seeing. His aunt Mary, one of the sweetest and probably the most unobtrusive person he had ever known, was ringing the front doorbell for an unannounced meeting with Mrs. Tessi. The timing of the visit was planned for midmorning on a Monday so as to ensure that Mario Tessi would be at work.

It was two weeks prior to Johnny's scheduled release from the hospital, and his mother thought it was time for her speak to Mrs. Tessi.

"Hello, what can I do for you?" said Mrs. Tessi, sounding cooler than she had intended. She had met John's mother on two other occasions and had taking an immediate liking to her.

"I'm here to talk to you about our children."

"Mrs. DeSimone, I'm not sure that we have anything to talk about. I believe that we have made that clear."

Mary decided to let the Desimone thing slide, realizing that they had been on a first name basis from the moment they had met. She saw no reason to further complicate things now. She pressed forward.

"Please, it will only take a few minutes of your time. It is very important to both our children."

"Come in." She led Mary to the living room and asked her to be seated.

"My husband and I have made a decision, and there is nothing you can say that will change that."

"This is what bothers me, Mrs. Tessi. You and your husband have made this decision and have not told your daughter of it. If this were her decision, I would not be bothering you, but that is not what has happened."

"Your son hurt my Serena, and we will not allow that to happen again."

"You know my son, he has been here many times. Serena has spent time at our home also. I never saw a time when they were not very happy, very much in love."

Mrs. Tessi knew that to be true.

"I don't know if you know this, but Johnny has been in the service. They sent him to Korea."

"Yes, Father Pasquale has told us of this and his wounds. How is he doing?"

"Very well, he is being released from the hospital in a couple of weeks. He has told me that if being apart is what Serena wants, he will accept her decision, but he wants to hear that from her. You can't take this one last chance from them."

"Mrs. DeSimone, I cannot make any promises, but I will talk to my husband."

"That's all I can ask. Let me give you a number you can call."

"Listen, I've been in hospitals for over four months, I've had three operations, killed myself in rehab, and now you're telling me I can't walk out of this place. There's no way I get wheeled out of here."

"Regulations Private DeSimone, just be happy that today is your last with army regs. I'm only a nurse. If it were up to me, you could do cartwheels out of here."

"Sit down, cus', I've got the wheels."

"Don't you have a job? You're here all the time."

"I can study for the bar anytime, but I'll only get one shot at wheeling you out of the military."

"Who's watching my car?"

"Manny got the day off. He told his boss he wanted to pitch the company one last time."

A few minutes later, they passed through the front door, and Johnny raised his hand, signaling Tony to stop.

"I have it from here." He got up and headed for the Caddie.

"Hey, soldier, can a girl get a lift?"

He couldn't believe his ears. Is it possible?

He turned and found that it was possible. Walking toward him was the last piece he needed to put his life back together.

———

Serena was beautiful even with eyes filled with tears. She wasn't alone in this; the three tough guys from Gloucester were also fighting back tears. It took ten minutes before they finally got into the car and headed home.

Serena explained how she had, just the week before, found out what her parents had done.

"I'm so angry with them for what they did. I don't know if I can ever forgive them."

Johnny turned her so he could look directly into her eyes.

"You can forgive them. Everyone gets to make one mistake."

CHAPTER FIFTY

The Confessional

"Forgive me Father, for I have sinned. It has been over a year since my last confession."

"What is it my son?"

"I have murdered a man, he did my family harm, and I took the law into my own hands."

"You do understand that no matter what this person was guilty of, that in the eyes of God, you have done the wrong thing?"

"I do, Father, but nothing can change that now."

"Do you intend to go the police and confess your crime to them?"

"No, Father, I will not be doing that."

"You know then, that I cannot give you absolution?"

"Yes, Father, I understand."

"Then what is it you want of me?"

"I needed to confess my sins and I have done so."

Life Going Forward

Epilogue

Tony and Terry were married the following June with Johnny and Serena following one month later. Tony passed the bar exam on his first try and worked at Clark, Kenney, and Clark until the summer of 1956 when he did, in fact, hang out his shingle. Being an optimist coupled with his confidence in his cousin, the shingle read Silina and Silina Attorneys at Law. The following spring, Johnny graduated from Suffolk Law School, joined the firm; and not to be outdone, he also passed the bar on his first attempt.

Serena continued to work at Massachusetts General until the arrival of Marco, the first of their three children. Not to be outdone, Tony and Terry had four children. The two cousins wanted their children to grow to know one another as they had, so they settled in South Medford. This worked on many levels since it was a short commute to their law office in Cambridge, close enough for visiting the North End and Gloucester, and had a heavy concentration of Italian residents.

True to their mantra, they never got involved in defending people with ties to organized crime. They became successful enough so that Johnny was able to dedicate time to do work as a prisoner advocate. If an inmate could convince him that he or she had been wrongly convicted of a crime, he would work pro bono in an effort to get the conviction reversed.

This work later led to Johnny crossing paths with his army friend from Tokyo, Nate Henry, whose brother had run afoul of the law during the time of racial unrest in the South, but more on that later.

Recognition of the Gloucester High School Football Program

This book is fiction, but not pure fiction. What I mean by that is wherever possible, I tried to make the story mirror actual events. I worked hard to stay relatively accurate with regards to times and dates during World War II and the Korean War. I had the Red Sox winning the pennant in 1946, and Eddie Popowski managing the Roanoke Red Sox in that same summer. I did the same when it came to the Gloucester High School football team in the fall of 1944. When I made a phone call to the reference department at the Sawyer Public Library in Gloucester, I was hoping to be told that the Gloucester Fishermen had an extremely successful team some sixty-four years earlier. History told me that this was not the case. The team's record was 1-5-2. I was also told that the Fishermen had an additional game with a score of 1 to 0 in their favor, but since I didn't know how that could happen, I chose to exercise my poetic license and disregarded it altogether. (A forfeit perhaps?)

I did discover something else during that phone conversation; that the current Gloucester High football team had won the Eastern Mass Division 2A Super Bowl the previous fall. As it turned out they returned to the Super Bowl this fall in search of a second consecutive title. Regrettably they lost a highly competitive game to an excellent Duxbury High team.

I'm sure that the players, coaches, and fans were disappointed with the loss. I know how that feels because fifty-three years ago my high school baseball team lost the championship game for the 1955 Eastern Massachusetts title.

I can share with you something that I've learned from experience. More important than the championships won or lost are the lifelong friendships that are made with the members of your team.

Please allow me to offer congratulations for what you have accomplished in both 2007 and 2008.

Ron Calareso.

ACKNOWLEDGMENTS

It's difficult to know where to start. The first book I wrote was nonfiction. It was the story of my life and that of the Calaresos and Magliozzis that came before and after me. While it was nonfiction, the main reference sources for the book were my mother and I. When I started this book, I had the mistaken opinion that, since it was fiction, I could sort of make it up as I went along. When I got into it, however, I found myself wanting it to be, to a certain extent, historically accurate. This led to far more research than I had ever anticipated.

Much of the research was done by me on the Internet, which while a good source, has its limitations. Early on in the story, the Great Depression had a major impact on the lives of the people being depicted in it. I found myself in the Naples branch of the Collier County Public Library, trying to gather data, which was applicable to the time and place in the storyline. It was then that I went to the reference desk and enlisted the aid of Carol Ann. Carol Ann put me onto a book written by Charles H. Trout entitled, *Boston, the Great Depression, and the New Deal.* With the aid of this book, I was able to be far more accurate with regards to dates and events than I could ever have hoped to be on my own. If you should ever want to get it 100 percent accurate, I would suggest you read Mr. Trout's book to do so.

Carol Ann and Mr. Trout were only the beginning. There were Stephanie Buck and Martha Oaks at the Cape Ann Historical Museum and Ann from the Sawyer Library of Gloucester. Then there was Abby of the Boston Red Sox media office who supplied information on the Sox minor league affiliates in the 1940s

People were just eager to help. Let me give just a couple of examples: I needed to confirm the address of a Boston Police precinct in Boston's North End. I called the desk sergeant and asked for the exact address. After giving me the information, he asked why I wanted the address. When I told him I needed it for a book, he simply replied, "Whatever." As I mentioned in the dedication, I made two trips to Gloucester to look around and take a few photographs while working on the book. During the first of those visits, after taking photos of the monument of the Gloucester Fisherman and the memorial plaques honoring the Gloucester fishermen lost at sea, I wanted to enlist the aid of a passerby to take a picture of me at that site. I hailed down a woman out on an afternoon walk and asked her help. Like so many others, she couldn't have been nicer. She took two shots and then directed me to one of the memorial plaques and the name of her daughter's father-in-law. His name was one of the most recent additions to memorial. I believe the name of his boat was *Italian Gold*.

And then of course are the many contributions of my underpaid (if underpaid means not paid at all), but highly appreciated staff. That would be my wife Pat and daughters Michele O'Brien and Paula Conrad. Pat proofreads and makes suggestions, Paula reads and edits, and Michele lends her considerable talents to the finishing touches on the interior and exterior templates of the book. Where would I be without them?

Get Published, Inc!
Thorofare, NJ 08086
21 August 2009
BA2009233